Crown of a King, Book Three
of The Carolingian Chronicles

Crown of a King, Book Three of The Carolingian Chronicles

J. Boyce Gleason

Yet A Little While PUBLISHING

Yet a Little While Publishing

CONTENTS

CONTENTS

CONTENTS

I dedicated this book to my father Burdette Gleason, known to most as "Bud" but to his family and close friends as "Vince." He was a humble, soft-spoken man who dedicated much of his life to public service, mostly in education, first as a teacher and principal in the New York State school system, then as the administrator of its Board of Cooperative Educational Services and finally as the superintendent of schools in Corning, New York.

While he wore other hats throughout his life, he was most proud of being a Marine. Like many who serve, he didn't talk much about his tours in Korea (unless he was with someone who'd been in combat), but you had the sense that his training and experience had a profound effect on his sense of purpose, his work ethic and his commitment to duty and country.

He was always measured with his words, careful of to listen to others, but resolute in pursuing what he perceived as right. He didn't buy into elitism in any form and had close friends from all walks of life. He also had a unique gift which I'll call, "the voice of command." He didn't use it much, but when he did *everyone* listened.

To say that he had a profound effect on me would be an understatement. I've spent most of my life trying to live up to the kind of man he was. I share this calling with each of my five siblings. It's an unstated thing among us but something we all understand. The greatest compliment you can give one of us is, "you remind me of Vince."

I'll admit, I haven't come close but I'm a far better man for his influence that I would have been without it and I've tried to pass on to my children the values that he and my mom imbued in the six of us. I am always delighted when I see traits of them in my children.

My dad lived a good life, dying too soon of leukemia at age 79, but not a day passes that I don't wish he were still here. I'd love to hear his voice, his laugh, ask his advice, or just hang out with him a while on the patio by the lake, sipping a martini. I love you, Dad. Semper Fidelis.

Area more or less under FRANKISH dominion in the time of CHARLES MARTEL

Royalty

King Childeric (Elevated by Carloman)

The Church

Pope Zachary (His Holiness the Pope)
Bishop Boniface (Legate to the Holy See)
Bishop Sergius (Legate to the Holy See)
Bishop Aidolf of Auxerres
Bishop Heddo of Strasbourg
Bishop Reginfried of Cologne
Bishop Witta of Buraburg
Bishop Milo of Reims
Bishop Gewilib of Mainz

Regional Nobility

Alemannia

Theudebald (son of Godefred)
Lantfrid (son of Lantfrid, son of Godefred)
Comte Sudiger of Nordgau
Comte Eingard of Kurbayern

Austrasia

Charles Martel, mayor of the palace (d. 741)
Childebrand (stepbrother to Charles Martel)
Carloman (son of Martel & Chlotrude)
Pippin II (son of Martel & Chlotrude)

Hiltrude (daughter of Martel & Chlotrude)
Gripho (son of Martel & Sunnichild)
Gunther (a knight loyal to Pippin)
Arnot (a knight loyal to Pippin)
Laurent (a knight loyal to Carloman)
Gerold of Vinzgau (a knight loyal to Pippin)
Emma of Vinzgau (Gerold's wife)

Aquitaine

Duc Hunoald
Waifar (son of Hunoald)
Comtesse de Loches (Catherine)

Bavaria

Duc Odilo (son of Godefred)
Tassilo (son of Hiltrude and Odilo)
Sunnichild (second wife of Charles Martel)
Hans (son of Eta)
Eta (a commoner)
Tobias (a commoner)

Neustria

Bertrada (daughter of the Compte de Laon)
Aude (daughter of the Compte de Laon)
Lord Ragomfred the Younger
Lady Ragomfred (Miette)
Lady Gagnon
Lady Didot
Lady Talon
Lady Hélène
Agnès (a commoner)

Salau (a knight loyal to Childeric)
Lady Brevet
Jean-Pierre (a knight)
Julien (a knight)

Saxony

Duc Theodoric

Twelve Counties

Compte Drusseau
Lady Drusseau

Transjura

Frederic (a knight)

Vienne

Theodoenus (a knight)

Allies

Lombardy

King Liutbrand
Prince Aistulf (King Liutbrand's successor)

1

Quierzy
745 A.D.

The rhythmic stomp of marching feet echoed off the low rolling hills that bordered the eastern road. As the army grew nearer, one could hear more discreet sounds; officers shouting to maintain order, horses nickering at the slow pace, and plated armor scraping and clanging against metal shields. A boisterous crowd gathered outside the gates to welcome them home, cheering the mounted cavalry knights with their colorful household banners.

A warm, bright, spring day lent a festive air to the occasion and the villagers threw flowers to their favorites among the ranks. Archers and pike men followed next in crisp lines with their crossbows and long spears held high. Young girls with colored strips of cloth in their hair whistled and waved at the remaining columns of infantrymen, who carried their shields and broadswords strapped high across their backs.

There was a swagger to these men. Like the cocksure sons of noblemen, confidence permeated their collective stride as if God Himself had blessed their weapons. No one need ask if the Franks had vanquished the hateful Saxons; it was shouted aloud in every step they took.

A vain commander would have led his army into the city, but Pippin rode cloistered among the ranks of the cavalry, his face somber as if the celebration surrounding him didn't reach his ears or the flowers thrown his way didn't warrant his attention.

He looked short next to the immense height of his uncle Childebrand, yet no one could mistake Pippin's broad shoulders and massive arms as anything but those of a master swordsman even at a distance. Only twenty-nine years old, he carried his command as if he had been born to it – which, as the son of the late Charles Martel, he had been.

"Aren't you even a little happy to be home?"

Childebrand's question caught Pippin off guard. Thinking in retrospect, he supposed he had grown quiet as they drew nearer to Quierzy. For his uncle's benefit, Pippin smiled. Childebrand was always worried about him – especially his bouts with the blackness. For much of Pippin's life Childebrand had shouldered the burden of them whenever they had surfaced but, for now, they were just a memory; the corners of his mind remained clear.

"I will miss being out on campaign," Pippin said. "Life in the field is simple: you take care of your men and you defeat your enemies. Here, I'll have to listen to every noble who has a grievance to air; I'm never sure who is friend or foe, *and* I'll have to contend with Carloman's king." Although it had been two years, the thought of Childeric on the throne still made Pippin furious. He shook his head. "Not something I look forward to."

"I was talking about seeing your son."

Pippin chuckled, his smile becoming genuine. ""Charles? I can't wait to see how much he's grown. It's hard to believe he's almost three."

"And Bertrada?"

Pippin's grin faltered. "I'll be glad to see her as well."

The neutral response clearly didn't sit well with Childebrand. The man's face grimaced into a scowl. "I just don't understand the difficulty between you two."

Pippin sighed, trying to ignore the sinking feeling in his stomach. "Nor do I, uncle."

"You should have married her when little Charles was born."

Pippin nodded; it was an old argument and one he couldn't seem to solve to anyone's satisfaction. He loved Bertrada. At least he loved what they once had been, but their relationship had changed. He wasn't even sure that Bertrada still cared for him. He had thought the babe would make them closer – and in a way it had – but she had closed off a part of herself and Pippin had doubts that she would ever let him back inside.

Childebrand's next argument would be that they didn't need to love one another – that marriages of state were about politics, not romance – but for once, his uncle let the silence stand between them and Pippin was thankful that he did.

As they drew nearer the gate, Pippin could see a crowd of nobles gathered on the rampart. He scanned the cheering faces, searching for Bertrada. Although her absence didn't surprise him, he still felt a stab of disappointment.

His eyes, however, did land on Miette. The Lady Ragomfred stood apart from the crowd to one side of the rampart, her arms folded across her stomach as if waiting impatiently for him to arrive. Childebrand noticed her too and grunted his displeasure.

Pippin groaned, knowing his uncle's silence now would be short-lived. He could almost feel the admonitions fomenting inside Childe-brand as anger and frustration distorted his face.

"Go ahead and say it –"

"Send that bitch back to her husband! She'll be the death of you."

Although the rebuke stung, Pippin was accustomed to it. It had been a constant refrain since he had offered her a haven from the king's violence. As Childeric's mistress, she had been beaten close to death for her perceived disloyalty. Pippin's offer of protection had become a symbol of his break with the throne. Half the court thought she shared his bed. And despite his efforts to deny it, the gossip continued un-abated. It was one of the reasons he preferred life out on campaign.

Pippin chuckled at the irony of his uncle's rebuke. "You're right, Childebrand. It's *so* good to be home."

After ensuring that his men were settled on the western side of the town, Pippin made his way back to the family compound. Originally built as a hunting lodge, Quierzy had become the residence of choice for Pippin. The accommodations were far more spacious and luxurious than those of the fortified palace in Paris and for Pippin it had a more sentimental association; it was the only place he had ever thought of as home.

The town had become a small city during his father's reign as mayor of the palace. Wherever Charles the Hammer rested his head instantly became the seat of government and commerce for all Francia. And since Quierzy was the man's favorite, the town had grown substantially to accommodate the court, their attending military contingents, and the merchants who came to profit from them.

It also had proved to be the perfect retreat for Pippin following his split with his brother Carloman. As the inheritors of their father's power, the two shared in governing Francia. Yet, when it came to elevating the latest Merovingian to the throne, Carloman had acted alone, overriding Pippin's objections.

Stunned by the insult to his authority and convinced that Childeric was a disastrous choice, Pippin had refused to bend his knee to the newly elevated king and left Paris, moving his court and his army to Quierzy.

The move had its intended effect. By making camp a week's ride from Paris, Pippin posed an ongoing threat to Childeric and no one, including Carloman, knew what to do about it. Pippin was too powerful to attack and too near to ignore.

Carloman had chosen to try the latter, perhaps hoping that eventually Pippin would capitulate. As a result, a political stalemate ensued. Half the kingdom acknowledged Childeric's reign, while half refused. Pippin was content to let Carloman stew in the pot he had stirred.

With the army's return, merchants filled the town square with brightly colored wagons and crowds of customers bargained for everything from salted pork to armor plating. A stone church adjacent to

Pippin's family's villa towered over the marketplace – a not so subtle reminder of its influence on the affairs of the Frankish state.

Pippin made his way past the church and climbed the broad stairs leading up to his family's residence. He ran his hand over the polished oak railing, comforted by its smooth familiar feel. Once inside the villa, he turned towards Bertrada's rooms.

He found her playing with little Charles, rolling a small wooden hoop across the floor for his enjoyment. When she saw Pippin a look of relief crossed her face, but only for a moment, before being replaced with a frown.

"Pip-Pip!" Little Charles screeched and ran to Pippin with open arms. Pippin scooped him up and twirled him before hugging his son to his chest.

"And how's my big boy?"

"I got toy." Charles held out the wooden hoop.

"Yes." Pippin laughed. "Yes, you do."

He turned to Bertrada. "I had hoped to see you on the rampart."

She waved away the suggestion. "I can't abide the stares of the women at court."

"People will think there's trouble between us."

"There isn't?" Her face blotched red with emotion. She stood and took Charles away from him, eyeing his clothes with disgust. "At least you could have bathed before coming."

"Bathed?"

"Don't you ever wash on campaign? There's blood on your clothes. It's in your hair!"

Pippin bit off his initial rebuke and tried to calm himself. He wiped his hands on the back of his tunic. "I suppose I should have. I just couldn't wait to see the two of you."

"The two of us?"

"Yes, of course."

"Then why have you allowed that woman to remain here?"

She, of course, meant Miette. "You know why."

"It's been three years. How long must you protect her?"

"As long as her life is in danger."

Charles began pulling on Bertrada's blouse. "Maman! Maman!"

With a sigh, Bertrada sat, leaving little Charles to stand in front of her. She unbuttoned her blouse and offered him her right breast. He latched on to her nipple and began to suckle. Bertrada scowled up at Pippin. "Don't start."

Pippin tried to keep his voice calm. "I thought you were going to wean him while I was away."

"He needs me!"

"He's almost three. In a few years, he'll begin warrior training. You can't leave him on the tit forever."

Bertrada's face flushed with anger. "I *know* you are going to take him from me! God's blood, the thought consumes me. All I think about it is you taking this sweet little boy from me and turning him into a monster who doesn't even notice the blood on his hands."

Bertrada began to cry. "And then what will become of me? He's all I have."

"That's not true –"

"It's not? Can you honestly say that I would be here if it weren't for him?"

It was a question that his younger self would have dismissed outright, but Pippin was no longer sure. Bertrada's revulsion for his family had become more virulent after the birth of Charles, and Pippin was beginning to doubt that he could reclaim their former relationship.

"Please, Bertie. I just came home. Can't we have a moment without quarrelling?"

Bertrada closed her eyes and seemed to calm herself. When she opened them, they appeared more compassionate. "I'm sorry. It's so hard for me when you're gone. I feel so alone. I doubt myself. I doubt you."

She offered him a half smile. "Go bathe and put on a clean set of clothes. We can talk at dinner. I've ordered a small feast for the household in honor of the army's return."

A sense of relief flooded through Pippin at her change in tone. He took a step towards her. "Bertie, I just –"

She held up a hand. "Bathe first."

* * *

He hesitated only a moment before taking his leave. He found a servant to draw him a hot bath and headed up to his quarters on the next floor of the villa. Bertrada's greeting wasn't all he had hoped it would be, but he had seen worse. There were times when she had refused to greet him altogether. If it weren't for little Charles, Pippin wondered if she would acknowledge him at all.

They once had been so good together! He remembered summers when they had spent more time naked than clothed. He longed to hear her laugh again, the way she did when they were younger – without the reservation or hesitation he now heard in her voice.

He was sure she had said "blood on your hands" on purpose. It was her favorite lament about his family, that and "They butcher people because of their faith." Nothing he could say would assuage her sense of outrage.

Pippin watched as a servant – a boy named Gerard – patiently carried pails of hot water into the room. The tub was a monstrous copper affair that would allow Pippin to completely submerge under the water once it was filled. He stared as the steam rose off the liquid surface, trying to connect the luxury of his apartments with his life on campaign. He suspected Bertrada was right: he couldn't remember bathing, even once.

He ordered a flagon of ale and began to take off his boots and the rest of his clothes. He had to peel the shift off his back; it felt as if it had become part of his skin. When he was naked, he stepped into the tub and ever so slowly sat down into the near scalding water. He scrubbed his flesh with soap and kneaded it into his scalp until he was thoroughly covered and then slid into the silence beneath the water's surface.

He latched on to the quiet, unwilling to let it go. He held his breath, allowing the stillness and the heat to permeate his body. In time, he began to relax. When he could hold his breath no longer, he surfaced, blowing out his pent-up air and wiping away the hair and water from his eyes.

Miette was sitting at the edge of his tub.

As always, she was breathtaking. Dark eyes and black hair contrasted with pale features that seemed to glow with an inner light. Shapely and petite, she knew she was beautiful and never hesitated to use it to her advantage.

"Miss me?" She smiled.

"Milady Ragomfred," he acknowledged, trying to keep the smile from his face.

"It's so good to see you," she quipped, leering at his nakedness.

Pippin made no effort to cover himself. He knew it was a game for her and his only defense was not to play.

"I watched you from the rampart." She ran a finger along the side of the tub. He marveled at her ability to make such a casual gesture suggestive. "You looked so alone amongst all those men. You would think that after such a victory you would be celebrating."

Pippin could feel his body reacting to her and stood to fetch a towel. The less she had to work with, the better. She smirked as he dried himself. He crossed the room and found a clean shift to wear. "Bertrada is holding a feast tonight. Does that count?"

She followed him and pressed her body to his back. "I was thinking about something more immediate."

Pippin chuckled and pulled the shift over his head. "How goes your training?"

Miette scowled, giving up the game. "The Lady Hélène is a cruel taskmaster, but I seem to have some talent for it. She will never forgive me for the death of Agnès, but perhaps with time I can balance the scales."

"That's better than Childebrand. He wants me to send you back to your husband."

A hint of fear touched Miette's face. "Surely, you won't agree."

"Not while Childeric is in power."

Her body visually relaxed and she tried to play the coquette once more. "Then we are destined to be together for some time."

Pippin laughed in spite of himself. "Yes. It seems that way."

"We should learn to make better use of our time." Again, she drew close but this time her face was serious. "I missed you, Pippin."

Pippin tried to appear unmoved, but in truth he enjoyed their banter and found a great deal of comfort in her welcome. Not for the first time, he pondered indulging himself in her attempts at seduction. She was so close! He could feel the heat emanating off her and felt his body respond to it, urging him forward. For once, he let himself languish in the feeling, his heart pounding at the thought of her nakedness. She raised an eyebrow as if daring him to take the last step between them.

It took every bit of Pippin's restraint to turn away from her.

"One day, Pippin..." she warned.

He stopped and turned at the door.

"One day soon, you will bed me. And when you do, it will be your idea."

Pippin smiled and bowed deeply at the waist. "I missed you, too, milady."

* * *

"Bishop Boniface arrived an hour after you did," Gunther spat. "He's got that prick Aidolf with him."

Gunther had never been fond of priests, let alone bishops. The man even hated attending mass. In fact, Pippin wasn't really sure that his lieutenant was Christian. Pippin had left a brigade in Quierzy with

Gunther to keep an eye on the king and his allies among the Neustrian nobles while he was away campaigning in Saxony.

"Aidolf, *the Bishop of Auxerres*," Pippin said with emphasis, "heads one of the most powerful monasteries in the kingdom. He has more land and wealth than half the duchies. And he has a bigger army than most as well."

Gunther shrugged. "He's still a prick. They are in the small sitting room near the kitchen."

"Did you –"

"Yes, I kept the boy out of sight."

"Will you ask a servant –"

"To bring wine and meats? Bertrada ordered refreshments the moment the bishops arrived."

Pippin was not surprised that Boniface had come to see him. The Church had sided with Carloman over his refusal to acknowledge Childeric. While he and Carloman had tried to remain civil, the hostility between their factions was growing.

Carloman's Knights in Christ – like Carloman himself – believed themselves to be "holy warriors" defending their religion. They looked upon Pippin's obstinance as an assault on their faith. They saw it as their sacred duty to insist upon obeisance to Childeric. More often than not, violence was the result.

The fact that Boniface had solicited the aid of the Bishop of Auxerres and timed their arrival so closely to Pippin's return suggested that the politics of court were coming to a head.

Boniface was a logical intermediary between the two brothers. He had been a close advisor to Pippin's father, Charles, and now served in a similar capacity to Carloman. He also was a legate to the Holy See in Rome.

But one factor weighed in for Pippin's benefit. Boniface was also his godfather. If anyone could help find a solution to their stalemate it was him. Perhaps he could be persuaded to see the legitimacy of Pippin's rejection of Childeric.

The two bishops were still standing when Pippin entered the room. He bowed, formally. "Your Excellencies, I beg your forgiveness for my inadequate welcome. I only just returned from campaign and was not aware until now of your visit."

"Milord mayor." Bishop Aidolf extended his ring for Pippin to kiss. He was a short arrogant man used to having his way. As form demanded, Pippin bent to kiss the ring even though Aidolf's intent clearly was meant to show Pippin his place.

Rather than repeat the same gesture with Boniface, Pippin smiled and opened his arms wide to wrap them around the big bishop, slapping him on the back in welcome. "It is good to see you, godfather. You look well for such an old man."

Boniface smiled in return. "I hear your campaign in Saxony was successful."

Pippin waved them to seats at the table. "Theodoric is still more outlaw than nobleman, but he knows how to count troops. We had twice as many men and after a day's bloodshed, he suddenly had a change of heart. He's also building a new castle at Seeburg and I don't think he wanted to see it burnt down."

"Perhaps there is hope for him yet."

Aidolf cleared his throat. "As much as your campaign in Saxony is…interesting, I would suggest we have more important matters to discuss."

Pippin frowned. "Important to whom?"

"Your refusal to acknowledge Childeric has created a rift that imperils the kingdom. We've come to see it rectified." Aidolf waved his hand as if they were discussing something already decided.

"Or?" Pippin asked.

"Or we will take steps to –"

"If I may," Boniface interrupted. "I think it would be more productive to discuss how we might find an end to the divide between you and Carloman."

"I would like nothing more." Pippin waved two servants into the room. One carried a tray of meat and cheese. The second brought cups of wine. "But may I ask on whose behalf are you negotiating? Are you here as representatives of the Church or of Carloman?"

"For the moment, our interests are the same." Boniface helped himself to the wine and several slices of meat. "This dispute between you and Carloman has gone on long enough. We seek to unite the kingdom under Childeric. Your refusal to acknowledge him as king undermines his legitimacy. And it serves no purpose. When your father was mayor, I once imagined that he, himself, would succeed to the throne. His untimely death and the discovery of one with the royal blood destroyed that hope. Carloman had no choice but to raise Childeric to the throne. He is a true Merovingian and deserves your loyalty."

Pippin tried to keep his voice calm. "Carloman and I have worked in concert over the past two years. We campaigned together last year to punish Hunoald of Aquitaine for burning the church at Chartres. This spring, I confronted the Saxons while Carloman went to Alemannia to punish Theudebald. We've put down every duchy in rebellion since my father's death. After Carloman finishes with Theudebald, there should be peace in the kingdom. What need have I for Childeric?"

Bishop Aidolf cleared his throat. "Childeric has been crowned king. He has been anointed with the holy oil. Your refusal leaves the kingdom in a quandary. As mayors of the palace, you and Carloman control all the military might of the kingdom. With only one acknowledging the king, it leaves the legitimacy of the throne in question."

Pippin scowled. "Not to mention the legitimacy of the Church that anointed him."

Aidolf nodded his head in acknowledgement. "My point exactly."

"Childeric's legitimacy should be in question," Pippin said. "The man is incompetent, self-indulgent, and deceitful."

"He would not be the first king to be so described," Aidolf said.

Pippin's anger was growing with each exchange. "It is you who have made the mistake here, Your Excellencies. You approached me before elevating him to the throne and I refused to sanction it. You ignored my protest and raised him anyway, assuming I would fall into line. And now, when I won't, you pressure me into sanctioning it rather than to admit to your error. You are compounding the problem rather than addressing it."

"We see you as the problem, Mayor," Aidolf said. "You are the only one challenging this decision. You are the one in rebellion."

Pippin's voice dropped to just above a whisper. "I would be very careful of using such a term, Bishop. It will only lead to bloodshed. I have raised arms solely in defense of the kingdom. I and my nobles have kept the roads safe for trade and travel and we have upheld order. Making accusations like 'rebellion' could cause a war you cannot win."

"You have to see that your choices undermine the Church," Boniface said.

"They were your choices, Boniface."

"What about Lady Ragomfred?" Aidolf asked. "The entire kingdom knows you are bedding her. Are you really willing to risk excommunication over a woman?"

It was an old charge and Pippin was prepared for it. "She is a hostage, nothing more."

"A hostage?" Aidolf exchanged an incredulous glance with Boniface. "You take hostages from Neustrian nobles? They are your allies!"

"As you well know, Lady Bertrada was attacked on the King's Road. She has implicated knights in the service of Lord Ragomfred and Childeric himself. To ensure Bertrada's safety, I've taken Lady Ragomfred as a hostage to avoid further bloodshed."

Aidolf stood, his anger visible. "Do you deny committing adultery with her?"

"I have never slept with Lady Ragomfred. I'm not sure Childeric can say the same."

"Are you accusing him?"

"If you insist on this course, I will have to. And I should remind you, I have the witness."

Boniface stood and put his hand on Aidolf's shoulder. "Emotions are running high. Let us retire for now to the church rectory. The Lady Bertrada has invited us to a fete this evening to celebrate the army's return. Perhaps we can all consider ways to further our discussion then."

It was the last thing Pippin wanted for Bertrada's fete, but he kept his voice neutral. "I look forward to it."

As the two bishops left the room, Aidolf paused at the door, his face red with fury. "You *will* accede to our wishes."

"Not if Childeric is king," Pippin said. He waited until the door had closed behind them before throwing his cup of wine against the wall.

* * *

Bertrada had outdone herself. The main hall was decorated with banners of his green and white colors to celebrate the army's return. The huge fireplace blazed with giant logs to ward off the evening's chill. Tables displaying a choice of meats, cheeses, and bread lined the wall. And a large iron pot by the fire kept warm a stew of lamb and vegetables. Servants carried trays filled with cups of wine and ale so that no hand was empty.

There were perhaps forty people already in attendance when Pippin entered. A hearty cheer greeted his arrival and he waved to acknowledge it. He then bowed to Bertrada, took her hand, and raised it above their heads. The cheers grew louder and Pippin took great delight in her responding smile. Being Quierzy's host seemed to be the one role where she was happy. Without asking his blessing, she had taken over running the household when Pippin moved his court to Quierzy. And, as the daughter of a comte, she was well acquainted with its responsibilities. No one had ever felt a need to question her authority.

Holding his arm, Bertrada led him through the crowd to greet each of the guests personally. Pippin reveled in the gesture. She was a breath of elegance in her long black dress and gold necklace. The simplicity of the combination set off her blue eyes and blond hair so that she seemed to shine in the firelight. Everyone they greeted was one of the dozens of nobles housed within the residence – the inner circle of Pippin's court.

When the tour of the room ended, Bertrada led Pippin before the fireplace and waited until every eye in the room was upon them. As the room grew quiet, she stepped aside to give him the floor. Taking her cue, the nobles applauded. Pippin marveled at her ability to command a room without even speaking.

Taking a cup of wine from a nearby tray, Pippin cleared his throat. "Every homecoming is a cause for both celebration and for grief. To-night, we celebrate our success in defeating the Saxons" – cheers and whistles interrupted him – "and we celebrate our reunion with those who guarded our home front." He nodded to Gunther. More cheers engulfed him.

"But we also grieve for those who did not return with us: Jean-Baptiste de Blois and Henri de Soissons gave their lives for the peace of the realm." Pippin raised his glass to the silence that took the room. "To those we miss."

"Salut!" Gunther called out.

"Salut!" the room echoed.

"I would also like to thank the Lady Bertrada for hosting us this evening. I don't know where I would be without her."

More cheers. As they were about to subside, Childebrand shouted, "Marry her!"

Pippin smiled to acknowledge the jibe and the room erupted with laughter. Glancing at Bertrada he could see she was embarrassed.

He noticed that most of the guests were wearing a green band around one of their arms. When he mentioned it to Bertrada she chuckled and pointed to Catherine de Loches.

"That's her doing." She led him toward the comtesse who, as always, was commanding the attention of everyone around her.

Despite three years together, Pippin had yet to put an age on the woman. She had known his father, that much she had admitted, and she had two children still under fifteen, but beyond that Pippin hadn't a clue. She carried herself with an elegance that demanded respect but had the intellect to deserve it. Pippin had taken her hostage after sacking the city of Loches, only to have the comtesse renegotiate her standing by using a family treasure she had kept hidden from her husband. Rather than return to Loches, she had insisted that her children be raised as subjects in Pippin's court.

To his surprise, she was also Lady Hélène's sister.

As he and Bertrada approached, Catherine's eyes beamed with delight. "Milord mayor!" She kissed both his cheeks in greeting.

"I'm told I have you to thank for these mysterious green bands everyone seems to have on their arms."

"Actually, you can thank Carloman. I borrowed the idea from him. His Knights in Christ are very visible, parading around Paris in those red and white doublets. So much so, it appears as if our supporters don't exist. I thought it might be appropriate that your subjects carry some symbol of their fealty. Some wear it on their arms, some as a patch on their clothing."

"Was there any resistance to it?"

She smiled. "I can be very persuasive. Of course, once the nobles started wearing them, each of their subjects wanted one as well. Every linen merchant this side of Paris has been sold out of green cloth for a month."

As flattered as Pippin was about such a display of loyalty, he wondered about its consequences. He could see it setting off conflicts between his men and those aligned with Carloman.

Catherine answered his reservation before he could voice it. "It will engender some fighting, but people need to see that your power extends beyond Quierzy. All they see now are Carloman's knights."

Bertrada took him once again by the arm to guide him. "We should acknowledge our special guests." She nodded to the entryway where Bishops Boniface and Aidolf stood.

As they crossed the room Boniface met them halfway. "Lady Bertrada, you look stunning tonight." Boniface took her in his arms and kissed both her cheeks.

"Your Excellency." She broke away and curtsied to Aidolf. "Welcome, Bishop."

"Did I hear talk of marriage?" Boniface grinned. "I would be happy to wed the two of you. It's long overdue."

"When the time is right it would be an honor," Bertrada said. "How long will you be staying in Quierzy?"

"Unfortunately, we leave tomorrow."

"That is regrettable. I've always valued your counsel."

"I'm proud to be of service." Boniface made a small bow.

She turned to Bishop Aidolf. "To what do we owe the honor of your presence, Your Excellency?"

"Affairs of state, Milady." Aidolf smiled vacantly. "Nothing that would concern you."

Pippin saw crimson blotching Bertrada's cheeks and cleared his throat. "It seems the Church is pressing me to acknowledge Childeric's claim to the throne."

Bertrada's eyes flashed. "I would think that was between you and Carloman."

Aidolf puffed out his chest. "*King* Childeric has been anointed with the holy oil. It is already his divine right to rule."

"If that were the case, then why would you need Pippin's acknowledgement?"

Aidolf's eyes narrowed as he considered Bertrada. "As I said, Milady, this is nothing that concerns you."

"Are you aware that Childeric sent men to kill me? He murdered several nuns at the Abbey at Chelles."

"That incident has never been verified."

"I was there."

"It has not been corroborated."

"There were dozens of nuns present."

"You can hardly expect the Church to condemn a nascent king on the testimony of a handful of hysterical women." Aidolf waved his hand dismissively.

The color drained from Bertrada's face.

Pippin's voice was barely above a whisper, but it carried the menace of a feral animal. "Get out."

"I beg your pardon?" Aidolf's face carried a wealth of disdain.

"You mistake your place here, Bishop. Get out of my home."

Boniface held up his hand in a placating gesture. "Now, Pippin –"

"The only reason he is still standing is out of respect for you, God-father." Pippin signaled to Gunther. His lieutenant stepped forward.

Boniface interceded by grabbing the Bishop of Auxerres by the arm and ushering him from the room. Before they left, Boniface quickly bowed to Bertrada. "My apologies, Milady."

Silence took the main hall, disturbed only by the crackling of the fire. Pippin reached out a hand for Bertrada.

Without meeting his eyes, she held up her hand to stop him and kept her voice low. "There was no need to threaten him. And your outburst only made his point that I am not capable of handling such discussions."

Still caught up in his anger at Bishop Aidolf, Pippin was confused by Bertrada's rebuke. He had thought he was defending her. "Bertie, I'm sorry, I –"

"Please give our guests my apologies." She strode from the room with her back straight and her head held high.

* * *

After months sleeping on the ground, Pippin had trouble adjusting to a night in bed. The depth of his mattress and the sheer weight of his blankets kept him struggling to find a place of comfort. It was just too soft. When he did sleep, his dreams were populated by both Bertrada and Miette. Neither of them was clothed.

He startled awake in the early hours with a crick in his neck. The house was still dark and quiet. He struggled to escape his bed and padded naked across the room to a washstand, where he splashed water on his face.

When he turned, Bertrada was standing in his doorway dressed in a nightshift.

She looked startled to see him awake. "I...I'm sorry. I thought to just look in on you. I didn't think you'd be awake."

"I'm glad you did."

She shook her head. "I shouldn't be here."

"No. Please, stay." Afraid she might bolt, Pippin walked slowly toward her, making no sudden moves. What light there was showed a silhouette of her body through her shift, showing him much of what he had dreamed just moments ago. As he drew nearer, she raised her hand to ward him away, but Pippin took it in his and kissed it. She didn't retract it.

"I did miss you," Bertrada whispered.

"I missed you, too."

"I know I can be difficult."

"The world is difficult." Pippin risked putting his other hand on her waist to draw her closer. Again, she let him.

He held her lightly, afraid to do more, but she sighed and rested her forehead on his chest. He trembled with delight and his arms encircled her in a soft embrace. He held his breath, afraid she would retreat, but she put her arms around him and pulled him close. He nearly wept with relief.

"I just wish we could go back in time to the way we were," Pippin ventured. "I miss our old life."

She hesitated before responding. "Those days are gone, Pippin. We were young and naïve and you weren't mayor of the palace with the fate of the kingdom in your hands."

"I still miss it."

"As do I." She began to cry. Pippin held her for a time and then lifted her chin to kiss away her tears. And then, he was kissing her lips and pulling her to him with a hunger he could no longer restrain. He was surprised to find that her passion matched his. Her kisses became insistent, aggressive.

He lifted her and carried her to the bed. Once there, she struggled to pull her shift over her head to match his nakedness. With eyes lidded in passion, she found his erection and pulled him toward her. In a moment, he was inside her.

In that moment, everything fell away from him; all his reservations, his guilt and fears melted within their embrace. He was at once exhilarated, humbled, and grateful as their coupling intensified.

And as quickly as it began, it ended in a flurry of climaxes and suppressed shouts. Pippin lay beside her on his too soft bed, allowing their breathing to return to normal.

"I didn't expect that," Pippin whispered.

"Nor did I." She chuckled, her hand tracing a line down his chest. "I should say that I'm sorry for how I treated you today. I was needlessly cruel."

"You're here now." As he stroked her hair, Pippin marveled at how languid his body felt, as if all the tension he had been carrying suddenly disappeared into the mattress beneath him.

"I know you're a good man, Pippin. I don't like the violence that comes with being mayor, but I recognize you are not like Carloman. You would never have hung that boy."

Pippin leaned his head back against the bed frame, blinking back the tears welling in his eyes. It was a huge concession for her to make. Carloman's hanging of Duc Heden's son had been the cause of her break with him. Pippin had tried to insist that the fault was Carloman's alone, but for Bertrada, the act had become a symbol of his family's history of violence, in which Pippin was complicit. They had repeated the quarrel so many times that Pippin could recite her half of the argument as well as she could.

"I am surprised to hear you say that."

"You can thank your assassin, Lady Hélène."

Following his father's death, Pippin had learned that the Lady Hélène was indeed Charles's assassin. The wealthy widow of a Neustrian nobleman, Hélène had hidden in plain sight as a lady of the court. No one had suspected that she was an acolyte of a secret cult of the Gascon Church where "justice" was the predominant principle. She had chosen Charles as her ally in the cause.

Of late, she had adopted the role of protecting Bertrada and little Charles following the attack on the King's Road.

"She is not my assassin...but I do appreciate her watching over you while I was away."

"She has a unique perspective. It has helped me better appreciate the role you play as mayor. She talks a lot about justice and combatting evil."

"So does Carloman."

"But she is more discerning. Carloman always equates good with the Church." Bertrada sighed. "I just wish the bloodshed would end. I wish that you wouldn't be gone for months – while Charles and I wait here, praying that you return alive and whole."

She paused and Pippin could feel the tears leaking from her eyes onto his chest. When she began again, her voice was choked, full of emotion. "And I wish that you weren't the instrument of so much death. I shudder when I think of your hands – the hands that wield your sword in battle – playing with little Charles."

Pippin sighed. It was the opening salvo of their quarrel. Rather than argue, he tried to have her see it from his eyes. "All my life, there has been nothing but war – in every part of the kingdom. It's the consequence of weak kings – or corrupt ones. My father believed he would be a better king than the Merovingians he served. His objective was to unite the kingdom. If we could do that, we could eliminate the constant bloodshed."

"And the pagans – don't forget killing the pagans."

Pippin hesitated. This was where their argument always turned against him. Charles had allied himself with the Church from his earliest days and the Church had always demanded that he suppress the pagans – forcing them to renounce their faith at the point of a sword. It was a practice favored by many of the nobles at court – especially in Neustria and Austrasia. During the last decade, Carloman had been their greatest champion.

She was waiting for him to defend his family – as he usually did at this point – with arguments about needing the Church's resources and the unifying nature of one religion throughout the kingdom.

If he did that, the spell would be broken. She would leave his room and the silence between them would begin anew.

He wanted to explain that there were always trade-offs to sustaining power, that he couldn't stop the purge of pagans even if he tried. Such a stance would risk losing the Church's support as well as many of the nobles most loyal to him.

Yet, he couldn't lose Bertrada. Not again. If she could concede a point as she had done earlier, then so could he.

"You're right," he said carefully. "It isn't 'just,' as Lady Hélène would say. I won't persecute them. I won't force them to convert."

She lifted her head to search his eyes. Pippin held her gaze and said, "I swear."

She kissed him and laid her head on his chest. He could feel the tension leave her body. "Thank you," she whispered.

Pippin held her for hours, staring into the darkness, praying the night wouldn't end. He knew their troubles weren't over, but for once the two of them had been able to set them aside. And for that, he was grateful.

2

Canstatt

Carloman lingered in sleep, refusing to open his eyes and let her go. She had visited his dreams before, always in the early morning hours, her face and dark hair shrouded in ephemeral haze. This time, she strained to reach him, but her arms were too distant. She called out to him, but her words were too faint. Carloman tried to speak, but his mouth wouldn't cooperate. He grew desperate as she receded further and further into the haze. Lunging forward, he shouted for her to wait.

A strangled cry passed his lips and Carloman opened his eyes. Alone in his tent, he sat up and wiped a line of drool from his cheek, wondering who the woman could be. When he stood, he discovered an erection pushing out against his shift. He stared at it with surprise. He hadn't had one in two years. It gave him a feeling of expectation.

He put on a robe and sandals and threw back the flap to his tent. A heavy dew covered the ground and his breath misted in the morning air. Despite the early hour, the camp was already coming to life with men stoking fires, platoon leaders rousting soldiers, and lines forming at the latrine trench.

Carloman hated being back in Alemannia. This was the third time in three years that he or Pippin had confronted the rebel Duc Theudebald for fomenting rebellion, attacking priests, and defying the Church. Carloman vowed this would be the last.

A small twitch at his jawline betrayed the fury Carloman harbored for the pagan. It was far from a fleeting emotion; he had kindled and nurtured it like a blacksmith at the forge, stoking his rage until it burned white hot within him. Fury kept his mind clear. Fury kept his faith strong for the work he must do as one of God's chosen.

His calling to be the Blade of Christ had redefined him, elevating him from the cautious deliberate man he once was into a man of righteous vision and deed. His will was God's will, his voice, God's voice. He had been blessed to walk a divine path.

His epiphany had come three years earlier. Unhorsed during a desperate cavalry charge, Carloman had found himself alone behind the enemy line. Rather than panic, he had been filled with a holy euphoria. The sounds of the battle had quieted and the fighting around him slowed. His sword became an extension of his will and he moved with a lethal grace deeper and deeper into the enemy ranks. No one could stand before his killing dance. He had become death incarnate. The hand of God was upon him.

Within this revelation, Carloman's understanding of the world seared to its essential form. The politics of court, the Church, his marriage, his brother, and his life, all became meaningless. He had been called. He would become Christ's champion – his sword on earth – to rid the kingdom of godlessness and paganism.

The euphoria of that moment, however, drained from him like blood from an open wound. Desperate to be filled again with its righteousness, he fasted, performed penance, and held daylong vigils, praying for the surety and the passion it once had provided. But no amount of prayer sufficed. He felt empty, a mere ghost of the man he had been.

One day during the flogging of one of his men for blasphemy, Carloman had grown infuriated by the weak blows being delivered, He stepped forward to whip the man himself. As the first stroke fell perfectly across the man's shoulder blades, Carloman felt a thrill. He watched enthralled as a line of blood welled across the man's back. With each subsequent crack of the whip, a wave of righteous anger surged within him until he was once again filled with the holy rage. He latched on to that anger – that blessed fury – to sustain him in his holy war against paganism.

The latest front in that war was in Alemannia.

Carloman sat with Laurent, his newest champion, to take his morning meal. The third son of a Neustrian nobleman from Orleans, Laurent was a swordsman's swordsman, known for his fluid grace upon the battlefield. He was slightly taller than Carloman with a lithe body and long arms, but it was the speed of his blade that set him apart.

Unfortunately, his champion was a man of few words, grunting, "Yes, milord" and "No, milord" into the spaces Carloman left for him to join the conversation. After a few attempts to engage the man, Carloman let the discussion drift into silence. At least he could enjoy the eggs that had been cooked for him.

A commotion nearby drew both men to their feet. They followed the clamor outside until they found several of his men surrounding a lone woman and taunting her from all sides. From the animal skins she wore, she was likely pagan, but despite the ridicule and jostling, she held herself as poised as any noblewoman. She had long dark hair with something woven through it that clacked eerily as she moved.

The men were pushing her from one side of their circle to another, spinning her into disorientation and grabbing at her breasts as she came near them.

"Enough!" Carloman said.

When it became clear that the men couldn't hear him over their taunting and laughter, he nodded to Laurent, who leapt into the circle and commanded the men to stop.

"A pagan, milord," one of the men called out to explain. "See?" He pulled off the animal skin that covered her upper body and she stood bare chested before them. Her entire upper body, save for her breasts, was covered in tattoos. But rather than hide her nakedness in shame, the woman stood unbowed before their stares. She looked at Carloman as if he were the one who should be embarrassed.

That's when he recognized her: the woman from his dream. He stared, disbelieving, a quiet trepidation stealing over him.

"Bring her to me." He turned toward his tent.

Laurent recovered her clothing, threw it around her shoulders, and started to follow. When some of the men fell in line behind them, Laurent barked a command that they return to their duties.

Once inside his tent, Carloman lit torches. He was filled with apprehension. How could she be here? What did it mean? He tried to recapture a sense of command by sitting on the elevated chair he used for settling disputes between his men. Laurent brought the woman in, forced her to her knees before Carloman, and then left to stand guard outside.

Seeing her up close, there was no question she was the woman from his dream. Although attractive, what made her compelling was her assuredness. She looked up at him with piercing grey eyes as if he were a supplicant, not her.

"My name is Carloman. I rule here in the name of the king," he said, trying to keep the apprehension from his voice. "Who, in God's name, are you?"

The woman looked back to where Laurent had exited and then stood, the white trinkets in her hair clacking as she did. Carloman shivered, realizing they were small bones.

"I am Asa." She spoke carefully, her accent only serving to compound her mystery.

Carloman's hands gripped the arms of his chair. "Are you a witch?"

She barked a laugh. "I am many things, but not that." She walked through his command tent taking note of its cross and the prie-dieu on which he knelt to pray.

"But you are pagan?"

"That is what some call it."

"What do you call it?"

She shrugged. "It is faith, like yours."

The insult angered him. "I can assure you it is nothing like mine."

"Yet, we both worship what we cannot see and cannot know."

Carloman stood, using his height to tower over her. "There is only one true God. The lord Jesus said, 'I am the way and the light. No one comes to the Father but through me.'"

She chuckled. "All gods make such boasts."

She had spoken so casually, without fear, as if her words weren't blasphemous. Carloman's backhand took her across the face. Her head turned with the blow. When she looked back at him, there was a trickle of blood on her lip. Even then, her eyes were defiant.

"Why are you here?" he demanded.

"The Fates brought me to you."

"For what purpose?"

"I am a seer. I see the shadows of the future and the past."

"A charlatan's boast."

She smiled and wiped the blood from her lip. "I will show you." Her hand reached up to cup his face. Carloman flinched away from it. She chuckled at that. "No harm will come to you."

Despite his anger, he was curious, so he let her hand touch his damaged cheek. She looked into his eyes like she was searching for his soul. After a moment her eyes widened, and she stepped back. "You've been touched by the gods!"

Carloman froze in his place. He had never spoken about his epiphany to anyone. He stared at the woman, fear spiking inside him.

"What do you mean?" The evasion sounded weak to his ears.

"You must know of what I speak."

"I am not touched."

She scoffed. "Are not the gods worshipped among your people?"

"There is only one God." Carloman began to pace; he needed space to think. "And, of course, we worship Him."

Carloman sat back down in his chair. Was she of the devil? Had she cast a spell over him? His piety struggled with his curiosity. She could *see* his epiphany within him. "What else can you see?" he whispered, blood pounding in his ears.

"To see more requires augury." She began to disrobe, her breasts swinging freely in the torchlight. "I will need fire and blood."

Carloman jumped to his feet, retrieving the skins she had discarded. "No. I forbid it."

She shrugged. "As you wish." She rewrapped the skins around her and turned to go.

He held up his hand. "I haven't dismissed you."

She smiled. "I am not yours to command."

"Why did the Fates send you?"

"For that, I must petition the gods."

"Pagan rites are forbidden."

She shrugged. "There is a clearing by a stream to the north of your camp. I will wait there until sundown tomorrow. If you do not come, I will return to my home in the mountains."

She opened the tent flap and Laurent stood in her way, his eyes questioning Carloman.

With a wave of his hand, Carloman let her go.

* * *

All day she plagued his thoughts and when he slept that night, he dreamed of her again. It was a never-ending loop of doubt, curiosity, fear, and lust. He awoke the next morning at dawn drenched in sweat. He immediately sent for Laurent.

"Break camp. I want to head south. Theudebald can't hide forever."

Laurent looked surprised. "You've word of him?"

"No. But he isn't here."

"Milord, we've only just begun to resupply. Our men are out foraging, and we need the food. It would be preferable to delay for at least a day or two to ensure we have enough supplies for the march ahead of us."

"I said break camp!" The words came out with more heat than he intended.

"Of course, milord." Clearly stung by the rebuke, Laurent bowed his head and turned to go.

"Wait." Carloman chided himself. He had let the witch unsettle him. He pictured her in the clearing by the stream waiting for him. Well, she could wait. He could withstand her temptations. "I'm sorry, Laurent. There's no reason to go."

"Yes, milord." With a look of confusion, his champion took his leave.

Clearly, the woman had bewitched him. That was the only explanation. His assuredness, his confidence in God's will had weakened in her presence. She had used dark forces to leech his strength. But she also had promised to leave and return to her mountain. All he had to do was let her go.

He went to look after his warhorse, but a stable hand assured him that the steed was well tended. He went to have his armor polished, but a smithy's son already had bent to the task. He walked the perimeter of the camp, surprising the pickets, who stiffened at his approach. When his tour was complete, he checked with Laurent to see if any of the scouts had returned. None had yet to make it back to camp.

And still she occupied his thoughts.

He returned to his tent and knelt at the prie-dieu before his crucifix. He closed his eyes, bowed his head, and prayed. *"Credo in Deum Patrem omnipotentem, Creatorem caeli et terrae."* The Apostles' Creed, ingrained in him as a child, had always soothed his temper and calmed his spirit. His shoulders relaxed with the rhythm of its words. *"Et in Iesum Christum, Filium Eius unicum, Dominum nostrum."*

An image of the witch came to him. She was sitting before a fire, her eyes closed as if she, too, were lost in prayer. He watched as she swayed in time to his words. And then, as if sensing his presence, her eyes opened and returned his gaze.

Carloman jumped away from the prie-dieu. She *was* a witch! How else could she have invaded his prayer?

Furious, he bolted from his tent and waved off a concerned look from Laurent. Finding his warhorse, he had it saddled and rode north out of camp. He pushed the mare, matching her pace to his fury. When he found the clearing, the witch was sitting as he had seen her, facing a fire with her back to an ash tree.

Carloman rode hard to her place by the ash, as if to run her down. He wanted her to fear his wrath. Just short of the fire, he reined in. The woman barely looked up to acknowledge his presence. She leaned forward to add branches to the fire and, from a pouch, she drew a handful of crushed plants and threw them onto the blaze. They gave off a pungent odor.

He dismounted. "What have you done to me?"

Her eyebrows arched. "I 'do' nothing. I am a seer, blessed and cursed with sight beyond the veil."

"We burn witches like you at the stake."

Her face was unreadable, but she nodded. "Yes. This, I have seen; I will die by fire. But it will not be by your hand."

"How can you know that?" He waited for an answer, but she looked at him as if he hadn't been listening.

The smoke from the blaze swirled around them. There was a bowl beside her filled with blood. After a moment she pointed to the ground. "Sit."

Instead, he began to pace. Again, she ignored him, focusing her attention on the fire. After a few moments his anger abated, and he began to feel foolish. He sat near her by the fire. Only then did she look up. "Why have you come?"

"To stop you from bewitching me."

She shook her head. "You came because the gods have touched you and you want to understand why."

In truth, he did, but was reluctant to admit it. "I saw you in my dreams."

She raised an eyebrow, and a smile touched the corner of her lips. "Many men say such things."

"It was before I met you."

She nodded, her face growing serious. "I saw you too. That is why I came."

The fumes from the fire smelled strange and made him cough. He watched as she drew the smoke to her with her hands, immersing herself in it and breathing deeply.

She picked up the bowl and dipped two fingers into it, using the blood to draw vertical lines on her face. She offered him the bowl.

When he shook his head to decline, she shrugged and set the bowl beside her. He felt odd, like he was watching her from a distance. He tried to concentrate by focusing on the fire. It seemed brighter than it had a moment ago. He watched the intricate dance of its flames as they curled and flared in successive waves. He couldn't tell how long he stared, but it felt like more than a minute.

"We begin." She discarded the animal skin covering her. Her nakedness unsettled him, but she treated it as if it were customary. With her arms held out toward the fire, she began to chant in a language he didn't understand. There was a rhythm to it, and she swayed in a circular motion to its beat. She next held aloft a pouch before the blaze much as a priest would lift a chalice and then poured its contents on the ground before her. Smooth stones like those found in a riverbed cascaded before her. When he looked closer, each had a marking carved into its face.

"What are those?"

"Odin stones. A gift of the gods. The runes provide a path for to those willing to see."

She returned to her chant, inhaling deeply the strange smoke from the fire. After a few moments, her chanting stopped and her eyes opened. They had a faraway look to them. Still swaying, she leaned forward to study the rune stones before her.

She touched one stone, then another, aligning them into a pattern. With a sudden start she sat up, muttering, "No, no, no," under her breath. Abruptly, she gathered the stones and recast them.

"What is it?" Even his voice sounded strange to him.

She searched among the spilled stones, frantic in her intensity. "No!" She gave him a horrified look and struggled to her feet, weaving as if drunk. She backed away from him, holding up her arm before her as if she was being attacked. Her hands dove into a pack by the tree and came out with a knife. She turned to face him.

"Murderer!"

Confused, Carloman staggered to his feet. He too felt unsteady. Smoke from the fire danced over her nakedness and he couldn't look away. She held the knife as if she had never used one and Carloman easily caught her by the wrists and pinned her against the tree. She struggled and he felt the length of her body beneath his.

"What did you see?" Anger pulsed through him.

She hissed between clenched teeth, struggling to free herself. "Murder! I saw murder!"

"I am a soldier. Killing is a cost of war."

"No!" Her eyes found his. "You kill innocents. And you've come to kill again."

The smell of the fire mixed with the scent of her. He was furious and aroused at the same time, his blood surging through him. "I came to wage war!" he shouted. "I don't kill innocents."

"I have seen it!" She renewed her struggle.

"Witch!" Almost against his will his hips thrust forward and ground himself against her body, thrilling in the promise of relief it offered. Her struggles only enhanced his passion. He thrust again.

Abruptly she stilled beneath him. "Will you ravage me as well, Carloman?"

He stopped. Appalled and livid at the same time, Carloman flung the woman to the ground. "Get away from me, witch!" She landed awkwardly, her limbs splaying out wide. Carloman's eyes locked on the dark patch between her legs.

Using her elbows, she sat up, doing nothing to hide her body.

Shaking his head to clear it, Carloman found her clothes by the tree and threw them at her. "Clothe yourself, temptress!"

She stepped into her animal skins. "I am a seer. Nothing more. But ware what I see! The touch of the gods can be powerful – too powerful – for mere mortals to bear. Death stalks the earth with you, Carloman. He surrounds your every step. Your god may have touched you, but that will not absolve your sins. Go home. If you stay, more innocents will die."

Carloman left her and returned to camp, his humiliation growing unabated. He should have seen her for what she was – a witch and a temptress. She had poisoned his thoughts and weakened his resolve.

He needed to cleanse himself, to purge the sin from his soul. He hurried back to his tent. From a compartment in his prie-dieu, he pulled a whip. Caressing its dark leather handle, he dropped his robe and he knelt before the cross. With a vehemence worthy of his sin, he snapped it over his shoulder, grunting as the lashes scored his back. He struck himself again and felt welts lift from his skin.

"Yes," he whispered through gritted teeth. "God's will be done." He struck himself again and again, praying for the archangels to blot out her memory. He embraced the pain, letting it fuel his fury until rivulets of blood poured down his body. And then he flogged himself more for having been so weak.

As evening fell and the day died, Carloman emerged from his tent covered with blood. Laurent raced to succor him. Too weak to resist, Carloman allowed his champion to tend his wounds. But the relief Carloman felt was palpable. His soul had been replenished and his fury restored. He was once again the Blade of Christ.

* * *

Carloman and Laurent stared out at a broad valley stretching for miles to the east. Flanked by steep hills to the north and south, it looked as if God Himself had plowed a giant furrow into the countryside. The resulting landscape was lush and verdant, bursting with wildlife; even the air was filled with the wet loamy scents of spring.

The valley also was filled with the Aleman army. By Carloman's count, Theudebald had mustered roughly two thousand men, mostly spearmen supported by a small cavalry. Given the number of women and children he could see, the valley was also likely their base camp. A number of wooden framed structures dotted the rows of tents barracking the men.

Carloman gave himself a satisfied nod. He would punish Theudebald at last.

By now, the pagan rebel should have seen his army and realized there were only two options – fight or surrender. Carloman didn't care which choice the man made. One way or another, Theudebald would answer for breaking his oaths.

"Our men are in position, milord," Laurent said.

Carloman turned to face his men. They were arranged in two broad columns with his cavalry on their flanks.

"Men of God!" he shouted. His words were echoed by men stationed periodically to relay his words so that everyone could hear him.

"Men of God, we have travelled far to do the Lord's work. Our mission here is a holy one. It is a sacrament. Directed by God, we act in His name and carry His blessings onto the battlefield. Your swords, your pikes, your bows are righteous instruments blessed by His hand.

"Today, we fight pagans who reject God's word, abjure His teachings, and mock us, His servants. Today, we fight pagans who relegate the one and true God to the level of their pathetic nature deities – as if the Almighty were but a river nymph or a god of thunder. It is one thing for pagans to be ignorant, unknowing of the Lord's holy word. It is another for them to know His word and reject it. It is an evil we cannot abide.

"Let there be no doubt; we face a creature of Satan sent to undermine us. Like a catching disease they infect the devout with their practices and beliefs; they use magic to seduce our women and subvert our children. Like a succubus in the night, they malign our bridal beds with their seed and corrupt that which is pure."

Emotion lifted Carloman's voice, filling it with his rage. "Who here has not been touched by the plagues of sickness they spawn? Who here has not seen their fields wither from the pagans' ungodly ways? Who here can say that the pagans' existence is anything but a scourge on our holy Christian homes?

"The time has come to end this travesty. Three times we have come to Alemannia to right this wrong. Three times we have been met by pagans willing to kneel before the cross when we arrive and profane the word of God when we leave. Many of these pagans have kissed the cross and claimed they are Christian, but it is a lie. They still pray to the morning sun and worship the phasing moon. They still carry potions and herbs to do their magic and hold perverse ceremonies in the night, naked before the stars."

He paused to wipe a trickle of mucus that ran from his nose across his upper lip. "They are sin itself. And that sin threatens our way of life and the Church we have sworn to protect. I have seen their ways up close. I have seen their practices and ceremonies. Their so-called 'holy men' are not holy. They are the work of the devil. They even sent one of their temptresses to me in an attempt to turn us away from our task.

"We will not be turned away!" Many of the men banged their spears against their shields. "We will not be deterred." More banging. "We will fight the enemy and purge the land of their stain." The banging became rhythmic. "We will protect our wives and our daughters from their ravaging and save the Church from their blasphemy! We will unite the kingdom under the will of the one true God."

Shouts of "Hu-yah!" sprang from the men.

"Let us pray." Carloman dismounted and knelt. An aging priest stepped forward to take his place. In unison, all the armed men dropped to their knees.

"Holy Father." The priest's voice belied his age and carried across the ranks. "We ask you to cleanse these souls of all past sins and any they commit on the battlefield today. They battle in Your name and with Your blessing to defend the kingdom from the pagan scourge before us.

We beseech You to bring all those who perish in this effort to Your side and assure them a hallowed place in heaven." He made the sign of the cross. "In the name of the Father, the Son, and the Holy Ghost. Amen."

"Amen," chorused the ranked soldiers.

Carloman remounted his warhorse. "For Francia!" he shouted.

"For Francia!" the men shouted.

"Let's take them into the valley," he said to Laurent.

As they descended to face the pagan army, Carloman could see Theudebald's men racing to form their army into ranks. They matched his two-column formation but had scant cavalry to protect their flanks. Once they reached a point one hundred yards away, Carloman signaled for his men to halt. He listened as the ranks marched four more disciplined steps before stopping as one. He smiled, knowing their precision would send a message of its own.

"Signal that we want to parley."

Laurent raised a hand, and a flag of truce was lifted. In moments a reply signal came from the enemy camp. Carloman and Laurent rode out to a point midway between the two armies.

Alone, Theudebald rode forward astride a wild-eyed, black stallion that suited its rider; it fought against its reins and chomped at its bit. A hardened man in his forties, Theudebald was a block of a soldier that had seen his share of battles. Like Carloman, his face was damaged. The Aleman's cheek carried a scar from his left ear to the corner of his mouth, giving the man a ghastly permanent smile.

Theudebald came to a stop before them. His defiance couldn't have been more pronounced if he had spit in Carloman's eye. "Why are you here, Carloman?"

Carloman struggled to contain his rage at the man's impudence. "I am here to accept your surrender."

"You want me to kneel? I'll kneel. You want tribute? I'll give you tribute."

"Your time as ruler of Alemannia has passed, Theudebald. The time of all pagan rulers has passed. I claim Alemannia for the Church."

"You flatter yourself, Carloman. You are far from home with half an army. Do I need to remind you that you barely won last time?"

Carloman raised his right fist, and a horn blew. On either side of the valley, other horns replied, and two new lines of Frankish troops filled the hillsides from the north and south. Carloman had split his army in advance of entering the valley and sent them to outflank the pagans. They had Theudebald's army all but surrounded and had the advantage of higher ground. The pagan army's fate was sealed. Many of the Alemanni dropped their weapons at the display.

Theudebald spat on the ground between them. "If I am gone, who do you think will rule in my stead? You? You and your brother come with your armies and demand tribute and then go back to your castles west of the Rhine. *I rule here*. Just as my father ruled before me."

"No longer," Carloman said. "Only Christians will rule here."

Theudebald's face grew dark and threatening. He brought his horse close to Carloman. Laurent moved to intervene, but Carloman stayed him with a hand signal.

"If you insist on this," Theudebald hissed, "this war will be never-ending. I will exhaust your armies and drain your treasure. I will fuck you just like I fucked your sister."

Carloman was stunned by the boast.

"She didn't tell you? Oh, I fucked her good. That bitch couldn't get enough pagan cock from that simpering cousin of mine, so I gave it to her – even while she was pregnant."

Theudebald kept speaking, but Carloman could no longer hear him. The pagan no longer mattered. As on the day of his epiphany, the world around Carloman slowed and his senses heightened. He could hear the wings of a bird flapping overhead and saw a trickle of sweat slide down Theudebald's jawline. Almost of its own volition, Carloman's sword flew from its scabbard, and he pointed it at Theudebald's throat.

"Milord?" Laurent called out in surprise.

"You'd violate the truce of parley?" Theudebald scoffed, holding his arms wide to emphasize that he was unarmed.

Carloman's lips curled into a smile. "Behold the will of God!" He thrust the blade past the pagan's chin into the man's brain.

"Milord!" Laurent looked stunned. "What have you done?"

Carloman's voice sounded distant, almost as if it were apart from him. "Enough of this. Kill them. Kill them all."

Seeing the hesitation on Laurent's face, Carloman turned his horse, screamed his battle cry *"Michaeli Archangelo!"* and spurred into the Alemanni ranks.

Horns echoed off the hillside and Carloman's troops followed him, descending on the Alemanni from all sides. Unprepared for battle, many of the Alemanni fell where they stood. Others scrambled for discarded weapons but found them too late.

Euphoria carried Carloman forward as he cut his way through the enemy ranks. He was again the Blade of Christ, raining down judgement on the pagans before him. No one was spared from his wrath. Shouting incoherently, he took the lives of all who stood before him: men, women, and children. A young boy of no more than ten years held up his hand to ward off Carloman's sword, but the blade sliced through it, severing small fingers from the boy's hand. The digits flew into Carloman's face just as his backhand blow took off the child's head.

Nothing could stop him. He fought until there were no more Alemanni left to kill. When it had ended, he strode across the length of the battlefield, blood and viscera covering his face and armor, satisfied that his judgement had been swift. He was surprised to see a number of his knights retching.

Laurent sought him out. His champion looked ghastly pale in the afternoon light. "What is it?" Carloman asked. "What is wrong?"

"Many were unarmed, milord. The women and children..."

"They were pagan."

"Yes, but –"

"But what?"

"Milord, they were innocents!"

The word struck Carloman like a stone.

3

Quierzy

Just after dawn, Pippin followed the smell of frying bacon down to the kitchen. He went alone because Bertrada had returned to her rooms an hour earlier to avoid attention.

While the kitchen would prepare a large meal of meat and eggs for the household, Pippin knew the cook would serve him alone. He sat down to some boiled eggs and bread while waiting for the bacon to cook.

Gunther poked his head through the door and, seeing Pippin, pulled up a chair next to him. "I thought I might find you here." He waved to the cook, who brought him his own plate of eggs and bread.

Pippin clapped him on the shoulder. "It's good to be back."

Gunther's eyes registered surprise. "I thought after last night, you'd be grousing over Aidolf's insult."

"You had the right of him. He is a prick."

"Boniface sent word that he'd like to talk with you alone."

"Won't change how I feel about Childeric."

"Didn't think it would. But you should know your refusal to acknowledge him is causing problems. Carloman's Knights in Christ are going out of their way to punish those who refuse to bend a knee to Childeric. In Paris, they're forcing people to take loyalty oaths at sword point."

"Are there any Knights in Christ in our camp?"

Gunther chuckled. "Nah, I made it clear long ago that you wouldn't tolerate that secret horseshit."

"Are these loyalty oaths to Childeric taking place on the streets or in people's homes?"

"Both, as far as I can tell. They started with nobles already in Carloman's camp but have begun spreading their kindness to our followers."

"Ask Childebrand to lead a few patrols of ten to twenty knights into Paris. Tell them to arrest anyone demanding such oaths."

"There'll be fighting."

Pippin nodded. "Someone needs to remind them that I still rule here."

"What about Carloman? Maybe he ordered the oaths."

"I would hope he's smarter than that."

"If he's not?"

"Then, I'll deal with him when he gets back from Alemannia."

The chef brought them a plate of sizzling bacon and the conversation halted while the two attacked it like it was a band of Saracens.

When the last of it had been eaten, Pippin set aside his plate. "How was Bertrada while I was away?"

Gunther wiped his mouth against his sleeve. "She runs a tight household."

Pippin raised his eyebrows, waiting for more.

"Ah, you know how she is. She hasn't been herself since the attack. She never lets the boy out of her sight. And she never goes anywhere without Lady Hélène."

"Has the lie held?" Although his inner circle knew the child was his, Pippin had decided to keep the boy's birth secret, to prevent further assassination attempts. Most nobles at court thought the babe was Bertrada's nephew, by her sister Aude. They had concocted the story when Aude and her husband, Tedbalt, left for Rome to manage his family's estates there. Even with the lie in place, Pippin had asked Bertrada to keep little Charles out of sight to avoid speculation.

"The lie holds. Can't say how much longer it will. It would be a lot easier if you would simply marry the woman."

"It would be." Pippin nodded. "Tell me about Childeric."

"He seems to be enjoying your standoff. While you and Carloman were away on campaign, he pandered to the Church bishops, promising to return lands taken from them by your father. He regularly holds court among the nobles beholden to Carloman. Ragomfred provides him with all the treasure he needs, and he's adopted the Knights in Christ as his personal guard. He uses them to dispense justice as he sees fit. My guess is that he's the one behind the loyalty oaths."

"Are the nobles falling in line?"

Gunther nodded. "Some have. Childeric does have the Church's blessing."

"How many from our camp?"

"More than I'd like to admit. Not all of those loyalty oaths are forced."

Pippin ran his hand through his hair. "We're losing ground." It was just as Miette once had warned him; he was being isolated by Carloman, the Church, and the king. Over time, they would woo the nobles supporting him to realign with Carloman until one night his back would feel the wrong end of knife. He needed to change strategies.

"Tell Boniface I'll meet with him at noon."

* * *

At the last second, Miette ducked beneath the long staff swinging toward her head and spun to her left, her own weapon whirling to counterstrike. Instead, a blow to the back of her legs swept her feet out from beneath her. With an audible grunt, she landed hard against the packed soil. She rolled to her right to regain her feet but stopped when the butt of her opponent's long staff shoved her back to the ground.

Pippin applauded. Miette had lasted far longer than he had expected. Lady Hélène bowed formally in victory with her long staff held horizontally before her. Miette slowly got to her feet, leaning heavily on her weapon. The two had sweated through a pair of linen shirts and pantaloons, typically worn by men.

"How goes the training?"

Miette grunted. "I have bruises on my bruises."

"It goes well." Hélène accepted Pippin's kiss to both her cheeks. "We've come a long way in two years."

Pippin had to admit the changes in Miette were substantial. Her arms and legs had clearly defined muscles. She looked lethal, her body toned and as strong as most men.

"Want to try your luck?" Miette goaded him with the end of her long staff.

He smiled. "It's not my weapon of choice."

"Afraid of me, milord mayor?"

He chuckled. "Always."

Their banter drew a look of disapproval from Hélène. "How may we serve you, milord?"

"If you would walk with me, I would like a word with you, Lady Hélène."

"My life is to serve."

Pippin nodded to Miette and he and Hélène walked away in silence until they were well clear of the training ground. "I'm glad to see you have reconciled with Miette."

Hélène scowled. "I've neither forgiven her for the death of Agnès nor forgotten it. But, as I believe in atonement, training Miette in the dark path is one way both she and I can redress such a loss."

Devotees of Hélène's sect of the Church committed their lives to a path for achieving one of the seven virtues. The "dark" path, the one Hélène chose, was the path to justice. As Pippin had come to understand it, Hélène wasn't an assassin for hire, she administered justice in God's name.

"For what do you have to atone? You didn't kill Agnès."

"I should have prevented her death. I had grown soft."

Pippin doubted that Hélène had ever been soft. "Her death should be laid at Childeric's feet, not yours."

"I owe penance for so much more." Hélène looked away. "I spent my life without her."

"It was a great loss. I owe her and you a debt for protecting Bertrada. In fact, that's why I've sought you out. I wanted to thank you for watching over both her and Charles. If I might ask, how did she fare while I was away on campaign?"

Hélène hesitated. "Are you asking about her health or your relationship with her?"

"Both, I suppose. She seems fragile to me. Charles is three years old and she has yet to wean the boy."

Hélène frowned. "Is that so surprising? She rejected you and this way of life only to have it forced upon her. Being the boy's mother is the only choice she has had the ability to make."

"I'm only trying to protect her and little Charles."

"Nonetheless...it is by your choice that she is here. And when you take Charles away to be trained as a warrior – just as you were trained – you're taking away the only choice she's made."

Pippin told her of Bertrada's visit during the night and the compromises they had made.

Hélène nodded. "That's good to hear. I have tried to help her see that the kingdom needs your protection the way she has needed mine. She struggles with the violence that surrounds you. She's very fearful about what it will do to you and what it will mean for your son."

"Charles can't afford to be weak."

Hélène laughed. "*Le Magne*? He won't be."

Pippin laughed at the nickname. "As much as I value your role protecting Bertrada and Charles, I would like you to return to Paris as the Lady Hélène the court has known."

"You want me to spy on Childeric." It wasn't a question.

"I need eyes on the Neustrian nobles as well. You have always had the ear of those at court."

"They will suspect that we are allied. They know I helped Bertrada – it's how they found us at Chelles. Plus, I've spent a great deal of time in your court."

"Tell them that you were here for Miette while she was being held hostage. You have stayed to provide her company."

"Then why would I leave now?"

"Tell them we had a falling-out. Make up a story that they'll believe."

Hélène bowed. "I am at your command, milord."

Pippin affectionately put his hand on her shoulder. "How can I repay you for your service?"

Hélène grunted. "Stop courting Miette."

Pippin felt his cheeks flush with embarrassment. "I don't know what you mean."

"Yes. You do. You openly court her."

"That's ridiculous!"

"Is it?"

"I admit she's very attractive. But –"

Hélène mimicked Miette's voice. "Want to try your luck, milord? Afraid of me, milord?" Her voiced dropped while she imitated him. "Not my weapon of choice, milady."

Pippin laughed self-consciously, hating to admit she had a point. "I'll do my best to keep my ardor contained."

"I thank you, milord." Under her breath she muttered, "As will the rest of the kingdom."

* * *

Although officially a legate to the Holy See, Boniface came dressed in the plain brown robe of a parish priest. Pippin met him in the same sitting room they had met with Aidolf. As before, Pippin had ordered plates of fruit and meats and as before, Boniface made use of them.

"I want to apologize for Bishop Aidolf's row with Bertrada last night. That was very unfortunate, and I hope it didn't deter from the evening's festivities."

Pippin waved away the apology. "We need to talk frankly, Boniface."

"Please do."

"All my life, I've known you to be a good judge of men. How is it that you have turned a blind eye toward Childeric?"

"Not all kings are good men. In fact, most aren't. I do have misgivings about Childeric. But, here, in Francia, the mayors are the true power behind the throne. *You* administer the government. *You* lead the military. You already hold all the power. Why is acknowledging Childeric so difficult?"

Pippin shook his head. "Childeric will never be satisfied with that. He already is usurping Carloman's authority."

"And your feud is helping him. Can't you see that by forcing the court to choose sides – and going against the Church – you're undermining your own authority? You've already fought off rebellions in four parts of the kingdom. How many more will you endure before you see your strategy is not working."

"Appeasing him will not work. He wants more. He openly tried to kill Bertrada to weaken me." Pippin could see his argument wasn't moving Boniface. His godfather just looked at him like he was waiting for Pippin to see the light. All his life, Pippin had never opposed Boniface or Carloman directly. He always had put the interests of the kingdom first – and for that, they thought him manageable. They needed to understand how far he would go to stop Childeric.

He stood. "Understand this, Boniface." His voice was a menacing whisper. "I will lay waste to all of Francia before I acknowledge him. On my father's grave, I so vow."

Boniface looked up in surprise and then frowned in thought. After a moment, he waved Pippin toward his chair. "Sit. Please, sit, Pippin. There are matters of importance we need to discuss." He waved Pippin closer as if sharing a secret. "There are some things you need to understand. We live in a precarious time. For years, the emperor in Constantinople has been withdrawing his support of the papal see. He has already abandoned the exarchate of Ravenna, leaving the pope to defend the

Church's land against the Lombards. Naples, Calabria, and Liguria all have fallen to King Liutbrand.

"Pope Zachary still rules in Rome but fears that, over time, he will lack the resources to defend the papal enclave and the Basilica of Saint Peter. He needs support from the west, but as long as you and Carloman are preoccupied by rebellion, there is little chance it will be offered. He sent his legate Sergius to stop the Bavarian revolt, but you and Carloman refused him. Now he is asking us to support Childeric in hopes that naming a king will bring legitimacy to your rule and peace to the kingdom."

"Have the Lombards threatened him directly?"

"Not directly. But, as you well know, they are ambitious. It will only be a matter of time."

"Carloman and I will not let the Basilica fall to the Lombards. Of that I can assure you. I can't say the same for Childeric. Should he gain control of the kingdom, his only concern will be for himself."

Pippin's mind whirled, trying to find a compromise to offer Boniface. Instead, he chose merely to buy time. "Tell Sergius we need to meet. Carloman has called for a church council in two months at Estinnes. Ask Sergius to be there and I will talk to Carloman when he comes back from Alemannia."

"Agreed." Boniface hesitated, appearing to weigh his next words. "If we are speaking frankly, I must address the issue of Lady Ragomfred."

"I will not release her. Childeric nearly killed her."

Boniface nodded. "Privately, Ragomfred acknowledges his failure to protect her."

"Privately?"

"For the last few months, I have been negotiating with him to avoid a petition to the Holy See to have you excommunicated." Boniface held up his hand to stop Pippin's protest. "Clearly, his bluff to make you acknowledge Childeric failed. And that leaves Ragomfred in a very difficult place. If he continues to pursue it, his wife could implicate

Childeric. But having made the allegation, he's now being pressured by the Neustrian nobles to see it through."

Pippin grunted. "His problems are no concern of mine."

"Of course, they are," snapped Boniface. "Being tried for excommunication would severely damage your credibility as mayor. It is in everyone's interest for this dispute to end."

"Save for Lady Ragomfred."

Boniface nodded. "That is where my private conversations have borne fruit. While Ragomfred refuses to publicly implicate Childeric, privately, he recognizes he failed to protect her. It is also – according to him – 'inconvenient' for him to not have a wife."

"Because it hides the fact that he sleeps with men?"

Boniface raised an eyebrow.

"I thought we were speaking frankly," Pippin said.

Boniface waved his hand to dismiss the allegation. "I have negotiated a potential solution. If you will swear before me on the Holy Bible that you have not slept with Lady Ragomfred, her husband will pay you ransom to release his wife – with assurances that he will protect her from Childeric."

"And why should I believe him?"

"That I can't answer save that he is clearly more afraid of you than he is of Childeric."

Pippin grunted. "He should be."

* * *

Pippin returned to the kitchen and retrieved a basket he had requested the cook prepare and then made his way up to Bertrada's rooms. He found her playing on the floor with Charles and suggested the three of them go out for a walk.

It was a surprisingly warm day and he led her to down the north road to a place where a footpath meandered off to the right.

Her smile was radiant. "Our place."

They took the path until it forked and followed the left – more difficult – route. With Charles draped across his back, they climbed up over steep rocky terrain before descending to a small waterfall and a secluded pool.

In the past, Pippin had kept the undergrowth around the water cut back to provide space. It now was overgrown, and Pippin had to clear it so the three could sit. He worked up a sweat using his sword to chop the underbrush but eventually had enough space to spread a blanket by the water. Once they were seated, he pulled a flagon of wine from the basket and together they unpacked what the cook had readied for them – a loaf of bread, hard cheese, and half a roasted chicken.

Little Charles, however, wasn't willing to sit. He kept running toward the pool, so Pippin stripped down to his underclothes to play with him in the water.

"Be careful!" Bertrada winced as he dipped Charles up to his waist. The boy let out a nervous squawk and Pippin rubbed his forehead against the boy's belly until Charles laughed outright. Then Pippin held him at arm's length and swept him through the water to get him used to the cold temperature. Charles laughed and laughed, and Pippin soon found himself laughing with him. He held the boy close, watching him slap the water with his hands, covering them both.

In time, Bertrada stripped down to join them. She tiptoed into the water until it came up to her waist and then dove deep, swimming underwater to surprise them by bursting into the air next to them. Charles squealed with delight. Bertrada wrapped her arms around the two of them, holding Charles between them, their heads just above the surface.

It had been so long since Pippin had felt such peace. His emotions surged and, caught off guard, he struggled to contain them. Bertrada saw it and her eyes too welled with tears. He kissed her. She pulled him close, wrapping a leg around his.

"I love you," he whispered. Bertrada nodded and kissed him again, a long languorous kiss that suggested something more intimate.

Charles batted at their faces, and chuckling, they kissed him as well. They climbed out of the pool and returned to the blanket to let the sun dry their bodies.

Charles broke the bread and handed a piece to Bertrada. Within minutes they had devoured most of the food and lay back on the blanket. Pippin lazily caressed Bertrada's arm. "We should marry," he said.

Bertrada sat up. "Are you asking me or telling me?"

Pippin rolled toward her, propping his head up with his arm. "Asking. Will you marry me?"

Her face flushed red and she looked away. "One day together does not mend all that's gone between us."

"I know." He sat up and pulled her to him, wrapping his arms around her shoulders. "But you and Charles are the one joy in my life. I may never be the man you want me to be. And my life will always be tied to the kingdom. But I promise you I will seek peace where I can find it...and that includes the peace I find with you."

"What about Miette, your Lady Ragomfred?"

"It's you I love, Bertie. I always have. And despite your doubts, I know you love me. I vow to commit my life to you and Charles just as I've committed it to the kingdom."

Tears leaked from her eyes. "I am doomed to love you, Pippin. And I believe you are a good man who will rule justly. But I know what it will take for you to become king." She pulled partly away from him. "That is what you desire, is it not?"

Pippin had shied away from that question for much of his life. To own such an ambition could set events in motion whether you desired them to or not. Lady Hélène had been the first to ask the question aloud. He had always demurred. Looking into Bertrada's eyes, he knew, for once, he could not.

"I will take the throne and it will be a better, more peaceful kingdom for it." For years, Pippin had suspected that it was to be his fate, but saying the words aloud seemed to seal it. It was no longer a choice, no longer a possibility. He would be king.

She took his face in her hands and looked into his eyes. The sadness he saw there was nearly overwhelming. She shook her head. "I know you will make a fine king. But there will be little peace. It will be the death of you and I fear of me and Charles." She kissed him and laid her head on his shoulder. "But I can't imagine a future without you. I will marry you, Pippin, although I suspect we will find little of the good life you seek. But I do love you and will stand by your side and have your children."

Charles climbed into his mother's lap and the three of them sat in the quiet of the afternoon, listening to water spilling into the pool from the rocks above.

* * *

Every morning when the cock crowed, Miette leapt out of bed, hungry for the challenge posed by the day ahead. Although Hélène's training regimen was grueling, it had the profound benefit of quieting the voices screaming in her mind – the ones that kept reminding her that she was without a home, without resources, and very likely a dead woman if Pippin sent her away.

The fault was her own, of course. Every choice she had made since marrying into nobility clanged in her head like a death knell. She had chosen to become the king's mistress, indulging him in his violent need for domination; she had flaunted the tryst in front of her husband, and she had helped Childeric's men hunt Bertrada. And then, on impulse, she had betrayed them all by disclosing secrets to Pippin and thwarting the attack on Bertrada. This last act was the only reason she still drew breath.

Despite her tutelage, it was clear to Miette that Lady Hélène had not forgiven her for the death of Agnès. Instead, Hélène had offered Miette a chance to redeem herself by following Hélène's "dark path" in the search for justice.

That Hélène was a cruel tutor was an understatement. Every morning for the past two years, they started with a light breakfast followed by a slow, strictly controlled flow of martial poses that challenged her both mentally and physically, then came sparring through hand-to-hand combat and with the long staff. Prayer followed the combat and then a brief meal at midday. The afternoon was spent honing skills with a knife and short sword – for which Miette found she had some talent – and a regimen of lifting water pails, sprinting across the practice yard, and her nemesis – the stairs.

The stairs up to the rampart at Quierzy weren't necessarily long, but they were steep, and if you had to run up them and back down twenty times, they could break your will. Always the last of Hélène's regimen, the stairs were the challenge that Miette detested most. Just the thought of them still on the horizon of her day had her groaning in anticipation.

"Two more!" Hélène shouted one evening.

"That was the last!" Miette complained.

"Not tonight. Two more."

Miette refused to let Hélène see her frustration. She turned to the stairway and forced one foot to follow the other until she was done. "Why do you put me through this?" she asked when she had finished.

"A better question is 'why do you agree to it?'"

Miette frowned. "You know, I can't go back. This" – she waved at the stairs – "is my only way forward. But why, after Agnès, would *you* agree to this?"

With a sigh, Hélène sat on one of the stairway steps and patted the place next to her. She waited until Miette was seated before starting. "I have committed my life to justice. And in an odd twist of fate, I see the spark of it in you. On the day you brought Childeric's man Salau to the nunnery to kill Bertrada, you had everything to gain by letting him succeed. It would have kept you in good graces with Childeric and it would have eliminated a rival for Pippin's affections. Yet, in that critical moment, you chose to stop him. You acted in opposition to your interests."

Miette flushed with the memory. "I couldn't do it."

"But why not?"

Miette searched for an answer and came up with nothing. "I don't really know."

"I think you recognized that taking an innocent life is unjust. Killing Bertrada would have been wrong. You knew it and chose to act on it. You set aside your selfish considerations and chose to do what's right."

"You give me more credit than I'm due."

Hélène shook her head. "Each of us is ruled every day by our wants and desires – our pain and our fears. If you're hungry, you eat. If you want to indulge yourself with a bath, you do. The same is true for our ambitions. You wanted to be nobility, so you married a nobleman twice your age. You wanted power and influence at court, so you slept with Childeric to achieve it. Your ambition – and your fear of him – drove you to carry out his order to hunt Bertrada."

Hélène paused. "But in that moment when Salau was close to killing me and Bertrada's life hung in the balance, you chose to be just. You put your life at risk to stop him. Whether you understood it or not, you undertook a selfless act – a noble act. That is why Pippin spared you and it is why I choose to train you."

Miette felt only doubt. "I don't think of myself as 'just.' I'm not even sure I know what that means."

Hélène laughed. "It isn't always obvious."

"Then how am I supposed to know? You call it justice, but I violated a command from the king. How could that be just? Don't I owe him fealty? Am I not supposed to follow his commands?"

"Not all commands are just. You recognized that when you saved Bertrada."

"So, I'm supposed to guess?"

"There are principles to guide us. They take time to understand and require us to reassess the roles we play and the rules by which we live."

"Give me an example."

Hélène's eyes squinted in thought. "Under the law, you are your husband's property. But according to the principles of the dark path, you're not."

Miette almost laughed aloud. "Tell that to my husband! He'd have me drawn and quartered just for saying it. And I'll wager, the church would agree with him."

"In the Gascon church, each of us is considered a 'child of God.' Once you perceive yourself and your fellow man in such a way you cannot unsee it. It redefines how you see yourself and them."

"As children of God."

Hélène nodded. "Salau's attempt to take Bertrada's life violated the rights she is due as a child of God. You sought to correct that imbalance."

Miette frowned. "But that would put everyone on the same level, peasants, priests, and nobles alike."

"In God's eyes, they are on the same level."

"That can't be right."

"You were a commoner before you married Lord Ragomfred –"

"And I was treated as such! Becoming a noblewoman changed my life."

"No doubt. But did it actually change who you are? Did it change how God sees you?"

Miette frowned. "Then what about fealty? Don't we owe service and fealty to our liege lord?"

"Fealty is an agreement of service for protection. It should be respected as long as it is just."

Something was bothering Miette. She could follow the argument, but it still seemed at odds with what she knew of Hélène. "How, then, do you justify murder? You were Charles's assassin, were you not?"

"That is more complicated still," Hélène acknowledged. "In addition to respecting the rights and dignity of our fellow children of God, each of us has a duty to the land in which we live – a shared responsibility to make it – and our collective lives – more just. To some, this can be their family, their town, their duchy, the church, or the kingdom. I chose the dark path to create a more just kingdom. My commitment to Charles was in service of that ideal."

"That seems convenient. It allowed you to murder anyone who got in his way."

Hélène shook her head. "Charles understood my path. He chose carefully."

"And Pippin?"

Hélène had a faraway look about her. "That remains to be seen."

* * *

Pippin couldn't sleep and contented himself with watching Bertrada snore softly in the sliver of moonlight that illuminated his room. He savored the moment, basking in the contentment her presence brought him. She had been so distant for so long he had abandoned hope that such a moment was possible.

He knew that the peace between them was still fragile, yet she was here beside him and that was enough for now. He had surprised them both with his marriage proposal, but she had agreed. They now just needed time to make their decision public. Bertrada first wanted to tell her family and Pippin promised to give her ample time to send for her parents in Laon.

While their relationship was finally on good terms, he was under no delusions that they were on safe ground.

She had expressed some of her fears earlier that night, asking about his sister Trudi – how she fared alone in a duchy on the other side of the kingdom. "Although it was terribly romantic for her to fall in love with a rebel so far away from her father's court, I can't imagine how she survives. She is a woman alone in a foreign land."

Pippin chuckled. "She is a duchesse, married to a charismatic duc and the mother to his heir. She is as safe as a woman can be."

Bertrada was not to be deterred. "She's not just any woman. She's the daughter of Charles Martel. There's little love for your family in that part of the kingdom and if anything happens to her husband, Odilo, her life will be in jeopardy."

Pippin shook his head. "From what I have heard, she's already gained support from many of the Bavarian nobles. She held off a siege from Theudebald while Odilo was away. She's not one to be taken lightly."

"Still, her son, Tassilo...just like our Charles...holds a legacy to power that makes him a pawn in a much larger game. I worry that the same forces dragging you into these endless wars will afflict them."

Pippin didn't disagree. And although he feared it would take them back into their long-running argument, he told her so. "It is one of the things I fear most. When we defeated Odilo, I made Trudi promise that she would forbid Tassilo from challenging Charles over their legacy."

"Do you think that will be enough?"

Pippin shook his head. "It's all I can do for now."

"Then, I will pray for them."

At some point, she had snuggled under Pippin's right shoulder, and they had fallen asleep. He awoke sometime later with his arm numb. Although he feared waking her, he shifted her.

She opened her eyes. "Hello there."

He kissed her in response. At first, she fell into his embrace, but then she pulled away with a yawn. "I've got to check on Charles."

"I'll do it." Pippin leapt out of bed, fearful that she wouldn't return. He threw on a shift and padded barefoot down the flight of stairs to Bertrada's rooms. He had to pass through her bedroom to reach Charles's bed and was surprised to find Bertrada's bedding awry. He thought she had come straight to his rooms.

His arm still tingled, and he shook it to restore its feeling. Squinting in the darkness of Charles's room he took the four paces to his son's bed. Something near the head of the bed caught Pippin's eye...the light was wrong. It was too dark. He grew still and peered into the blackness. Something – someone was there. They too had stopped moving. Fear for his son pierced Pippin like a blade and he threw his body toward the darkness, praying he hadn't come too late.

4

Regensburg

Although Regensburg had outgrown the massive stone battlement built by the Romans in the first century after Christ, the fortress still defined the city. Constructed to secure the empire's northern Germanic border, the bastion's size matched the Romans' ambition, towering over the Danube River that roared less than one hundred paces from its gate. Turrets anchored each corner of the building, whose vast stone walls faced the four winds. Huge wooden double-arched gateways graced each wall, providing access to the keep.

Over the centuries, a city had spilled into the eastern countryside creating a muddle of houses, shops, and meandering streets. Homes and businesses inside the fortress were considered the "old town" while outside the gate regions took various names, depending on the mercurial whims of their residents.

Near the city, the riverbed narrowed dramatically, forcing the already swift current to churn with such violence that its sound had kept Trudi awake for the first three weeks after her arrival in the Bavarian capital. Oddly enough, after three years, she now found the sound comforting, like the thrumming of rain on a rooftop or the rhythmic pounding of waves upon the shore.

Having come to marry Duc Odilo, she worked hard during those three years to make Regensburg her home and to win the hearts of the Bavarian nobility. This last was incredibly difficult given that she was the daughter of Charles Martel and sister to Carloman and Pippin. The

Franks always had been unpopular in Bavaria, but when her brothers defeated Odilo in combat at the River Lech, she felt the wrath of her new kinsmen as if she herself had gone into battle with them.

Trudi endeavored to heal those wounds. She ordered a hospital built for those injured on the battlefield and personally assisted in their care, cleaning and wrapping wounds, changing bandages, and staying through the final hours of those who died.

She tended to the spiritual wounds of the court by accompanying Odilo as he awarded treasure to the sons of nobles slain in battle and feted the courage of those who survived. She was aided in this cause tremendously by the celebrity of their new son, Tassilo, who, as the future duc, still drew crowds of onlookers every time they left the palace.

Ironically, part of Tassilo's celebrity was rooted in the fact that he was the grandson of the hated Charles Martel. As mayor of the palace, Charles had been the ruling power behind the Merovingian throne. Since the office of mayor was inherited from one generation to the next, Tassilo stood to inherit part of that legacy. With only one other grandchild in the family, her son's claim would have to be taken seriously. That kind of power meant wealth, standing, autonomy and, most importantly, relief from the Church's hegemony.

With time, Trudi's efforts to charm the local nobility bore fruit. By spring of that year, the darkness that permeated Regensburg after its loss had dissipated. Trudi took advantage of the warmer weather by hosting local festivals. She spared no expense, celebrating Christian and pagan holidays alike.

She had even made a few allies among the nobles. Count Sudiger of Nordgau and Eingard of Kurbayern – both pagan nobles – had regularly sought her counsel. As for the Christians, Trudi's and Tassilo's presence dramatically changed the standing of the small Christian minority. Much to the delight of Bishop Gaibald – who recently had been named to head Regensburg's new diocese – the attacks against Christians had dwindled to a rarity and his priests could walk most city streets free from harassment. For once, Trudi thought, life in Regensburg was good.

At least it had been until Carloman slaughtered the Aleman nobility.

The news arrived in the middle of the court's monthly day of appeal when Odilo heard the grievances of his nobles and pronounced judgement. It was always a contentious affair and well attended for the theatre it provided. Odilo was known for his sense of humor in dispensing justice and for creating innovative solutions to the problems posed by his subjects.

During one such exhortation, a servant entered the hall and stood behind Odilo's seat, waiting for him to finish. When Odilo had finished his oration, he turned to wave the servant forward. The young man stepped up to whisper into Odilo's ear. Trudi leaned forward but couldn't hear his words. Odilo frowned before nodding and sent the boy away.

"It seems we have an unexpected guest," Odilo announced to the hall.

A young man of no more than twenty was ushered into the hall accompanied by two Alemanni soldiers. He was covered in sweat and the dust of a hard ride. Trudi could tell by the young man's face that he was exhausted.

One of the Alemanni soldiers stepped forward. "My lords and ladies, may I present Lantfrid, son of Lantfrid, son of Godefred."

"Nephew!" Odilo called in greeting. "I am both surprised and delighted by your presence. I have almost completed my duty here. May I suggest that you rest and bathe before we meet?"

Odilo's nephew bowed low. "I apologize for my appearance, milord duc, but my news is dire and cannot wait for such pleasantries."

That drew everyone's attention. Odilo leaned forward. "Then let's hear it, son."

"I come to report that Mayor of the Palace, Carloman, and my uncle Duc Theudebald met with their armies on a field outside Canstatt."

At the mention of Theudebald's name, anger gripped Trudi and she grabbed the arms of her chair with white-knuckled force. Theudebald once had ravaged her in her own home and had yet to pay the price for it. She detested the man and silently prayed that Carloman had killed him.

Lantfrid recognized that he had captured the attention of the room and so raised his voice so all could hear. "With a force that had surrounded the Alemanni, Carloman offered to parley under a flag of truce. Duc Theudebald accepted and while they parleyed, he was slain by Carloman's own hand."

Trudi's relief at the news was short-lived. Shouts of anger erupted from the Bavarian nobility, forcing the young man to wait before he could continue. Odilo held up his hand for silence.

Lantfrid paused until the room had quieted and began again. "Given that they were surrounded, most of the Alemanni had disarmed. Carloman nevertheless ordered his army to attack. They butchered the Aleman army and its nobility where they stood, women and children as well."

A collective gasp greeted this news. "How many survived?" Odilo asked.

"Very few, milord. I was notified by the wife of my cousin, who fled to bear witness."

"How many dead?"

"Over two thousand."

This time, silence greeted the exchange. While Trudi hated Theudebald, she was staggered by the slaughter of so many, especially the women and children. She had known Carloman to be ruthless, but such butchery was unthinkable.

Odilo appeared shaken by the news. "Is there more?"

"I ask asylum until I can assert my claim to the duchy."

Trudi held her breath. The request put Odilo in a difficult place. If he granted it, he would be defying Carloman publicly and siding with the Alemanni. But for Odilo to deny the boy – his own nephew – in front of the nobles of his court? It would be seen as an act of cowardice.

Fortunately, Odilo didn't hesitate. "I'm appalled at your loss, nephew. You may, of course, reside here. Your asylum is granted."

The decision was applauded, but quickly the cheers became shouts of anger. Like a wave, the nobles stood, row after row shouting their rage at the butchery. Given that a number of the noble Bavarian and Alemanni families were intertwined, Odilo wasn't surprised that many in the room called for war and vengeance.

He stood and the room quieted to hear him speak. "The appeals are finished for today. I ask my council to stay so that we may address this outrage."

The angry voices grumbled; they clearly wanted more from him in the moment, but Trudi was glad he took a step back before making another rash decision. She rose to leave Odilo to his councilors and to develop a plan she could present to him when they were alone.

As she stood, however, the eyes of everyone in the hall fell upon her. To a person, they were filled with suspicion and anger. Trudi's heart sank. No longer did they see the Duchess of Bavaria who had nursed their wounded back to health and graced their duchy with an heir. She was once again Carloman's sister and all the goodwill and amity she had built over the past three years was gone.

Although filled with despair, Trudi took an extra moment to smooth out her dress. She refused to run from this room. She would not cower or show weakness. She turned to her husband with all the dignity she could muster and offered him a curtsey. "Milord." She then turned to the gathered nobility in the hall and nodded before walking slowly from the room.

* * *

Odilo was furious, that much was obvious. "What was Carloman thinking?"

Relieved that he had finally returned to their rooms, Trudi touched his arm to calm him. He had been cloistered with his council for over two hours and she was afraid about what he might have promised them. "That's something we should understand before reacting."

He turned and looked at her, his eyes wide with incredulity. "How much more is there to know? He murdered two thousand people. Women! Children! And most of the Aleman nobility! How can we let that go unpunished? We must respond."

"Not until we know more. It's one thing to grant asylum to your nephew, but quite another to pick up arms. You won't beat Carloman in combat. At the very least hear him out."

"You saw the nobles in that room. What kind of options do you think I have?"

"You are the duc. It is your choice. They may not like it, but they will follow where you lead."

Odilo was unmoved. "We have to respond. What is to stop them from doing the same thing here?!"

Trudi shook her head. "This is about Theudebald. He is the evil Carloman is fighting. Don't equate yourself with that rapist."

That quieted him some and he came close to wrap his arms around her. "I hate him as much as anyone for what he did to you, but what Carloman has done is unthinkable."

Trudi had nothing to add. Odilo was right. There would have to be some sort of response, but for the life of her, Trudi couldn't think of what – short of war – would suffice. They could have lived with Carloman killing Theudebald; the man was a monster and most Bavarians knew it. But the slaughter was unforgivable. Given the intermarried families of Bavaria with the Aleman nobility, the massacre was personal. And the killing of innocents was appalling in its own right.

There was a knock at the door. Trudi pulled away from Odilo's embrace and crossed the room to open it. She found a newly bathed and coiffed Lantfrid waiting in the hallway. Now that he was no longer covered with dust, Trudi found Lantfrid to be a handsome young man with long brown hair and blue eyes. He was slightly taller than Odilo but much thinner and more graceful. He sported no facial hair, which was odd for a man this far east. Although he carried himself with assurance, he seemed hesitant to look her in the eye. Two Alemanni guards stood behind him. Trudi ushered in Lantfrid but held her hand up to forestall the two guards.

"They must stay in my presence," Lantfrid said.

"Not in our private rooms," Trudi replied.

Lantfrid turned to Odilo. "Milord?"

"I'm afraid this is her domain, nephew. I can assure you; you are quite safe here."

Lantfrid motioned to his guards to wait outside. "Thank you for receiving me and for granting my request for asylum."

"It is the least I can do," Odilo said.

Lantfrid hesitated. "I was hoping we could discuss my future plans."

Odilo nodded. "Yes, of course."

Lantfrid hesitated again, as if he were waiting for something. "Milord?" He looked meaningfully toward Trudi.

"You want me to leave." Trudi said. "We have accepted you into our home, put ourselves at political risk on your behalf, and you insult me on our first encounter?"

Lantfrid didn't even blink. "I made those requests to your husband, which he has granted. It is with him I wish to consult about my future. I can't see the value a woman could bring to that discussion."

Ever the peacemaker, Odilo put his hand on Lantfrid's shoulder. "I can assure you she is as good at strategy as she is at wielding a sword. And my wife is very good with a sword."

"Yet, she is the sister of the man who killed my uncle and slaughtered my kinsmen."

"Your uncle deserved to be killed. He was an evil man." Trudi enjoyed seeing the shock on the young man's face. Before he could speak, she continued. "But there is no excuse for violating the truce of parley and we are appalled by the slaughter of innocents. *We* will aid your cause to assert your claim because you are my husband's kin and because *we* believe your cause is just."

Red splotches dotted Lantfrid's face. "No one speaks to me like this."

Odilo stepped in before Trudi could respond. "Nephew, I know you are grieving and rightfully outraged by the horror inflicted on your people. I want you to know that I grieve with you...but perhaps you should consider the fact that you are addressing my wife, the mother of my child, the mistress of this palace, and the duchesse of this realm. It rarely pays to insult your host, especially on your first day. You should also recognize that as the daughter of Charles Martel, she is much more valuable as an ally than an enemy and has every bit of his courage and tenacity running through her veins."

Odilo's speech did little to mollify the young man. He stood stock-still, taut with anger, staring at Trudi as if she were a viper. "My apologies to you, milord. Perhaps we can discuss this further at another time." Lantfrid turned on his heel and left the room.

Trudi waited for the door to close before grunting aloud. "So nice to make your acquaintance."

Odilo rounded on her. "You didn't have to goad him. This is going to be hard enough as it is."

Trudi was stunned. "He insulted me!"

"And I reprimanded him. But you didn't have to tell him his uncle was evil."

She fought back her anger enough to think about it. Odilo *had* defended her. So why was she so furious? "Theudebald," she said aloud. "Lantfrid reminds me of your half-brother: he has the same arrogance, the same disdain for women, and he is perfectly comfortable walking into our home and insulting me."

It took a moment, but eventually Odilo nodded. "You're right. They are alike in many ways, but Lantfrid's anger stems from learning that everyone he knew and loved was murdered by *your* brother. It's not surprising that he harbors anger towards you."

"Well, if he wants our help, he'll need to do a better job of hiding it."

Odilo took her back into his arms. "I'll speak with him."

He kissed her and although she had more questions for him, she lingered in the embrace, enjoying the comfort of his arms around her.

She tried to think about when they last had made love and couldn't remember. She kissed him again and made a mental note to remedy that, and soon.

When they broke away, she asked, "What did you and your council agree to?"

"I'm sending emissaries to the other duchies – Aquitaine and Hesse, as well as to the Saxons – to prepare for war."

Trudi's heart began to race. "Please, don't. You've already been down that road. You know where it leads. You won't beat them in combat."

"I said, 'prepare' for war." Odilo's voice held an undercurrent of anger. "What if this is just the beginning? What if Carloman intends to rid the kingdom of pagans one duchy at a time? We must prepare ourselves and, if need be, join forces with the other duchies to even the scales."

Trudi couldn't argue with his logic, so she didn't try. "At least talk to them. Talk to Pippin. You know that he has broken with Carloman. There may be a way forward without war."

Odilo nodded, but Trudi could see in his face that he didn't believe there was.

* * *

It had been two days since Lantfrid's arrival and the Alemanni massacre was still on the lips of everyone at court. Most were advocating war, and Trudi couldn't find much to fault in their logic. But, to her, the end was predictable: they would lose.

She didn't voice this opinion, of course. It would do little, given her birthright, to remind them of how outmatched they were. And, of course, it would serve to remind them once again how foreign she was to Bavaria.

Odilo had ordered a banquet for that evening to introduce Lantfrid at court. Trudi shuddered thinking about it. The silent stares of the Bavarian nobility had continued wherever she went but they paled beside the insinuations about her loyalty spread by Lantfrid. She couldn't quiet the fear – or the anger – building inside her.

Like Theudebald, Lantfrid was leading Odilo into a war he couldn't win, and Trudi feared that this time Odilo would be killed. It was as if a noose slowly was being tightened around her neck and she didn't know how to stop it. She hadn't felt this alone and vulnerable since Theudebald's rape.

When she had finished dressing for the banquet, she sent for Hans, the captain of her guard, and within minutes he appeared, moving down the hallway to her rooms with a soldier's lethal self-assurance. A tall man in his middle forties, Hans had long brown hair and a Roman nose. He was a commoner, skilled with sword and ax, but he had the one attribute Trudi valued most: loyalty.

She met him in the hallway and motioned for him to walk with her. "Have you heard about the report from Alemannia?"

"Yes, milady. All of Regensburg has heard it by now."

"And you now that Lantfrid has asked for asylum?"

Hans nodded.

"That man makes me feel the way that Theudebald did." Trudi could see her captain's eyes grow hard at the thought. He was one of the few people who knew of her rape. "I want two guards with me at all times and the same number guarding my rooms. I also want someone to watch Lantfrid, but it must be someone discreet. I don't want him – or Odilo – to know he's being watched."

"Yes, milady."

She waved to dismiss him, and he bowed to take his leave.

Making her way to the main hall, she set about the task of ensuring that the room was ready for their guests. The hall was small by Frankish standards but large for Bavaria. A long table was set for the meal on one side of the room while a fireplace blazed on the other to take away the spring air's chill. Two servants scrambled to lay out food and drink while two others hung an Alemanni banner next to their Bavarian one.

Trudi smiled when two of her guardsmen entered the room. Hans was nothing if not efficient. She pointed to a place on the wall not far from where she was to be seated.

The hall filled quickly. A musician played a lyre to help ease the conversation and soon the room was a lively mix of nobility drinking before the fire. Trudi circulated through the hall, greeting the guests. As she expected, her reception was cool. No one was rude or insulting, but neither were they welcoming. She smiled, talked of inconsequential matters, and moved on to the next guest.

The one exception was Comte Sudiger. One of the few pagan nobles who had supported her marriage to Odilo in the early days, the comte kissed her hand and smiled warmly in greeting. "You are as beautiful as ever, milady!"

A large rotund man with a broad face, the comte was softened by years of drink and good food. A greying beard did little to hide the fleshy jowls on either side of his face and his lips were already tinted red from wine.

Trudi returned his grin. The comte was a wealthy and powerful man, used to having his way. He owned an enormous estate twenty miles north of the city, but rumor had it that he lived in Regensburg much of the year to indulge his passion for gambling. His city house was a beautiful two-storied affair of brick and plaster overlooking the river.

"It is nice to find a friendly face here tonight," Trudi said.

The comte harrumphed. "It's as if you had accompanied Carloman to Alemannia, the way these nobles are reacting."

"To an extent, I understand their aversion, but I had thought by now people would know where my allegiance lies."

"One would think your son, Tassilo, would have made that obvious."

Trudi smiled. "He *is* my best argument."

He took her hands in his. "They will come around, milady."

Trudi nodded but wondered what would happen if they didn't. And what would happen if Odilo went to war and died? Who would be her allies? How would she protect Tassilo? She found herself assessing

Sudiger, trying to judge just how much she could trust him. He was well regarded among the nobles, especially those who were pagan; a voice like his in support would be exceedingly valuable.

"I owe you a debt of gratitude, Sudiger. You supported my marriage to Odilo long before the other pagan nobles at court."

"Who am I to stand in the way of true love?" His grin widened. "Such a marvelously romantic story: the daughter of the great Charles Martel leaves his court in the middle of the night to chase a rebel's love across the kingdom!"

She laughed. "It does have a bit of drama to it."

"If not for our rebellion against your brothers it also would have been shrewd politically: Bavaria would have been allied to the mayors of the palace; we would have a new duchesse to provide us with an heir, and that heir would stand to inherit part of Charles Martel's legacy."

"If not for the rebellion..." Trudi echoed. "They blame me for a war I begged Odilo to oppose. There was no need for so many to die. The weight of it haunts me to this day. This time, instead of Theudebald, it will be Lantfrid who sucks us in to war. And, when we lose, I again will bear the brunt of it. You saw it in the hall. I'm suspect in my own home."

"*If* we lose, milady."

"Is that a wager you are prepared to make?"

Sudiger's grin was expansive. "I always hedge my bets, milady."

It was the opening Trudi was hoping for. "How would you suggest I hedge mine?"

"Milady?"

"With all this talk of war, I am deathly afraid of something happening to Odilo."

"His death would be a great loss." Sudiger nodded. "I imagine you're also worried that if he dies, few in this room will support your regency on behalf of Tassilo."

"Am I so easily assessed?"

"Gamblers know how to read faces, milady. Plus, the subject has been on a few lips already this evening."

"What do you think?"

"It will be a challenge if it does come to pass. There is a great deal of support for Tassilo, but..." He left the implication hanging.

"Not as much for my regency," she said, finishing the thought.

"You have the Christian nobles, of course, but they number only a few. The pagan lords? They will need some persuasion. If it comes to that, I hope you will seek me out as your champion. My voice carries a good deal of weight."

Trudi had to restrain herself from hugging the man on the spot. "Thank you, Sudiger. That is a relief to hear. Now if I can only convince my husband to talk with Pippin before storming off to war, I will be able to sleep tonight."

5

Canstatt

It took three days to find and bury their dead. Carloman set pickets around the battlefield to ensure that the remains of his soldiers were unmolested while a grave was being dug. The one noble killed, Henri d'Ambose, was found and wrapped in linen to be brought home for burial.

Carloman refused to give the pagans access to the battlefield and his decision prompted several skirmishes with families frantic to find the bodies of loved ones. After several such attempts, he doubled the pickets to stop them.

Unfortunately, due to the steep hills on either side of the valley, there was little wind circulating. The stench of blood, feces, and decay grew so foul that fires had to be lit to dampen their effect; even so, most of his men wore strips of cloth to cover their faces to ward off the smell.

When at last the priest walked the burial site with his thurible to consecrate the ground, Carloman gladly gave the order for his army to vacate the valley. For him, the place felt accursed, and the army's leave-taking couldn't begin soon enough. When, at last, they climbed out of the valley, hundreds of pagans swept over the battlefield to search for their dead.

To manage what was left to the duchy, Carloman had left two Frankish comtes in command, granting them substantial estates and holdings and allocating them responsibility for maintaining public order. Comtes Warin and Ruthard each had sizable military retainers and were well known for their administrative skills.

To his dismay, the euphoria Carloman had experienced during the battle had vanished and, in its place, he experienced a growing sense of dread. He held fast to his belief in his role as the Blade of Christ and the surety of the decisions he had made, but his dreams at night were haunted by ghoulish nightmares and visions of the sybil brandishing a knife. He tried to decipher what was causing his disquiet, but when he did, his unease only grew stronger. Frustrated, he angrily pushed it from his thoughts.

Some of his commanders were avoiding him. Although they displayed no overt insolence – nothing for which to upbraid them – they refused to meet his eye and gave one-word answers to his questions. Even Laurent had barely spoken to him, communicating solely on military matters.

Their silence infuriated him. Who were they to judge? *He* was the mayor of the palace. *He* was the Blade of Christ. *He* was God's champion on earth. They had rid the kingdom of a pagan threat. The men should be proud of their victory.

As was their custom, Laurent rode beside him on the march. His champion had not repeated his rebuke about killing innocents and Carloman was glad for it. Its echo of the sybil's prophecy had hung in the back of his mind like a curse.

Laurent cleared his throat before speaking. "Morale is becoming a problem, milord. Twice the priest has voiced concerns over the number of men seeking absolution."

"War can be hard on men."

"He says it is a sickness of the soul. I've seen it myself in their faces. They look as if they have suffered injury. Even their march is listless."

That, Carloman had noticed. Rather than the meticulous march for which his army was known, their quick step had become more of a lazy shuffle. Not even the drums could spur them to greater precision. "One would think we lost the battle."

Laurent hesitated. "I'm not sure 'battle' is the appropriate term, milord."

Carloman rounded on Laurent. "What would you call it?"

"Slaughter."

"It was God's will!" Carloman shouted. Seeing the men around them react, he lowered his voice to a venomous whisper. "Tell me that the kingdom isn't better off for the death of Theudebald! Tell me we should continue to coddle these pagans who defile His holy name with their every breath!"

"I will not defend Theudebald, milord. The others…" Laurent let the implication hang in the air.

"We are at war with paganism. They are a scourge on our land. There can be no quarter given, ever!" Carloman could barely contain his outrage. "Perhaps I need a new champion." He gave spurs to his horse to distance himself from Laurent. How could the man fail to understand? They had a duty to God to uphold.

A crowd had formed along their path out of the valley. A peasant woman stood in front with a child in her arms. She waited for Carloman to reach her and held up the little girl for him to see. Carloman leaned forward to bless the girl, but she didn't move. It took a moment before he realized that the child was dead, nearly cut in half by a blade.

"Murderer!" the woman screamed. "Murderer!"

Carloman froze in his saddle. Soldiers moved in to seize her, but the crowd pulled her away and soon she was lost among them.

With an effort, Carloman dismissed the episode with a wave of his hand. Being vilified after a battle was commonplace and he didn't want to falter in front of his men, but the thought of the dead child stayed with him throughout the day.

The woman appeared again on the second day, touching off looks of incredulity among his men.

"How did she get ahead?" one man asked.

"Witch!" declared another. Hundreds crossed themselves to ward off the potential of evil.

Carloman was unmoved by the display. Armies moved slowly; it would have been easy for her to surpass their progress.

The woman again held up her dead child and again called him "murderer." This time, at a nod from Carloman, one of his soldiers drew sword and cut her down where she stood. She lay in a bloody heap on the ground next to her dead daughter.

Although glad to be rid of the nuisance, the sight of the mother and daughter renewed Carloman's sense of dread. This time it wasn't so easily set aside. Adding to his discomfort was a persistent stench of death. It stayed with him even after leaving the valley. It was as if the dead of the battle were following him. Shuddering, he made the sign of the cross.

On the third day another woman appeared by the side of the road. As they grew closer, Carloman recognized the sybil by the bones in her hair. She said nothing but stared into his eyes with a sadness that was palpable.

Later that night, two soldiers committed suicide; on the next night there were four more. Each night the numbers grew as they made their way to Strasbourg.

By the time they reached the city, twenty soldiers had taken their lives and a pall of despair hung over the army. Carloman ordered the men to camp outside the gates while he and the rest of the nobles entered the city. Annoyingly, the mysterious stench of decay that had followed him accompanied him into the city.

He hoped that Strasbourg would be an opportunity for renewal. The men would have a chance to rest and enjoy the city to break the melancholy that plagued them. His renewal would come through prayer.

The site of a former Roman fort, Strasbourg was the crossroads for much of Francia and offered a convenient place for his army to rest and resupply. In addition to its broad fortifications and vibrant market, the city was also the home to Saint Étienne's cathedral, the seat of a bishopric, a convent, and a monastery. In many ways, it was a holy city.

He ordered his men to forage and resupply while he and his commanders retired to the bishop's residence. Carloman had sent word ahead to ensure that their hosts would be well prepared to receive them.

Just entering the city lifted his mood. People gave them wide berth but bowed and knuckled their foreheads as they rode through the marketplace. He imagined that, to a peasant, armed men of noble birth would be quite frightening, especially if they were still bloodied from battle.

Bishop Heddo greeted them warmly at his large and spacious residence, ordering servants to tend to their horses and belongings. "Be at ease here, Mayor, my home is at your disposal. I have ordered baths drawn for you and your commanders and a feast has been organized for this evening after mass."

The bishop was a lean man in his forties with greying hair dusting his temples and goatee. He was shorter than Carloman but exuded a confidence that suggested he was still in command of the room despite Carloman's presence.

Wanting to remind his officers of the holiness of their mission, Carloman held up his hand to interrupt the bishop. "Your generosity is well received, Bishop Heddo. But, while my men are getting settled, I would spend a moment of prayer in your cathedral. Although we have succeeded in our mission to break the pagan hold over Alemannia, our army has been plagued by a weakness of faith. I wish to pray to the saints for guidance."

The bishop's smile was broad. "Of course, of course. I'll take you there myself."

Saint Étienne was a small cathedral compared to Saint Denis but well known for its relics: a piece of Christ's cross and a bone of its patron saint, recently brought from the Church of Hagia Sion in Jerusalem where Saint Étienne's remains were housed. The bishop led Carloman to a small and relatively private alcove dedicated to the Virgin Mother.

"May I join you in prayer, my son, or would you prefer to be alone?" the bishop asked.

Carloman pointed to the floor next to him. "I'd be honored if you would lead me in the Litany of Saints. It has always restored my faith in troubled times."

Heddo's Latin was poor, but Carloman embraced the words, supplying the supplicant responses to echo the bishop's invocation.

"*Kyrie, eleison.*"

"Kyrie, eleison."

"*Christe, eleison.*"

As the litany progressed, Carloman immersed himself in the rhythm of its call and response. It allowed him to step back from his thoughts and drift in the prayer. As the muscles in his back and neck relaxed, relief flooded through him. This world had always welcomed him. This world, he knew. He felt more at home within the walls of a church than at any of the residences he shared with Greta.

He wore a holy relic, the finger bone of his patron Saint Lambert, encased in a wooden tube that hung from a chain around his neck. A gift from Boniface on his elevation to knighthood, Carloman pulled it from beneath his tunic and held it in his right hand. He extended his open left hand in supplication.

"*Pater de caelis, Deus.*"

"Miserere nobis."

"*Fili, Redemptor mundi, Deus.*"

"Miserere nobis."

A shaft of light from one of the windows fell upon his outstretched hand and a feeling of peace came over him. It was disturbed only by a small itch on his scalp. Carloman tried to ignore it, but it persisted and disrupted the rhythm of his responses. He moved to scratch it with his left hand but couldn't seem to reach it; his hair was so tangled and matted from months on campaign. Carloman had to dig his fingers through his hair to reach the offending area.

"*Omnes Sancti et Sanctae Dei.*"

"Intercedite pro nobis."

"*Propitius esto.*"

"Parce nos, Domine."

His index finger touched something. It felt like a large worm. He tried to pry it out of his hair, but it remained entangled. His concentration for the prayer faltered. *What was it?* He finally pried the offending object loose from a knot and moved it into the shaft of light.

"Oh God, no."

Blood drained from his face as recognition set in. It was a child's finger. The pagan child who had tried to stop Carloman's blade with his hand. The shock of it, in this holy place, shifted Carloman's perspective, elevating the unwelcome thoughts he had quashed for a fortnight and giving a face to his disquiet. "You kill innocents," the sibyl had said.

His mind returned to Canstatt. He saw the small boy's hand reach out to stop his blade, only to have his fingers severed and his head taken from him. Carloman watched with horror as he murdered women, children, and defenseless soldiers. He saw the joy in his own face at the slaughter. A girl maybe ten years old. A boy maybe twelve. A woman with a babe in arms. All fell by his sword. Blood and viscera covered his face and body in an unholy mask of gore. He was a monster, a demon, the angel of death.

His saw his life's work, the mountain of death dealt by his hand and by his command and it staggered him. There was a certainty about this new perspective. He had been wrong, horribly wrong. Within the cold light of his new understanding, he saw his calling for what it was: an act of hubris.

There was nothing that could justify such butchery. He had damned himself to hell. All of this he saw in an instant and its implication broke his mind.

He started screaming and threw the severed digit away in horror. His revered relic, the finger bone of Saint Lambert, followed. Carloman ripped it from his neck in disgust. It was a mockery – a celestial jape at his expense.

His hands went to his hair, frantically searching for the boy's other digits. He dug deep, pulling out whole tufts of his hair at a time. He had to get them out. Had to.

Bishop Heddo was slapping his face. A stronger blow brought Carloman to himself and he stopped screaming. Looking into the bishop's eyes, Carloman saw concern and fright. He tried to reassure Heddo that he was well, but the thought of living the rest of his life with such horrific knowledge was too much. He doubled over, keening at the weight of his sins. Nothing could cleanse such a stain.

"Carloman! Carloman!" Bishop Heddo was holding him upright. "How can I help you?"

The question sparked a thought. Carloman latched on to it with all his strength. He tried to calm himself, drawing in deep breaths. "Will you hear my confession?"

"Of course, my son."

A wave of nausea swept over Carloman. He leaned onto Heddo's shoulder and retched onto the altar.

* * *

Heddo did not become a bishop by accident. It had taken him years of plotting and scheming to be elevated. He had a talent for helping others succeed, which he found often led to his own success. But he also was good with managing upheaval. Where others might panic, he had always kept calm and focused. He viewed change within the Church as an opportunity – and more often than not had benefited from it.

He had no idea, however, of what to do with Carloman. The shock of seeing the most powerful man in the kingdom screaming incoherently had left him stunned. He wondered if the man was possessed.

Heddo had been delighted by the note from the mayor announcing his stay. Carloman was a benefactor of the Church and it was an honor to receive him. But asking for "guidance to restore and renew our faith after an arduous campaign" was recognition of a higher order. Few bishops could claim a personal relationship with a mayor. Not even Chrodegang of Mayence, the pompous bastard.

It was both an accolade and a distinction within the Church itself. One only had to look at the impact such a relationship had on Boniface's standing with the Holy See to know how valuable it was.

He knew instinctively that Carloman's crisis would be a defining moment in his career. How he handled the mayor had the potential to establish himself as a pillar in the Church. But first, he had to get Carloman out of sight. Rumors about the mayor being possessed would be disastrous for both the kingdom and the Church.

Carloman had quieted after being promised a confession. So, he led the mayor to his own rooms and ordered servants to clean up the altar and to bring up a bath to his chambers. He dismissed all his attendants and sent word to Father Peter, asking the priest to say that evening's mass.

Carloman was still keening, although not as loud as he had in the cathedral. Heddo helped the mayor disrobe and encouraged him to enter the tub. He then bathed the man himself as Carloman rocked back and forth like a child.

The most difficult part of the bath was cleaning Carloman's hair. Not only was it tangled and matted, but every time Heddo touched it, Carloman cried out and tried to tear out another cluster of it. Remembering the mayor's claim that the Litany of Saints had soothed him, Heddo began reciting it from memory in a soft voice. Although his eyes weren't focused, Carloman eventually began to provide the appropriate responses.

That the mayor could recite the litany reassured Heddo. If Carloman was indeed possessed, he wouldn't be able to voice the names of the saints aloud.

He combed out Carloman's hair and tied it back behind the mayor's head to hide the damaged areas. He then helped Carloman out of the tub, put him in a robe, and ushered him to his own bed. Heddo gave him a draft of sleeping medicine the doctor had provided for his own use. After a moment's thought, he gave Carloman two doses.

Heddo sat at his bedside for nearly an hour until the potion took effect. Only then did he send for Carloman's second-in-command.

* * *

Carloman woke in a plush bed in a luxurious suite of rooms, making him wonder where he was and how he had gotten there. As the room was filled with bright sunlight, it was clearly well past noon. He was surprised to have been bathed as well. *Who had done this?*

He started to get out of bed to search for answers, but the memory of the previous night slammed into him like a warhorse. Visions of the slaughter at Canstatt flooded his mind and he sat back down on the bed as the full weight of his sins fell upon him. He put his head in his hands thinking, *I don't know if I can live with this.*

Bishop Heddo entered the room. "There you are! I'm glad to see you awake."

Carloman stood and tried to compose himself. "I suppose these are your rooms, Bishop?"

"Yes, milord mayor. You were so distraught yesterday I thought it best to provide for your needs myself. At the time, discretion seemed to be appropriate."

"Did anyone see –"

"No. I was the only one present. I told your second-in-command that you had taken ill and had retired for the evening."

Carloman nodded as a wave of sadness washed over him. "I thank you for your discretion, Bishop, but it doesn't matter. I am truly damned."

Heddo led him to a nearby sitting area in his suite of rooms. "Now that would be my area of responsibility and I suggest we not condemn you just yet. Why don't we sit?"

Carloman sat.

"Yesterday, you asked me to hear your confession. Would you like to offer it now?"

Carloman nodded.

Heddo made the sign of the cross and waited.

Carloman mimicked the gesture and began. "Bless me, father, for I have sinned."

Carloman told him everything: the epiphany, his hubris in naming himself the Blade of Christ, the murder of Theudebald, and the massacre of the Alemanni. He described in detail the death of the boy and the innocents he had slain. He told him about the sybil and the woman whose child had been cut in half. He didn't stop, purging the breadth of his sins until he couldn't suffer them anymore. "I'm so sorry," he said, weeping into his hands.

The bishop put his hand on Carloman's shoulder. "Be at peace, Carloman. I will help you through this. War can be difficult."

"That's the point." Carloman shook his head. "It wasn't war. Many of them didn't have the chance fight. There were innocent women and children among them."

Heddo frowned. "I didn't say your sins weren't grievous. Your penance will indeed be a harsh one, but you must remember that you are not an angel. You are not the Blade of Christ. You are a man – just a man – who has known war for much of his life. Although death is a natural outcome of war, the effect of battle on those who live is significant. War can warp a man's mind."

"I don't think I can shoulder this burden."

"You should not. You must atone for your sins. Only then can you be forgiven."

"How?"

"That will require further thought. I will help you through this, but for now, you must remember who and what you are. You are mayor of the palace. You need to act like one. You can begin your penance with an all-night vigil before the altar of the Blessed Mother and ask for her forgiveness."

* * *

Heddo was dumbfounded by Carloman's confession. Pagans were a threat to the Church and the kingdom. Of course, they should be put down. His actions at Canstatt were a blessing, not a curse. He couldn't understand why Carloman had judged himself guilty in the eyes of the Lord. It must have been the sybil that Carloman had described. Perhaps, as a pawn of Satan, she laid a spell on the mayor.

Regardless of the reason, Carloman's confession was an opportunity. If Heddo could guide Carloman through his penance, he could guide him through the affairs of state. He just had to maintain a balance between propping up the mayor and controlling the man through his penance.

The brother, of course, would be a problem. It was fortuitous that Carloman had come to him before confronting Pippin. It was rumored that the two of them were due to attend the church council at Estinnes. By stopping in Strasbourg, Carloman had given him time to prepare for that encounter. But first, he would have to get the man back on his feet and acting like the mayor he was born to be. Nothing less would suffice.

* * *

Heddo's first problem was what to do about Laurent. Carloman's second-in-command was rightfully concerned over the absence of his superior. Heddo had put him off during Carloman's nightlong vigil, but now he needed the mayor to reassure his champion that all was well. Unfortunately, Carloman didn't look in command of himself, let alone an army. Exhausted and still weeping after his all-night vigil, Carloman didn't look capable of reassuring anyone. Heddo had to get the man under control.

"Wash yourself and put on a clean robe," he commanded. "You need to act like a mayor even if you don't feel like one."

"I must resign my post," Carloman said. "I am unworthy of leading these men. If anything, I should beg their forgiveness."

"Nonsense!" Heddo used his most commanding voice. "You are the son of Charles the Hammer, mayor of the palace. You will behave like it."

Carloman's eyes widened at the verbal assault but shook his head. "I am not worthy."

Heddo tried a more congenial tone. "Carloman, you are in no condition to arrive at such a conclusion. You have barely begun your penance. Until that is done, you are half a man and incapable of making such sweeping decisions. There is the kingdom to run and the Church to uphold. You must consider your responsibility to each."

Carloman nodded and put his face in his hands to wipe away his tears. "Send for Laurent. I will speak with him."

While Heddo sent a servant to summon Laurent, Carloman cleaned his face in a washbowl.

Laurent arrived with a crisp formality. Fortunately, Carloman looked more presentable – less than his usual self – but presentable. His efforts to dismiss his second-in-command, however, proved more difficult.

"Milord, you must address the men. We have had four more take their own lives since we arrived."

Heddo responded. "The mayor has told me of the events at Canstatt and the toll it has taken on your men. We plan to hold a healing mass to address their spiritual needs tomorrow. Carloman, you said that you wanted it to be mandatory?"

Carloman's eyes widened but he nodded.

"There is a crisis to address, Laurent," Heddo continued. "The mayor stopped here in Strasbourg to allow some healing to take place. He has spent the night in prayer at a vigil before the Blessed Mother and today we agreed to hold the healing mass. He also has asked me to provide the Church's guidance for his mission going forward. I hope you can afford me the time to provide it by managing the army for the next few days."

Laurent frowned. "And the council at Estinnes? The mayor is expected."

"I will accompany you and the mayor to Estinnes."

Laurent looked to Carloman. Heddo held his breath until Carloman nodded his assent.

Although Laurent looked doubtful, he rose and bowed formally before leaving.

Heddo sighed in relief. Turning back to Carloman, he saw the mayor with his head in his hands. A lot of work, thought Heddo, and not much time to do it.

6

Quierzy

Fear flooded through Pippin as he leapt at the dark space in his son's room. It could only be an assassin. He had to get between the attacker and little Charles. Pippin's shoulder hit the man's upper body, but Pippin had miscalculated the distance and lost his footing. He clung desperately to the man's tunic, trying to drag the two of them to the floor, but lost his grip on the man's cloak. This turned out to be fortunate as the assailant's effort to stab Pippin fell short, only catching his shoulder as he fell.

He landed hard but swept out an arm, trying take the man's legs out from under him, but the assassin had stepped aside. Knowing he was vulnerable to an attack from above, Pippin rolled to his left, then quickly sprang to his feet. He still couldn't see much in the darkness, so he waited for any sign of movement. He heard a sharp intake of a breath to his left and without hesitation bent low, pivoted toward the sound, and kicked upward. His heel connected with the man's arm and spun him away. Howling with fury, Pippin rushed him.

For once, Pippin had the better footing. He drove his shoulder into the attacker's chest until they hit the wall. They were so close Pippin could feel the man's breath against his face. He slammed his forehead into the attacker's nose and grappled with the man's arm to avoid the knife. Pivoting toward the knife, he threw his left elbow back at the man's head. It connected. Pippin hit him again and again until he felt the man drop to the floor.

Still frantic over Charles's safety, he bent over the attacker to drag him from the room. The man moved. Pippin immediately dodged left just as a knife punched up to stab him. It barely missed his throat. Grabbing the man's knife hand, Pippin used his weight to turn the blade back on its owner. With a slow determined arc, he pushed the knife blade down until it rested just above the assailant's throat. With a final shove, he forced the blade through the man's neck.

Adjusting to the darkness, Pippin's eyes found little Charles standing atop his bed watching him. "Son, are you all right?"

Hearing his father's voice, Charles burst into tears.

* * *

Pippin called for a guard while carrying Charles out into the hallway. Pippin had to get him away from the corpse; the boy wouldn't stop crying. When the guard arrived, Pippin dispatched him to summon Gunther, Hélène, and Catherine.

He was about to take Charles up to Bertrada when she came downstairs in her nightgown. Her face grew instantly pale at the sight of them. Looking down, Pippin realized that he – and Charles – were covered in blood.

"Oh my God!" Bertrada put her hand against the wall for support. "Oh my God!" She began to weep.

"He's all right." Pippin held the boy out to her.

Bertrada snatched Charles from his hands and searched the boy for injury.

"He's well," Pippin insisted. "He's only frightened."

"I'm frightened!" she shouted. "This is what I fear most!"

He tried to reach out a hand to comfort her, but she shrugged it away and bolted up the stairs to his rooms.

"Christ! What happened here?" Gunther arrived in his nightshirt. He stood next to Pippin beside the body.

"That's what I want to know." Pippin scowled. "How does an assassin get this far into the compound?"

Gunther frowned at the rebuke. "I'll question the guards." He disappeared down the hall.

"It's one of Salau's men, "Miette said, looking down at the body. She and Hélène had arrived just after Gunther.

"Are you sure?"

Miette rolled her eyes. "Do you want to know where his tattoos are? Yes, I'm sure. He was one of the assailants that Childeric forced on me. Not the most subtle of men; I'm surprised he got this far without being stopped."

"It's likely that you'll find a guard or two dead," Hélène said. "Surprise isn't the same thing as stealth, but it can be just as effective."

"Do you think they know about Charles?"

"If they know where Bertrada's rooms are located, they know about your son. Someone here is giving them information."

Gunther returned, breathing heavily. "Two guards were found murdered. They were garroted. Someone clearly knew where they would be and when."

"Christ!" Pippin shouted. "Double the guard and keep one with Bertrada at all times. Hélène, will you stay with her tonight?"

"Yes, of course, milord." She looked pensive.

"What is it?" Pippin demanded. He didn't have the patience for polite conversation.

"We need better intelligence. And I fear my access is limited. May I suggest you send Miette to Paris with me? She can be your eyes and ears inside the palace."

Pippin shook his head. "I can't guarantee her safety."

"She has the ability to protect herself, even from Childeric," Hélène said.

Miette looked pale. "It's too dangerous."

"I can go with you to grease the wheel. I will vouch for your imprisonment and your fidelity. The two of us can carry the ruse."

Miette frowned. "I can't. I cannot be near Childeric. He nearly killed me. And I won't return to his bed."

"You won't have to," Pippin said. "I spoke to Boniface. Apparently Ragomfred's threats to have me excommunicated brought unwanted attention in Rome to Childeric's affair with you. Now, as king, he too faces potential excommunication. Childeric and Ragomfred have offered a solution to end the difficulty. I will swear on a Bible that we never slept together. Your husband will acknowledge your fidelity, pay ransom for your return, and shield you from Childeric. And Childeric will agree to abide by your husband's wishes that you be left alone." When Pippin finished, silence greeted him. "But I won't ask this of you," he said. "The choice is yours."

After a few moments Miette nodded. "You don't have to ask, Pippin. It's time I did something to earn your protection."

* * *

Pippin stayed to watch the body being removed and the blood washed away from the stone floor. Not that it will matter, thought Pippin. It wasn't likely that Bertrada would ever return to her rooms after the attempted assault. From experience, he knew it was best to leave her alone during times like this, so rather than return to his rooms he spent what was left of the night making an impromptu tour of the guards manning the compound. From the start, it was clear that Gunther had beat him to it. Their numbers had already doubled, and sergeants patrolled the halls to keep them at the ready.

He went to the kitchen early and, as usual, Gunther was there. He looked furious, stabbing at his food as if it were still alive. When he saw Pippin, he stood, spilling half his meal on the table. He bowed awkwardly, his face stricken. "Milord."

"Sit, Gunther. I know how much you care for Bertrada. If anything would have happened to her or Charles –"

"It would have killed me. So help me God, it would have killed me. I have failed you, milord. And I offer myself for whatever punishment you ordain."

Pippin paused to consider the man. Punishment would be wasted on him. He was as loyal and resolute as a soldier could be. It might send a message to others responsible for guarding the household, but then again, they all reported to Gunther. Sending a signal that he had lost faith in one of his top lieutenants would undermine the man's authority.

"I hold you responsible," Pippin said quietly. "And you must hold your men responsible. This can never happen again. No one will be safe from my fury if anything happens to either of them. But, for now we must resolve exactly how this happened and who betrayed us. I leave it to you to find him – or her."

"I've already begun, milord."

Pippin nodded. "I knew you would, Gunther. I trust you will see this through. Now sit down and eat your eggs. They're getting cold."

Gunther smiled weakly. "Thank you, milord."

If only Bertrada were so easy, thought Pippin. The cook brought him some eggs, bacon, and a biscuit, which he finished almost as quickly as Gunther. He slapped his lieutenant on the back and headed upstairs. It was time to face Bertrada.

He found her in his suite of rooms with Hélène. He could tell that they were in a serious discussion, so he waited by the door for them to finish. When they were done, Hélène touched her on the arm, but before she could turn to go, Bertrada pulled her into an embrace. When they separated, Hélène was smiling broadly, almost as if she were embarrassed. Before she left, she offered Bertrada a curtsey.

"That's not something you see very often," Pippin said.

Bertrada's face was a blank. "What is?"

Pippin tried to keep his voice light. "Hélène only curtseys at formal court functions. Here with us, she bows like a man if she does anything at all – actually, it's more of a nod than a bow."

A hint of a smile touched her lips. "Perhaps she sees someone worthy of a curtsey."

"In that, she would be right, milady." Pippin offered a deep formal bow.

The blank mask returned to her face. "You could have come yourself, rather than send Hélène."

"I didn't send her. I asked her to act as your companion so you will be protected wherever you are. I also doubled the guard."

She waved away his protest. "She's very convincing. You should reward her more often. She believes in you. She believes in us."

"As do I."

"She said that even if I were to leave you, Charles's life would always be in danger. She said we are safest in your care." Bertrada walked to the window and gazed out into the morning. "She also said that we were betrayed, that someone gave Childeric the location of our rooms and where the guards are posted. If that's true, they know, for certain, that Charles exists."

"That's likely the truth of it." Pippin held her gaze. "Marrying me is a way – not out – but forward. If you love me, as you say you do, if you believe in us, in Charles, we can move forward. We can acknowledge Charles as our son and raise him to be a leader of men. We can raise him to be king – a just king who understands and values the things we value. I can't change the fact that he is my son and Charles's grandson, but we can protect him and guide him to be a man we both admire. That is a promise I can keep."

Bertrada nodded. "I will hold you to it."

"So, you will still marry me?"

She smiled. "I will. Especially now that Lady Ragomfred is returning to Paris."

It was not lost on Pippin that Hélène had orchestrated this outcome for Bertrada more than for him. "You and Hélène are dangerous together."

"Just wait till after we're married."

"I'd like to announce the engagement at the church council at Estinnes. Carloman and Boniface will be there as well as much of the court. We can wed the next week."

"Will you acknowledge then that Charles is your son?"

"Yes. Childeric already suspects, so there is little reason to keep it secret any longer. There will be some talk, but yes, I will acknowledge him."

* * *

Miette had hoped that the attack would cancel her daily routine with Hélène. If anything, the woman drove her harder. She made her way back to her rooms, her muscles aching from exertion. In one way, the exhaustion helped her avoid thinking about her imminent return to court.

From the moment Hélène had suggested it, Miette felt as if she stood on the edge of a precipice. The idea frightened her to the point of trembling. While Hélène's praise had kept her – for a time – floating above the panic, her mind raced, calculating the breadth of the challenge before her. Could her husband truly keep her from facing Childeric? Would they believe she had not lain with Pippin?

She flushed just thinking about it. Alone in her room she allowed herself a small daydream about him. She pictured Pippin in the bath, as he had been after returning from campaign, except this time he stood and took her in her arms. Easing back into one of her chairs, she wallowed in the fantasy, tasting his lips on hers, feeling his hands caress her body, taking his weight as he pinned her to the floor, his body sliding into hers as he moaned into her ear.

She shook her head, chuckling at her desire. It had been so long since she had been with a man, she might be considered a virgin. She could have had anyone in Pippin's court, married or unmarried, but that would have been the end of any possibility with Pippin.

Damn that man! She knew he wanted her. He became aroused just talking to her. But, for the life of her, she couldn't get him into bed – or anywhere else for that matter. In the beginning, he had tried to deny his affections, but she had caught him out enough times that he had given up the ploy. Now he merely traded banter and japed, trying to avoid the obvious. She could not have made her desire for him plainer, but his devotion to that damned Bertrada – who barely acknowledged him for the better part of two years – was insurmountable.

And now she was returning to a husband that wouldn't – or couldn't – visit her bed. To say the least, her chances of intimacy at court looked bleak.

As if by magic, Pippin appeared at her door. Somehow just thinking of him had conjured his presence in her rooms.

"May I come in?"

Miette stood to welcome him, hoping that the flush had left her cheeks.

He looked hesitant, unsure of where to start. "I just want to make sure you are comfortable returning to court. Hélène surprised me with her offer and while I know she thinks you are ready, I'd rather know how you feel."

"I'm happy to do this for you."

"Are you sure you can –"

"It's all right, Pippin." She put her hand on his arm to reassure him. "It's time for me to find my place. And I would do anything to help you." She looked up into his eyes. She could see emotion welling up inside him.

"Bertrada agreed to be my wife." It came out as a whisper, as if he thought that would be a gentler way to tell her.

As much as she always knew this was the way it would be, it still hurt to hear it. She felt the loss as if he had been hers all along. "Congratulations," she said, but her voice cracked, betraying her emotions. And the realization that he had heard it loosened her control. A sob escaped her mouth; she desperately tried to catch it in her hand and found herself crying.

He tried to hold her, but she shook her shoulders to get away. She didn't want his pity. He offered her a kerchief, which she took and used to restore some order to her face.

"I'm sorry," she said. "That was unexpected. Please accept my felicitations."

"Miette, you must know –"

"No!" Anger took her. She held up her hand. "You must not speak of it. I know how you feel. I can see it in your eyes and hear it in your voice. But I also can see your love for her. And that must be our guide stone. I have always known that you loved her. And that if you had the choice, you'd choose her. I just –" Her emotions cut her off. "I just hoped you wouldn't have the choice."

She tried to collect herself, wiping her eyes and blowing her nose into the kerchief. "Ugh! I'm such a mess." When she felt she had restored some control she cleared her throat. "I love you, Pippin." She shook her head. "Isn't it funny you are only brave enough to say such things after it's too late? I love you and always will, but I will not interfere with your marriage. It wouldn't be just. And, thanks to Hélène, that's become very important to me."

The statement seemed to galvanize something insider her. "Hélène says that it is your destiny to be king. If you are willing to accept my oath of fealty, I wish to be a part of that."

Pippin's eyes shifted. Where they had been filled with emotion, recognizing their loss of a potential love, they now grew solemn. He nodded his head in acceptance and asked her to kneel.

When she had complied, he took her hands in his and with a solemn voice said, "Will you honor my commands and prohibitions?"

Miette bowed her head. "I will."

She and Hélène left for Paris the next day.

* * *

Pippin was in the main hall sifting through reports from Burgundy when Childebrand entered. His clothes were covered with blood. If it wasn't for the smile on his face Pippin would have been alarmed.

"Did you kill a boar, uncle?"

Childebrand shook his head and if anything, his smile grew wider. "We've been reminding those bastard Knights in Christ who really rules Neustria. We found five of them, all dressed up in their red and white vests, prancing around Paris as if they were lords of the manor. They've been terrorizing the local nobles with loyalty oaths and forced confessions.

"They had drawn a crowd in a public square where they were accusing a man of adultery. They had him and the woman bound and kneeling before a cross. They were getting ready to cut off his fingers one at a time until he confessed."

"Were there no nobles to stop them?"

"Everyone, including the nobles, seemed to be afraid of them."

"Did you stop them or did the man confess?"

"We sent the bastards on their way before anyone lost so much as a thumb."

Pippin waved at Childebrand's tunic. "Surely, that didn't require this kind of bloodshed."

Still smiling, Pippin's uncle shook his head and sat down with a loud grunt. "Nah, it was their counterattack. Those we stopped ran for their friends and returned with thirty or so to pay us a visit. It didn't go well for them. Even the crowd attacked them, throwing stones at their soldiers."

"What was their toll?"

"We let three live to tell their friends that the time of terror had passed."

"How many of ours?"

"Five."

"I'll need their names."

Childebrand nodded, face growing serious. "I'll have a priest make a list."

"Don't stop the patrols. And take more men, they will likely be better prepared next time."

"You need to talk to Carloman," said Childebrand. "These are his men. If they don't stop, these skirmishes will only get larger – and they'll become a lot harder to end."

"I'll see him at Estinnes and add it to my list of grievances." Pippin stood and began to pace. "I don't know if this is coming from Carloman or Childeric. Either way, it's a move to destabilize the territory and provoke us into civil war. Carloman takes the side of the 'king' and Church and leaves us isolated and untethered, fighting for nothing but my ambition."

Childebrand frowned. "A decent strategy, but I can't believe it is your brother."

"I'm no longer so confident of Carloman. Since Charles died, he has become someone I no longer recognize. He used to be careful and cautious, his strategies well thought out and debated. Now he acts as if he alone is mayor. He betrayed me with Gripho and again when it came to raising Childeric. His Knights in Christ are like the zealots of ancient Rome. They're starting to believe they are actually soldiers of God. And I'm beginning to think Carloman does too."

Childebrand let out a huge sigh. "I wish Charles was still alive."

"I do too. I miss him every day."

Childebrand got up to leave. He looked down at his tunic. "I suppose I should change."

Pippin chuckled. "A bath might help as well. Don't let Bertrada see you like that; I'll never hear the end of it."

"I'm telling you; you should marry that woman."

Pippin barked a short laugh. "I am, uncle. I'll announce it at the Council of Estinnes. We'll wed a week later."

Childebrand roared like a bear and threw his arms around Pippin, lifting him off the ground as if he were still a child. He twirled Pippin around and began to sing as if the two were dancing. Pippin laughed to see the delight on his uncle's face.

Soon they were both laughing. Childebrand put Pippin down and clapped him on the shoulder. "I told you!"

Gunther appeared at the door, his face somber.

"Come in," Childebrand called. "We're going to celebrate!"

Gunther shook his head. "There's a dispatch from the east."

"What is it?" Pippin sobered. He knew Gunther well enough to know the report was bad.

"It's Carloman."

7

Regensburg

Intent on keeping her promise to make love to her husband, Trudi teased Odilo before bed, giving him glimpses of her nakedness as she changed into a new shift. And when they kissed good night, she lingered in his embrace, running her tongue across his lips and tracing a line down the length of his back with her fingers. A boyish grin took his face and he pulled up her shift to slowly kiss his way down the length of her torso.

Once he was inside her, however, Odilo seemed to detach, forgetting she was there. His thrusting became aggressive and impersonal, as if he was trying to climax as fast as he could. She tried to reengage him, coaxing him over onto his back, but their coupling was still more methodical than passionate. In the end, neither of them found release. He grew soft, slipped out of her, and with a grunt, rolled over onto his side.

She lay awake for hours, her worries about Odilo and the potential for war magnified in the darkness, endlessly repeating in a nightmarish litany of loss, abandonment, and dread.

She was frustrated by the fact that she had no control over the events shaping the duchy. Lantfrid's quest to avenge the massacre had kept the nobles at court in a feverish state. The momentum was clearly boxing Odilo into a single option. His only recourse was to declare war.

Despite the support of the few Christian nobles, her growing isolation at court made her feel like a captive in her own home. It reminded her of Theudebald's siege. She was thankful to have Hans and his men to protect her, but she felt trapped, nonetheless. She wondered if it was worse for her half-brother Gripho, imprisoned in Neufchateau.

The thought of Gripho gave her pause. It sparked the beginnings of an idea and rather than seize it, she let it grow on her, exploring its possibilities and dangers, testing its merits, and weighing them against its weaknesses.

When dawn began to filter into their room, Trudi couldn't wait any longer. She shook Odilo. "I might have a solution."

He rolled over bleary eyed and squinted up at her. "A solution for what?"

"There is a conclave of bishops meeting next month in Estinnes. I'm sure Carloman and Pippin will be there. We will be there as well."

He sat up, rubbing life into his face. "To what purpose? We are better off coordinating with our allies, forcing Carloman and Pippin to fight us along several fronts at once."

"But what if we don't need to fight?"

Odilo groaned and climbed out of bed to find a chamber pot to piss in. "They didn't murder the Alemanni nobility to sue for peace. They're coming for each of us. We must gather our allies and remain united against the threat."

Trudi was undaunted. "Hear me out. What if this was not some grand strategy, but just about Theudebald? I can't believe that Pippin approves. And they both must know that the massacre will spawn a reaction. Unless they plan on fighting all the rebel duchies at once, they will be looking for a way to placate us." Trudi could tell by Odilo's face that he wasn't moved.

"What price do you suggest they pay for a massacre?" He scowled. "What could balance the scales? Simply restoring Lantfrid isn't enough. Such butchery requires a response."

"Demand that they free Gripho."

Odilo frowned. She could tell he was considering the possibility. Bavaria had gone to war on Gripho's behalf when Carloman had prevented his ascension to mayor. As a pagan, Gripho fundamentally would have changed the religious persecution within the kingdom. Odilo shook his head. "Carloman will never agree to that. It's what started the civil war in the first place."

"But Pippin might. He didn't support Carloman's war on Gripho. He's opposing Carloman over the Merovingian. Perhaps, in this, he will take our side. And if he does, Carloman won't want to fight all the duchies alone."

"Freeing Gripho won't balance the scales."

"You were willing to go to war for him once; why isn't he worthy of peace?"

The sun was up, filling their room with light. Odilo looked at her. For the first time in a long while his eyes sparkled with a hint of mischief. "It's worth a try."

"So, we're going to Estinnes?"

Odilo nodded.

"Then come back to bed. You need to finish what you started last night."

Odilo laughed and rolled onto the bed.

* * *

The next evening Odilo met with the Bavarian nobles to disclose his plan for the diplomatic mission to Estinnes. Fearing that she would be a distraction, Trudi chose to watch the proceedings from the back of the room rather than sit next to Odilo at the dais in the front of the great hall.

Odilo first notified the sitting nobles that calls for support had gone out to the nearby territories in the hopes of drawing the Hessians, Carinthians, the Croats, and Serbs into the war. Messengers were also sent to their allies in Saxony and Aquitaine.

Trudi had to admit that he was good at commanding a room. He looked completely at ease sitting at a dais before the crowd. His confidence and enthusiasm lifted everyone and his intensity was compelling.

But, when he described his plans for a diplomatic mission to Estinnes, the spell he had been weaving was broken.

Lantfrid was the first on his feet to object. "The murder of two thousand innocents cannot go unpunished. Are Bavarians so weak they must go begging to the Franks? Blood must be paid for blood!" A number of the nobles shouted in agreement.

Comte Sudiger stood and waited for the room to quiet. "Yet, my young friend, it is *our* blood you are asking us to spill. I concede that war may be inevitable. And, as you have seen, we are preparing for it – as are the Saxons and our allies in Aquitaine. We recognize the threat Carloman poses and will defend our homeland to the last man.

"But we won't throw lives away. We stood against the Franks just three years ago and many of our finest fell before their swords. The Alemanni, too, have bowed before their might. Your uncle Theudebald himself repeatedly knelt before Carloman and gave up his hands. The Franks are a formidable foe."

Sudiger paused. "If it is necessary, we will fight your war. But is it not worth a month or two to see if a different solution can be found?"

Trudi could have kissed the man. He had taken the burden of defending the mission from Odilo and had made a strong case for it. Although less vocal, many of the nobles in the room nodded their heads, agreeing with Sudiger.

Lantfrid's cheeks blotched red with emotion. "This is how you avenge the murder of my people? You negotiate? They violate the truce of parley; they slaughter unarmed men; they butcher women and children. And you negotiate?"

Shouts echoed his words and Lantfrid lifted his voice above them. "Any agreement you reach with the Franks condones their crime. Any offer to negotiate signals our weakness. You are letting your wife delude you, Odilo. The Franks speak nothing but lies and you are a coward to consider them."

A shocked silence took the room. Trudi held her breath as all eyes turned to Odilo.

For a few moments, Odilo did nothing but stare at the cup of wine in his hands. Then, slowly, he set the cup down and stood. When his eyes rose to meet Lantfrid's, they were hard and dispassionate. He purposefully made his way across the floor to where the young man stood. Although he kept his voice low, it could be heard throughout the hall.

"When you arrived on the heels of the massacre, nephew, I posed no judgement on you for where you were when Theudebald's army was slaughtered – why you were someplace other than with the nobles protecting your duchy. I didn't question why you alone survived Carloman's attack or why you alone are left to lead Alemannia.

"Instead, I gave you shelter; I fed you and clothed you. I grieved with you for the loss of your family and your people. I granted you asylum and my protection despite the potential consequence to Bavaria. I have called our allies to prepare for war and I championed your claim to rule in Alemannia."

Odilo stopped directly in front of Lantfrid. With a speed that surprised Trudi, Odilo's left hand shot out and grabbed his nephew by the throat. Lantfrid's two Alemanni guards tried to intercede but were restrained by nearby Bavarian nobles. The young man struggled with both hands to pry free of Odilo's grip, but Odilo only squeezed harder and soon Lantfrid's eyes began to bulge.

The fury in Odilo's voice was unmistakable. "And this is how I'm repaid? You think yourself brave to enter my hall and call me 'coward.' You forget that I am a son of Godefred. Better men than you have died for less at my hand."

Lantfrid was on his knees, much of the fight leaving his limbs.

"Odilo!" Trudi made her way to her husband's side from the back of the room. "Don't do this. I beg you. He's just a boy, your own nephew! Please, Odilo."

Odilo looked over his shoulder at her and growled. He released his grip and let Lantfrid collapse to the floor. He turned to one of his guards. "Take him back to his room."

Looking up at the nobles in the hall, Odilo spread his arms and shouted. "Anyone else?" His eyes searched the room looking for a combatant. "Anyone?" Hearing no reply, he continued. "I leave for Estinnes in the morning. Count Eingard of Kurbayern will lead the war effort while I am gone. In my absence, his word is my command." He paused for a moment and then waved his hand.

"You are dismissed."

* * *

They left in the early hours just after dawn. The air was cool and wet; a thick dew had settled over the countryside. A cohort of fifty men on horseback accompanied them, looking formidable in the early morning light as they rode in crisp formation before and behind their party. Begrudgingly, Trudi had left Tassilo behind in Eta's care. Travelling with a three-year-old would have slowed their progress considerably and he was safer staying behind in Regensburg.

Although Odilo seemed to have mellowed during the night, he had spoken little to her since his confrontation with Lantfrid. They rode together silently as they made their way to Danouwörth and the Roman road north.

"A question, husband?" she ventured, trying to bridge the silence between them.

A wry smile took Odilo's face. "Since when have you ever asked my permission to speak?"

"Oh, I don't know." Trudi tried to match his jocularity. "Maybe since you nearly choked your nephew to death in front of me."

The jest failed to amuse him, and a hardness returned to his eyes. "He deserved it." They rode in silence for a minute or two before he added, "What was your question?"

"Why did you select Eingard of Kurbayern to lead the war effort? I would have thought Sudiger a more suitable choice. He spoke against Lantfrid and certainly has proved himself a worthy ally."

"As has Eingard," Odilo said. "They are both capable leaders, although Sudiger is more oriented towards the politics of court than the battlefield. Eingard is first and foremost a soldier. He'll do what needs to be done to prepare us for battle."

Trudi nodded in agreement. She was fond of Eingard. He was as strong as a soldier half his age and carried himself with a military reserve that commanded respect. He was a quiet man who spoke rarely, but when he did, people listened. His light green eyes held the inner fire of a zealot, but, when it came to her and Tassilo, they always were alight with kindness.

Odilo wasn't finished. "I also worry about Sudiger. He is a very ambitious man."

Trudi laughed. "Aren't they all?"

"Some more than others. Sudiger is a powerful ally who has ties to many at court."

"You mean he owes gambling debts to many at court."

Odilo shook his head. "Don't let him fool you. He likes to play the poor gambler who is down on his luck. He has more money than all of us. And if there are debts owed, I'm certain he's the one collecting on them."

"After his insult before the court, what do you plan to do about Lantfrid?"

"I'll support his restoration to the duchy in Alemannia." Seeing her surprise, he smiled and added, "The gods know he can't stay with us!"

"What if Carloman and Pippin refuse to consider it?"

Odilo frowned. "I don't know. Godefred's family has ruled Alemannia for generations. I can't imagine the ducal seat without one of his heirs."

"Just make sure he doesn't stay in Bavaria," Trudi said. "Or I may be the one choking him to death."

This time Odilo laughed.

As the day warmed the dew lifted and the sky became a stunning blue. The absence of clouds gave it immeasurable depth, lending a magical air to the firmament. Trudi realized that she rarely had this much of Odilo's time and became determined to make the most of it. She stopped talking about politics and pretended that the two of them were just out for a ride in the country.

"It's too bad we're in such a hurry," she said wistfully. "The towns along the Roman road are quite romantic. It would have been nice to take our time to enjoy them."

"Has the armor-wearing wife of my youth gone soft?"

"Oh, I don't remember wearing too much armor around you." She smiled. "In fact, I don't remember wearing much of anything at all."

His grin widened. "I suppose we'll have to sleep at some point. I'm sure we can find one of your romantic towns in which to spend the night."

"Good, there is a new pagan marital rite I'm dying to try."

He laughed outright. "Your wish is my command, milady!"

"That's the Odilo I know."

Their conversation remained light throughout the early afternoon. As they rode side by side, Trudi felt like she was rediscovering the man with whom she had fallen in love. So much had happened since those early days that Trudi felt like they had become two different people. She was glad she had left Tassilo behind. There was something about the two of them, their attraction for each other, that needed to be rekindled.

When they had first met, Trudi had been enamored by Odilo's casual manner and quiet self-assuredness. He exuded a boyish charm that despite his years had seduced her from the start.

Now, she recognized a depth within him. Odilo carried the weight of his responsibility as duc. Although he was an ambitious man, what drove that ambition was not fame or wealth. It was Bavaria. He was committed to seeing a more secure and prosperous future for the duchy his son would inherit.

As the shadows of the day lengthened, whatever walls the years had erected between them fell away and a familiar intimacy took its place.

Odilo began to tell stories of his youth in Alemannia as a son of Gode-fred. Some were amusing, some sad. In one, he had been swimming with another boy when they both got out beyond their depth.

"It was my fault," Odilo said. "I was older and a better swimmer. I was flaunting my ability, diving into deeper water. He followed me out, trying to match me stroke for stroke. When he realized he'd gone too far, he started to panic and began flailing in the water. I tried to calm him and pull him to shore, but he grabbed me and tried to climb up on my shoulders, pulling the two of us under.

"He was all over me and it became my turn to panic. I wrestled with him underwater to push him away. When I came up for air, he was thrashing, desperately gasping for air, trying to stay above water. I could see the fear in his eyes. I remember looking to the shore for someone to save us, but we were alone."

Odilo frowned. "He lunged for me again, but this time I pushed him away. I had no more strength to wrestle him. I was gasping for breath myself."

"What did you do?" Trudi whispered.

"He started to go under and all I could think to do was to keep his head above water. I dove down to the bottom, stood on the lake bed, and reached up with my hands. Grabbing the back of his legs I pushed him up, trying to keep his head above water. I walked several steps towards shore and then ran out of breath. I had to let him go and resurface. This time, I kept away from him, sucked in a few breaths, and then dove back down again. He was still kicking, but I grabbed hold of him and lifted. It took six or seven tries, but we finally made it to shore."

"You saved him."

Odilo shook his head. "I put him in harm's way. I nearly killed him. Getting him back to shore doesn't balance the scales."

They rode for some minutes in silence, while Trudi pondered his story.

"You're a good man, Odilo." A mischievous grin stole across her face. "Now, where's that romantic town you promised me?"

8

Estinnes

The church council had yet to start and already Boniface felt it spinning out of control.

It was the latest in a series of synods he had spent years organizing to address a growing fragmentation of the Church throughout Francia. One could travel across the kingdom attending mass in every town and hamlet and experience no two ceremonies that were alike. He was determined to establish strict guidelines for parish priests, enforce greater organization among the bishops, and impose a code of conduct for their personal behavior. Too many bishops lived a secular life, enjoying the Church's wealth and prestige and spending their time drinking, hunting, and living with concubines as if they were nobility.

By far the most important subject he hoped to address, however, was the restoration of Church lands. Years earlier, Charles Martel had seized a staggering amount of Church property and wealth to fund his military campaign to conquer and unify the kingdom. The council had tried to pressure Carloman and Pippin into restoring the lands after Charles's death, but the civil war with Gripho had prevented it. Now at Estinnes, Boniface was seeking restitution.

Carloman had promised to address the subject at the synod and Boniface had recruited his allies to be among the bishops in attendance to hold him to account: Reginfried of Cologne, Witta of Buraburg, and Heddo of Strasbourg had all agreed to attend.

Unfortunately, all that preparation was being undermined. With the wealth and power of the bishops gathered in one place, nobles, who had political designs of their own, were arriving daily from across the kingdom to scheme and socialize during every meal and break from the council's itinerary. The small quaint village of Estinnes was being over-run by Frankish nobility.

With such a gathering, the presence of a mayor could easily over-whelm the council's focus, and this year both mayors would be attend-ing: Carloman to address the restoration of lands, and Pippin to meet with Sergius, legate to the Holy See.

Boniface had prepared as best he could for their presence but reports of the Alemanni slaughter threatened to disrupt the entire proceedings. The controversy was on the lips of every bishop and noble. Not every-one agreed with Boniface that it was murder. While he approved of conversion by the sword, he couldn't condone the massacre of inno-cents. And murdering defenseless women and children? It was a blight on Christ's name.

He had polled those bishops already present and many disagreed. They saw the pagans as a threat and the elimination of the Alemanni nobility as a chance for the Church to build a Christian duchy on the corpse of the pagan one.

That Carloman could order such a massacre greatly disturbed Bon-iface. Until recently, his godson was known to be a God-fearing man of careful deliberation. Now, he seemed a man without a conscience. Boniface recalled Carloman's threat to drown Tassilo in the baptismal font at the boy's christening. The act had alarmed him. The murder of two thousand innocents had him horrified.

Carloman had arrived a day earlier with his army in tow and usurped the two-story residence of a local nobleman. Boniface had arranged to see him on the eve of the council's first day to go over his plans for the meeting. When he arrived at the residence, however, it wasn't his god-son who greeted him; it was Bishop Heddo.

"Boniface! Come in. Come in! It's wonderful to see such an old friend." Heddo embraced him and led him to a sitting room where he waved Boniface toward a chair by the window. "Please sit. We have so much to discuss. The mayor has asked me to meet with you in his stead to prepare for the council meeting."

Boniface frowned. Carloman never before had used an intermediary and the idea rankled. "I am confused, Heddo. What is this? Where is Carloman?"

"He begs your forgiveness. Other pressing matters require his attention. I'm afraid that his ability to participate in the council also will be limited."

"Is he reneging on his promise to return our lands?"

Heddo sighed. "Fortunately, I have dissuaded him from another postponement. But I believe we've worked out a compromise that will suit the clergy and allow the mayors to continue defending the kingdom."

Boniface squinted his eyes in concentration. "How will it suit the clergy?"

"Carloman will restore ownership of the land to the clergy if they agree to lease the property back to the nobles. That allows Carloman's knights to maintain their estates, but they must acknowledge that the land belongs to the Church and pay regular stipends for its use. The Church will be compensated for the temporary loss of the land and, in a generation or two, it will revert to the Church."

"An interesting compromise," Boniface said.

"Thank you." Heddo smiled. "I suggest that you be the one to offer it, after Carloman refuses to return the land tomorrow."

"I don't understand."

Heddo leaned forward to speak in a conspiratorial whisper. "To gain the assent of these bishops, we need to make it look like they've pushed Carloman into a compromise. If we start with the compromise, the bishops will bargain for more. And as Carloman won't agree to more, this is the best we can get."

While Boniface agreed that the strategy was sound, he was offended that he was colluding with Heddo rather than Carloman. "Maybe he would agree to more, if I met with him."

Heddo shook his head. "He's refused further discussion. To be honest, I'm surprised he agreed to this. I had to argue for half the night. At the meeting tomorrow, he'll announce he won't return the land. If you step in to suggest the compromise, it will carry far more weight with the bishops than if I do it."

Boniface didn't like being manipulated. "And just how did you come to be the one negotiating this with Carloman?"

"On his way back from the Alemanni conquest, he asked me for spiritual guidance." Heddo handed him a letter from Carloman that confirmed the request. "Although he supports the Church in everything he does, the secular and military demands on him as mayor can be overwhelming. After an all-night vigil spent in prayer, we discussed his many responsibilities as mayor. I helped him focus on what was most important – sorting out the wheat from the chaff."

"And he's asked you to continue as his advisor?"

Heddo nodded. "Spiritual advisor. Now, let's discuss issuing a joint accolade from the bishops, honoring Carloman's victory over Alemannia."

Boniface nearly spilled his drink. "Victory?! I hardly think that's the word for what happened in Alemannia."

Heddo waved away his objection. "I'm speaking from the perspective of the Church, not his immortal soul. In one battle, Carloman has provided the Church with an opportunity to establish Christianity – in name and in practice – as the official faith of Alemannia. Surely, that is worth acknowledgement."

"We cannot condone the killing of innocents."

"Carloman and Pippin have been trying for years to bring that duchy into line. Those rebels agree to kiss the cross when they are forced to but pray before ash trees the moment our Frankish knights leave the field. They are hardly innocents."

"And the women and children?"

Heddo waved the question away. "We have suffered three generations of conflict with Alemannia. How many more will be lost if it continues for another three? Better to end it now."

Boniface shook his head. "I won't condone the slaughter of innocents."

After a moment of thought, Heddo seemed to shrug and bow at the same time. "I yield to your wisdom, old friend." He stood and went to a cabinet and pulled out a bottle. "Now why don't we celebrate your council with some of this port I've been saving?"

* * *

Thirty bishops arrived for the first morning of the synod. As there was no building large enough to accommodate them all, two tent pavilions had been erected on the grounds of the church. One was intended to provide food for the bishops while a second, larger pavilion housed two long tables for their meeting.

As with years past, the visiting nobles erected a row of smaller pavilions on nearby grounds that offered food and drink that was far more sumptuous than what was provided by the Church. Bishops often took their morning meals at the Church's tent and dined at night in the nobles' tents. During those evening hours, the nobles' tents also offered music and entertainment, giving the synod an atmosphere more like a carnival than a religious meeting.

Boniface knew better than to insist that the bishops resist the tempting fare offered by the nobility. For some, the revelry at the tents was the primary reason they came. In truth, he enjoyed them as well.

The weather was cooperating with a warm sunny day and a gentle breeze that kept the pavilion quite comfortable. Boniface waited for Carloman to arrive, but after an hour, he decided to start the synod without him.

Motioning for the bishops to be seated, he began the proceedings with a prayer for guidance. When it was finished, he stood.

"We, the leadership of the Frankish Church, gather here first in prayer and then in council to bring ourselves and our parishioners closer to God. We must be humble in this endeavor for we are His servants and work in His name."

Boniface surveyed the room before him. "Yet, as I stand before you, I must recognize that there are many gathered here who do not adhere to Sunday as a day of rest. There are many here who live with mistresses and concubines. There are men here who hunt and drink to excess.

"Like the nobility of the kingdom, we are powerful men, to be sure. We have worked hard to attain and sustain our bishoprics. We have access to wealth and to power. But how can we bring our flock closer to God when we, His servants, carouse like the youngest son of a duc?

"We must serve as an example. We must show our clergy and our parishioners that the way to reach God's home in heaven is through a life of piety.

"But can we preach piety if we are not pious? Can we preach chastity if we are not chaste? Can we preach a life of humility if we are not humble?

"We are men of God!" Boniface pounded the table with his fist. "It's long past time we acted like it."

The council argued long and hard over hunting and chastity. But those disputing reform were mostly noblemen who had claimed their religious titles using their families' wealth and military prowess. The council overruled their objections and agreed to hold bishops accountable for excessive behaviors.

The next item on Boniface's agenda was the standardization of the holy mass. But before he could broach the subject, Carloman stepped into the tent, his eyes downcast. He looked tentative – a man unsure of his place and himself.

"Welcome, milord mayor!" Boniface announced and stepped aside so that Carloman could sit at the head of the table.

Heddo, who was sitting to the right of Boniface, stood and began to applaud. "To the Christian conqueror of Alemannia!" he shouted and doubled the speed of his applause. Others followed and soon all the bishops were standing. Some were even cheering. Boniface was furious at the display and at Heddo for initiating it.

Carloman, however, looked relieved. He began to acknowledge many of the bishops in the room with a nod of his head.

"From this day forth," Heddo continued, "Alemannia will no longer be a pagan stronghold. It will be governed by Christians. Milord mayor has announced that two Frankish comtes, Warin and Ruthard, whose families were established in the region by Charles Martel, shall rule in the place of the pagan Theudebald."

Again, the bishops applauded. Boniface tried to interrupt, but Heddo wasn't finished. "I ask that the council issue a statement of acclamation to honor the liberator of Alemannia."

Boniface stood to regain the floor. "I suggest caution. Reports from the battlefield state that parley was violated and innocents were killed. It is not something for which the council should acclaim."

Instead of responding, Heddo turned to Carloman. "Milord?"

Carloman took a deep breath before answering. To Boniface, who had known the man since he was a child, Carloman's words sounded lifeless, as if they weren't his own.

"For some time, I have been concerned by the infedelitas of the Alemanni. Three times we engaged them to honor their vows and three times those vows were broken. We were left with no other choice. It was with a heavy heart, but – a majority of the prisoners had to be executed."

Heddo nodded. "It was the Alemanni who brought this on themselves. Over the years, many had declared themselves Christian and kissed the cross, only to renounce their faith when our armies returned home. What choice did he have?"

Several of the bishops were nodding their assent, including Boniface's allies Reginfried and Witta.

Boniface voiced his concern again, but the acclamation passed with Boniface abstaining. When he stood to regain the floor, however, Heddo interrupted once more.

"My apologies, Boniface, but we only have Carloman for a short time and I think it would be preferable to resolve the issue of the restoration of Church lands stolen by Charles Martel."

Again, nods of approval greeted this proposal. Heddo began his planned charade, advising the synod of Carloman's decision to continue holding Church lands due to the staggering cost of putting down the rebellions in the east and in Aquitaine. At the council's shocked response, he turned as if on cue to Boniface.

Although he hated being manipulated, Boniface knew that resolving the Church's land dispute took precedence over his personal feelings. "Perhaps I can suggest a compromise..."

It took several hours of haggling, but it was decided that the nobles would continue to hold the land in precaria and remit to each church one solidus – or twelve denarii – each year for each property. At the event of a noble's death, the land would revert to the Church. While it didn't fully satisfy the synod, much of the council recognized the compromise as a significant step forward. It too passed without dissent.

By the end of the negotiation, Boniface noted that Carloman looked more himself, sitting at the head of the table. His back was straighter, his demeanor more relaxed. It was as if the demons that earlier had occupied his thoughts had been purged. Boniface was happy to see it, although deeply concerned over Carloman's erratic behavior.

The rest of the day progressed more smoothly. Heddo kept quiet while Boniface presided over the meeting. Carloman grew more comfortable at the head of the table, offering insights and counsel. And after a spirited discussion about who should be allowed on the altar, the bishops passed a resolution addressing the standardization of the mass. Pleased with the progress they had made, Boniface halted the proceedings for their evening meal.

As he exited the tent, however, he discovered that his synod would be taking another unexpected turn. Odilo and Trudi had arrived seeking a conference with Carloman and Pippin.

* * *

"He is praying and cannot be disturbed." Heddo's voice sounded shrill to Boniface. He had tried to intercede as the proceedings had ended, but Heddo had rushed Carloman away and kept him under a close watch. He was now refusing all entreaties to approach Carloman.

Intent on keeping control over his council, Boniface chose to dine with Odilo and Trudi in the tent of Gerold of Vinzgau. His wife, Emma, was a distant cousin of Odilo's from Alemannia and sympathetic to their cause. The nobleman had agreed to host Odilo and Trudi during their stay at Estinnes.

That Odilo was furious was an understatement. "It is murder, Boniface! How can you call yourself a man of God and condone such depravity? The men were unarmed and Carloman killed them where they stood. And the women and children? He slaughtered them too. If that is not a sin, I defy you to show me what is."

Boniface struggled to find a point of view he could defend. To a large extent he agreed with Odilo. There could be no justification for the slaughter, but it put him directly in opposition to the synod and to Carloman.

"I agree that we need to examine what really happened in Canstatt," Boniface began.

"It was the will of God." Heddo strode into the tent. "Three times the pagans kissed the cross and three times they renounced their faith." His hand slapped the table.

"As did Saint Peter," Trudi said, her eyes cold with anger.

"You, who were raised in the faith, should know better than to question a prelate." Heddo waved her protest away. "Besides, your protest is too late, the synod already has lauded the victory in Alemannia –"

"Victory?!" Odilo shouted. "You are confused, priest. There was no battle."

Heddo snarled. "It is 'bishop' or 'Your Excellency' to the likes of you, pagan. Yes, we bishops have honored the conqueror of Alemannia. Now, go back to your hovel or you might be next."

Odilo turned to Boniface, his voice seething. "Is he telling the truth? Your synod condoned the massacre?"

Boniface had no recourse but to nod.

Odilo threw his flask of wine across the room and stormed from the tent.

Trudi broke the silence left in his wake. "You are begging for war, Boniface. All the rebel states will rise against this. God knows, I had no love lost for Theudebald, but there can be no justification of such slaughter. Bavaria is already preparing for war, so are Aquitaine and Saxony. Carloman and Pippin must move quickly to stop it or the next twenty years will be filled with bloodshed."

"It is the will of God," Heddo repeated.

Trudi turned to confront him. "I find it hard to believe that God would want Carloman to murder two thousand innocent souls."

"They were hardly innocent. They were pagans – pagans who accepted Christ and then blasphemed and committed heresy by returning to their so-called faith."

"Murder is murder, no matter how you dress it up."

"As I said, it is the will of God."

"But it is not mine." Pippin stood at the opening of the tent, his face cold and devoid of emotion. He was covered in dust and sweat and looked exhausted. Boniface wondered if he had ridden most of the day to reach Estinnes. Gunther and Bertrada, also covered in dust, stood behind him.

"Where is he?" Pippin spoke, his voice full of menace. "Where's Carloman?"

"He is in prayer and not to be disturbed." Heddo's voice sounded like a command.

Pippin ignored him and turned to Boniface. "Where is he?"

Boniface led him outside and pointed to the house at the end of the road. With a determined step, Pippin marched toward the house with Gunther, Bertrada, Trudi, and Boniface in his wake. Within moments, the rest of the tent followed.

"Carloman!" Pippin shouted as he approached the home. "Carloman!"

His brother appeared at the door. He put his hands up in a placating gesture. "Pippin, please. I –"

Pippin closed the last remaining steps between them and struck his brother in the face.

Heddo moved to intercede, but Gunther barred his way. "Let's let the boys work this out."

At first, Carloman's training kicked in and he mounted a spirited defense, but Pippin's speed and strength were overwhelming. He landed blow after blow on his older brother. Carloman tried to block them, tried to implore reason, but Pippin would not relent. "What have you done?" he shouted at Carloman. "What have you done?!"

Carloman's face grew bloodied but, in the end, it was his weeping that stopped Pippin's assault. Pippin looked down at Carloman, stunned.

"I've sinned. Oh God, Pippin, I have sinned." Carloman clung to his brother, his voice pleading through his tears. "I'm so sorry. I'm so sorry!"

It took a moment, but Pippin's eyes changed from fury to sympathy. He sat in the doorway and pulled Carloman into his arms. While his brother wept, Pippin stroked his hair and soothed him like a child.

"They were innocents," Carloman croaked. "Children."

"I know, Carloman. I know," Pippin whispered. "We'll fix this. We will fix this." He paused for a moment and then said, "I will fix this."

9

Estinnes

Pippin and Bertrada took Carloman upstairs to bed. Bertrada agreed to watch over him, comforting him in his hysteria. Pippin returned to the first floor, making way for his servants, who took control of the house, stocking its kitchen, preparing baths and beds for its new occupants. They even found a small bed for Charles.

Someone was pounding on the door. Pippin opened it to find a furious Bishop Heddo.

"I demand to see Carloman! He has appointed me his spiritual advisor." When Pippin started to close the door, Heddo used his shoulder to push into the house. "I insist that you take me to him." Pippin picked him up by his neck and threw him out onto the street.

A crowd of bishops and nobles had formed outside the house. Boniface was with them, as were Odilo and Trudi. Pippin signaled for his godfather to come inside. When Boniface entered the sitting room, Pippin didn't greet him; he simply waved him to a chair.

"Did the synod really condone the massacre?"

Boniface nodded.

"Tell them to rescind it, or they will never see the Church lands in my lifetime."

Boniface looked shocked and guilty at the same time. "I tried to stop it."

Pippin couldn't keep the fury from his voice. "Stop it? You and Carloman have driven us to this place from the start! Every decision you've made has been about the primacy of the Church and nothing else. Carloman murders thousands and your synod condones it? Good God, Boniface! You have launched a holy war and left me to wage it."

Boniface tried to speak, but Pippin cut him off. "You saw Odilo! Do you think Bavaria will just sit back and wait to see if we slaughter them as well? Do you think Saxony will, or Aquitaine?" Pippin sat and put his head in his hands.

Boniface nodded, for once contrite. "This is not what I had hoped would happen. If I can be of help..."

Pippin didn't bother to respond.

"How is Carloman?"

Pippin grunted. "Leave him to me. I will speak with him when he is able. I will let you and the synod know where things stand."

"I will speak to the council in the morning about rescinding the commendation."

"And tell that idiot Heddo to stay out of my sight. If I see any sign of him tomorrow, I'll tear his arms from their sockets."

Boniface appeared to be about to speak but Pippin cut him off. "Tell Odilo and Trudi I will see them now."

It took a second for Boniface to realize that he was being dismissed. Color rushed to his face in embarrassment. Pippin watched as his god-father stood. He was surprised by how old the man looked.

A few moments later, Odilo and Trudi entered without knocking, and Pippin could see the anger in each of them. He stood and crossed the room to take Odilo by the arm in greeting and then hugged his sister to his chest. The gesture clearly surprised them, and he bade them sit while he asked a servant to pour wine for the three of them.

"I suppose you are here to declare war." He couldn't disguise the weariness in his voice.

Odilo put down his cup. "We came to negotiate a peace."

Pippin let out a sigh of relief and sat back in his chair. "I'll admit I'm surprised but happy to hear it."

Odilo began to speak but Pippin held up a hand to stop him. "I know you are angry and have every right to be. I promise I will discuss terms tomorrow and I sincerely hope we can come to an agreement. But, for the moment, let's set aside our differences. We can save the kingdom tomorrow. It's been a long day for all of us. Let's enjoy this wine together and talk of more important things."

Pippin could see the confusion on their faces. "How's my nephew Tassilo?"

Trudi smiled and picked up his cue. "He's huge! Only three and he's already lord of the household."

Although it started with some awkwardness, the three of them relaxed into a warm conversation that lasted well into the evening hours. Aided by plenty of wine and a strict refusal to talk politics, the three of them reunited on a more familial level. Trudi boasted about Tassilo's popularity and Pippin shared embarrassing stories about her childhood. The threat of war still haunted their conversation, but their laughter for the moment held it at bay.

After they left, Pippin went upstairs to look in on Carloman. Bertrada sat at his bedside, a dour look on her face. She looked up when Pippin entered.

"Is he asleep?"

She nodded. "He wept for hours, begging me to forgive him."

"Did you?"

She shook her head. "I will never forgive him."

* * *

Pippin slept alone that night, just as he had every night since the report of the Alemanni slaughter arrived in Quierzy. Bertrada had retreated within herself to the point of barely speaking to him. The joy he had felt at their reconciliation had disappeared in an instant. She looked at him as if he were a stranger.

He had tried to speak to her about it, that he had no hand in it, but she just shook her head, refusing to engage with him in any type of explanation or excuse. With Lady Hélène in Paris, he had no one to intercede on his behalf, so he did the only thing he could think to do; he gave her time and space.

Although he originally had planned to arrive at the end of the council to meet with Sergius, the news from Alemannia changed everything. He ordered servants to pack immediately for the journey to Estinnes.

He was surprised when Bertrada intervened to supervise. He was even more surprised to find she and Charles planned to accompany him.

"I thought you would prefer to remain behind," he ventured.

"Are you withdrawing your promise of marriage?"

Pippin was stunned by the question. "No, of course not."

"You said that you would announce our engagement at Estinnes and that we would be wed a week later. You also promised to recognize Charles as your son."

Pippin wasn't sure how to react. He was delighted that she still wanted to marry, but he was wary of her remoteness. "I thought, given your reaction to the massacre, you were reconsidering."

A blotch of red touched her cheeks. "I'm with child." Her voice cracked and tears sprang to her eyes. She fought to suppress them. "Despite my reservations the marriage must proceed as planned."

"Your reservations?"

"While you insist that you aren't at fault in your family's tyranny, you are complicit. You always have been. You supported your father and your brother for a generation of conquest to unify the kingdom and through all that time you turned away from the torture it spawned.

"But you have promised me that you will no longer persecute the pagans and will no longer force them to convert, so I will hold you to that promise. And in turn, I will uphold my promise to wed you, Pippin. I will bear your children. I will continue to love the man I know, but the mayor" – she shuddered – "him, I abhor."

Lying in bed at the house in Estinnes, Pippin despaired for the life that awaited him. There was a chance he could avert a war over

Alemannia, just as there was a chance he could find his way back to Bertrada. But the odds seemed against him.

In his heart, he knew she was right about much of it. He never acted in or voiced any opposition to the forced conversion of pagans. He had done it himself. And now he was being called to account for it.

At the same time, he couldn't go back in time to change any of it. He could only move forward. He took solace in the fact that Bertrada agreed to marry him and that they would have a second child. That had to count for something.

* * *

He was eating a biscuit when his brother came down for breakfast the next morning. Carloman looked terrible. His face was covered with bruises and his eyes were puffy as if he had been weeping all night.

"Sit, Carloman."

Carloman sat. Pippin waved forward a servant, who put a plate of eggs, bacon, and biscuits in front of him. Carloman stared at the food but made no attempt to eat.

Pippin was content to let the silence mount, forcing Carloman to speak first. When his brother finally did, he looked at Pippin with hollow eyes. "Everything they're saying about me is true. I killed them. I killed them all."

Pippin nodded.

Carloman's voice cracked. "All that I imagined myself to be is a lie." Tears sprang to his eyes. "I murdered them and the guilt is crushing me. I – I can't bear the weight of it. It's too much."

"Last night, I told you I would fix this."

"No one can fix this."

"I will."

Carloman waited.

"You will resign as mayor and take holy orders."

Carloman's eyes welled up. He nodded and looked skyward as if searching for another path forward. "Is there no other way?"

Pippin folded his arms, trying to be patient. "You murdered two thousand unarmed men, women, and children – innocents. This is the way you atone for your sins. This is the way you protect our family name. This is the way you help me prevent a holy war."

After a long silence, Carloman nodded and sighed. "And Drogo?"

"You will invest your son Drogo with your territories. I will act as his guardian."

Again, he nodded. "It won't stop the war."

"No, it won't. But tomorrow you will send out a missive that says you held a trial of the Alemanni for treason and found them guilty. I want you to add a statement of regret because those you executed were Christian."

"You know they weren't."

"They kissed the cross after your last campaign, so, according to the Church, they are Christian. If we make this about their fealty instead of their religion, it may impede the incentive for war among the other pagan territories."

Carloman frowned. "I'll do it, but I doubt it will work. Odilo is already here. His allies won't be far behind."

Pippin sighed. "I know. But I'll try anything to avoid a holy war."

Silence again took the room. Carloman leaned back in his chair. Again, he looked skyward. "I was so arrogant. I thought myself the Blade of Christ here on earth. I was so sure I was right." He hung his head. "She even came to warn me, and I cursed her. Now, I can't stop seeing it: every death, every woman, every child."

"She?"

"A sybil, one of their priestesses."

For some reason, the admission bothered Pippin. It reminded him of something Trudi had told him, years ago. He stood to leave and laid his hand on his brother's shoulder. "You will find a way to atone, Carloman. Build the Church something big enough to warrant being forgiven."

* * *

Pippin saw Sergius next. The tall papal legate ducked through the doorway and strolled into the house, sniffing as if he smelled something foul. He proceeded to sit in the plushest chair and motioned for Pippin to take a seat as if he were hosting the meeting, not Pippin.

"I'll have red," he ordered a servant, before turning to Pippin. "Would you care for any wine?"

Pippin shook his head.

Sergius leaned back, resting his elbows on the arms of the chair and folding his hands into a steeple. "From the talk in the tents, we are either on the verge of a holy war or marching triumphantly towards a unified kingdom in Christ."

"Unless we move quickly, it is more likely the holy war," Pippin said.

"What does Carloman say?"

Pippin took a deep breath. "Carloman is resigning as mayor and will be taking holy orders. Before doing so, he will be issuing a statement that the Alemanni massacre was the consequence of a trial over fealty. And that those executed were Christians."

"An interesting fiction."

"Hopefully, it will slow down the drumbeat for war. I also will try to negotiate with Odilo but don't have much at my disposal with which to bargain."

"War is the last thing the pope wants."

"He's not alone in that."

Sergius frowned. "To the Church, the loss of Carloman is significant. I would prefer a solution that will keep him as mayor."

"There isn't one. He's a damaged man, Sergius. You can see it in his eyes. Besides, the politics require it as much as does his soul."

"So, with Carloman out of the picture, I suppose you now will be mayor of all Francia. How convenient for you."

"Drogo will continue to serve under my guardianship."

Sergius grunted. "How did we become so fortunate?"

Pippin bit back his retort. The man was so arrogant! It took a moment for him to cool his anger and remind himself that Sergius was just a game piece on the board.

"As you know, I refuse to support Childeric as king."

Sergius waved his hands again, dismissing the subject. "This again! He is already king. He was anointed with the holy oil."

"If he can be anointed with the holy oil, he can be unanointed."

"Highly unlikely."

"The Lombards are pressing the papal see, taking land and wealth. At some point you are going to need my help. And when you do, it won't be Childeric who comes to your aid, it will be me. So, the question you should be thinking about is 'what would entice Pippin to cross the kingdom to come to our aid?'"

The legate's response was swift. "You impudent little turd! It's too bad that you aren't the one taking holy orders. At least Carloman is a servant of the Church."

Sergius stood, towering over Pippin. "Do you really think the pope can be blackmailed? Until a year ago, half the kingdom wanted you excommunicated. And now you're on the verge of a civil war, without the strength of your brother, without the support of the Church, and without the support of your king.

"Even if you survive, you likely won't have the resources left to fight the Lombards. In all likelihood, it will be you needing the pope more than he will need you!"

Pippin kept his voice calm. "Perhaps you are correct, Sergius. You understand the papal see far better than I do. I am merely a soldier, but I understand war. And I understand what it will take to beat back the Lombards. I'm not sure you have another ally who does."

Sergius replied, "The arrogance of you Franks is always perplexing to me. I will convey your message to the pope, but I see little help in it for you. You have a king, duly anointed with the holy oil. For the sake of the kingdom, I suggest you bend the knee."

Just as he began the meeting, Sergius ended it.

* * *

Odilo and Trudi asked that they meet in the tent belonging to Gerold of Vinzgau. They wanted a witness to the discussion and felt that Gerold and his wife, Emma, made for a suitable, if not entirely neutral, party.

Pippin agreed and made his way to the tent with Gunther in tow. Gerold had emptied the tent of visiting nobles so that only they and the servants remained.

Pippin was surprised by the amount of food that had been prepared and gratefully accepted a flask of red wine. He was beginning to feel the strain of the day's negotiations.

He greeted Gerold, Emma, Odilo, and Trudi in turn and the six of them, including Gunther, sat at a round table for their discussion.

Having seen how anxious Odilo was to talk, Pippin waited for his brother-in-law to start.

"Where is Carloman?" Odilo said. "I don't see how we can start without him."

"I will speak for Carloman," Pippin said.

"I don't think you understand, Pippin. Bavaria, Saxony, Aquitaine, and many of the outlier territories are already arming. War is imminent."

Pippin tried to keep the frustration out of his voice. "I understand what is at stake."

"If you did, Carloman would be here. There can be no peace if he is not a party to it."

"Carloman resigned his office of mayor. He will be taking holy orders and joining the clergy." Pippin enjoyed seeing the shock on everyone's face. "His son Drogo will inherit Carloman's territories under my guardianship."

Odilo was first to recover. "Then you must answer for the slaughter of two thousand Alemanni – unarmed men, women, and children."

"I will attempt to do so." Pippin stood and took a large sip of his wine. He needed to move. "And I hope that you see Carloman's abdication as a first step in that effort. You should also understand that the Alemanni were executed for their lack of fealty, not their religion."

"That's a lie," Trudi cut in. "Carloman would never have murdered innocent Christian women and children."

Pippin nodded, to take her point. "You must admit, however, that Theudebald and his army have defied my dictates – as well as Carloman's – for years. They attacked your palace while Odilo was at war, they refused to pay tribute, and they harassed and defiled priests. They violated their fealty and had to be held accountable. Unfortunately, Carloman went too far. He defied the truce of parley, he killed Theudebald and murdered innocents."

Pippin leaned forward to put both hands on the table. "And now, he is no longer mayor. There is no threat to Bavaria. There is no threat to Saxony or Aquitaine. This was about Theudebald. He was the target. Carloman lost his way and now...has stepped down to atone for his sins."

Silence greeted his speech. He sat down and finished his drink and waited for a response.

"It's not enough," Odilo said in a quiet voice. "It will not be enough for Bavaria or our allies to know that Carloman has taken holy orders. The punishment doesn't fit the crime. And while I believe your words – Carloman has grown more violent over the past few years – we'll need more than assurances that we are not under threat. I will need something more to quell the calls for war. I need a concession that demonstrates you want peace."

Here it comes, thought Pippin. He knew there would be an ask.

"First, we want Lantfrid, son of Lantfrid, installed as duc of Alemannia. Second, we want Gripho released from Neufchateau and offered an appropriate position in your government."

Pippin pretended to frown but was elated by the demand. He had never wanted Gripho imprisoned and had promised Sunnichild that he would free her son once he had a chance.

"Both those demands are unacceptable," Pippin said. "There will be no duc in Alemannia. We already have given territorial rule to Comtes Warin and Ruthard. Gripho is also out of the question. He could potentially destabilize the kingdom."

"Then there is little to discuss." Odilo stood to leave.

Pippin raised his hand. "Perhaps we could find alternative means to demonstrate our desire for peace. Perhaps a reduction in tribute or a payment in gold."

They haggled for hours and eventually Pippin gave in to the demand for Gripho's release but held firm on Lantfrid. The last thing he wanted was another descendant of Godefred to be duc of Alemannia.

As the negotiation was wrapping up, Pippin nodded to Gunther and his lieutenant excused himself from the table.

"I have another bit of news I'd like you to hear," Pippin said. He waved for servants to fill the cups of all his guests.

"What is it?" Trudi asked.

Gunther returned with Bertrada and she walked over to stand beside Pippin.

"First, to peace in the kingdom." Pippin raised his glass, and everyone toasted with him. "Second, I'd like to announce that Bertrada and I are to be married one week from today here in Estinnes. I'd like you to join us if you are willing."

"Thank God." Trudi jumped up and took Bertrada into her arms. "I can't believe it took you two so long!"

"Will you stand with me?" Bertrada asked her.

"Yes! Yes, with all my heart."

"Then it is settled." Pippin clinked his flask against Odilo's. "I told you we would save the kingdom, today."

10

Paris

Despite Miette's fears over returning to Paris, her homecoming went without incident. Ragomfred received her cordially at the front door, kissed her on the cheek, and led her back to her rooms.

"I'm glad for your return, Miette."

Miette had rehearsed her speech to him with Lady Hélène. "As am I, milord. I know we have had our differences in the past but hope that our future can be less...tumultuous. After years of being isolated from my family and friends, I have no further desire to be an instrument of politics unless it is to enhance your name and the house of Ragomfred."

From the relief in his eyes, her husband understood that "an instrument of politics" meant her affair with the king. Although he had never been interested in her – he preferred men – her affair with the king had caused him some embarrassment among the nobles within the king's entourage.

Miette's return to court, however, was far more turbulent. Miette found herself both a pariah and one of the most sought-after guests in Paris. She was either considered a traitor or a victim depending on one's allegiance to Carloman's red or Pippin's green. Either way, as the former hostess to the king and the rumored lover of Pippin, Miette was the talk of the court. She, of course, loved her newfound status and quickly worked her way back into the salons of the leading families at court.

Hélène received far less attention. With a change of wardrobe as well as a shift in posture and demeanor, she transformed herself back into the widowed matron at court she was known to be and quietly returned home. She dismissed whatever role she was rumored to play in Miette's saga and described her stay in Pippin's household solely as a means to accompany Miette through her imprisonment. She also readily testified that Miette's chastity and Pippin's honor remained intact and that much of Miette's imprisonment was driven by the politics between Pippin and the king.

The first luncheon Miette attended was a small gathering of perhaps a dozen women, all prominent in Neustrian society. Of those present, Miette was best acquainted with Lady Gagnon, Lady Didot, and Lady Talon.

Although they all had snubbed her when she first married into nobility, their shift in allegiance came swiftly after she began playing hostess to the king. At first, Miette had carried a grudge, but with time, she grew to enjoy their company, especially their love of gossip. Now, Miette considered each of them a friend.

All three were older than she, although none had yet reached the age of thirty. They were handsome women, well dressed and coiffed, but not what Miette would consider as beautiful. Gagnon was renowned for having breasts the size of melons. Didot's best feature was her green eyes and Talon was nearly as dainty as Miette.

Miette kissed the cheeks of all three and settled in at their table for a plate of cheese, bread cakes, and pork slices. A fourth woman whom Gagnon introduced as Lady Drusseau also joined their table. She was younger than the other three and decidedly less confident.

After a bit of small talk about the weather, Talon turned to Miette with a malicious grin. "So, tell us about Pippin?"

"He is what he is known to be: a fierce warrior and a kind but serious man."

"Is he as short as they say he is?"

Miette stood and held up her hand above her head. "He stands about this tall next to me, but his chest is nearly this wide." She pantomimed hugging Pippin's chest."

"So...you got to know him *well*," Gagnon said.

"I did." Miette smiled.

"Is Lady Bertrada still living with him?" Didot interjected.

Miette coughed, hoping they didn't see her face flush. "She lives in his household, yes. But their relationship has been somewhat strained."

"Was that your fault?" Didot chimed in, leering.

Miette looked away. "No. I was never a factor...just a guest. I would not be surprised if they marry."

"They seem like such an odd couple," Gagnon offered. "She is so beautiful, and he is so dull. They say he suffers from the blackness."

"He does," confirmed Miette, "but he can also be quite charming."

All the ladies sat forward for that.

"No, no. Nothing like that. I was merely a guest in his home."

"They say he's violent." Lady Drusseau's interruption hit the conversation like a blunt instrument. "I pray for Bertrada."

Miette stiffened at the rebuke. "I believe Pippin holds his violence for the battlefield, milady. He was always a kind to me."

"That means nothing between a man and a woman." Drusseau waved her hand dismissively.

The three other women looked away as if they were embarrassed by her comment. Miette frowned, assessing Lady Drusseau more carefully. The woman's face was heavily powdered, more so than most women.

After the meal, the women got up to mingle with the larger group. Lady Drusseau stopped by the dessert table to pick up a small cake. Miette sidled next to her.

"How long have you and your husband been at court?"

Although startled, Drusseau answered quickly. "A year. The king invited us to live in the palace."

"He must think highly of your husband."

"As he does of yours, Lady Ragomfred."

"Please call me Miette."

"Only if you call me Charlotte."

The two women kissed each other's cheeks. Up close, Miette could see a bruise on Drusseau's face hidden beneath her powder.

Miette remembered when she had used powder to cover the bruises given her by Childeric and his men. An anger, deep within her, welled to the surface. The thought of Charlotte being beaten infuriated her. She put her hand on the young woman's arm. "Who did that to you?"

Charlotte looked as if she had been slapped. "I don't know what you are talking about."

Miette lowered her voice. "Yes. You do. Was it your husband, your brother, your father-in-law?"

Charlotte's eyes were tearing up and she bit her lip. "Please. Don't say anything."

"Who did this?"

Charlotte's face sobered. "Does it matter?" Her manner suggested otherwise.

"It does to me." Miette let go of her arm.

"It's nothing. It was my fault." Charlotte shook her head and walked away.

* * *

"I met the most interesting woman today," Miette said to her husband at dinner. "Lady Drusseau."

Their meals and interactions had been quite cordial since her return. For the most part, they talked court politics and she filled in her husband on the latest gossip. He never asked about her imprisonment in Quierzy or even hinted at her (or his) affair with the king. From what Miette could gather at court, the threat of excommunicating Pippin had drawn attention to Childeric's own behavior and increasingly become an issue with the Church.

Ragomfred swirled his wine in his flask before tasting it. "Yes, her husband has a large holding in the Breton March. A very wealthy man. He claims to be a descendent of Dagobert I through one of the old king's concubines. But that is a common boast: Dagobert had three wives and as many concubines while he reigned."

"Is Drusseau a knight?"

Her husband nodded. "He has a small retinue of soldiers here in Paris but maintains a large army in the Twelve Counties along the Breton March."

"Is he a big man?"

"Yes, a very imposing man – all muscle and sinew." Her husband imbued the words with relish and his eyes took on a gleam of their own. "They say he can cleave a man in two with his broadsword."

Miette smiled at her husband's obvious arousal. "His wife is lovely. We should invite them to dine with us."

"Yes, that would be advantageous. He is important to Childeric."

At the mention of Childeric's name, Miette grew cold, as if a wraith breathed over her body. She had been safe for so long, but here without protection, she felt unmoored.

Her husband saw her reaction and chuckled. "You know you can't avoid him forever, my dear. We belong to his court. We'll be at the palace next week. He's likely to be there."

Images of her degradation flew through her mind. Soldiers rutting her while the king masturbated above them, the humiliation of him raping her in front of his men.

Her hands began to shake, her heart slammed inside her chest, and she had trouble breathing. She desperately fought for control, sinking her fingernails into her right arm, preferring pain to her humiliation. She dug deeper until they drew blood and the anguish brought her some focus. It allowed her to calm her mind. She took three long breaths and looked up at her husband. "I'd rather not go."

Although he must have seen the panic take her, Ragomfred chose not to acknowledge it. His face was stern and unsympathetic. "Your absence would reignite the rumors, which I cannot allow. But I can assure you that as far as Childeric is concerned, it will be as if your dalliance never happened. It serves Childeric's interest to let the matter die, especially after all the talk of excommunication. I can assure you he will be nothing but a gracious host."

"When it comes to Childeric you can assure me of nothing."

The Drusseau dinner was quickly scheduled, and two days later Miette greeted Charlotte and her husband at the door of her home and ushered them into the dining area.

Ragomfred hadn't exaggerated about the size and build of Drusseau. He was tall, at least a foot taller than her husband, well muscled, and handsome to the eye. He also walked with a certain grace that spoke of years of training with a sword. A twist of desire stoked in Miette before she could squelch it. She had always been attracted to powerful men. She had to remind herself of Charlotte's bruises to stifle the lure of his presence.

Despite the day being warm, Charlotte wore a long dress with a scarf around her neck and gloves that reached up to her elbow.

Ragomfred and Drusseau clearly had met, but the two weren't well acquainted. And as the evening unfolded, Miette found herself doing most of the talking. Drusseau also had a diffident military demeanor that didn't promote conversation. His initial responses to Miette's questions were somewhat terse.

Undaunted, Miette made sure their flagons of wine never emptied and used all her coquettish charm to draw the man out. When she asked him questions about his lineage to Dagobert I, Drusseau's tongue began to loosen, and he regaled them with stories of his great-grand-sire and their fiefdom in the Twelve Counties.

Her husband joined the conversation and soon the two were comparing ancestors and stories of their families' military conquests.

Watching Drusseau, Miette found herself drawn to the man's self-assuredness. He certainly was handsome. She could see why Charlotte was conflicted about him.

When the men's conversation lagged, she gave Drusseau a wide-eyed look. "My husband tells me you are indispensable to the king."

The man smiled. "I will be once more of my men arrive."

"For the civil war?" Miette asked.

"If it comes to that," Drusseau said guardedly. "For now we're just shifting resources to where they need to be."

"I've heard there are already battles in the streets between Pippin's men and Carloman's Knights in Christ."

Drusseau smirked. "They aren't Carloman's anymore. At least not in Paris."

"Then whose are they?"

Drusseau smiled. "Let's just say, they report to someone who's indispensable to the king."

When the meal ended, the two men stepped outside for brandy while the women retired to the sitting room. Charlotte, who had hardly spoken throughout the meal, had no such trouble when they were alone.

"Why did you bring us here?" Her face was flushed with anger.

"My husband thought it would be advantageous."

"Do you always lie so easily?"

Miette nodded. "When it matters."

"Why does it matter now?"

"How often does he hit you?"

Charlotte shook her head in refusal, her eyes brimming with tears.

Miette leaned forward, putting her hand on Charlotte's. "You matter to me."

"There's nothing to be done!" Charlotte's voice seethed with anger. "And it is none of your affair."

"Show me." Miette's voice was soft but firm. "Show me where he hurts you."

Charlotte stared back, her lips pressing into a thin line. And then with a look of defiance she undid her scarf. A thick blue bruise marred her otherwise flawless skin.

She continued, pulling the top of her gown past her shoulder to her waist. Bruises marked her chest, her breast, and stomach.

Miette's eyes teared up in empathy. "No one deserves that."

"He is my husband," Charlotte said diffidently. She pulled up her dress and redid her scarf. "He has the right. There is nothing anyone can do."

"But you don't have to suffer alone."

"What would you know of my pain?"

Miette's eyes grew cold. "I have scars of my own."

Charlotte's eyes widened at her change in tone. "Perhaps you do."

"I may know someone who can help."

"No!" Charlotte's voice raised almost an octave. "It would only make things worse."

Miette retook her hand to assure her. "I won't do anything unless you ask me to."

* * *

The palace had been refurbished since Miette had been there with Pippin. Childeric clearly had an eye for the dramatic; the grand hall was decorated with rich tapestries of military conquests; the ceiling was filled with purple bunting and gold-leaf flourishes that made the room sparkle in the light of the thousand candles that lit the room.

Childeric's throne stood at one end of the hall on a raised platform; it was the only piece of furniture to be seen. Stanchions cordoned off the center of the room – a rectangle that ran from a place ten feet before the throne almost to the door – so that all eyes in the room could always see Childeric.

Nobles entering the hall escorted their wives on a tour around the rectangle, nodding in greeting to those guests who had arrived earlier and stood along the walls.

When Ragomfred entered with Miette, the room quieted to a hushed murmur of whispers. Despite the unsettled flurries in her stomach Miette managed a smile that took in the nobles lining the walls. She nodded to those familiar to her and greeted the women she knew by name. The murmurs grew in volume as she progressed through the room. When their tour had ended, her husband released her hand with a smile and she made her way to the wall where Ladies Gagnon, Didot, and Talon awaited her.

"Quite the entrance," Gagnon chided. "One would think you had slept with the king."

"Or Mayor Pippin," Talon added.

"Or both!" Didot laughed.

A horn played a fanfare and Childeric swept into the hall from a door behind his throne, an arm raised in salutation. Miette saw the lithe movement of his body, his long, braided hair and beard, and his bejeweled fingernails. It hit her like a physical blow, nearly bending her over double. She welcomed the obligatory bows and curtseys that followed his appearance as it gave her time to recover. Even so, when she stood, she felt lightheaded and nauseous.

Someone took her arm. She turned to find Lady Hélène beside her and nearly wept with relief. "I thought you might need a steadying hand. Walk with me until you recover."

Miette latched on to her arm. "Is it so obvious?"

"Perhaps to me. I'm impressed that you agreed to come to the palace so soon."

Miette shook her head. "I wasn't given much choice."

The nobles were lining up to pay their respects to the king. Miette saw Ragomfred heading their way and groaned. "Now, I'm going to have to face the bastard."

Hélène turned and kissed both her cheeks. "Remember your training. He no longer can hurt you. You know at least ten ways to maim and kill him if you need to. If that knowledge fails you, I find anger usually works just as well."

Miette envisioned three of the ways she could hurt Childeric and took enormous comfort in them. When Ragomfred arrived to collect her, she even smiled for his benefit.

The line was long but moved quickly. To pass the time, Miette imagined the seven other ways she could maim or kill the man. As they drew close to the throne, she felt ready to face him.

A stunning young woman with thin elven features announced each of the guests as they approached Childeric. Her long brown hair cascaded in waves of curls behind her back and her green eyes looked upon Childeric with adulation.

"The Lady Brevet," Ragomfred whispered to Miette. "She now serves as hostess to the king."

My replacement, thought Miette.

When Lady Brevet turned to find Miette, a small smirk took the woman's face. "The Lord and Lady Ragomfred," Brevet announced in a loud voice, her eyes triumphant.

Miette only felt sorrow for the woman. She turned to Childeric and curtsied, meeting the king's gaze. His eyes were the same dark pools that had captured her on their first meeting. Miette imagined slitting his throat.

"Ah! The Lord and Lady Ragomfred reunited at last," Childeric cooed. He addressed Miette directly. "I hope your captivity wasn't too uncomfortable."

"Any time away from my husband is a tragic loss," Miette said.

"And how is Mayor Pippin?"

Miette's mind saw her knife plunging into the king's eye. "He is well, Your Highness."

Whenever Childeric spoke of Pippin, his tone grew mocking. "Does our short mayor still have his big sword?"

Ragomfred squeezed her arm in warning and Miette's imaginary knife found Childeric's armpit. She used her best coquettish smile and said, "I've learned, Your Highness, that those who have the biggest swords also know how to use them."

The king's eyes opened wide at the obvious sexual reference, and she could see the old sparks kindle Childeric's need to dominate her. "Have you met my new hostess, the Lady Brevet?"

Miette almost laughed at his attempt to taunt her with his new lover. Instead, she curtsied to the young woman. "It is my pleasure to meet you."

Childeric was growing more animated by the second. "Oh, you must get to know each other. Perhaps the two of you could join me for a game...of cards or some other amusement."

Shock, fear, or jealousy, and perhaps a desperate need for Childeric overwhelmed Brevet's face. The old Miette would have laughed in triumph at the woman's comeuppance, but now, she only could see the manipulation. It made her sick. Given half a chance Childeric would degrade them both to the point of depravity.

I could kill him, thought Miette. I could bring my knives to his game and end his reign.

Her husband cleared his throat to gain Childeric's attention. His look suggested caution and Childeric, with a scowl, nodded. He waved his bejeweled fingers to dismiss them.

Miette curtsied and her husband bowed. As they walked away, she imagined cutting off the king's testicles. The thought made her smile.

* * *

An invitation arrived the next morning asking Miette to join Lady Hélène at her home in Paris at Miette's earliest convenience. Miette dropped everything she had planned for the day, put on a modest gown, and took a carriage across the river to Lady Hélène's apartments.

An elderly woman led her through a large plush sitting room filled with artwork, past a study filled with sculptures of naked women, and into to a large square room empty of furniture.

Hélène was waiting for her there, dressed in pantaloons and a short chemise, holding two long staffs. "I hope you didn't think your training ended just because we came back to Paris."

Miette laughed and stripped to her undergarments. "Do you have an extra pair of pantaloons?"

"You don't need them. There's no one here but you and me. And all my servants are women." Hélène tossed her a long staff.

Miette caught the wooden pole and immediately spun to the attack. Hélène stepped back to deflect the onslaught and the two traded a series of blows, none of which landed cleanly. Miette could have laughed, she was so pleased. She loved the feeling of strength that invaded her body when she sparred. A gleam of sweat soon covered the two of them as they danced over every square foot of the floor.

Miette caught Hélène with a blow to her shoulder and a second one to her mid-thigh. With a grimace, her mentor doubled her effort and Miette soon found herself using every move she had just to play defense. She ducked under a blow meant for her head just before Hélène pivoted with her and took out her legs.

They spent over an hour training. When Hélène finally brought it to an end, the two women were covered in sweat.

They collapsed in a corner of the empty room and Hélène batted her staff against the door. The old woman who had greeted Miette appeared with a tray filled with flasks of water.

"I didn't think I'd miss this." Miette drained half the flask in one quaff.

"You need to train. The path requires it. You can't ensure justice if you aren't prepared to deliver it."

"I've some news for Pippin. A knight named Drusseau has taken over Carloman's Knights in Christ – at least in Paris. He's become indispensable to Childeric and has an army and a lot of property in the Breton March. He's positioning men and resources for civil war."

"I'll send word to Childebrand. He seems to come here more often than Pippin."

Miette nodded. "Drusseau beats his wife."

"They all do."

Miette frowned. "Did your husband?"

Hélène winked. "Why do you think I'm a widow?"

Miette laughed at the jest and then wondered if it was a jest. "I can't help thinking she deserves better."

"She does. It isn't just."

"She begged me not to do anything. I told her I would do nothing unless she asked me to."

"Did she tell you it was her fault?"

Miette nodded.

"Then, she'll never ask you."

"But even if I wanted to, how could I stop it? Her husband is huge and powerful. He knows as many ways to kill someone as I do. And he has an army behind him."

"Perhaps you can't."

The response angered Miette. "How does doing nothing serve justice?"

"I didn't say you should do nothing. I said perhaps you can't stop him."

11

Estinnes

Pippin's "solution" to the Alemanni massacre threw Boniface's synod into an uproar. Every bishop present objected to it, many shouting their displeasure. Carloman was seen as their mayor and a man of God. Taking the tonsure would leave the kingdom in the hands of Pippin – a man the bishops equated more with his father, the hated Charles Martel.

Rather than fight for order, Boniface instead called for a halt to their proceedings. He needed to talk to Carloman. And he needed to talk with him alone. Everything he had worked to achieve was coming undone and he would no longer accept someone else's word for it. He was glad Pippin had chased away the meddling Heddo, but he would be damned to accept the report of Carloman's tonsure without having spoken to Carloman himself.

He found his godson in the first place he looked, kneeling at the altar in the Estinnes chapel. It was still early morning, and the small chapel was dark with only a single shaft of light coming through a window high on the eastern wall. Dust particles floated in its illumination above the altar before it fell on Carloman's outstretched hands, folded in prayer.

Coming from the unruly cacophony of the synod, the quiet of the chapel filled Boniface with a small measure of peace. He embraced it, waiting in the nave for Carloman to finish, knowing the respite would be short-lived. When at last Carloman made the sign of the cross, Boniface stepped forward and placed his hand on his godson's shoulder.

"Walk with me, son."

Carloman stood and together they walked out of the chapel and into the morning light. Boniface tried not to react to the sight of Carloman's face. The man's eyes were sunken and shadowed, his skin was pasty, and he looked as if he hadn't slept in a fortnight.

Boniface led him to the well-groomed gardens of the church court-yard where flowers were just beginning to bloom. "I spoke to Pippin about your decision to take the tonsure. I must say I'm surprised and concerned."

Carloman nodded. "It's the only way I can fully atone."

"Clearly, you are having a crisis of faith. And I worry that you're being manipulated in that crisis, first by Bishop Heddo and now by Pippin."

"Pippin sees it clearly. He has his own motives but is right about what must be done."

"Surely there are other ways without giving up your role as mayor."

Carloman shook his head and sat on the first bench that crossed their path. He tugged on Boniface's sleeve to draw the man beside him. A great sadness seemed to well within him and when he spoke, his voice cracked with emotion. "It's the only way. I'm not fit to be mayor. In my hubris, I believed I was doing the work of God."

"For most of your life you have!"

"No!" The sudden fury in Carloman's eyes brought Boniface to silence. When he spoke, Carloman's voice dropped to a whisper. "Not our God. He would never countenance such evil. All that I have achieved is my ruin. I have sinned – mortal sins, Boniface – sins I cannot even bear to describe. I can't continue."

Carloman drew from his pocket the wooden canister that contained the finger bone of Saint Lambert. He handed it to Boniface. "You gave me this at my elevation to knighthood. I took it as a symbol of my worth as a man of God. It has now become a symbol of my sins against mankind."

Tears leaked from Carloman's eyes. "I've butchered thousands in His name. Innocents." He winced, speaking the word. "I took their lives in the midst of a holy furor that flooded my being. Only it wasn't holy; it was my pride and my pride alone. To show me, God sent a sign of my vanity – the finger bone of a child I had murdered in Canstatt. That is the true measure of my service."

Boniface shook his head. "You have been a faithful servant of the Church, a true man of God. You cannot let this one incident define your worth."

"Their murders do define me. I can't get them out of my head. Each killing leads to another, to another, and another; I am never alone in my thoughts; I'm chased by the souls of those I butchered. Pippin is right. I can no longer be mayor. I have sinned against God and my fellow man. I must atone."

The pain he saw in Carloman's face was palpable and Boniface briefly wondered at his own role in leading his godson to this place. But, in that moment, there were greater implications to the kingdom than his godson's soul. "The Church needs you, Carloman. It needs your leadership. Pippin doesn't carry your depth of faith; he doesn't always advocate for the Church."

Carloman patted Boniface's knee. "I'm not abandoning the Church. My brother still takes my counsel even if we don't always agree and Drogo will succeed me as mayor. As Pippin has no children, it's likely Drogo will one day rule over the breadth of the kingdom. I will be there to be his guide."

"Pippin and Bertrada are to wed," Boniface cautioned. "If they have children, Drogo's future role may be in doubt."

Carloman shook his head. "The way those two have coupled for years, they should have had a dozen children by now. Bertrada is barren. You should see how she dotes on her sister's child! She acts like it's her own. Surely, if she could have a child, she would have had one by now. I pity my brother. Anyone other than Pippin would have found a more fertile bride by now, but he is besotted with the woman. Be at peace,

Boniface. Drogo will be mayor and I will always have influence over the kingdom's affairs."

* * *

Returning to the bishops, Boniface spoke with reverence about Carloman's need to atone. When the bishops began to object, he displayed the holy relic Carloman had returned to him as evidence of his godson's despair. Just the presence of the sacred relic silenced the synod. In the hands of a church or a cathedral, the artefact would bring thousands of pilgrims each year and guarantee the wealth and power of a diocese for generations. It was priceless. That Carloman had returned it was as stunning as it was profound.

Boniface asked the bishops to stay for the ordination ceremony and requested that, as a representative of the pope, Sergius conduct it.

Sergius, however, insisted that, as a former mayor, Carloman should be ordained officially in Rome. He could conduct the rite of tonsure – cutting Carloman's hair to signify his departure from his life in the laity to his new life in the Church – but the ordination itself should be administered by the pope's own hand.

Given that the tonsure ritual is brief, Boniface suggested that the ceremonies be conducted in succession. Carloman would go first, followed by a rite of commendation where Pippin would take Drogo's hands within his own, and then Pippin and Bertrada would wed. As no one had an objection, he scheduled the services for the coming Saturday. With the council's agreement, Boniface closed the synod and turned his attention to Pippin's upcoming nuptials.

Although marriage was available to any two people who simply made vows of commitment to each other, to be married in the Church was another matter. It required the consent of a priest and – given Pippin's now singular role as mayor – Boniface wanted to ensure that whatever leverage he could gain from performing the ceremony be gained.

Bertrada agreed to meet with him in the same church courtyard he had used to speak with Carloman. When she arrived, she opened her arms wide in greeting and hugged him to her chest. Turning her attention to the garden, she delighted in the early flowers and the small hedges that defined the lawn. They sat next to each other on the bench at the center of the courtyard. The day was turning warm and birds returned again and again to a small decorative pond nearby. A lone grey cat sat next to the pool, waiting for one to come close, but each time a bird drew near, it flitted away before the cat could pounce.

"Why now?" Boniface asked, once the opening pleasantries had been satisfied. "You and Pippin have been together for so long; what has changed that brings you to ask for this sacrament, now?"

Bertrada's face grew serious at the question. "I have always loved Pippin. But, until recently, he wasn't his own man. He was either his father's son or, subsequently, mayor of the palace. He was pulled in so many directions by the politics and by the fighting that he hadn't grown into the man he was meant to be." Her cheeks blotched red with color. "Or perhaps the man I'd hoped he would be."

Although Boniface had known Bertrada for years, he found her answer astonishing. Most women would have thrown themselves at Pippin at the slightest provocation. Yet, here, Bertrada had waited until Pippin had proved himself worthy of her. The delay was *her* choice. Not his. "He will expect children."

Bertrada's hand stole to her stomach. "Yes. Of course."

"Are you able to bear them?"

Bertrada's eyes hardened at the question. "We'll find out soon enough."

"If you cannot have children, Pippin's succession will be jeopardized. I know that you care for your sister's child, but the Church will not support her son as a successor. We will ask both you and Pippin to name Drogo. Can I have your promise that you will abide by that request?"

"Pippin and I will have children of our own."

"I'm asking if you cannot."

"Pippin and I will have children of our own."

Boniface swallowed an oath of frustration. He wasn't sure if Bertrada was demurring due to the politics or simply obsessed with having a child.

He decided to change course.

"You will, of course, agree that your children will be raised in the Church."

Bertrada nodded her assent.

Boniface laid his hand on her arm and said sternly, "You need to affirm it, Bertrada."

"Yes, they will be raised in the Church."

He had hoped that Bertrada might be an advocate for the Church in influencing Pippin, but Boniface couldn't seem to pin down her politics. If her commitment to the Church was as limited as Pippin's, they would be a formidable couple to persuade about anything. Recalling her willingness to stand up to Bishop Aidolf, Boniface realized she might well be formidable all on her own.

"You should know that you are choosing a hard life. Your children – and you – will become targets of your husband's rivals. You will never be completely safe."

Bertrada nodded her head. "I would have to have been blind not to see the portent of the last five years."

"There also is great responsibility that comes with being a mayor's wife."

Bertrada looked down at her hands. "I know what's in store for me. But being mayor is Pippin's cross to bear. I don't aspire to be the mayor's wife; I aspire to be Pippin's wife."

Boniface chuckled. "But he is mayor. I don't see the distinction."

Bertrada's eyes grew hard. "Neither did Carloman. He lost himself in his role as mayor. He believed he was inviolate, above reproach. In Canstatt, he abandoned his values and his humanity. I won't let Pippin forget who he is and I won't condone the violence that goes with him being mayor."

* * *

Pippin woke up with a raging hangover. He, Gunther, and Boniface had drunk wine well into the early hours of his wedding day, singing bawdy songs and telling tall tales from the battles they had fought. Boniface had some of the best stories from his years in Frisia, where he fought pagan warlords, just to have his sermons heard.

Despite the pain in his head, Pippin couldn't help smiling. For once, the Fates' wheel was turning in his favor. Bertrada had agreed to be his bride; his feud with Carloman appeared to be finished; like his father before him, Pippin would be the sole mayor of the realm and the holy war with the pagan states over the massacre at Canstatt would be avoided.

Part of him, of course, didn't trust his luck. It had happened too fast. And as with most good fortune, he wasn't sure he deserved it. Bertrada's reservations also continued to fill him with doubt. Even so, he found himself thinking there might yet be a chance that he could be happy.

Bertrada had banished the men from the house they were occupying, so he, Carloman, and Gunther bathed in a large stream just outside town in the shadow of a large escarpment. The current was brisk, the water cold and shoulder deep. The three of them doffed their clothes and threw themselves in to splash away the week's dirt and grime. Pippin chuckled at the sight; it reminded him of being out on campaign with his father when he and Carloman were boys.

"Do you remember that night in Sancerres when Old Tibault's daughters caught us swimming in the Loire?"

Carloman laughed. "We didn't know they were there until they were in the water with us."

"Élize," Pippin said. "The one who swam to me was Élize."

"Noémie," Carloman said. "And Gunther got the chaperone."

Gunther chuckled. "Lilli. Now, she was a lovely woman."

"How old were we?" Pippin asked.

"Maybe sixteen or seventeen," Carloman said. "You would have been fourteen."

"I dreamed about her for years."

"You kept thinking it would happen every time we went on campaign. You bathed more times that year than a Roman courtesan."

"There was a time," Gunther said, "when your father was just as innocent. I remember the first time he met your mother." He laughed. "I thought he would piss himself. She was the daughter of a duc and as beautiful as they come. He was convinced Chlotrude was destined for much greater men and would never be seen with a bastard son like him. And if truth be told, I agreed with him.

"Yet there we are at her father's house and she's smiling at Charles and touching his arm, flirting shamelessly with him. And he couldn't see it!" Gunther winked. "When it came to women your father wasn't all that brave. She's the one who eventually seduced him. To this day, I blame her for all the wars we fought. If it wasn't for her, he would have never thought himself worthy enough to make his claim as mayor."

As they dressed on the shore, a wave of melancholy swept over Pippin. It had been years since he and Carloman had laughed like that. They had been close once, before the weight of the kingdom fell to their shoulders, before the Church exacted its tithe on Carloman's faith.

They could never go back to the way it was. Too much had been said and done. But, before they parted, Pippin embraced his brother. "I pray you find peace in the clergy, Carloman."

Carloman's eyes welled. "You were right to come for me, brother. I had fallen too far to recover on my own."

They parted ways. Carloman had an instructional meeting with Sergius and Pippin needed to retrieve Bertrada. The ceremonies were due to begin within the hour.

* * *

Pippin had seen a fair number of spectacles in his life – his father's wedding to Sunnichild, Carloman's wedding to Greta, Gripho's elevation to knighthood – he was pretty sure that his wedding to Bertrada would not be ranked high among them. While the church at Estinnes aspired one day to become the site of a cathedral, it could hardly lay a claim to such grandeur now.

Designed to look like the shape of a cross, the small stone church featured two side altars – the left a tribute to the Blessed Mother and the right to Saint Peter – while the main altar was framed by an intricate wooden reredos that both housed the tabernacle and screened the church sacristy from the congregation.

He and Trudi were seated on Saint Mary's altar while Sergius presided over Carloman's tonsure ceremony on the main altar.

Wearing a brown robe and kneeling, Carloman was surrounded by nearly every bishop who had attended the synod. Each of them carried a smoking thurible of incense that swung back and forth above Carloman's head as they circled him, clinking their chains rhythmically and sending a cloud of noxious smoke over the altar.

One by one the bishops completed their circuit, bowed, and retreated to a line forming behind Sergius. When the line was complete, the pope's legate stepped forward to confront Carloman.

"Take heed, Carloman! Today you renounce all worldly habits and manners and come under the jurisdiction of the Church. Do you accept the Holy Ghost to guard you against the love of the world?"

Carloman bowed his head. "I accept."

"Will you leave your family and worldly possessions?"

"I will."

"Will you strip yourself of worldly attire and manners?"

"I will." Carloman pulled down the robe off his shoulders so that it gathered at his waist.

Sergius presented Carloman a plain, white surplice. "This garment is a symbol of the new man you will become, made by God in true righteousness and holiness. Its whiteness is a symbol of the constant need for renunciation of the world and penance to keep your soul pure and unsullied.

"Will you accept this holy apparel?"

"I will accept it."

Sergius placed the garment over Carloman's head. Carloman pushed his arms into its sleeves and, standing, let the surplice fall to his knees. He then stepped out of his former robe and knelt once again. An acolyte brought out a pair of shears and presented them to Sergius.

The legate held the shears aloft for the congregation to see. "Tonsure is a sign that sets the clergy apart from the world. It symbolizes our commitment to a purity of heart, to service in the name of the Lord, and to an undivided heart to tend His holy bride the Church."

The former mayor bowed and Sergius began to cut the hairs on the crown of his head. When he finished, Carloman stood.

"Welcome, Brother Carloman!" The two embraced and the congregation broke into a polite applause.

Drogo was next to the altar. The young man bowed, made the sign of the cross, and then knelt before Pippin, proffering his hands. Pippin took them into his own and they quickly recited the litany of commitments required by commendation.

When this last was finished, Drogo went to stand beside his father on the altar to Saint Peter and Pippin and Trudi walked before the tabernacle, where Boniface was waiting beneath a canopy held aloft by four acolytes. Pippin tried to steal a glance at Bertrada but she wouldn't meet his eye.

"Do you have the ceremonial dowry?" Boniface asked.

Pippin nodded and handed him a pouch with thirteen solidi. Boniface turned to face the altar and quickly blessed the gold coins.

"Now the ring?"

Pippin handed it to him.

Boniface faced the congregation and held the ring aloft. *"Orémus. Bénedic, Dómine, ánulum hunc, quem nos in tuo nómine benedícimus: ut, quæ eum gestáverit, fidelitátem íntegram suo sponso tenens, Per Christum Dóminum nostrum."*

He gave it back to Pippin, who in turn took Bertrada's hands in his and placed it on her thumb. "In the name of the Father," Pippin intoned.

"*In nomine Patris,*" Boniface echoed.

Pippin next placed it on her index finger. "And Son."

"*Et filii.*"

And then again on her middle finger. "And Holy Ghost."

"*Et Spiritus Sancti.*"

Last he put it on her fourth finger. "I marry you, wife."

"*Lo te esposy, mohler.*"

When he looked up, Bertrada was smiling and her eyes held his with a warmth he had not seen in many years. It eased the doubts in his heart and soothed the fears that still haunted him. But, he saw, too, that Bertrada was a vastly different woman than the girl he had courted years ago. There was a depth to her eyes, an independence of thought that he knew would challenge him for the rest of his days. She might be his wife, but she would never be truly *his*. She was her own woman.

"May the Lord our God bless your marriage," Boniface said, handing her the ceremonial dowry. He added, in a voice that carried to the congregation, "And may your union be blessed with children."

As one, the congregation of nobles stood and applauded. Pippin felt a little embarrassed when the cheering started. Bertrada began to laugh, and the cheers only grew louder.

Pippin let her enjoy the moment, then held up his hand for silence. Eventually the congregation complied and he waited for the nobles to be seated before speaking.

"I thank you all for witnessing my marriage to Bertrada. This day has been long in coming and for many" – he nodded to Gunther – "long overdue. I would also like to acknowledge something else that is long overdue." Pippin paused. "I have a son."

Silence greeted him, as if the congregation couldn't comprehend the words he had spoken.

"What did you say?" Carloman's astonished whisper carried the room.

Pippin ignored him. A servant led little Charles to the altar, where Pippin lifted him into his arms. "Bertrada and I have a son. May I present Charles, son of Pippin, son of Charles the Hammer."

The church erupted in cheers.

12

Miette arrived at Lady Hélène's apartment for her training session but batted away the long staff being proffered to her. "There's a plot to kill Childebrand."

"Where and when?"

"I don't know."

"What do you know?"

Miette began to pace. "Not much. I overheard my husband talking about it with Drusseau. Apparently, there are Knights in Christ posing as Pippin loyalists. They plan to ambush Childebrand when he thinks he's on safe soil."

"Have you heard any names or how many there are?"

Miette shook her head. "They were whispering and grew upset when I entered the room."

"Anything further about their plans for civil war?"

"Drusseau has sent for the military contingent he has stationed in the Breton March. It's unlikely that anything significant will happen until it arrives."

"Except Childebrand's murder. With Pippin away, that would clear the way for Drusseau's men to take Paris in the king's name."

"We've got to warn Childebrand."

Hélène nodded. "We need to do more than that. Keep listening at home and see if you can identify any gossip around the city. One of those hidden Knights in Christ will boast about their plans."

"What are you going to do?" Miette asked.

"First, I'm going to push you to your limit." Hélène tossed Miette the long staff. "When we're finished, I'll warn Childebrand. And then, I'll do what Lady Hélène always does in times like this."

Miette waited for her to finish.

"I'll throw a party."

* * *

Miette was desperate. She had visited every salon in Paris and had no information to show for it. Even the Ladies Talon, Didot, and Gagnon had little to offer. The only thing anyone wanted to talk about was Lady Hélène's upcoming soirée.

It was only as a last resort that Miette called upon the Lady Drusseau. She had barely gained Charlotte's trust and didn't want to lose it by questioning her about her husband's politics, but she had run out of options.

The couple had taken up residence at the palace in the rooms reserved for Childeric's favorites. When Miette made her way to the residential wing of the palace, Charlotte greeted her with surprise and anger. "You shouldn't be here!" Her whisper had an urgency to it that left Miette unsettled.

"I haven't heard from you. I wanted to know if you're all right."

"Of course, I'm not all right. And now my husband will be suspicious. You should wait until we are in someplace public."

Miette could tell the girl was panicking. "I'm sorry. I don't mean to upset you. I will go."

Charlotte welled up. "No. Please. Come with me." She grabbed Miette's hand and led her back to her rooms. As they made their way, Miette found herself surprised by its opulence. Every room was richly decorated with elegant furniture, linen brocades, sculpture, and tapestries to rival any house she'd seen. Drusseau clearly was wealthy, far wealthier than she had thought. They passed through what Miette took to be a library that housed a collection of weapons that rivaled Hélène's.

Charlotte led Miette up into her room and shut the door. And then, to Miette's surprise, she burst into tears.

Miette hadn't the slightest idea what to do. She had never spent much time in the company of women. All her efforts as a young lady were focused on manipulating men. She tentatively put her hand on Charlotte's shoulder and was surprised when the poor sobbing girl fell into her arms. Miette patted her back, worrying that the woman would ruin her blouse with all those tears.

It took several minutes but Charlotte finally stopped. She sat up and dried her eyes with the backs of her hands. "I'm sorry. I've been so afraid for so long…"

"What has he done?"

Charlotte shook her head and Miette worried she would weep again. "The things he makes me do – I can't speak of them." Her face flushed. "I tried to refuse, but he beats me until I give in. Now, I do whatever he wants whenever he wants it. But even that is not enough. I must pretend that I like it." Her tears started again. "I'm so ashamed!"

"Don't be." Miette took her hand. "All you've done is protect yourself. The only one who should be ashamed is your husband."

"What am I going to do? I can't live like this."

"First, you do whatever it takes to stay alive. I will try to find a way to help you."

"No one can help me." Charlotte started wringing her hands. "It's even worse than you can imagine."

"How could it be worse?"

"He wants me to bed the king."

Miette thought her heart had stopped. She found it difficult to breathe. "You mustn't!"

"How can I refuse?"

"I will find a way."

Miette was making her way back to the entrance when Charlotte's husband stepped into the hallway and grabbed her by the arm. Drusseau twisted it, causing pain to shoot down her shoulder. He backed her up against the wall, his size and strength overwhelming her.

"Why are you here?"

The menace in his voice frightened her. "To see Charlotte."

"But why?"

"We've become friends."

"Charlotte doesn't have friends. Neither do I. Why are you here?" He twisted her arm again and the pain grew worse.

"I don't know what you mean!"

"Oh, I think you do. You see, I know all about you, Miette." He said her name like it was a curse. "Childeric told me of your betrayal. He told me you slept with Pippin. You may have fooled your husband, but I'm not such an easy mark."

"It's not what you think. Please!" Miette couldn't seem to breathe, and her heart was pounding so hard, she thought it would break her chest.

"Tell your lover, his time is short. And you better stay away from my wife or the next time Pippin finds you by the side of the road, you won't be breathing."

He released her and stalked away. Unnerved, Miette stumbled from his residence and made her way back home, her mind reeling with humiliation. She had cowered before the man! All her training, all her boasting to Charlotte had been a lie. She was a coward. She was so frightened she wanted to crawl into her bed and hide. With hands shaking, she locked herself in her room and wept, ashamed of the weakness she displayed.

* * *

Hélène's soirée was unique to the season because she had invited nobles from both the red and green camps. She asked her guests to leave their weapons and symbols of loyalty at the door and required everyone to wear a mask. These last, she supplied from a great carton by the front door. There were dozens of examples: great elaborate ones with feathers and ribbons as well as plain black ones that simply covered a guest's nose and circled their eyes.

Hélène was busy with other guests when Miette and her husband arrived, but Miette's mentor nodded her head in acknowledgement and frowned to express her displeasure. Since her confrontation with Charlotte's husband, Miette had ignored all invitations from Hélène and had not been to her home once for their practice sessions.

Miette chose one of the plain masks from the carton. She had no wish to stand out and even less of a wish to be recognized by Drusseau. Her husband chose an elaborate owlish mask with gold trimmings and feathers around the eyes. The moment they entered the ballroom, he bowed to take his leave of her. For once, she didn't mind the slight; she preferred to be alone.

She wandered through the crowd, acknowledging people she recognized but not caring to engage. Although she sensed a certain amount of excitement in the room, she herself was removed from it. In fact, she had felt disconnected since her encounter with Drusseau, It was as if she wasn't really present in her own body. She was like a ghost or an apparition, gliding through the world, unable to be seen or touched.

People from the two camps mingled with each other, albeit cautiously, keeping their discussions away from the politics at court. The masks seemed to help with this. Miette hadn't crossed half the room, and yet people already were laughing and sharing toasts as if the civil war weren't imminent.

She saw Drusseau and Charlotte across the room and mirrored their movements to ensure she kept her distance from them. Without warning, Lady Gagnon grabbed Miette's arm and pulled her into a circle with Didot and Talon. The three of them squealed as if Miette were a long-lost relative and quickly began their practice of disparaging the other guests in attendance.

"Look at the duchesse de Tricot flirting with a man half her age."

"You would too, if your husband was twice yours."

Miette couldn't seem to catch their enthusiasm for the sport. She watched as the women drank copious amounts of wine and gossiped, but she didn't join in. After a time, she realized she wasn't even listening to what they said. She felt as if she was disappearing altogether and quietly drifted away from her friends.

She saw Childebrand across the room. His size made him easy to recognize. He was in a corner with a group of soldiers, regaling them with his stories. She smiled to herself as the giant waved his arms and contorted his face. Although he had never liked her, she appreciated his value to Pippin. He was selfless and wholly Pippin's man. After a bit of observation, she guessed the names of two of the masked soldiers with him, Jean-Pierre and Julien; they were good men, also loyal to Pippin.

"Are you avoiding me?" It was Hélène.

Miette nodded. "Yes."

"May I ask why?"

Miette felt relief in telling her. "I'm not worthy of your faith in me." She felt her face flushing. "I'm a coward."

Hélène merely raised an eyebrow, waiting for her explanation.

"Drusseau assaulted me," Miette said, frowning. "Well, he twisted my arm. And I was so scared I could barely breathe. I forgot all my training, all my capability, and nearly wet myself while he threatened me. I'm not who I thought I was. I'm not who you think I am. Although I appreciate your belief in me, I'm unworthy of your instruction, Hélène."

"Did I ever say you wouldn't fail?"

Miette grunted a laugh. "I was so scared I didn't even try. You can't fail if you don't try."

Hélène nodded. "You might be right. Not everyone has a capacity for violence. But remember, violence without purpose isn't just. Perhaps you didn't perceive a purpose."

"He was threatening me."

"He was 'twisting your arm.'"

"I was frightened, scared out of my mind." Miette shook her head. "I'm not who you think I am."

Hélène sighed. "Perhaps not. But, for now, I will withhold judgement. I saw you challenge Salau. I believe if the need is great, you will answer the call."

Miette grunted her doubt. "Why on earth did you throw this soirée? What did you hope to accomplish?"

"We need to know where and when the trap is laid," Hélène said. "People talk at parties. Whether it is too much drink, too many egos, or too much in the way of flattery, soirées like this one bring out secrets. Have you overheard anything?"

Miette shook her head no, ashamed that she hadn't even tried.

"Let me know if you do." Hélène left to greet some new guests and Miette returned to losing herself in the crowd. As time passed, people drank more and the mood began to change. Several arguments broke out and it became clear that the evening's truce might be in jeopardy.

Miette saw the Lady Brevet flitting through the room, greeting guests and dispensing the favor of her presence to those she deemed worthy. Miette smiled, thinking of herself in that role. As Childeric's hostess, she had been so sure of herself.

When their eyes met, Brevet smirked and sauntered closer. "Why, if it isn't Pippin's whore."

The remark didn't touch Miette; nothing touched her, she was only an apparition. "Peace, milady. I wish you no harm."

"What harm could you possibly do me?"

Miette saw the bruise on Brevet's cheek that her mask and makeup had not fully covered. "Did Childeric give you that?"

The shock on Brevet's face was enough to confirm it.

Miette lowered her voice. "Your time is short, milady. I beg you to find a way out. They will cause you grievous harm, believe me, I know."

"You know nothing, you ungrateful bitch! You betrayed Childeric, and for what? To spread your legs for that bastard Pippin? You think he can protect you? After tonight you won't be so condescending. After tonight, you'll see how quickly the Fates' wheel can turn." Brevet spun on her heel and stormed across the room.

Tonight? Miette's mind raced. The trap was here, tonight! She frantically searched the room for Hélène but couldn't see her anywhere. She had to warn Childebrand. She started to work her way through the crowd. He was still in the corner where she had last seen him, still regaling his soldiers. With men around him he would be well protected – but something about them now struck her as odd. She stopped to watch. They seemed tense, their laughter forced. Jean-Pierre and Julien looked downright nervous.

She began to make her way toward them, still frantically searching for Hélène. At the same time, part of her mind seemed to break away on its own. It calmly analyzed the threat and ran through the possibilities. There were four soldiers. They must have weapons, most likely knives as all swords were left at the door. A part of her wanted to scream, but the quiet part of her mind knew that if she did, it would likely create the diversion the soldiers needed.

She had three knives on her. A small one in each sleeve and a bigger one strapped to her thigh. Even with a fourth, she couldn't fight all of them. Childebrand would have to help, but he needed a weapon. She saw one of Hélène's statues off to her right, a nude, about the size of her forearm. Without breaking stride, she lifted it off the pedestal.

She was maybe ten steps away when she shoved her way past a woman who bellowed, "Good God!"

One of the soldiers looked up to see what was happening. He couldn't miss Miette; she was moving directly toward them. His eyes locked on hers and he knew that she knew.

"NOW!" he shouted. The three soldiers before Childebrand pulled out their weapons.

Miette's first knife took the one who shouted in the throat. Childebrand instinctively stepped back, and Miette tossed him the statue as she sprinted toward the attack. Jean-Pierre turned to stop her, swiping his knife in a wide arc toward her stomach. Miette used her momentum to slide beneath the blade and closer to Julien, who had turned to attack Childebrand. She pulled her second knife from its strap on her leg and slashed the back of Julien's leg, severing his hamstring. She felt great satisfaction when he fell to the floor. She stood and turned back to Jean-Pierre, hedging to the right, away from Childebrand and the other soldier.

She kept her blade low, trying to assess Jean-Pierre. She could see he was frustrated. His plans were going awry, and the odds of success had dimmed. Moving to the balls of her feet, she readied herself for his expected lunge. When it came, she stepped past it to his left, grabbed his extended arm, and stabbed upwards, catching him in the armpit. He backed away, not realizing that his life was spilling onto the floor.

Miette turned to see how Childebrand fared. He was standing above the fourth soldier, whose head now sported a crater the size of a small statue. The entire confrontation had taken only seconds to unfold. Many in the crowd were just turning to see what had happened. Childebrand stared at her like she was some magical beast that had appeared in the room before him.

Jean-Pierre collapsed. As all eyes turned to him, Miette took the moment to melt into the crowd behind her. She moved slowly, letting the curious push past her.

"He bested four men by himself!" she said to no one in particular. "Four against one and not even a scratch on him! The Lord must be with him!"

She repeated the mantra as she walked backwards through the crowd. She heard others repeat her words. She felt a hand on her elbow. It was Hélène. She held out a handkerchief to Miette. "There's blood on the side of your face."

Miette tried to dab it. "Let me," Hélène said. Her hands were gentle but thorough as she wiped clean the splatter from Miette's mask and her cheeks. "How did you know it was the soldiers?"

"Lady Brevet boasted that tonight would turn the tables. I went to warn Childebrand and noticed the soldiers around him looking tense and nervous."

'What happened to you being a coward?"

Miette shrugged. "I don't understand it myself. It was like a part of me detached to deal with the attack. The other part is still scared witless."

"Well, I'm glad you were here. I was on the other side of the room. I wouldn't have made it in time."

"Do you think they will try again?"

"Not tonight. Not with everyone watching."

"How did they think they would get away with it?"

Hélène shrugged. "Had they succeeded, they all would simply attest that it was an argument gone bad."

"And now?"

"Julian will be questioned and whoever commanded him to do it will be hung."

Miette spied Drusseau across the room. Even with a mask, his face looked ashen. "My money is on Drusseau."

Hélène nodded. "Have you figured out how to save Charlotte?"

Miette shook her head. "Not yet."

13

Estinnes

Protocol demanded that Pippin consummate his marriage to Bertrada immediately following the wedding ceremony. After Boniface announced the mass had ended, many of the nobles began to clap and stomp their feet in expectation that Pippin would lead them in a parade to his temporary residence, where they would serenade the couple with bawdy songs and imitations of orgasmic pleasure while he and Bertrada performed the bedding ritual.

True to form, Pippin led them out of the church onto the steps outside, but much to the nobles' disappointment, he abruptly kissed his wife, left her with Boniface, and rode with Gunther and Drogo to the outskirts of Estinnes, where Carloman's army was stationed.

Armies without leaders were dangerous things, and Pippin was sure that Carloman's decision to take the tonsure would be a shock to his commanders. He and Gunther had discussed the challenge of taking command of a rival army. Even more challenging would be Carloman's Knights in Christ. By making their service a religious calling, his brother had created an army of zealots. Trying to curtail their cult and integrate them with his army in Quierzy would be problematic. Pippin couldn't afford to wait even a day before bringing them into line.

As they entered the camp, soldiers came to tend to their horses. Pippin dismounted and asked to be taken to Laurent. He was quickly led to a large tent where Carloman's champion was housed.

Laurent bowed to acknowledge Pippin and led him and Gunther into his tent. In the torchlit interior, his face looked peaked. "Is it true, milord? Did Carloman take the tonsure?"

"It's true." Pippin nodded. "His hair was shorn this morning by the pope's legate. He will leave in the morning to take his vows in Rome."

Laurent made the sign of the cross. "May the Lord grant him peace."

Pippin put his hand on Laurent's shoulder. "That is my hope as well. He was greatly troubled by the attack at Canstatt."

Laurent recoiled at the reference, the pain on his face evident. He looked away and shook his head. "It was murder. And all of us will pay for that sin."

Pippin shook his head. "No, Laurent. Let my brother carry that burden. It was by his command. His alone. I know many of your men are suffering. I will need your help to save this army. As the sole mayor of the realm and Drogo's guardian, I'm here to take command."

To his credit, Laurent immediately knelt before Pippin and offered his hands. Pippin took them in his own and the two recited their oaths of commendation. When they were finished, Pippin motioned for Laurent to stand. "Call the commanders to order, we start now."

Laurent brought together Carloman's commanding officers and formed them into two long lines before Pippin. He took the place of leadership before them.

Pippin stepped forward in the waning light of the day. "This morning, my brother Carloman abdicated his position as mayor of the palace, renounced his family and secular life, and took the tonsure to pursue a life among the clergy."

He waited for that news to be absorbed. He pointed to Drogo. "I have taken his sons hands in mine and will serve as Drogo's guardian. As sole mayor of the kingdom, I'm here today to take control of the army. I ask each of you to offer your hands in commendation." One by one, they stepped forward, knelt, and proffered their hands.

Now that he had their stated allegiance, he began the more difficult part of his endeavor. "My first command is that you remove all vestments signifying allegiance to the organization called the 'Knights in Christ.'"

An abrupt silence met his order. Pippin folded his arms and waited. He watched the anxious looks each of the commanders gave to one another. After a moment's hesitation, Laurent stepped forward and took off his armored plates and removed his red doublet displaying the white fleur-de-lis. He laid it on the ground, restored his armor, and returned to his position. Although there was some grumbling in the ranks, a second knight stepped forward to comply. Then a third did as well. In a wave of obeisance, the rest of the commanders removed their red and white symbols of allegiance.

Pippin breathed a sigh of relief and ordered several soldiers to gather the vestments into a large pile and then nodded to Gunther, who stepped forward with a torch and set them aflame. Pippin could see the fury in every eye. He positioned himself between the commanders and the burning vestments.

"I am today disbanding the Knights in Christ. From this day forward, there will be no loyalty oaths other than those given to your liege lord, no rank other than that given by your liege lord, and no bond beyond the bond of commendation. Any and all ties given through the Knights in Christ are voided. And anyone who continues their association with the Knights in Christ will be killed for treason."

Pippin paused in the stunned silence, wanting to ensure that message be heard and understood.

"I know that many of you are men of profound faith. I do not place myself between you and our God or between you and your priest. But in this army, our faith is not a weapon; our devotion is not a cause, and our mission is not a holy one. We fight for Francia. It is that simple. FRANCIA!" he shouted, letting them see his own passion.

"I know about your rituals. I know about your vows. But I also know that ripping the heart out of a goat does not make you a weapon of God."

Pippin lowered his eyes and let his emotions leak into his words. "My brother lost his way. In his arrogance he thought himself the Blade of Christ. In his passion he murdered men, women, and children." Pippin looked up. "And at his behest, *you* murdered innocents, thousands of them. The cost of that arrogance rebounds against you. I know you have felt the wrongness of it. Many within your ranks have taken their own lives. It was wrong and it put the kingdom on the verge of civil war." Pippin shook his head. "It ends here."

"I will be merging this army with the one in Quierzy. You will have new commanders and your responsibilities will be assigned based on your performance. No longer will rank be associated with levels of faith and devotion. Show me your *worth* and you will be rewarded in kind.

"I expect you to convey these words to your men. I expect them to know and understand that the Knights in Christ no longer exist. I expect them to embrace commendation and our mission for Francia without hesitation."

Pippin walked in silence before them, meeting each of their eyes in turn.

"I value you above your faith. I value you above your devotion to the Church. I value you. Don't let me down."

Pippin nodded to Laurent, who dismissed the commanders while he and Gunther retrieved their horses to ride back to Estinnes.

Gunther spat. "You know that little speech won't be enough."

"I know." Pippin sighed. "You'll have to make an example out of some of them."

"Even so," Gunther said.

"Even so."

* * *

Bertrada wasn't surprised that Pippin left her on the steps of the church. He had told her of his plan before the ceremony. She let Boniface wave off the score of nobles hoping to escort her home, relieved that she wouldn't have had to play the role of a bride on her way to her nuptial bed with half a village in tow.

Instead, Boniface led her back to the sacristy so that he could change out of his ceremonial vestments. When they entered the church, however, a large throng of bishops, who moments before had witnessed her vows, were now in a heated debate on the altar. Heddo was at its center, Carloman by his side.

"This can't be good," Boniface said under his breath and went to investigate. Bertrada followed.

Heddo turned on them when he saw them approach. "Did you know about this, Boniface? Did you know Pippin had a son?"

Boniface shook his head. "I was told that the child was Bertrada's nephew."

Heddo turned toward her. "You lied! Pippin hid your son from everyone until after Carloman abdicated. He knew Carloman wouldn't step down if Drogo's legacy was in doubt."

Bertrada was stunned by the vehemence of this charge. She didn't get a chance to respond, however, as a number of the bishops began echoing Heddo's complaint and calling for sanctions against Pippin.

Carloman looked at her, his eyes filled with betrayal. "I trusted Pippin. I stepped down at his request. I gave him guardianship over Drogo. And this is how he repays me? He's shut Drogo out of succession!"

"That was not our intent."

"Then why did he name the bastard Charles?!"

It was not that the term was unexpected. Bertrada had long ago known that Charles's birth out of wedlock would raise the disdain of some. She just was stunned that Pippin's own brother would be the first to use it. She saw the impact the word had on the group of bishops and anger poured through her at the indignity. Every one of these bishops had clambered to be on the altar at their wedding and here they stood, their faces twisted with malice, castigating Pippin and her son.

Bertrada stepped onto the altar and all discussion stopped.

In a soft voice, Boniface said, "Milady, outside a specific rite, women are forbidden –"

"Silence!" Bertrada turned to Boniface to let him see the fury within her. She let it carry her forward to face Carloman; the bishops gave way before her.

Bertrada shook her head, her eyes welling with emotion. "After all you've done!" Her words came out with a passion from the depths of her soul. "You alone warred against and imprisoned your own brother and stepmother. You, alone, hanged that Thuringian boy. You ignored Pippin's objections and raised the Merovingian to the throne. And it was you who massacred thousands in the name of your faith and put the entire kingdom on the brink of civil war.

"And still, Pippin came to you in your hour of need. He brought you to your senses, held you in his arms to succor you, and kept away those who would use you for their own purposes." Bertrada waved her hand at Heddo and the bishops gathered around him. "He gave you a path forward. He showed you a way to atone. He gave you a life worth living."

Righteousness surged in Bertrada's voice. "We hid Charles to protect him from the man you named as king. We didn't want to acknowledge Charles out of fear for his life because you refused to see the kind of man Childeric is.

"And until recently, that ruse worked. Unfortunately, a traitor disclosed Charles's identity to Childeric and an assassination attempt soon followed. Pippin was able to foil the attempt, but secrecy is no longer of any value. My son, my 'bastard' son, is in danger every day of his life because of you.

"You alone are the betrayer. You dismissed Pippin's views since the day you both first became mayors. You have used your faith as a weapon against the weak and innocent. You have committed atrocity after atrocity and soiled our name and your father's name with your 'holy' murders."

Bertrada's face was flushed. "I loathe the man you have become, Carloman. You are no man of God, for no God would have you as you stand before me."

Carloman's face had become pale through the course of her harangue. He seemed too stunned to respond.

Sergius stepped forward and put his hand on Carloman's shoulder. "Be at peace, Carloman. You have renounced this world. You accepted the Holy Ghost to guard you against it. You left your family and worldly possessions and stripped yourself of worldly attire. It's time to turn your eyes to the world of God. There is nothing more for you here."

Carloman nodded, his eyes still on Bertrada. "Yes, Sergius, you have the right of it. There is nothing more for me here." His voice had been filled with loathing. Bertrada couldn't tell if was for her or himself.

* * *

Although Gripho's rooms at Neufchateau were comfortable, they were a prison, nonetheless. Situated high on a hill, the castle had broad stout walls overlooking a large lake. Not that Gripho could see much of it through the three narrow slits in his wall, but he had a decent bed, a desk, a prie-dieu, which he never used, as well as a bath and a chair.

The castle itself was built in two sections. The first, where he was housed, was in the shape of a rough rectangle. It was isolated from the rest of the castle and provided a limited space for him to exercise in an interior courtyard. The second section, where Comte Gabriel and his family lived, was a six-sided affair that matched the topography of the hilltop. That section had access to the outside world. Gripho's did not.

At first, he had eschewed the friendship offered by Gabriel, but after several months of boredom had settled in, he welcomed the old man's overtures to play a nightly game of jeu de moulin. Gabriel was well into his sixth decade and enjoyed reminiscing about his years as a knight in Charles's army. His penchant for talking often segued into the affairs of state and through him, Gripho had learned of the aftermath of the siege at Laon. He knew that his two brothers had split the kingdom between them. He knew they had defeated Odilo and the Saxons and he knew that they had feuded over raising the Merovingian to the throne.

Although he found Gabriel somewhat dull minded, he preferred dull minded to his isolation. He, of course, had considered several ways to take the man hostage in an effort to escape but knew them to be unworkable flights of fantasy.

Gabriel had assigned a young boy named Thomas to bring Gripho meals and to provide fresh linen and bathwater for his room. It only took a month for Gripho to seduce him. And once the boy had learned how to accommodate him, Gripho humped him like a rabbit.

He had grown a beard during his captivity, and it descended now well onto his chest. His hair, too, was as long as a woman's. He toyed with the idea of growing his fingernails, like a Merovingian, but found them disgusting when they started to curl inward.

Days became meaningless to him, as did weeks. He lost all track of time and only counted the changing seasons. With no one but Gabriel to talk to, he aired his grievances to the wind and his walls, railing aloud against his mother, who had abandoned him, against the priests who tried to rule him, and against his two brothers, who had stolen his birthright. How he hated them and their arrogance!

Over time his complaints became an endless loop of frustration, and he howled at his betrayers. He wondered often if he was going mad. Day after day after day was the same. To avoid the monotony, he began to sleep during the day and stare into the darkness at night.

The snakes came at night. At first, they teased him, coming just outside his vision. He'd turn his head to find them, but they were too fast. They would disappear before he could find them. But then they started slithering across his floor in waves. He heard someone shouting in fright, but there was no one but him in his room.

When he received word that Pippin was coming, he began to tremble. He had always been afraid of Pippin. He had seen his half-brother's rage on a battlefield. No one could stop him. He convinced Thomas to smuggle him a knife, which he hid under his bed. But then an odd thought took him: What if Pippin was coming to free him?

He had to think about it for most of the day before deciding it might be best to find out what Pippin had in mind before trying to kill him.

The idea of freedom intrigued him. He would agree to anything to get out of Neufchateau...anything. He bathed, put on a clean shift, and trimmed back his beard. He let Thomas comb and tie his hair but became so aroused he bent the boy over his chair before Thomas had finished. Afterwards, he wiped himself off with a towel and sent the lad away. Watching him go, Gripho wondered if it would be the last time he would see Thomas. He felt a vague sense of loss at the idea.

It was Gabriel who came to retrieve him. When they passed through the locked door that separated the two sections of the castle, Gripho felt faint. Gabriel took him by the arm to steady him and the two walked down a spiral staircase and into the main hall of the castle. Pippin was there waiting for him.

Upon seeing Pippin, Gripho began to cry. "Are you here to kill me?"

"Brother?"

"Please don't kill me!" He tried to rein in his thoughts; they didn't seem clear.

"No, Gripho. I'm here to set you free. Carloman is no longer mayor and I promised Sunnichild I would free you if I could."

Gripho nodded, relief flooding through him. "Did you kill Carloman?"

"He took the tonsure. He's going to Rome to take his vows."

"So, it's just you and me?"

Pippin shook his head. "Those days are gone. I alone am mayor. I took Drogo's hands in mine. And if you are willing, I will take yours as well."

Just get out! Get out! Gripho's mind was screaming. He lifted his hands to Pippin. "Anything to get out of this place."

Pippin was looking at him strangely. "Are you well, Gripho?"

The question frightened him. He couldn't let anything get in the way of leaving. "Yes. Yes, of course. I'm well."

* * *

For Gripho, the journey from Neufchateau to Paris was nothing but a relief. Just being outside, riding in the ranks with the men and talking – talking! – had done wonders. At first, he had trouble with his emotions, but his thoughts were becoming clearer. And the snakes had retreated outside his sight.

He had been careful with Pippin; only once did he try to clarify what his role would be. He had ridden next to Pippin and asked it outright.

"What do I get?"

Pippin didn't even bother to answer; he just raised his eyebrow.

"What do I get for giving you my hands in commendation?"

"A duchy."

"So, I'm no longer a mayor?"

Pippin shook his head. "A duc."

Although Gripho had been furious, he swallowed his anger and moved back among the ranks. They were supposed to have been equals! Who was Pippin to overrule the great Charles Martel? And now Pippin had a boy child. Where would that leave him?

Gripho watched as Pippin and Bertrada hugged and kissed each other and spoke like little babies to Pippin's bastard. It made him want to vomit. They were never his family. It had all been politics from the moment Charles took his mother Sunni from Bavaria.

God, he hated her! She was the reason he had been imprisoned! She was his betrayer. If she hadn't abdicated, he would have defeated Carloman at the siege of Laon.

Pippin spoke glowingly about her as if she had always been there for him. Well, fuck her. And fuck Pippin! He thinks just because Carloman took the tonsure, he has rights to all the kingdom!?

For the moment, he had to play the dutiful brother. He had to pretend that he was happy to be Pippin's man. But one day he would bugger the arrogant bastard. The thought brought him a chuckle. Maybe he would bugger Boniface too! That made him laugh aloud. They were all so stupid not to see it. One day soon, he would have his day. As Charles's son, he deserved half the kingdom. And he would find a way to have it. With all his thoughts of buggering, he wondered what Thomas was doing.

14

Wurzburg

Two weeks into their journey, Trudi reminded Odilo that the Roman road back to Regensburg was lined by romantic villages and towns that deserved their attention. She was very happy when he agreed with her assessment. He had set a steady pace for their return trip and they both needed some rest. If the promise of a romantic evening could bring some respite, she was more than happy to suggest it.

At dusk, they stopped at a small inn called "The Painted Horse" in Wurzburg by the river Main. Odilo sent his men to camp outside the town, while they took rooms at the inn. Trudi ordered the servants to prepare a hot bath and they went downstairs to dine. They enjoyed a fine bottle of red that Odilo had purchased in Estinnes along with a succulent meal of cooked lamb.

"Let's enjoy the rest of this trip together, husband. It's very rare that I get you all to myself."

Odilo smiled. "We've made good time; I suppose we can slow down a little."

"Good, you look exhausted, and I smell like I've spent a fortnight on the road."

"It has been a fortnight."

"My point, exactly. How's a woman supposed to seduce her husband when she smells as bad as the horse she's riding?"

When they returned to their room she made for the bath, slowly stripping off pieces of her clothing for his benefit. She enjoyed watching him watch her, seeing the delight that every discarded garment brought to his eyes. She was naked by the time she reached the brass tub and dipped a toe in to gauge the water's temperature. Happy with its warmth, she stepped in. "Are you going to just stare or do you plan to join me?"

Odilo ripped off his clothes. Trudi laughed as she sank into the tub. It was too small for what she had in mind, but the thrill of watching Odilo scramble to get out of his clothes was worth it. He hopped into the tub, and she struggled to make room for him, scooting to one end and placing her feet on either side of him. When they were settled, their knees stood between them like sentinels.

"Now what do we do?" he asked.

"Now you tell me you love me." She had meant it playfully, but the words struck a serious chord within her and a wave of emotion took her, love so powerful she almost wept.

She saw the emotion touch his eyes as well. "I thought I'd lost you," he whispered.

"I know," she said.

"After Theudebald –"

"After the rape," she corrected.

He nodded. "After the rape, I thought you were gone to me."

"I was." Trudi held his eyes, letting him see her pain, letting him see the damage it had cost her. "At first, I blamed you. But it wasn't you who hurt me. Your fault was in trusting a man so evil. And I've forgiven you for that."

She could see the shame he still carried with him and leaned forward to reassure him. "The love I feel for you now is different. It's older and wiser." She grasped his hand. "But it's just as strong and, in many ways, deeper than the love we first shared."

His eyes brimmed with tears. "I love you," he said.

She pulled herself up by the edges of the tub and straddled his torso so that she could kiss him. It was a gentle kiss, but his arms circled her and pulled her to him in a more passionate embrace. Their kiss became urgent, almost desperate as she sought to show him the depth of her feeling.

His erection grew beneath her, and she relaxed her legs to let it rub against her, coaxing it along with slow undulating movements. She delighted that she still could affect him so.

And then he was inside her. Confined as they were, it was left to her to move above him, thrusting against him while he guided her hips with his hands. She lost herself in the motion and water splashed over the sides of the tub.

She looked into his eyes and found him still staring back at her, his eyes brimming with love. And suddenly she felt whole, complete, as if every trial in her life was meant to lead to this moment. This was love beyond anything she had known.

Her orgasm came over her so quickly, it surprised her. It held her in wave after wave as it coursed through her, and she moaned aloud. Just as it began to subside, she felt him release into her.

She kissed him and they lay still in the water. She didn't move, didn't want to let the moment go.

"You've got to get up," he said.

"No. I want to stay here forever."

He chuckled. "But I can't feel my legs."

She stood up in the tub and laughed. "Come on, old man, I'll help you up!"

"Next time let's aim for the bed." He groaned. "Either that or ask for a bigger tub."

* * *

Trudi awoke first and found Odilo's head resting on her shoulder. She let him sleep, watching his chest rise and fall with each breath. She curled his hair around her fingers and whispered softly in his ear. "I love you, Odilo, more than you know. You've made me whole again. And I never thought that would be possible. Thank you for listening to me and stopping this war. I can't afford to lose you – *we* can't afford to lose you."

Although she knew he'd be furious, she let him sleep long into the morning. When he woke, they went downstairs to enjoy a hearty breakfast. By the time they regained the Roman road, the sun was high and bright. Fortunately, a cool breeze came from the west. At times it was so cold it raised the hair on Trudi's arms.

Odilo set a determined pace through the rolling farmland, but the mood of the whole troop was light. It was nice to be back in Bavaria.

"What do we do about Lantfrid?" Trudi asked. "Your compromise with Pippin leaves him without a title or territory. He won't go quietly. And I'm nervous he'll never leave."

Odilo frowned. "It will be up to Lantfrid to claim his birthright. Because Carloman dissolved the duchy and gave Warin and Ruthard stewardship over Alemannia, Pippin won't have to defend it. He'll trust the two comtes to deal with Lantfrid.

"They're well equipped with men and arms and won't be bested easily. With the vast majority of the Alemanni nobles gone, Lantfrid will have little support to confront them. My guess is that the land grants to Frankish nobles are just beginning. In five years, there will be more Franks this side of the Rhine than Lantfrid can count."

"So how are we going to get him to leave? I don't want him in our palace."

"He won't return to Alemannia without an army at his back, so I'd expect he'll want to stay in Bavaria until he can raise the treasure to afford one. I'll find a landed estate for him in Danouwörth or someplace to the west where he can plot his return to power. He won't be in the palace long."

"Why should you help him at all? He called you a coward."

Odilo frowned. "Although I rule Bavaria, I'm still a son of Godefred. Our family has ruled Alemannia for over a century. Lantfrid has the right of succession and should rule. He's a hateful nephew but I am compelled by family loyalty to defend his right, just as I defended Gripho's right to succession."

There were times Odilo reminded her of her father. He had a way about him that was from a different time. Trudi shook her head. "Lantfrid won't thank you. He'll fight your compromise. He'll whip your nobles into a frenzy at the Frankish threat. How are you going to reassure the nobles that the massacre of Alemannia won't happen to Bavaria?"

"It will be a challenge," Odilo said. "If the Alemanni nobility can be so easily replaced, what's to prevent a similar strategy in Bavaria? Letting Canstatt go unpunished sets a very dangerous precedent."

"But it was Carloman who led the massacre. And, because of it, Pippin forced him to step down and take the tonsure. And to further show faith with Bavaria, Pippin set Gripho free."

"Do you think that will be enough?"

Odilo smiled. "When we fought the last war, all we asked for was Gripho's right to succession and a Merovingian on the throne. Now we have both. We may have lost the battle, but we have gotten what we wanted. With Carloman going to Rome, we may even have solidified Tassilo's rights to succeed as well. I'm hoping that will be enough to convince the nobles."

Trudi frowned. "Don't doom Tassilo to a war with Drogo."

"That possibility will exist whether we wish it or not," Odilo said.

"Who among the nobles will oppose you?"

Odilo shrugged. "Eingard of Kurbayern will likely advocate for war. It's the one answer soldiers understand."

"And Sudiger?"

"He'll want something for his support. He's too ambitious to give it away."

"What will you give him?"

"Treasure, land, armed men if I have to."

"He's always been supportive of me."

Odilo smiled. "That's because you, milady, are power personified."

Trudi raised an eyebrow in question.

Odilo shook his head, chuckling to himself. "You've never fully understood it. Sudiger has never met a woman like you. Let's discount for a moment that you are the daughter of Charles Martel and sister to Carloman and Pippin. Let's ignore the fact that your son is in line to succeed them.

"How many women do you think he knows who could best him with a sword? How many women does he know who can debate the politics of the kingdom with every noble in the realm? How many can request the presence of a papal legate and have the pope comply?

"You, my love, are a prize for which any man in the kingdom would pluck out an eye. Why do you think Aistulf and Carloman tracked you all the way across the continent?"

Trudi grew cold listening to her husband's description of her. "Is that what you think of me?"

Odilo shook his head. "I fell in love with a Christian girl wearing a pagan amulet who loved me more than the kingdom her father had conquered. I didn't fall in love with Charles Martel's daughter. I fell in love with you."

* * *

The Wormit River meandered lazily to their west as Trudi and Odilo ambled on horseback through the countryside approaching Danouwörth. It was the last leg of the Roman road they would travel. Once they reached Danouwörth, they would follow the Danube east to Regensburg.

Trudi couldn't help but recall the last time she had travelled this road. She had been with Bradius and the memory of him haunted her.

Riding next to Odilo, part of her felt guilty wallowing in the recollection of her former lover, but the warmth of Bradius's memory suffused her. They passed places where the two of them had stayed or stopped to eat. It had been a magical time and it filled her with love for him. They passed an inn where she and Bradius had stayed the night, and Trudi flushed with the memory of their lovemaking there.

She looked to Odilo to see if he could see the change in her, but he just smiled and returned his eyes to the road ahead. His look lightened her heart. She knew she loved him deeply. That recognition seemed to satisfy her anxiety. Her heart was big enough to love them both.

In a duel of swords, Aistulf had killed Bradius in Danouwörth and the closer their party came to that fateful city the more nervous Trudi became. Her mind howled at the memory. She tried to remain calm, but fear clawed at her. She wanted to run, to hide, or to weep.

A woman alongside the river stopped to watch them pass. As Trudi grew near, their eyes met, and the woman drew a rune of warning in the air. Tattoos snaked along the woman's arms and bones adorned her hair. Knowing her as a sybil, Trudi's fears spiked even more.

Suddenly, she had trouble breathing and thought her heart would explode in her chest if she had to continue much longer. Thankfully, the growing darkness forced Odilo to stop for the night before reaching the city.

That night at dinner, she drank several cups of wine in hopes it would help to calm her fears. But even that made her think of Bradius. When they went to bed, they didn't make love, but she clung to Odilo as if he were her bond to this life.

In her dreams, Death stalked her. He wasn't in a hurry; he knew she couldn't escape. Trudi ran and ran and ran but always he was there just a few steps behind her. Unable to withstand the fear assailing her mind, she turned to face the threat. Instead, she found Bradius waiting for her.

"Oh, my love!" she exclaimed, leaping into his arms, but it was Odilo who held her. She hugged him to her chest, weeping, but a wetness spewed across her chest. Looking down she saw blood. Bradius stood before her, a small hole through his torso.

"I'm sorry," he said, but it was Odilo who spoke.

She wanted to scream, but no voice came from her throat. She began to run but knew that Death still stalked her. She ran and ran and ran.

A sybil stood before her drawing runes in the air. "Ware what I see!" she shouted.

When she awoke, Odilo's head was on her shoulder. Trudi nearly laughed at the relief she felt at the end of her nightmare. She curled her fingers in his hair and whispered words of love in his ear.

His skin felt unusually cold, and she pulled a blanket up around him, but his body didn't move; it laid limp against her.

"Odilo?!" She tried to wake him, shaking his shoulders, but he didn't respond. She rolled him over and knelt beside him. She felt his face and put her lips near his. He wasn't breathing. "ODILO?!!" she screamed.

But he was gone, and her screaming had just begun.

15

Paris

Miette held the hood of her cloak low over her face and took a circuitous route to Hélène's home to avoid being seen. When she finally arrived, it was Childebrand who greeted her at the door, an enormous smile on his face.

Miette chuckled to herself. One positive outcome of the assassination attempt was that she had befriended Childebrand. He had been stunned by her ability with a knife and grateful for her appearance in his hour of need.

She had spent days in the salons of Paris dismissing her role in his defense. While she admitted to being there and even to being close to the action, she steadfastly refused to acknowledge that she played any role at all in saving anyone, let alone Pippin's uncle. She merely repeated her assertion that he had bested all four men on his own. For the most part, people believed her. They were far more willing to accept that story than believe a petite noblewoman bested three knights in under a minute.

Fortunately, the rumors about her were quickly overwhelmed by reports of Carloman's abdication. Everywhere Miette went, people were talking about the surprising turn of events. Most had greeted the destruction of the Alemanni army with celebration and were confused by Carloman's decision to take the tonsure.

Childebrand led her into Hélène's dining room, where her mentor greeted her with a cup of wine.

"What do you have for us?" Hélène motioned for them all to sit.

Miette threw back her cloak and nearly drained half the cup. "Rumors are flying everywhere. 'Pippin castrated Carloman.' 'Carloman is vying to become pope.' 'Pippin has named himself king.' 'Pippin has freed Gripho and Sunnichild and is creating a pagan duchy in Alemannia.' The speculation is endless."

Miette finished the cup in a gulp. "Nobles associated with Pippin are rejoicing at the news, of course, while those associated with Carloman have begun to panic. Everyone believes Pippin is coming to imprison the king."

"What does your husband say?" Hélène asked.

"He is beside himself with anxiety; he and Drusseau spend long hours plotting into the night." Miette didn't mention how much she stayed clear of them, not wanting to further enjoy the wrath of Drusseau's anger. "From what Ragomfred has told me, the Knights in Christ here in Paris plan to protect the king at all costs. Drusseau believes defending him will give them legitimacy. They're fortifying the palace and digging defensive positions along the left bank leading to the bridge."

Childebrand nodded. "It won't matter if Pippin drives them out."

Miette frowned. "He'll have a harder time than you think. Drusseau's reinforcements from the Twelve Counties have arrived. I think he believes he can challenge Pippin."

"Against the combined armies?" Childebrand grunted.

"He must have some reason to believe he can prevail," Hélène said.

"He's taken charge of the Knights in Christ here in Paris," Miette said. "Perhaps he sees some advantage there."

Hélène turned to Childebrand. "Did questioning the knight who attacked you lead to anything?"

"The bastard won't talk. The most he'll admit to is that he is a Knight in Christ and took a holy oath that supersedes his allegiance to me."

Hélène frowned. "Drusseau seems to be the key. Miette, you'll have to probe your husband for more on him. We need to know what he's plotting."

* * *

Pippin approached Paris from the north at a leisurely pace with Gripho and Drogo at his side. He wanted all the Neustrian nobles to see the full weight of the combined armies before he had to use them. Integrating the men at Quierzy had gone smoothly; he had taken the knights he knew to be solid and moved them into positions of leadership. He realigned the regiments so that they would be blended. He expected some fighting and resistance, but all armies suffered from such nuisances.

He had learned from Childebrand that there were still pockets of rebellious knights in the city: those who refused to bend the knee and a considerable number of Knights in Christ who had pledged allegiance to the king – and only the king.

As they drew into the heart of the city, a celebration of nobles wearing his green greeted Pippin. Horns blared, drums beat, and pipes blew around them as they advanced. Childebrand was with them. He had already taken many of their hands in commendation and Pippin motioned for the nobles to ride with him into the city. There were far more than he would have imagined prior to Carloman's abdication.

They planned to completely occupy the city and force a reconciliation, hopefully without bloodshed. Based on Childebrand's input, Pippin left the palace alone, knowing that he could deal with Childeric later. Once inside, they split their legions into four parts to take the city and met limited resistance in three sectors. Only the left bank was fortified against them. And from the reports Childebrand provided, there were well over a thousand knights encamped there.

Under a flag of truce, Pippin went to investigate. He took Gripho and Childebrand with him.

A large knight wearing the vestment of the Knights in Christ rode forward. He had a look of arrogance on his face to match Theudebald's.

"That would be Drusseau," Childebrand offered.

Pippin was puzzled. "How is it that I've never met the man?"

His uncle shrugged. "Charles never liked the Twelve Counties. He said the Black Mountains were haunted. As long as the counties paid tribute and they kept the Bretons at bay, he pretty much left them alone."

Pippin nudged his horse forward. Childebrand and Gripho followed. Pippin nodded in greeting. "Drusseau."

"Milord Pippin."

"Why are your men encamped here?"

"We have pledged loyalty to the king and have vowed to protect him."

"And who is threatening him?"

"Why, you are, milord."

It was an interesting assertion to make. And it forced Pippin to consider the politics of attacking Drusseau's encampment. If he did, it would look like he was, in fact, attacking the king. Having just prevented one civil war, Pippin had no intention of causing another. At the same time, he couldn't just leave a rival armed force inside Neustria. He needed a compromise that he could live with.

Pippin leaned forward in his saddle. "As long as the pope acknowledges Childeric, he is under no threat from me."

Drusseau nodded. "Well said. But, after your brother's violation of parley, how can I accept your word for that?"

Pippin shrugged. "If you wish, you may station a garrison to guard his person and the palace, but your encampment must be vacated and your men returned to the Twelve Counties."

"I'm afraid that's not enough."

Pippin smiled as he turned his horse to go. "You have till morning to decide whether it is or is not. If your encampment is still here at dawn, it will be considered a hostile force and attacked."

"You must also acknowledge Childeric's legitimacy and offer your hands in commendation." Drusseau's face looked fierce with determination.

Pippin shook his head, chuckling at the man's audacity. "Until morning, Drusseau."

* * *

Ragomfred burst into Miette's rooms in a frenzy. "Come with me at once!"

She could see the man was clearly afraid. "What is it, husband?"

"Just come!" He turned and stalked out the door.

Miette followed him down the stairs into the grand hall, where she found Drusseau dressed in full armored plates with a broadsword across his back, pacing back and forth. Fear lanced through her. She stopped at the entrance, considering whether to flee.

Drusseau saw her and barked, "Come here, woman!"

Her husband urged her forward. "Be quick, Miette. We need answers."

At first, fear gripped her and Miette's legs refused to cooperate. She tried to find the separate place in her mind – the calm disconnected place – but it eluded her. Cursing, Ragomfred took her arm and pulled her across the room.

Standing before Drusseau she curtsied, unable to raise her eyes to look him in the face. "Milord."

"Your husband tells me that Pippin doesn't really understand politics, that he is more comfortable on the battlefield than at court. Is that true?"

"My husband would know better than I about –"

Drusseau slapped her across the face. "I don't have time for your lies. You slept with the man!"

Tears came to her eyes. She shook her head. "I never –"

He slapped her again. This time, she fell to the floor, humiliation wracking her frame.

Drusseau waved at Ragomfred. "Good Lord, man, get her up."

When she was back on her feet, Drusseau leaned in close to her face. "Is what your husband said true?"

She fought for control, taking in deep breaths. Still looking down she said, "No, it's not. He understands politics, he's just not motivated by them."

"What motivates him?"

"Justice." The word seemed to sing within her. It tapped something deep. Like a clarion call it demanded a response. She lifted her eyes to meet Drusseau's. "He believes in justice."

Drusseau grunted. "What in hell does that mean?"

She smiled, wiping away her tears. "It's complicated."

He hit her again, but this time it felt distant, as if it couldn't touch her. She met his eye again.

He looked confused. "And the part about the battlefield?"

She shook her head. "I've never seen him fight, but he never loses. They say he's violence incarnate."

"She's right," Ragomfred said. "Everyone says that. The man's a beast."

Drusseau growled and started again to pace. "It makes no sense! He knows I have him trapped. I saw it in his eyes. If he attacks me, he's attacking the king. It would start a civil war! He'll be a pariah! He can't be that reckless."

"What did he say?" Miette asked.

"He said if we still were encamped by morning, he'd attack."

"Then that's what he'll do," Miette said. "He doesn't lie."

Drusseau didn't hit her. He turned to Ragomfred and led him across the room. Although he whispered, he spoke with such urgency that Miette could hear him clearly.

"We'll pretend to acquiesce. Pippin agreed that we could maintain a garrison to protect the king and the palace. That will be our command center. A cadre of the Knights in Christ will rejoin his army and secretly reconnect with their peers. I'll agree to send the rest of our troops back to the Twelve Counties but remove them instead to somewhere outside the city where they can be mobilized once Neustria is vulnerable."

"When will that be?" Ragomfred asked.

"Whenever Pippin sends the army to war."

* * *

Just before daybreak, Pippin and Gripho sat with the full might of the combined armies at their backs to watch Drusseau's men clear their encampment. Although their progress was orderly and professional, it was clear that many of the Knights in Christ wished to stay and fight.

Pippin was glad to see that Gripho comported himself professionally. When he had freed his brother from Neufchateau, Pippin had been worried about the young man. His thoughts didn't seem too coherent, and he tended to laugh at odd times.

As they made their way to Paris, however, Gripho had slowly returned to his belligerent self.

"I'm surprised the man acquiesced," Pippin said. "The Knights in Christ are so zealous they rarely back down."

"He's not one of them. You can see it in his eyes," Gripho spat. "He's just using the Knights in Christ to challenge you. My bet is he wants to be mayor."

"Then why withdraw?"

Gripho grunted. "He's ambitious but not stupid. He's far outnumbered, and he knows it. I'd watch that one. He'll be back to fight another day."

When the last of the troops were vacating the area, Drusseau rode up to meet them. His face was a mask of nothing but anger.

"Milord mayor, Gripho."

"Drusseau."

"We have complied with your demand; will you honor our agreement?"

Pippin nodded. "The Knights in Christ will be allowed to continue guarding the king and palace."

"Then I and my men shall retire." He turned to go.

"Before you depart, may I offer a new bargain?" Pippin said.

Drusseau seemed surprised and turned back.

"I grant you that I don't have Carloman's zeal for the Church or for Childeric, but I now rule of all Francia. My brother willingly took the tonsure; his son Drogo offered me his hands in commendation; and the kingdom now is unified under one mayor."

"And one king," Drusseau interjected.

Pippin nodded but continued. "I have no interest in battling you and the Knights in Christ. I've enough trouble keeping the nobles of the independent duchies in line. But I cannot tolerate a rebel force within the kingdom...including yours...or any who might claim a separate allegiance – even to the king."

Pippin paused. "You've judged me once and rightfully concluded that I am true to my word. Unless we can come to an agreement, I will come for you and these men."

"What do you have in mind?"

"I need every capable knight to defend the kingdom from the threats without. I can't afford to fight endlessly those from within. I need you and your men. The Twelve Counties already protect the kingdom from the Bretons, but you also occupy a strategic part of the kingdom critical to our defense."

Drusseau laughed derisively. "Strategic part of the kingdom? Why then is this the first time I've heard of it? You Austraisians don't come near the Twelve Counties and you barely recognize us as Franks! Your flattery is wasted on me, milord."

Pippin nodded. He couldn't blame Drusseau. They had ignored the Twelve Counties for generations. "I blame my father for that. It would have made better sense for the Twelve Counties to be a military buffer between Neustria and Aquitaine. But Charles carried a deep and enduring hatred for Aquitaine. He thought he didn't need the Twelve Counties. He despised Duc Eudo and took every chance he could to wage war with him. It was his passion.

"But it was a poor strategy. If Charles was off in the east, Eudo had free rein in the west. You've seen recent evidence of its failings. While Carloman and I were away in Saxony and Alemannia, Eudo's son

Hunoald sacked the cathedral at Chartres. Carloman and I both had to campaign in Aquitaine last year to seek justice."

"I don't see how this affects me."

"By locating a regiment between the Sarthe and the Loire, it will deter further aggression from the south. I want to reinstate the Breton March and make Gripho its duc."

Gripho looked surprised. Pippin continued. "By assigning my brother, it provides the March with the prestige and authority to raise troops and treasure. I want you to be his second. I will provide a thousand men – to include the Knights in Christ who ride with you – if you raise the rest of a regiment from the Twelve Counties. Gripho can take the old fortress in Le Mans; I'll provide the treasure to restore it. And he can lead the March from there."

Gripho smiled, albeit sarcastically. "Master of the March!"

Drusseau leaned forward, a quizzical look on his face. "I already have the Twelve Counties. Why would I agree to play nursemaid to your brother?"

Pippin sighed. "Because I will eventually come to the Twelve Counties to demand your fealty. And if you don't bend the knee, I will take your head. If you accept my proposal, you can play much the same role as you are now in a far wealthier Twelve Counties with a greater role in the kingdom and a stronger military contingent at your back. I see no need for further bloodshed. It's time to end the civil war. If Carloman and I can make peace, so can you and I."

Drusseau frowned and, after a moment's consideration, addressed himself to Gripho. "If milord will have me, I will task a cadre of my men to accompany you back to the Twelve Counties. I must remain here to oversee the protection of the king and palace."

Gripho nodded. "Ride with me as far as Saint Denis. You can brief me on the status of the Twelve Counties before returning to manage the king's protection."

Apparently satisfied, Drusseau dismounted and knelt before Gripho, offering his hands. Gripho dismounted and took them in his own.

* * *

Gripho rode out of Paris with Drusseau, a huge smile on his face. He was so giddy he had trouble preventing himself from laughing out loud. Such a buffoon! Pippin had let him get away so easily – and with an army!

Oh, he had been impressed with Pippin's bribe to Drusseau. His brother had used a clever bit of theatre backed by a very real threat to sway the knight. Gripho had watched the man's eyes grow wide with greed while he considered the offer. The wealth and power Pippin proffered was considerable.

What his fool of a brother hadn't considered was that he had no intention of being "Master of the March" or any title short of "mayor of the palace." He was Charles Martel's son! Carloman had tried to deny him his birthright and now so had Pippin. And there was only one answer to such betrayal – war.

"You are an ambitious man, Drusseau."

"Milord?"

"Oh, I know what you were planning. It was clever, using Childeric to take direct control of the Knights in Christ here in Paris and have them pledge loyalty directly to the king. Given Carloman's loyalty to both the crown and the Knights, it would have put him in a delicate position to remove you."

"My only concern was for the safety of the king," Drusseau said cautiously.

"But then Carloman abdicated, and you were left with Pippin, and you recognized that he wouldn't hesitate at all. So, it was very clever, trying to trap him like that. Had it been anyone else, it likely would have succeeded. And you would be left as the sole protector of the king with an army to defend him in the heart of Neustria."

"The threat to Childeric's person seemed real."

"Oh, it still is. But when confronted by Pippin, you didn't choose to ensure his safety at all costs, *you* acquiesced to save your army. And now you're sending me to the Twelve Counties with only a 'cadre of men.' Where are you planning to hide the army?"

"I don't understand, milord."

"I think you do. You aren't going to the Twelve Counties, at least not until you see how all the cards fall. You didn't abdicate, you retreated. You've still got the Knights in Christ, you're still guarding the king and palace, and you've kept your army intact. You'll just keep them nearby to mobilize when they're needed."

Drusseau didn't respond, so Gripho continued.

"Neither of us is going to the Twelve Counties." That clearly surprised Drusseau. "If you believed that story he told you about the Breton March, you aren't as smart as I think you are. He won't be sending us any new troops or treasure; he wants us isolated. Pippin is trying to keep us out of the way while he consolidates power. Once he has, we'll be easy pickings for him."

"How do you know this?"

"He's my brother. All he's ever done is betray me."

Drusseau rode for a few minutes, considering Gripho's claim. "He lies well, your brother."

"It's a family tradition."

"Then why should I believe you?"

"You don't have much of a choice. Once you encamped on the left bank, you set yourself against Pippin. Do you really think he would offer you a title and wealth after you challenged him? He's not that generous. Believe me, I'm giving you a way out."

"What would you have me do?"

"I want you to finish what you started. You're the knife pointed at Pippin's back. Once he is distracted by war, Neustria will be yours for the taking."

"What war?"

"The one I'm going to start in Saxony and Bavaria."

16

Regensburg

Trudi was nearly incoherent when her entourage reached Regensburg. All she could do was weep. Odilo was dead. It was so unexpected, so intertwined with the location of Bradius's death that she couldn't accept the fact of it. It was an illusion, a dream, a nightmare. Odilo couldn't be dead. He couldn't.

Trudi's eyes recognized the events around her, but her thoughts couldn't be contained in the corporeal world. Odilo's death swirled in her mind alongside Bradius's and she relived them again and again, powerless to make them stop.

Odilo's body had been wrapped in linen and placed on a cart. The doctor had said there was no malice, no accident; Odilo had died of dropsy. The declaration was meaningless to Trudi; they always said dropsy when they had no idea what happened. Word was sent ahead and a contingent of nobles met them outside the gates to lead them into the city.

Drummers lined the road inside the city walls and played a funeral cadence. The nobles led them to the palace, where much of the city stood in the courtyard waiting in silence. The nobles placed his body on an elevated bier of wood, surrounded by flowers.

As pagans didn't wait to dispose of their dead, Trudi wouldn't be given time to rest, to bathe, or to even to comb her hair. She was forced to stand and watch as one by one, the nobles advanced, kissed their fingers, and then touched the body of her late husband.

Sudiger came to her and stood by her, his large frame providing her with some stability. "Please accept my sorrow, milady. He was a good man and a great leader. His strength will be missed."

When the nobles had finished their procession, members of the palace household came forward. They too kissed their fingers and touched his body. She saw Hans and her guardsman step forward. She saw Eta, holding Tassilo.

The realization struck her that her son wouldn't remember Odilo and the knowledge hit her like a physical blow. How could she bear this?

Sudiger touched her elbow. "Milady?"

She looked up at him and he nodded toward the bier. It was her turn. She hesitated, not wanting to make the journey, but a gentle push from Sudiger propelled her forward. The shrouded figure seemed unreal to her, as if it couldn't be Odilo. He wasn't there, she told herself. Not here, not now. She raised her right hand and kissed the first two fingers and then touched them to the side of his corpse. It wasn't him, not him, it couldn't be.

A pagan lore master stepped forward, his face painted in streaks of black. He bowed to Trudi and turned to raise his face to the sun. He spread his arms wide. *"I call on Ansuz, the Ash, the World Tree, the Tree of Life!"*

"The ash which binds us," intoned the crowd.

Trudi returned to her place beside Sudiger and an acolyte with a burning taper stepped to the bier and laid it against the wood. Flames licked the edges of the logs as smoke seeped upward. It flowed around Odilo's corpse in an ephemeral shroud.

"Yggdrasil, you who link all the worlds of creation."

"You are the source for humankind."

It was then that the finality of his death took her. This was the end. It was too soon. She would never hold him again, never see him again, never feel his touch. A sob escaped her, and her body shook. Panic consumed her, and she folded forward, bending at the waist. Sudiger's arms wrapped around her, lifting her erect. "Not now, milady! Stand strong for us. Stand strong for Bavaria."

His words reached her, and she responded to the duty they implied. She stood, stifled her tears, and swallowed her sobs, but her mind remained adrift between the worlds.

"*Take your divine breath to Odilo,*" the lore master chanted. "*Take him to Utgart, the land of the dead.*"

She saw Odilo's face in a succession of flashes. The first time he rode into Quierzy, his rumpled casual grace among the perfectly groomed Bavarian horsemen. The surprise in his eyes when they speared the boar and the amazed look he gave her when she severed its head.

She saw the curl of his smile when they shared the rite of communion and the love in his eyes when they wed. A thousand images assaulted her, and she wallowed among them, knowing it was her last goodbye.

"*He has known both joy and sorrow.*"

"*Let his soul find peace and his body renew the earth,*" the crowd responded.

The entire bier was ablaze, its black smoke staining the sky. The lore master took a pouch from his belt and pulled from it a handful of dust. He held it aloft and let it sift through his closed hand, watching as the wind lifted it into the air.

* * *

When Eta brought Tassilo to her, he was so full of emotion at seeing her, he burst into tears. "Mama!" he wailed, and he reached for her, burying his face in her shoulder. "Mama!" he cried over and over. She wrapped her arms around him and whispered his name, rocking him back and forth like she had when he was an infant.

Her emotions were nearly as overwhelming as his. She couldn't believe how much she missed him. When she had left with Odilo for Estinnes, she had thought it would be good for her and her husband to have time alone together, but she hadn't counted on how much she would miss her son.

Odilo's death only made this feeling more acute, as she recognized how fragile life could be. Every moment was precious. When Tassilo's crying stopped, she kissed away the tears on his cheeks. "You've grown so big!" she exclaimed.

She took him for a walk through the palace gardens. He held her hand and she walked slowly so that his short legs could keep up with her. Although he was three, he was still a shy boy, clinging to her and Eta's shift if a stranger appeared.

Eta had taught him a song and he sang it for Trudi, his voice high and light. He missed several words, so she joined in to sing it with him and they clapped together when it was finished.

She pointed out several flowers and they picked the best to make a bouquet. He insisted on carrying it for her. When they came to a bench, the two sat next to each other.

"Mama, where is der Vati?"

Trudi froze. Der Vati was his name for Odilo. She felt tears welling inside her and, despite her attempt at controlling them, several leaked from her eyes. How could she tell her son that der Vati was gone forever? That he would never again be held in his father's arms or kiss him good night. She longed to shield that from him. She couldn't find the words to explain it to him. She barely could explain it to herself.

She was about to give up when she had a sudden inspiration. "*He would tell you that he is in Utgart.*"

"Where's that?"

She pulled him onto her lap. "Well, he believed there are three worlds all joined together by Yggdrasil, the great world tree. There is the land of the gods." She held her hand high. "The land of humankind, where we live." She lowered her hand. "And Utgart, the underworld." She lowered it further still. "Der Vati's soul went to Utgart."

"When will he come home?" There was fear in the boy's voice and Trudi choked up hearing it.

"He's – he's going to stay there," she said, kissing his head. "But he is always with us. His body lives in the trees around us, the earth beneath our feet, the air we breathe, and the water we drink. You can always talk to him, and he will always hear you."

"But I want to see him!" Tassilo insisted.

"I do, too." Trudi hugged him. "I do, too." Her mind howled in anguish. They had lost him forever. She couldn't imagine their life without him. They stayed like that for a long time, his short legs hanging off to the side of hers, kicking idly.

When he grew older she would tell him of his heritage, again and again, until he knew it by heart. She could give him that much and maybe it would allow her to remember too.

"Your father was a brave, brave man," she said. "He was a champion of his faith and a noble warrior for his people. He was loved by some, feared by many, but understood by only a few. I was proud to be one of them. And I loved him very much.

"As a nobleman, der Vati lived his life with principle. He was Bavaria's duc for twenty years. He ruled wisely, defending the weak and dispensing justice. He ruled with compassion, humor, and honor. He was my first love and my last. And I will miss him to the end of my days."

* * *

It only had been two days since the funeral, but Sudiger insisted Trudi take Odilo's place before the council of Bavarian nobles. "Don't let them see you as weak."

Trudi washed her face, combed her hair, and sat at the head of the dais, dutifully reporting on the deal her husband had struck with Pippin. When she was finished, silence filled the room.

Lantfrid stood. "Are you mocking us with this proposal?"

The question caught Trudi off guard. "I –"

"It's a coward's agreement," Lantfrid shouted. "Your brother butchers my people, steals our land, and the best you can come up with is to let your half-brother out of prison? It's laughable."

She'd been so proud of Odilo's accomplishment, she'd forgotten it would be challenged. She silently cursed herself. Of course, Lantfrid would stand against it. He had the most to lose and had been opposed to the plan from the beginning. But she could tell the nobles also were skeptical. They needed to hear from her the answer as well. "Bavaria fought wars over Gripho's right to succession."

"Which you haven't guaranteed. All you've done is seal the fate of Alemannia. The Franks will steal our land and your priests will swarm over our countryside. And in exchange, we get your assurance that Bavaria won't be next. How can we trust you? You're the sister of our enemy."

They would have believed Odilo, she thought. But, of course, Odilo was gone. Without him by her side, her word was suspect. Without him, she was Pippin's sister. It was her worst nightmare come to life. She refused, however, to let the success of Odilo's embassy to Estinnes be ignored.

"Odilo achieved everything we set out to accomplish. Carloman has abdicated and Gripho has been freed. The truth of it is Pippin doesn't want war. Carloman acted alone and now he's been forced to abdicate. Pippin is sole mayor of Francia."

"I care nothing for your two brothers." Lantfrid's face was flush with anger. "Alemannia should be mine. My family has ruled it for generations. This is not a settlement. It is piracy!"

Several nobles grumbled their assent.

Trudi was exhausted. And the obstinacy of these nobles frustrated her. She tried a different tack. "Bavaria went to war over Gripho's imprisonment. We mustered the largest army ever raised this side of the Rhine. We fought with the Alemanni, the Slavs, the Hessians, and the Thuringians, and still we lost.

"Yet with a single embassy, Odilo and I freed Gripho – not with blood – but with peace. We watched the abdication of Carloman and we gained the assurance that Pippin does not seek war with Bavaria. How much more can we expect?"

Eingard stood, his height and military bearing commanding attention. Trudi braced herself. Odilo had warned her that the man would oppose the agreement.

"It is good that Carloman abdicates. It is good that Gripho is free. But where is the justice for the two thousand dead? How do we console the survivors of our cousins to the north? How do we tell ourselves that it cannot happen here when we see the Franks seizing the land and wealth of those they slaughtered? There is no reasoning with such people! War is the only answer."

Shouts of agreement echoed his conclusion. Trudi could feel the room turning against her. She desperately looked to Sudiger, hoping the man would step in, but he merely stroked his beard as if in deep thought.

His refusal to stand in her defense both surprised and hurt her. She felt abandoned. Yet, her instinct for survival held. She refused to give in to the despair that assaulted her. She drummed her fingers on the dais, letting her anger build.

"I greatly respect your opinion, Comte Eingard, as did my husband. You've been a great champion of Bavaria. It is amusing to note, however, that Odilo predicted you would stand in opposition. 'To soldiers,' he said, 'the answer to every question is always war.' He didn't believe that and neither do I.

"There is a time and place for war. Had Pippin ignored my husband, had he allowed the massacre to go unanswered, had he not bargained with us in good faith, I would be calling for war myself. But Pippin did not ignore us. He forced Carloman to abdicate and he freed Gripho to show us good faith. He offered us peace.

"Lantfrid has questioned my loyalty in front of you in much the same way he called my husband a coward. Without Odilo at my side, he believes my loyalty has shifted to my brother. But Lantfrid ignores the fact that I pledged my life to Odilo. He ignores the fact that I now serve as regent to my son, the future duc of Bavaria." She let her voice underscore this last. "He ignores the fact that I have held the sons of

Bavaria as they died in my arms after the battle at the River Lech. I have consoled the widows of that war and succored those who were injured and maimed. I may have been born the daughter of Charles Martel, but until my son is of age, I am not only Bavarian, I am Bavaria!"

She stood. "I thank you for your counsel and will consider our next steps."

As she left the room, she saw Lantfrid and Sudiger talking in earnest in the corner of the room. "Not a good omen," she whispered to herself."

* * *

Returning to her rooms at the palace, Trudi closed the door and leaned against it. Why didn't Sudiger stand with her? He knew she would be vulnerable without Odilo. He had let her founder before the nobles like a wounded lamb before wolves.

She slid down the length of the door until she was seated and let herself cry. She was alone, desperately alone. The magnitude of her plight daunted her. She had bought herself some time with the council, but not much else.

When her tears subsided, she stood, washed her face, and combed her hair. She refused to let despair conquer her. She sent for Hans.

"From now on, you must consider everyone – even nobles we consider friends – to be a potential threat to Tassilo. I want the palace to be a fortress. Take whatever steps you need; recruit whatever men you require and make it so. I want you to secure the armory as if we are under siege and ensure that no one is given access without my express permission."

"Yes, milady." Hans bowed, but the question in his eyes begged an answer.

Trudi felt he deserved one. "With Odilo dead, the potential for war over the massacre in Alemannia is growing. The nobles are questioning my loyalty and my ability to rule and there are too many among them who feel empowered to take matters into their own hands. If they do,

Tassilo's life is in danger and so is mine. We can no longer take our security for granted. I'm trusting you to keep us safe."

"You have my word, milady." He bowed to take his leave.

She knew that wouldn't be enough. She needed to forestall the crisis. She sent for Comte Eingard. He arrived within the hour. A servant led him to Trudi's sitting room. If he thought the summons unusual, no sign of it crossed his face.

"Milady, how may I serve you?"

"Please." She motioned for them to sit. The comte sat on the edge of his seat with his back straight.

"I'd like you to take control of the army and the city guard."

He nodded as if he was an obvious choice.

Trudi continued. "Despite our disagreement over the correct response to the massacre, you have always been a loyal subject and a friend. I find myself in a situation where I need both."

Trudi took a deep breath. "I believe there may be an effort at insurrection and that my life and Tassilo's are in jeopardy. I've instructed the palace guard to act accordingly, and I am asking for your support in quashing any nascent rebellion before it starts."

Eingard's face showed no reaction to her plea for help. "You are perceptive, milady. The massacre in Alemannia weighs heavily on the minds of our nobles. Should you refuse to prosecute war with your brother, there are many nobles willing to challenge your regency and Tassilo's succession."

His eyes squinted in concentration. "Will you declare war on your brother?"

Trudi shook her head. "I will not. Odilo gave his word."

"Then you are asking me to place my loyalty to you above my conscience."

Trudi nodded. "You are one of my husband's most trusted allies."

Eingard stood. "I will consider it, milady. I do not know if the nobles will choose to wage war on your brother, but if they do, I will not oppose them whether I am your man or not. I can and will insist, however, that you and your son be kept safe should that decision be made. Unlike your brother Carloman, I do not condone the killing of innocent women and children."

Trudi tried not to panic. Two of her husband's most trusted allies had refused her pleas for help in the last twelve hours. Had she already lost her hold over them as regent? She had to know more. Despite the late hour, she sent for Sudiger.

An hour went by; then two. When a servant finally announced him, the sun had set and the palace rooms were lit by candlelight. Although furious that it had taken Sudiger so long to arrive, Trudi calmed herself and took a moment to fix her hair and straighten her clothes before waiting in the sitting room for him to appear.

When the servant showed him in, he bowed deeply.

"Thank you for coming," Trudi said.

"How may I serve you, milady?"

Trudi's despair couldn't wait for small talk. "Why didn't you stand with me before the council? Why leave me stranded when I needed you most?"

Sudiger motioned to the set of chairs beside them and looked questioningly at Trudi. Embarrassed at her lack of etiquette, she nodded her head and they sat.

Sudiger leaned back in his chair, interlacing his fingers over the huge belly bulging before him. "You've been gone for two months, milady. Much has been discussed while you were away. Lantfrid has argued persuasively for a call to arms and many of the nobles have vowed to answer it. We've also heard from relatives in Alemannia who have suffered great losses or who have been driven from their land by the Frankish usurpers. How can we stand aside and do nothing? Your agreement with Pippin was cleverly made, but it may not be enough to sway the council."

The earth seemed to shift beneath her. He wasn't just describing her situation; he was explaining his refusal to help. She had thought they were friends, but even he was lost to her. She couldn't shake the fear that her regency hung in the balance. If the nobles sided with Lantfrid,

Tassilo's legacy was in jeopardy. Her mind chased possibilities. She desperately tried to think clearly. Odilo had said that Sudiger would need to be bribed with land, treasure, or both. It was worth a try.

"You've always been a friend, Sudiger. And like Odilo, I prefer to reward my friends for their loyalty. Is there anything I can offer you to help you reconsider?"

Sudiger leaned forward, his eyes glistening. "There is, milady. There is."

"Name it."

"Let me be candid. Just as you had feared, you now find yourself alone among nobles who question your loyalty and your right to serve as Tassilo's regent. Your son's life might even be in danger."

Trudi's stomach clenched at the thought. She had to find her way through this. "What do you suggest?"

"An alliance of sorts." He licked his lips. "You need someone to provide you with the standing to continue your regency for Tassilo. You need a champion who will vouch for your loyalty and defend your interests and the interests of your son." Sudiger paused. "I can be that champion."

"At what price?"

He stood and held his hands out to her. She rose to take them.

"Be my bride. Not only in name, but in truth."

Trudi took a step back, but he held her hands firmly.

He grinned as if she had no choice. "If you wish to survive the years between now and Tassilo's ascendency, you will marry me. You will have my child to ensure the family's legacy and I will be the solution to your dilemma."

He had planned this from the beginning. He had befriended her, promised her aid, and then let her be buffeted by the political winds so that she would be desperate. The thought of marrying him made her want to scream, especially now that she could see him for what he was. Odilo had told her Sudiger's price would be high. She never imagined how high it could be.

She reeled with the implications of her situation. Everything he had said was true. She had no friend to turn to and no allies to call. He was her best chance of survival, but the thought of bedding Sudiger disgusted her. It would desecrate the love she had shared with both Odilo and Bradius. At best, it was coerced rape.

Her voice shook with the effort of hiding her nausea. "You are, of course, correct in your assessment of my situation. I will consider your proposal and let you know of my decision."

His eyes looked doubtful. "Don't delay, milady. You don't have the luxury of time and I won't be dallied with like some pimpled-faced suitor. I'll expect your answer within the week."

Like a man who had won the night at cards, Sudiger's eyes gleamed with victory. He stood, bowed, and left.

17

Paris

Although Pippin would have preferred to return to Quierzy for the winter months, his instincts suggested that the political situation in Paris required a more forceful position. But other than the continued presence of the Knights in Christ in the palace, he could think of no reason for this anxiety: he had taken the city in a clear show of force, expelled the only armed camp to threaten it, and solidified his hold on the government, the army, and the city itself. There should be nothing to fear.

He established a compound on the left bank to house his family and to manage the government. As in Quierzy it included Pippin's closest lieutenants and advisors as well as a guard unit large enough to secure a fortress. East of Saint-Germain-des-Prés and south of the bridge near the palace, it comprised a row of houses that took up an entire block. His army was encamped just outside the western end of the city near the Rouvray Forest.

He and Bertrada had agreed to attend a reception in honor of the army's return at the home of Hélène. When they arrived Pippin tried to embrace the celebratory mood, but he couldn't shake the feeling of anxiety that plagued him. Feeling short of breath, he excused himself from the conversation and found a quiet spot to breathe.

"Here, try this." Bertrada handed him a tall flask of wine. She was with Hélène and he was pleased that she looked happy. Thankfully, her nausea had passed, and she could eat normal food again. The roundness of her belly was starting to show, and she unconsciously had one hand atop it.

"Is my mood that obvious?"

"Maybe to me. You're also not sleeping well. What's bothering you?"

"I'm not sure. Everything seems to be settling into place. I'm no longer at odds with Carloman; I've avoided civil war with Odilo and the eastern duchies, and I've neutralized, for the most part, the Knights in Christ. Yet, I can't shake the feeling that I'm missing something."

"We're not done with the Knights," Hélène said. "And Drusseau is as dangerous a man as I've met. I know you've made a deal with him and Gripho, but I don't trust him to uphold it. He's moved into the palace, a place where we can't touch him, and he's still in control of the Knights in Christ. He's what I worry about."

Bertrada playfully pushed Hélène. "I was trying to get him to relax!"

Childebrand joined them and gave a bear hug to the newlyweds. "There's my favorite couple! It's about time you two finally wed." He tousled Pippin's hair. "I'll bet Carloman shat himself when he heard about little Charles."

"He wasn't happy," Bertrada said. "But he has no right to be bitter."

"He lost his way," Pippin said somberly. "The fervor of his faith took him to a place beyond reason. It will take him a long time to atone."

"Let's focus on something less morose," Bertrada pleaded. "Tell me, Childebrand, I heard you defeated four soldiers by yourself?"

A twinkle took the large man's eye. "It wasn't me. I clouted one of them with Hélène's statue, but the other three?" He paused for effect. "It was Hélène's pupil, Miette."

Both Pippin and Bertrada were speechless. Hélène seemed to glow with pride.

Childebrand laughed. "You should have seen her! She was so quick. A knife in the throat, one across a hamstring, and a third in the armpit; it was over before anyone knew what was happening. And then, quiet as a church, she melted into the crowd like she'd never been there at all. I got all the credit. She even tossed me the statue."

"She has been very helpful in rooting out information," Hélène said. "She was first to identify Drusseau as a threat."

Pippin could see a coldness enveloping Bertrada while the conversation centered on Miette.

"I think Childebrand has grown soft for her." Hélène laughed and playfully shoved the big man.

Childebrand looked offended. "And what if I have? Can't an old man dream?"

Gunther joined them with Catherine in tow. The two seemed an odd couple – the disgruntled military veteran and the elegant Comtesse de Loches.

"I know what kind of dream you've been having," Gunther said.

Hélène groaned. "And I was just beginning to like you, Gunther."

"He's an acquired taste, sister," Catherine offered, "but we have yet to celebrate the new babe Bertrada's carrying. Let me rectify that." She bowed to Bertrada. "To the babe!"

"To the babe!" they all shouted and lifted their cups. Pippin could have kissed Catherine. Bertrada's eyes had softened, and she even smiled.

"You look lovely, my dear," Catherine said to her. "I wish I had that glow about me when I had my two. My husband used to call me the Gascon witch."

Gunther chimed in. "I'm surprised he was that generous!"

They all laughed, and Pippin was surprised to feel the tension leaving him. He wondered what had changed. Everyone around him continued their banter and he marveled at the peace it gave him. And with that peace, he understood.

After Charles's death and the loss of everyone he loved, he had felt alone for so long. But now he had Bertrada, and little Charles...and this collection of people; he just hadn't recognized them for what they were. For the first time in a long while, he tilted his head back and began to laugh.

* * *

Although most of the city had embraced Pippin wholeheartedly, there was a small but virulent minority that held fast to their vows to Childeric and the Knights in Christ. Given Pippin's agreement that the Knights would guard the palace, it quickly became the center of their existence.

Masses were said there, Childeric held court there, balls were thrown there. They ate together, prayed together, and celebrated together, effectively separating themselves from the rest of the city. Drusseau fanned a siege mentality that kept "the faithful," as he called them, whipped into a furor. They became of one mind that they were aggrieved, persecuted, and unfairly judged by Pippin and his followers. Every knight among the faithful believed that civil war was inevitable and that the only question left to them was when it would come. For most, it wouldn't be soon enough.

As Ragomfred's wife, Miette was thrust bodily into this cloistered world of grievance. Their life centered around the palace and she was no longer permitted to visit salons unless they belonged to one of the faithful. As a result, she could no longer gossip with Ladies Gagnon, Didot, and Talon. They weren't among Ragomfred's chosen people.

Childeric, who ruled with divine right, was worshipped inside the palace as if he were a god himself. Knights and their wives struggled to get close to him, preening to get his attention. He chose a select few who were permitted into his presence to fawn over him and praise his every word. Any who failed to please him were exorcised from his presence and shunned within the palace.

Given the nature of this obsession, Miette couldn't help but feel vulnerable. She feared being forced once again to submit to Childeric's whims. There would be no one to stop him. If anything, the faithful would think her mad to refuse.

Although Miette took some solace that she no longer held Childeric's attention, she hated that his focus was centered on Lady Brevet and Charlotte. She could see the toll it was taking on both women. The joy and arrogance that was present in Brevet when they first met was gone.

The woman looked haggard and beaten. Charlotte looked worse. Her hair was disheveled, and her clothes rumpled. Her eyes held a vacant stare and her cheek twitched at odd moments.

Miette had tried to figure out how to get Charlotte out of the palace, but she was barred from going near Drusseau's rooms.

Miette's husband was of no help to her. Throughout the winter months he continued to debate with Drusseau about when to challenge Pippin. The two men seemed resigned to the fact that nothing would happen until the spring. Drusseau even had sent his military units back to the Twelve Counties for the winter.

They didn't tell her this, of course; she had to piece together the information from conversations she overheard from her husband and their servants. Drusseau always was careful around her, suspecting that she was a spy, and on more than one occasion he'd questioned Ragomfred as to why he'd bothered to pay her ransom. She would have loved to be the one to explain to him that Ragomfred needed her to hide his clandestine trysts with men.

One morning, she was left alone at the palace while Ragomfred met with Drusseau. The two walked along the rampart while they discussed strategies. Miette took a seat in the garden to wait for their return. When they did, however, they were so engrossed in their conversation they walked right past her without seeing her.

"Why is Gripho taking so long?" Ragomfred complained. "We haven't heard from him for months."

Drusseau's words were muffled. All she heard was "Saxony."

Miette frowned. What had Saxony to do with Gripho? She strained to hear more, but the two men had walked past the range of her hearing.

"Miette?" Charlotte touched her arm.

Miette was so surprised she jumped. "Charlotte!" She pulled the woman aside. "How are you?"

Her eyes looked hollow. "They ruined me."

"The king?"

She nodded. "The things they did...I can't – I can't –"

"Shhh. You don't need to explain."

"You never came for me."

"I tried. I just couldn't find a way." Miette hugged her to her chest. "I will get you out of here. There has to be a way."

"There is," she said, looking down, "but I'm not strong enough."

Miette followed her eyes and saw red slashes across Charlotte's wrists. "Please don't. I'll get you out; you'll be safe. I just need time."

Charlotte's eyes rose to meet hers. "I don't have much left."

* * *

Miette made her way to Pippin's compound, careful to avoid being seen. The weather had grown so cold that it pierced through her cloak as if she had nothing on. When she arrived, Childebrand, Hélène, and Pippin were already in the great hall engaged in a deep discussion. She made for the fire to warm herself.

She was still uncomfortable in Pippin's company. She wasn't sure whether it was because of Bertrada's perpetual scowl or the hurt she felt looking at Pippin. She still desired him, and it bothered her that she had so little control over herself.

When she felt sufficiently warm, she set aside her cloak and joined the conversation.

"Odilo's dead," Hélène said by way of greeting.

"And your sister?" Miette asked Pippin.

"She lives, but we don't know if she has control over the duchy or if the peace agreement we made still holds."

Miette frowned. "Who brought the report?"

"Sergius. He said Trudi is negotiating with the Bavarian nobles for control. Beyond that, we know nothing."

Miette's mind raced, trying to piece together the scraps of information she had gathered from her husband. The news from Bavaria was relevant.

"What is it?" Hélène pressed.

"I think Gripho's in Saxony."

Pippin looked surprised. "How do you know that?"

"I don't, for sure. I've only pieces of information, but they're beginning to make sense. We've known for some time that Drusseau was looking for a moment when you'd be vulnerable to attack. We just didn't know what kind of attack. We always assumed it would be by assassination."

"There have already been two attempts," Pippin said.

"But I overheard Ragomfred ask Drusseau about Gripho, and Drusseau mentioned Saxony. What if they're counting on Gripho to enlist Theodoric to be their distraction?"

Hélène frowned. "If there's a revolt in Saxony, Trudi won't be able to hold Bavaria. The east will be engulfed in war."

"And if Pippin takes the army east, Neustria will be vulnerable to an attack by Drusseau's army," Miette concluded.

Pippin swore under his breath. "Where are his troops?"

"The Twelve Counties. He sent them back for the winter, thinking nothing will happen until spring."

"Then we need to be ready by then. First, we need to confirm that Gripho isn't in the Twelve Counties."

"What if he's gone?" Childebrand asked.

Pippin frowned. "There'll be war." He looked into Miette's eyes. "Well done, Miette."

She blushed and looked away. In the old days, before his betrothal, she would have had a quick retort to throw his way, but not now.

When Pippin took his leave to meet with Sergius, Miette turned to Childebrand and Hélène. "I've got a problem."

Hélène raised an eyebrow, waiting for her to continue.

"I need to take Drusseau's wife out of the palace."

Childebrand looked puzzled. "Whatever for?"

"Drusseau and Childeric are raping her," she said, her voice lowered, "much in the way he raped me."

Childebrand's face reddened. "You can't just steal his wife."

"Pippin stole Miette," Hélène said.

"And that almost got him excommunicated. I don't think he'll want to do it again."

"We have to do something! She's trying to kill herself," Miette pleaded.

"There's nothing to be done until Drusseau rebels," Childebrand said. "When he attacks our men, his life and all his possessions will be forfeit."

"You need to take her, now." Miette looked to Childebrand.

"And how am I supposed to do it? The palace is guarded like a fortress."

"Hélène and I will get her out. You just have to stop him from taking her back."

Childebrand scowled. "No. The timing isn't right. We need to lure Drusseau out of the palace. Until then this will only end in bloodshed, and most of it will be ours."

* * *

Pippin had no desire to meet with Sergius. The man wore his arrogance like a shield. Still, given that he had left Estinnes for Rome and then returned so quickly was an indication that much had changed.

The pope's legate was so tall that he had to duck to enter the room. He sat in the first chair available and waved for Pippin to sit as well.

"Did Carloman speak his vows?" Pippin asked before the legate could speak.

Sergius nodded. "Yes, the deed is done. I've come at the pope's urgent request. King Liutbrand of the Lombards is dead."

A wave of sadness engulfed Pippin at the news. It didn't come as a shock; Liutbrand was far from a young man, but Pippin had lived much of his childhood in the Lombards' court – and the king had been so fond of him that he adopted him as his son. Although ambitious, the king had been a stabilizing force on the Roman peninsula, subjugating his cousins in Spoleto and Benevento. He had been tolerant of the pope but looked upon the emperor in Constantinople with disdain.

"I'm sorry to hear the news."

"As you can imagine, so was the pope, especially now that Aistulf has risen to the throne."

Pippin understood the pope's trepidation. Where Liutbrand had been judicious, Aistulf was impulsive.

"As you know, Aistulf is not the statesmen the king was."

"That's an understatement."

"He's already threatening to take papal territories. The pope has sent me to request that you intervene on his behalf."

Given his previous exchange with Sergius, Pippin was content to wait and watch the legate squirm.

Sergius cleared his throat. "His Excellency has indicated that he might be open to discussing the very delicate situation you described in our last meeting."

Pippin still didn't respond.

"He made no promises, but should you intercede, His Excellency has indicated that he would consider an appropriate title to indicate the high regard with which he holds you."

"And what title might that be?" Pippin asked.

"Patrician of Rome!" Sergius said it with a flourish, as if that would make the title more impactful.

Pippin was stunned. "This is what Pope Zachary sent you all the way from Rome to tell me?"

"The need is urgent."

"And yet you insult me with an empty title when I made my demands plainly to you in Estinnes."

"You do not make demands of the pope!"

"Is there anything else?" Pippin stood. "I have other affairs to attend to."

Sergius looked surprised at Pippin's obvious dismissal, and his arrogance began to falter. "I may be willing to negotiate other means of rewarding your intervention – land, treasure?"

Pippin was now furious. "You may be the pope's emissary, Sergius, but you are no longer mine. I don't trust you to speak on my behalf to the pope. I will send an emissary of my own, asking his holiness a simple question – the same question I put to you in Estinnes but was clearly ignored. How the pope answers will determine the extent to which I will intervene."

"But that will take months!"

"Yes," Pippin said. "In the meantime, I've got other priorities. Your presence here is no longer welcome."

Sergius looked stunned. He leaned over Pippin, using his height in an obvious attempt at intimidation. "You dare to insult a legate of the Holy See?!"

Pippin almost laughed at the ploy. "Get out, Sergius. And don't come back. You are no longer welcome in my court."

18

Regensburg

During the week after Sudiger's proposal, Trudi queried noble after noble to gauge their support, knowing her regency hung by a thread. It was clear that Lantfrid had used the two months she and Odilo were away to sow the seeds of rebellion. Only the Christian nobles expressed support, but they were too few in number to make a difference.

Sudiger had arrived midweek to ask for an answer and she put him off, begging for more time due to her grief. His answer was blunt:

"I don't tolerate deceit, milady. I know you've been seeking nobles to come to your aid. And," he said, smiling, "you've only found a handful. You're out of options. Either marry me or lose your regency."

He leaned in, just inches from her face. "And let me be clear. When you do marry me, it won't be a marriage of convenience. I expect you to give yourself to me willingly. I prefer not to use stronger measures, but if I must?" He left the threat hanging in the air. "We'll announce the engagement at the next council meeting." He grabbed her chin. "And make sure there's a smile on your face when we do it."

Once he had departed, she collapsed in her chair, humiliated. She thought about the girl she once had been – the armor-wearing daughter of the great Charles Martel. She had been willing to stand up to the most powerful man in the kingdom to refuse to an arranged marriage, yet here she was, willing to consider marrying a disgusting man to protect her son's legacy. The young girl she had been had nothing to lose. Now a child weighed in the balance, and she would do anything to protect him. The conflict that raged within her was over accepting that fact. She had a new appreciation of the demands made on her father and Sunnichild. They too had made compromises to protect their family.

If only Odilo had not died so soon! Part of her was still angry with him. He should be here with Tassilo. Her son needed a father. She tried to think of Sudiger in that role and shuddered.

In her mind, she heard Sunnichild saying, "You have more power than you know," and wanted to laugh at the absurdity of it. But she didn't laugh. Her mentor was worthy of more respect than that. Sunnichild had fought to the very end for her son and always on her terms.

At week's end, she knew she was out of options and stood before the Bavarian council with Sudiger poised at her side expectantly. He licked his lips as if he were about to feast on a great meal. She had never felt more alone. Sudiger had told several knights in the room of his proposal and word had spread throughout the capital that she soon would wed the comte from Nordgau.

She wanted to weep. She barely had been named regent and already was failing Tassilo and her husband's memory. And the thought of willingly bedding Sudiger appalled her.

She was about to start the meeting when Eta came to the door with Tassilo in her arms. Stunned, Trudi went to her and whispered, "Why have you brought him here?"

Eta looked surprised. "Comte Sudiger said you requested his presence at the council meeting."

A shiver ran down Trudi's spine. The bastard was reminding her of what was at stake; refusal would put her son's life in jeopardy. She looked at Sudiger and his only response was to smirk in acknowledgement.

She kissed her son, a cold fury sweeping over her. With Sudiger, her son's life would *always* be in jeopardy.

She signaled for Hans and whispered instructions in his ear. He approached two of the Christian nobles and together they left the room.

"Be seated," she commanded and waited for the nobles to take their seats. Sudiger remained standing until she nodded her head to him as well. Although he frowned, he took his seat.

"I stand before you today as regent of Duc Tassilo." She nodded toward her son. "It is my responsibility to keep the duchy safe and prosperous until the day he comes of age. I address you today with that in mind.

"There are many in this room calling for war to avenge the massacre in Alemannia. I am not one of them. My husband, Odilo, and I negotiated a settlement with the mayor of the palace that forestalls the need for war, and I have given my word to uphold it.

"As the daughter of Charles Martel" – she caught several faces frowning at the name – "I am no stranger to war and have no hesitation in waging it. You know this, as I've been tested before. When Odilo was away fighting at the River Lech, I withstood a siege to this city. Lantfrid makes a good case for his succession to the duchy of Alemannia but fails to acknowledge that it was his uncle Theudebald that I faced. Instead of fighting alongside Odilo, he chose to raid our armory and lay siege to our palace. That is the Alemannia for which you are beating the drums of war."

She watched Lantfrid shift uncomfortably in his seat as a number of the nobles looked his way. "I've been told that if I oppose Lantfrid's war of vengeance, there will be a challenge to my regency." She took a deep breath. "If it avoids a senseless war, I welcome such a challenge. What kind of ruler would I be if I coveted the power to rule Bavaria above the interests of Bavaria itself?"

She glanced at Sudiger. "I've also been told that, if I wish to persevere, I will require a champion at my side to protect my regency, my life, and the life of my son."

She paused. "Unfortunately, no one has volunteered to be that champion."

Heads turned to Sudiger in confusion. The comte, too, looked perplexed. A murmur swept through the council.

Trudi waited for their attention to return. "One noble, however, has offered me a chance to barter my body for that protection. He offered me the chance to bear his son, so that his progeny would be in line for succession after Tassilo." She sneered. "You can imagine how safe Tassilo would be after such an arrangement." She heard a few chuckles in response. "Finally, this noble wants me to sanctify his arrangement with the rite of marriage. I will not."

Sudiger stood, his face contorted with fury. He grabbed her arm, whispering, "You stupid bitch! You will pay for this!"

Trudi wrested her arm from him and walked to the aisle near the door, raising her voice to speak directly to the nobles. "Again, what kind of leader would I be if I yielded so easily under pressure?

"I have put the palace and the armory under guard and enlisted a number of nobles to defend my regency in the face of this council's desire for war."

Several nobles were standing and shouting their objection. Trudi shouted over them. "I will not give up Tassilo's legacy without a fight. I will not barter my body. I will not sanctify it with marriage. I will not produce another man's heir. I refuse to yield on behalf of Bavaria!"

As if on cue, the doors to the hall opened. Hans led dozens of armed soldiers into the room. They marched down the aisles past her to position themselves between the nobles and Trudi and they created a perimeter around the hall.

Trudi walked to Eta and picked up Tassilo. She carried him to the exit and escorted him back to the palace surrounded by a phalanx of guards. There, she waited for the hounds of hell to break loose.

* * *

The standoff became a public curiosity. People gathered outside the palace to see whether anyone would attack. Days passed and then a week, but not one came. Slowly, the crowds receded. The only people to come and go were guards securing supplies.

After the second week, Eingard of Kurbayern came to visit. The comte came alone and approached the palace weaponless. Trudi sent word to admit him and to have him wait for her in the great hall. For effect, she donned the plates of her armor. While she knew it wouldn't impress a military man, she hoped it would convey her willingness to fight for her regency.

She enjoyed putting them on and tried to think of the last time she had worn them. It had been years. She adjusted the leather straps to accommodate the slightly wider hips she had earned birthing Tassilo. And then, satisfied with the result, she made her way to the great hall.

"Comte Eingard," she said, striding into the room with a confidence she didn't feel.

He stood. If he was surprised to see her in armor, he didn't reveal it. "Milady."

She motioned for them to sit. "How may I help you?"

"The council met after your announcement. It was quite a spirited discussion. Many nobles were appalled by Sudiger's ultimatum. We recognize the precariousness of your situation and were impressed by your defense of Tassilo and the palace."

Trudi waited for him to get to the point.

"While it was agreed in principle that Lantfrid has a right to reclaim Alemannia, we have decided to wait until spring before choosing to aid him in that quest. If there is to be an expedition, I have been chosen to lead it.

"As I promised, my one stipulation is that you and the future duc were not to be harmed. The council has agreed and, once the Alemanni situation is decided, we will decide the question of your regency. Until then, the council will rule Bavaria."

Trudi held up her hand. She needed time to think. Her immediate concern, that Tassilo's life was in danger, may have been resolved, but she had lost her role as regent. Although the council had promised to reconsider the decision, it was unlikely that her regency would be restored. If the council rescinded it once, they could again.

"And if I refuse?"

Eingard shrugged. "Unless you can overwhelm the members of the council, there is little to be accomplished by opposing. I have guaranteed you and your son's safety. What more can you achieve?"

"I can refuse you the armory."

Eingard nodded. "That is one of the reasons I am here. I have been trying to avoid the spilling of Bavarian blood. The nobles you have recruited will not be able to sustain an organized siege of the armory and still protect the palace. There just aren't enough of them. And while I respect the strategic effort to stop our aid to Lantfrid, it will only lead to the death of our fellow countrymen."

"If you truly want to avoid spilling Bavarian blood, you could refrain from attacking the armory."

Eingard smiled. "Having seen how you respond to threats I am hoping we can come to an amicable agreement. Civil wars are unpredictable, and I worry that if it should spiral out of control, no one will be able to guarantee the safety of you and your son."

It was a fair point. She doubted that her nobles could withstand a concerted attack on the armory and once the fighting started, it might lead to the doors of the palace. Trudi wasn't ready to give up on her regency, but she didn't see a clear path to keep it.

"What of Sudiger?"

Eingard shook his head. "He has a substantial following, but his effort to use you to seize control over the regency tainted his influence. He made a bid to lead the council in your absence but was defeated by a narrow margin." Eingard frowned. "You have made a powerful enemy, milady."

"Sudiger will always be a threat. Should you choose to fight for Lantfrid, we'll be vulnerable the moment you leave for Alemannia."

"I can only tell you that the council was adamant about you and your son's safety."

She liked Eingard. He negotiated in a way that forced her to listen. And his reasoning was sound. She could see that there was little advantage in starting a civil war over an armory that she couldn't long defend.

"You are very good at this, Eingard."

He nodded in acknowledgement.

"Since you're waiting until spring to decide if you'll aid Lantfrid, there is no need to attack – or defend – the armory. I would suggest that we let the winter months pass us by before we conclude that part of our discussion."

Eingard nodded.

"And, as long as Tassilo's and my safety are guaranteed, I accept that the council will rule until the Alemanni matter is resolved."

"Thank you, milady." He stood.

They grabbed forearms to seal their agreement.

"I am not your enemy, Eingard."

"Nor I yours."

19

Paris

Pippin made his way to the main hall of the compound to meet with Gunther and Childebrand. The day did little to help his mood. Grey clouds covered the sky, leeching the colors from the landscape, and the air was like a cold, wet shroud that sapped the life from all it touched. Gunther had just arrived from the Twelve Counties to report on Gripho. Pippin wasn't hopeful that he would bear good news.

"He never arrived at the palace of Le Mans," Gunther said.

Pippin's thoughts turned black. Gripho had betrayed him. There would be no peace. "And Drusseau's men?"

"They're there but couldn't be less hospitable. You would have thought I was Saracen by the way they greeted me."

The news confirmed a report by the Bishop of Würzburg, who had arrived the past week fleeing from Bavaria. He had reported that Gripho had issued a call to arms from Saxony and that the entire eastern region, including Bavaria, was in revolt. The pagan nobility had seized control, and Trudi was being held as a prisoner in her own palace. The war Pippin had sought to prevent seemed inevitable.

"We should mobilize before they can pool their resources," Childebrand said.

Gunther nodded. "It's the right strategy. Fighting their armies individually is far preferable to facing them together."

"We'll need reserves for a revolt this large," Pippin said. "Even with the combined army of eight thousand men, it won't be enough. Send messengers throughout Austrasia to meet us at Cologne. We'll head first to Saxony and then, if need be, sweep south towards Alemannia and Bavaria."

Pippin called upon the Neustrian nobles to gather with him at the Rouvray Forest. Only those nobles who had pledged their hands to either him or Childebrand appeared. Those who had pledged directly to Childeric refused his call.

Pippin led them across the bridge to the Isle de la Cité and was confronted before the palace gates.

"State your interest!" a guardsman demanded.

Pippin waved off Childebrand, who was about to run the man through. "I wish to speak to Comte Drusseau."

With a grunt, the guardsman spun on his heel and disappeared through the gate. Several minutes later, Drusseau appeared. He was dressed in an elegant robe and accompanied by three men-at-arms.

"Milord Pippin!" Drusseau bowed formally. "To what do I owe this honor?"

"You refused my call to arms."

"Forgive me, milord, but I thought it was agreed that I and the Knights in Christ would protect the king, while you protected the kingdom."

"The kingdom is in revolt, and I require all able-bodied men-at-arms to join us – including the bulk of your Knights in Christ and your men in the Twelve Counties. You may leave a contingent of knights behind to protect the king, but the real threat to his person is not here; it is in the east."

"If you are speaking of your brother Gripho," Drusseau countered, "I hardly consider him a threat. He hasn't spoken out against the king. The only one who has done so is you, milord."

"Nevertheless, he has declared war."

"Against you, milord. Not against the king."

"So, you have chosen to side with him?"

"As I recall, milord, you asked me to offer my hands in service to your brother. Do you wish me to renounce that vow?"

"He has renounced his to me."

"Yet, your father declared that you both have a right to succession. This looks to be a civil dispute between you and your brother. I wish to remain neutral and, as His Majesty's protector, I refuse to leave my post to get involved."

"He's a slippery one," Childebrand whispered.

For the second time, Pippin felt that Drusseau had outflanked him politically. He could delay the army's departure and attack Drusseau and the palace – which would still look like he was attacking the king – or leave Drusseau in place and leave for Saxony.

Delaying would risk having his military face the superior force of a combined Saxon-Bavarian army. Departing would leave Drusseau with the support of the nobles who remain behind and his army in the Twelve Counties. He could potentially take control of Neustria.

Pippin scowled. "Refusing my call will have consequences, Drusseau. I can't afford to delay our departure. I will leave a regiment behind under Gunther's command to ensure the safety and security of Neustria." It was a regiment he needed in the east, but the risk to Neustria was too large. "We will revisit your 'neutrality' when I return. And I can assure you, I will return."

"Then Godspeed, milord Pippin." Drusseau smiled broadly as he bowed.

"Fuck that bastard," Childebrand whispered under his breath.

* * *

Pippin returned to his compound, trying to hold his fury in check. Drusseau's arrogance and insolence gnawed at his composure. On a battlefield, Pippin would have already killed him, but here? Here, he could play the politics of court as if it were a musical instrument and keep Pippin dancing to his tune.

Every turn of the road had been a challenge. It was as if the world was conspiring against him. He and Carloman had beaten back the rebellions, only to have Carloman massacre the Alemanni. He had negotiated a peace with Odilo only to have Odilo die unexpectedly. He had freed Gripho and given him and Drusseau a substantial role in the ruling of the kingdom, only to be betrayed. He growled as he ascended the stairs to his room. As soon as he was alone, Pippin picked up a chair and smashed it against the floor until it broke into pieces.

"Feel better?" Bertrada stood in the doorway, a look of concern on her face.

Embarrassed, he dropped the remains of the chair. Growling in frustration, he tried to let go of his anger. "I'm sorry."

"You don't need forgiveness from me," she said, "but you owe that chair an apology."

Pippin laughed and with a sheepish smile, he took her into his arms. She had become the one constant in his life. It struck him that he'd never seen her more beautiful. Where hard lines once had defined her countenance, her face now shined with happiness. There was also a stateliness about her that hadn't been present when she was a girl, and her pregnancy lent a beatific grace to her stature.

"What troubles you, my love?"

He sighed in response. "For the first time in my life, I thought peace in the kingdom was a possibility, but clearly, I was mistaken. War is inevitable. Gripho is calling on the eastern duchies to rebel."

"You can't stop it?"

"I've tried. Nothing I do seems to matter."

"When do you go?"

"We leave in two days. Can you and Charles be ready by then?"

She pulled away from him, her face pale. "I – I can't."

"Why not?"

"I'm too far along." Her hand caressed her swollen belly. "And there's been some blood."

"We'll put you in a cart."

She shook her head. "If I leave, I'll lose the child."

A sudden fear gripped him. "But it's not safe here! I'm leaving a regiment, but Drusseau is sure to attack. I can't afford for you to be here. You'll be a target."

She put her hand to his cheek. "I'm always a target. Leave Hélène with me and we'll be fine."

Pippin shook his head. It was another impossible choice. Either way had its dangers. He couldn't afford to lose her.

"I can't go with you, Pippin."

Looking into her eyes, he could see her resolve. And he knew better than to force her compliance. He had lost her heart once; he would never lose it again.

He nodded in acceptance. "I will call on Hélène."

She kissed him but he couldn't escape the feeling that he might lose her. They had finally found a small window of happiness, and he prayed that they might keep it. Everything with this war was slipping from his control.

She kissed him again, this time more urgently, teasing his tongue with hers and hooking her heel around his leg. She pulled his hips toward her and he felt his body respond to the warmth of her. A familiar ache spread through him and he groaned her name.

"What you doin'?" Little Charles was pulling on Bertrada's shift. The servant assigned with watching him had led him into the room unannounced. She looked horrified for having interrupted them. "I'm so sorry!" she blurted out.

Bertrada laughed and Pippin picked up Charles and held him between the two of them.

"I'm going to miss you two," Pippin said. Bertrada was kind enough to ignore the tears in his eyes.

* * *

The next morning Pippin met with Bishop Burchard of Würzburg. A big man with thinning hair, the bishop was an English disciple of

Boniface. The two had spent years doing missionary work in Hesse and Thuringia. Like Boniface, Burchard had huge, calloused hands and looked more like a blacksmith than a man of the cloth.

Pippin welcomed him and the two sat in his sitting room. "I hope you have found our accommodations here comfortable?"

"Quite. We bishops in the east live a more Spartan life than do those here in the west. You could have left me to sleep on the floor and I would be at ease."

Pippin decided he liked this man. "Does Boniface always recruit missionaries who are as large as he is?"

Burchard chuckled. "There is some value to being as big as the local chieftains. They value men with large bellies." He rubbed his own for emphasis. "It's a sign that you are powerful enough to enjoy more than your fair share of food."

Pippin offered a wry smile. "Then you must have been considered a very powerful man." They both laughed.

Pippin grew serious. "I want to thank you again for your account of the rebellion brewing in the eastern duchies."

"Pagans, milord. It is the pagans who are rebelling."

"As Würzburg is in Bavaria, I was hoping you could provide some news about my sister, Hiltrude."

Burchard had a pained look on his face. "I'm afraid what news I have isn't good. She's lost her regency. The Bavarian nobles backed Lantfrid's claim to the duchy in Alemannia and have risen to the call to arms issued by your brother Gripho. Absent that call, her regency might have survived. She and Tassilo, however, remain in the palace under guard. From what I've heard, they are safe for the time being."

"Who is governing in her stead?"

"The council, milord. Although, Comte Sudiger seems to have his hand in every directive issued."

"How universal is the uprising?"

"Gripho's blood ties to the Agilolfing family has solidified the opposition. They see him as a pagan mayor, equal in standing to you and

Carloman. Now that he has claimed his birthright, they've flocked to his banner. The massacre of the Alemanni nobility was the opportunity he needed."

Pippin shook his head. He had underestimated Gripho. In his mind, Gripho was still a boy who was barely tested on the battlefield. He couldn't imagine that nobles would follow him. The pull of the Agilolfing ties and the lure of a pagan savior seemed to be enough to throw the entire kingdom into war. He should have left him in Neufchateau.

Pippin realized he hadn't spoken in a while and that Burchard was politely waiting for him to return to himself. "Will you be returning to Würzburg?"

The big man looked pained. "For the moment, no. While a devotee of the martyrs, I have no intention of becoming one. If I and my priests had remained, we would be captured and become a symbol of pagan superiority over the Church. I have no interest in playing such a role. I'll return when the rebellion is finished."

Pippin nodded. "Sometimes a tactical retreat is the best strategy. Would you be willing to take on a mission for me?"

Burchard frowned. "What sort of mission?"

"I need to send an embassy to his holiness the pope."

At that, the big man sat upright in his chair. "I would be honored. But may I ask why me? You could send for Sergius or ask Boniface. What value do I bring?"

"I would prefer to keep Boniface here and, to speak plainly, I no longer trust Sergius to deliver my messages or to convey the pope's wishes accurately."

"When would you like me to leave?"

"As soon as possible." Pippin waved to a guard at the door and a clergyman was ushered into the room. He was a short, stocky man with greying temples who looked as hardened as a plowman. Of his features, however, his eyes were the most compelling. They were as grey as a wolf's eyes. And they looked as fearless. "This is Chaplain Fulrad. I'd like him to accompany you. I'll send you a small contingent of men to guard your passage as well, but Fulrad is there to protect your person."

"I hardly need such attention," Burchard said.

"With the east in revolt, it's wise to take precautions. Fulrad is the son of Fulrad, my weapons master, and one of the finest swordsmen in the kingdom. I was disappointed when he chose the clergy over the military, but you could be in no better hands for your journey."

"And what is my embassy to ask of His Excellency the pope?"

"I want you to ask Zachary whether it is good or not that the king of the Franks should wield no royal power."

Burchard's eyes squinted with thought. "A dangerous question, milord."

"That's why I'm sending Fulrad with you."

* * *

Pippin left Gunther in Paris with a single regiment of two thousand men to hold the city while he and Childebrand took the remaining three regiments east toward Reims. Despite his misgivings, he had left Bertrada and Charles behind under Lady Hélène's watchful eye.

It was unusual for the army to mobilize so early in the spring. A winter chill still hung in the air and the skies remained grey for most of the day. Pippin set a stiff pace, intending to catch the Saxons before Theodoric was ready, but the weather seemed to sap the men's mood with every step.

On the third day of their march Childebrand pulled his mount beside Pippin's. "There were more desertions today."

"How many?"

"A dozen knights and their retinues. All former Knights in Christ."

Pippin nodded. He expected some betrayal from the zealots. Quashing the religious order wouldn't be easy, and with Drusseau holding the palace, there was bound to be some that would desert. Still, it wasn't a good sign. They clearly believed that Drusseau would prevail. Either that, or they wished to be martyred.

"Make note of their names. There'll be consequences."

Childebrand grunted. "Not soon enough."

They rode in silence for a few minutes before Pippin asked, "How is Miette?"

If Childebrand was surprised by the question, he didn't show it. "She's a surprise, that one. I can see how she captured your eye. At first, I thought she was just a trollop dressed as nobility, but there's much more to her than I realized."

"Yes, there is." Pippin was glad he could speak of her to Childebrand without getting a tongue-lashing. He still cared for Miette, even if he couldn't be with her.

Childebrand was warming to the subject. "In addition to grooming her to be an assassin, Hélène has put some strange ideas in her head. She's got this fixation on 'justice,' as if that's how the world should work."

"It can make for an interesting discussion," Pippin said, thinking of his many debates with Hélène.

"Well, based on her notions about that, she's bound and determined to liberate Drusseau's wife."

Pippin didn't understand. "Liberate? From where?"

"The palace. Apparently, Drusseau and Childeric are using her the way they used Miette. And Miette's not letting it go. She wanted me to take her from her husband the way you took Miette."

Pippin shook his head. "Not a good plan."

"That's what I told her. But she and Hélène have this idea about justice that –"

"Hélène's involved?"

"Well, yes and no. She agrees with Miette that Drusseau's wife needs to be saved but believes, as I do, that it won't work unless Drusseau rebels. Then his life and wealth are forfeit."

A knot formed in Pippin's stomach. He hadn't planned for this. "Miette won't wait. Listening to reason was never her strongest trait. And Drusseau's a proud man. He'll spare no resource to find them."

Childebrand frowned. "If she succeeds it will endanger Bertrada and Charles."

"My fear, exactly."

20

Paris

Miette was furious with Childebrand's decision to delay saving Charlotte. He hadn't seen the look of despair in the woman's eyes or seen the scars laced across her arms. He didn't know how close she was to madness.

How could he? He had never suffered the kind of ruin that Childeric was capable of dispensing. He had never been broken so far that his own degradation would be considered a reward. He had never known shame and humiliation so absolute that death itself was a reprieve.

Her anger at his ignorance touched off the horror of her own memories at Childeric's hands. Shame welled within her at her initial naivete; she had reveled in the wantonness of his games until their depravity escalated beyond her control. Then the game became how much of her dignity he could destroy. She recoiled with the memory of him masturbating above her face while his men violated every orifice in her body.

Miette quieted the trembling that had taken over her hands. She couldn't wait until Childebrand decided the "timing was right." She had to save Charlotte now.

Unfortunately, when she approached Lady Hélène, her mentor agreed with Childebrand. "Part of administering justice is knowing when to do it. If we attempt to take her now, we'll likely fail. Then, no one would be served. And if we succeed, where will we take her to keep her safe?

"They already suspect you so your home will be the first they search. And the leap to me is not a large one, so mine will be next. We must wait for the right moment to get her out. Have patience."

Miette nodded her head but remained unmoved. She refused to wait. She would find a way to free Charlotte, even if she had to do it alone.

Her biggest obstacle was Drusseau. For some reason, the man paralyzed her with terror. What good were all the skills she had learned from Lady Hélène if she cowered before men like him? Her weakness appalled her. She would have to ensure the man was away or distracted.

But try as she might, she couldn't devise a strategy where she could control all the factors necessary for a quiet escape. She had an idea but would just have to invent her plan as it unfolded.

She was confident that she could make her way into the palace: her husband regularly took her there and often left her to her own devices while he conducted his affairs. Sometimes he sought out Drusseau to discuss political strategy, others he searched for more discreet encounters with other men. She never knew beforehand which kind of visit it was to be. Either way, she'd have no more than an hour to retrieve Charlotte and effect their departure.

She used her next two visits to survey and explore the palace. She noted the presence of guards, stairwells, servants, and exits. She watched as guests arrived, where they went, and where they stopped to converse. She memorized the rhythm of the place: when people ate, prayed, conversed, and celebrated.

When at last she was ready, she waited patiently for Ragomfred's next visit. It came early one morning, just a week after Pippin's departure.

Miette and her husband swept through the front gates as if they were royalty themselves. He was well celebrated among the faithful even if she was viewed with some suspicion. After greeting several other couples who had just arrived in the outer courtyard, they made their way into the palace itself.

Ragomfred promptly excused himself for parts unknown: Miette assumed in search of male companionship. She casually nodded to passersby, making it look as if she were heading toward the palace garden, but at the last minute she ducked down a servants' stairway to the lower level.

After the initial shock of seeing her in the lower level, the servants, of course, immediately averted their eyes and Miette had no trouble working her way through the underbelly of the palace to its far end, where the living quarters were housed.

Childeric's rooms were on the topmost floor while Drusseau and the other favored nobles were housed on the floors below.

As it was still early in the day servants were working their way through the rooms collecting chamber pots and replacing linen. Miette climbed the stairs alongside them, passing several rooms on her way. She could see some of the nobles still dressing and tried to move quickly past their doors to avoid being seen.

When she finally reached Charlotte's rooms, she hesitated, listening at the door to determine if Drusseau was still there. Hearing nothing, she took a deep breath and strode inside as if she were as confident as Hélène.

Charlotte was dressed in nothing but an undergarment tunic. Her hair was matted and tangled. Although she was sitting in a chair by the window, her eyes didn't seem to register what was outside it. A servant was trying to straighten her bed. With a wave, Miette dismissed the woman and knelt beside Charlotte's chair. Charlotte had yet to acknowledge her and Miette feared that she was so befuddled, she wouldn't recognize her.

"Charlotte, it's Miette. I've come to take you away from here."

It was as if her words had to seep through Charlotte's ears to reach her. The woman slowly shook her head. "It's too late. There's nothing left of me."

"Then there's nothing to lose." Miette took off her clothes.

That got Charlotte's attention. She turned her head and looked up at Miette quizzically. "What are you doing?"

Miette, down to her undergarments, threw her dress on the bed and started pinning her hair up onto her head. "I'm taking you away from here." She reached into her bag and pulled out two sets of servant's clothes. She tossed one to Charlotte. "Here, put these on." Charlotte didn't catch it and it landed in a heap on the ground.

Picking up the one for herself, Miette quickly stepped into it. "Come on," she chided. "We don't have much time."

Charlotte still hadn't moved.

"We could try just walking out the front door," Miette explained. "My guess is that your husband has standing orders for the guards to stop you. Plus, I'll be recognized, and we won't get too far before they track us down.

"My way, two servant girls leave with baskets to buy bread, and no one notices until we're far from the palace. Of course, to succeed, you'll have to dress the part and cover your hair." She put on a servant's cap and then an apron. "Or you could just sit there until Childeric sends for you and watch him ejaculate on your face."

Charlotte turned, her hands trembling. "We'll never get out. They'll catch us."

"Let me help you." Miette moved behind her and began to wrestle the woman's hair into coherency. She had most of it pinned up when she heard heavy footsteps behind her. Miette's hands froze in place, and it took every bit of her courage not to run.

"So, you've decided to dress," Drusseau sneered from the doorway.

Miette forced her hands to continue but she had trouble breathing.

"I suppose I should be grateful. People have been asking for you at court."

Miette realized he thought she was a servant. Keeping her head down, she turned, curtsied, and made to leave the room.

"No. Stay, I want her dressed." Walking to the bed, he fingered Miette's dress. "Although, she's got better than this to wear."

Miette kept her face hidden behind Charlotte and resumed fixing her hair.

Drusseau returned to the door. "Wear something special. Tonight, we'll be celebrating with the king."

After he left, Charlotte needed no more convincing. Miette finished pinning up the woman's hair and helped her step into her servant's clothes. Once her apron was in place, Miette took her by the hand and led her downstairs.

Heading back through the servants' area, Miette couldn't help but notice how frenzied the staff had become as they went about their tasks. The underground was alive with commotion. Servant boys ran through the corridors with panicked looks on their faces and everyone had their hands full. In the kitchen pots were banging and cooks were shouting. It was as if half of Neustria was coming for dinner.

Miette stopped a young servant boy. "What's going on?"

"They're closing the gates. There's going to be a battle."

Miette swore under her breath. Drusseau must have decided it was time to attack. Her mind raced as she sought an alternative to escaping through the main gate. She couldn't find one. They were trapped. They could make their way back to Charlotte's rooms and change back into their normal clothes, but Miette couldn't bring herself to leave Charlotte again.

"What'ya think you two're doing? Having a holiday?"

It was an older woman, clearly someone in charge of the servants. Miette, however, had prepared for such an interruption. "Lady Ragomfred requested us to attend her in the garden."

That drew a harrumph from the woman. "Well, her traitorship will just have to wait. There's too much to do and too few hands to do it. I can't afford for the two of you to spend the morning getting tea for the likes of that whore. Come along! I've got bedpans to clean and they won't be cleaning themselves now, will they?"

Miette wasn't ready to give up the ruse. They'd have to play along. She ducked her head and curtsied. After a moment, Charlotte mimicked her, and the matron led them down a long corridor to a room where dozens of chamber pots were stacked. The smell was overwhelming.

A small doorway was open. Miette poked her head outside to find a staircase leading down to a small landing by the river. A lone woman knelt on it cleaning chamber pots in the current.

"Well, get yerselves going!" the matron shouted. Miette grabbed two chamber pots and, giving one to Charlotte, headed down the stairs. Charlotte scurried after her.

"What do we do now?" Charlotte whispered.

"First, we get out of these clothes." Miette removed her apron and began pulling off her dress. Seeing Charlotte hesitate, Miette gave voice to the urgency she felt. "Hurry! We don't have much time."

Fortunately, Charlotte began to obey. The servant still on the landing had dropped her chamber pot and was backing away from them up the stairs. Miette grabbed her by the collar and dragged her back down. "Not 'til we're gone," she cautioned.

Turning back to Charlotte she asked, "Can you swim?"

"No."

"Time to learn." Miette pushed her into the Seine.

* * *

The shock of the cold water and the strength of the current were overwhelming. Miette, who had learned to swim as a young girl, worried that she had made a fatal error in judgement. She fought to the surface and searched for Charlotte, while battling desperately against the pull of the river. She found Charlotte downstream from her, struggling to keep her head above the surface. Her arms flailed uselessly, and panic filled her eyes.

Miette let the current pull her toward Charlotte, careful to keep her distance. She had been warned enough as a child that drowning people will take their saviors down with them if given half a chance. Miette kicked against the current to come up behind Charlotte. The woman tried to grab her but fortunately, Charlotte's lack of skill in water prevented her. Miette grabbed the back of her tunic and kicked toward shore.

It had been years since she had last been in the water and she began to tire far sooner than she expected. "Don't fight me!" she shouted at Charlotte. "You're making it harder. Let me do the work!" Charlotte, however, continued to struggle, desperately trying to take hold of Miette's arm. Still far from shore, Miette began to doubt her ability to make it. A burning ache seized her legs and arms while each kick barely moved them closer to shore.

Charlotte lunged again and this time grabbed hold of her arm. The additional weight began to pull Miette under. With all her might she pulled Charlotte close and punched her in the face. Stunned, Charlotte released her arm and Miette, again, kicked toward shore with Charlotte in tow.

The current took them well over a mile from the Isle de la Cité before they reached a dock on the west bank of the river. Straining her neck, Miette could see no one nearby to help them. She pulled Charlotte to a ladder and waited while the woman pulled herself out of the water. Miette followed and collapsed on the pier, too exhausted to stand.

When her body no longer felt like it was made of stone, she sat up and looked to Charlotte. The woman was shivering nearby, her arms wrapped around her legs.

"For someone ready to take their own life, you sure fought for it out in the water," Miette chided.

Charlotte's eyes squinted and she nodded. "You're right. I don't want to die." She shivered. "Especially not out there."

"I'm sorry about that. I didn't see any other way out. At least we didn't have to wash the chamber pots."

A smirk took Charlotte's lips, and then she lowered her eyes. "Thank you for coming to get me."

Miette stood and extended her hand to Charlotte. "It was the right thing to do, but we've got to keep moving. We're still in danger."

Their hair wet, their undergarments thin, and their feet bare, they looked like two street urchins. Miette guided them through back alleys and side streets to keep from being seen. Although she didn't expect her husband or Drusseau to discover their absence for some time, she didn't want to draw attention unnecessarily. Drusseau eventually would track them down. The fewer people who saw them, the better.

She made for Pippin's compound. Being situated on the west bank, it was the closest refuge she could imagine. With Pippin and Childebrand gone, however, she might not be as welcome as she hoped.

They arrived after an hour of walking. Their journey had completed their appearance as street urchins – their feet were bloodied, and their tunics smeared with mud – but Miette felt nothing but euphoria. She had freed Charlotte! She approached Pippin's compound triumphantly.

A guard with a pike barred her way. "Keep moving, *putain*. There's nothing for you here."

Miette was stunned. "Putain?! Do you jest? Stand aside, or I'll have you whipped!"

"I said, 'keep moving,' woman!"

"I am the Lady Ragomfred! I demand to see the Lady Bertrada."

"And I'm his holiness the pope. Keep moving." He used the heel of his pike to propel her down the street.

Furious, Miette pivoted back toward him and caught the end of his pike in her hands. The guard tried to pull the weapon away from her, leaving his lower body open. Miette savagely kicked the side of the man's knee. As his leg gave way, she slammed her elbow into his face. Blood spouted from his nose.

Howling with rage, he shoved her away with his left arm and brought the point of the pike down to face her. Miette crouched, waiting for him to strike.

"What the hell is going on here!" Gunther stood in the doorway.

"This bitch attacked me!" the guard said, trying to hold back the blood from his nose.

Gunther turned to confront her. "Move along now before – oh sweet Jesus!" He rolled his eyes. "With all this commotion, I should have expected you would be at the heart of it. Come along, Miette. I'll send for Bertrada and let her decide what to do with you."

"I have news for you as well," Miette said, "and there's little time to waste."

Gunther growled. "What's so important?"

"They've closed the gate to the palace. Drusseau's regiments are preparing to attack from the east."

"And how do you know that?"

Miette nodded her head toward Charlotte.

Gunther looked at Charlotte trying to see through all the mud and disheveled hair. His eyes widened in surprise. "Oh, my lord! What have you done?"

* * *

While Gunther left to prepare the army, Bertrada sent Miette and the Lady Drusseau to bathe before meeting with them. This gave her time to consider her options before dealing with the problem they represented. It also gave her time to send for Hélène.

News of the attack was unwelcome. No matter how hard she tried to avoid it, war seemed to follow her. She had hoped that the regiment Pippin had left with Gunther would forestall a revolt from the Knights in Christ, but clearly Drusseau's ambition overrode any hesitation they might have had.

She had never met Drusseau but Gunther believed him to be a formidable opponent. "It's harsh along the Breton March," he'd said. "With the Bretons on one side and the Gascons on the other, they're constantly at war."

And now, Miette had taken the man's wife and brought her here. What was she thinking? She tried to control her anger. Pippin had started this; he was responsible. He should have never brought Miette into their home at Quierzy. It had filled Miette's head with ideas – ideas that Pippin could love her, ideas that she could live a life apart from her husband. Was the woman always going to be a thorn in her side?

She shifted uneasily; the pregnancy was far more uncomfortable than her last.

After an hour, the two women entered Bertrada's sitting room. They each had bathed and been given one of her dresses to wear. Bertrada frowned at how good Miette looked in it.

"Milady Bertrada, may I present the Lady Drusseau?" Miette announced.

Bertrada welcomed them and despite the early hour offered wine. Once they had been seated and served, she decided to be blunt. "Why have you come here, Miette?"

"My apologies for adding to the burdens of your condition, Bertrada, but we are desperate. Charlotte is suffering from the same fate that I endured at the hands of Childeric. She's been raped, tortured, and broken. I couldn't stand aside and watch them destroy her any longer. Unfortunately, my efforts to bring her out of the palace were thwarted by the closure of the palace gate; our only escape was by way of the Seine. Without clothes and resources, we were vulnerable and our ability to escape impaired. I knew your compound was nearby and sought help."

Bertrada didn't trust Miette, but she believed she spoke the truth about Charlotte. She kept her face neutral. "Do you seek refuge?"

Miette's eyes flared. "Do you not offer it?"

"I would like to know more about Lady Drusseau's situation."

"Her situation is obvious. Her life is in jeopardy, and she's in need."

Bertrada stiffened. "Yet she remains the property of her husband. Isn't he within his rights to demand her return?"

"By law, yes. By God, no."

"That makes no sense."

"If you believe that we are children of God, we can't be property. How can a child of God be someone's property?"

Bertrada scoffed. "Are you daft? Who told you that?"

"I did." Hélène strode into the room. She looked at Miette. "Is it true that they've closed the palace gate and the attack is imminent?"

"Yes," Miette said.

"Then we all must go. You as well, Bertrada."

Bertrada was confused. She had hoped that Hélène would help her deal with Miette. "Why must I go?"

Hélène shrugged as if she was stating the obvious. "The compound is vulnerable and capturing you would give Drusseau leverage."

"Does having Charlotte give us leverage?"

"It depends on how much her husband cares for her. From everything Miette has told me, probably very little."

"Then why are we saving her?"

Hélène's eyes grew hard "For the same reason I helped you when Childeric's men threatened your life."

The rebuke shamed her. Hélène was right, of course. That damned Miette always brought out the worst in her. She shifted uncomfortably and nodded her assent. "Where will we go?"

"The only safe place now is with Gunther's regiment. And it will be safe only so long as the regiment survives."

* * *

Although Gunther had known that Drusseau might attack with the military units from the Twelve Counties, he was surprised, nonetheless. Attempting to seize Neustria was a brazen move, even for Drusseau, and completely reliant on the failure of Pippin's campaign in the east. If Pippin returned with even half his army, Drusseau would still face a force twice the size of his own. And if Gunther was confident of anything, it was that Pippin would return with far more than that.

The regiment Pippin had left him was well blooded. He had drilled the men over the past two months, weeding out the poor commanders and balancing the units so that he could count on them equally if the need arrived.

Early scouting reports put the number of troops from the Twelve Counties at five hundred more men than Gunther but fewer cavalry. That alone didn't give him pause; he would put his men up against any troops he had seen in his forty years of fighting. His problem was that he likely would be fighting on two fronts. Drusseau's decision to close the gates of the palace meant that he was sending the eight hundred men guarding the palace into the field.

The solution, as he saw it, was to leave the city and relocate to a more defensible position. Unfortunately, Pippin had ordered him to stand his ground if Drusseau attacked.

That command left him with few options. To concentrate his forces, he had withdrawn all the troops patrolling the city and called up the men-at-arms housed by nobles still loyal to Pippin. He ordered defensive barricades dug east of his position, facing the city, to match those in the west facing the troops from the Twelve Counties.

He had begun to feel like he had control over the things he could control when an aide sent him running to the picket line.

"What's going on here?" he bellowed.

One of the guards stepped forward. "The Lady Bertrada is asking for you."

Gunther frowned. Coming to the eastern picket, he found the Lady Hélène, Bertrada, little Charles, Catherine and her two children, as well as Lady Drusseau and Miette.

"This wasn't the plan," Gunther said.

"It is now," Hélène said.

"You can bring in everyone but those two." He pointed to Miette and Charlotte.

"I don't like it any more than you do, but I won't abandon either of them. This is the only way."

Gunther could see the resolve in her eyes. "We are going to be attacked on both sides in a matter of days. You're bringing them directly into harm's way!"

"We're already in harm's way, Gunther." Bertrada stepped forward. "Now, stop making this difficult and order your men to provide us quarters. You will admit these women. It's the only solution. If you don't, we'll be captured within the day and become leverage against Pippin. Surely you can see that."

Gunther didn't like it, but he couldn't refuse Bertrada. "All right. Let them in and see that they get tents in the center of camp." Assessing their number he added, "Better yet, give them my tent."

"Thank you, Gunther." Bertrada and Charles made their way past the guard.

Miette turned to Charlotte. "You must stay with Hélène. She can protect you."

"You are not staying?" The woman looked near panicked.

"I can be more useful at home. No one knows I helped you escape. If I return home they won't know where you are. Stay with Hélène. She can protect you far better than I can. If you're with her, you'll be safe."

Hélène put her arm around the Lady Drusseau and led her into the camp. "Come with me. We can protect you here."

Gunther watched them go. Only Miette remained by his side. "A hell of a mess you started, Miette. I hope you know what you're doing."

"It was the right thing to do."

Gunther grunted. "At least you won't be staying."

Miette leaned over and kissed him on the cheek. "I love you too, Gunther."

"None of that!" he groused playfully, but in his heart, he knew that taking Lady Drusseau was a mistake. Hélène knew it too. Behind the resolve in her eyes, he'd seen fear. And there was one thing Gunther knew for certain: Hélène didn't fear anything.

21

Regensburg

Although Trudi trusted Eingard, she didn't trust his ability to control the other nobles, especially with Sudiger fomenting dissent. She fortified the palace with a much greater contingent than she had when facing Theudebald three years earlier. She also had stores of grain and food brought in to forestall any siege during the winter months.

Her distrust of Sudiger was so strong, she believed there was nowhere safe outside the palace. As a result, she refused to leave it. At first, it was a relief, a sense of security, but over two months, she began to feel like a prisoner.

She sent for Tobias, just for the sake of his companionship. The wine merchant who had saved her after the death of Bradius arrived with his family in tow and Trudi gave them rooms in the palace. His wife, Mila, was stunned by the opulence of their surroundings and frightened to be in the company of nobility. Trudi did her best to put the woman at ease but knew after the first few days that it would take a great deal of time for her to be comfortable.

Ever her eyes and ears, Tobias informed her that she had far more support among the common folk than she had among the nobles.

"People are tired of war, especially with the Franks. They had hoped your marriage to Odilo was a symbol of peace."

"And the massacre?"

"They remember Theudebald laying siege to your palace, milady. They know he's a bastard."

While Trudi appreciated Tobias's words, they gave her little in the way of solace. Isolated as she was from the nobles, she had no way to influence what was going on at court. So, she decided to concentrate on keeping her household and the palace guard in good spirits.

Over the winter months she had the palace decorated with greenery and held banquets for the few nobles who supported her. She hired troubadours to entertain the commoners in her service. As a result, the palace took on a festive air.

Their revelry lightened Trudi's despondency for much of the winter. But early in the spring, before the streams began to thaw, one of the palace soldiers disappeared. At first, everyone believed that it had been desertion, but a day later he was found dead outside the palace. Another day later, two soldiers on leave vanished. Trudi ordered all those defending the palace to remain inside unless they were accompanied by at least two people. Most of the men quickly agreed to the change.

When even more men were found murdered, Trudi decided that she needed to devise some sort of counterstrike. It had to be Sudiger or Lantfrid. Only they would employ such a plan to weaken morale inside the palace walls. She had ideas for an ambush but needed more information as to how her own men had been lost. She queried some of the men as to where the soldiers were going that made them vulnerable, but no one would tell her. They looked away, almost as if they were embarrassed, and mumbled that they didn't know.

Trudi called for Hans. When he arrived, she confronted him directly. "Where are these men going that leaves them so vulnerable to attack?"

Hans, too, stumbled over his words.

"Out with it! Do you think I ask this lightly? Men are dying out there."

Hans reddened. "It's, uh, it's –"

"Yes?"

"It's Trudiville, milady. They're going to the whorehouses."

Now it was Trudi's turn to redden. When she first arrived in Regensburg, she had banished the prostitutes to a place outside the city. The women retaliated by naming their new home after her and attaching the Frankish "ville" to the ending rather than the local term "burg."

"You mean they're risking their lives for sex?"

It would be impossible for Hans to look any more sheepish. "Yes, milady."

Trudi began to pace. She had suspected that the murders weighed against the morale of the men, but this? She hadn't given it a thought. And, of course, their trips to Trudiville were how they were being targeted.

"Is there a way, Hans, for you to resolve this situation quietly so that the men don't actually have to leave the palace?"

"There might be, milady. I could bring –"

"A way in which I don't have to know?"

Hans nodded.

"Good. Then do that but make sure it is discreet and doesn't make us vulnerable in the process."

"Yes, milady."

"And don't tell anyone I know about it!"

"Yes, milady." Hans bowed to take his leave, trying to suppress the smile on his face.

* * *

Her seclusion within the palace began to wear on Trudi. She grew bored, restless, frustrated, and despondent. Her nightly glass of wine with Tobias quickly became two and then a bottle. They drank so late into the evening that she slept in most mornings. If it weren't for Tobias, she wasn't sure she would get up at all.

She tried to fight it, donning her armor and taking to the practice field for sword training and hiring storytellers to amuse her and Tassilo. But, after weeks of such effort, these distractions, too, became drudgery and she fell further into despondency. She gained weight, her skin grew red and blotched, and her hair became tangled and uncontrollable. She didn't bother to dress most days, choosing a simple tunic with a shawl to sustain her.

Late at night she fantasized about Odilo or Bradius, trying to recall their touch with her hands. Although she welcomed the relief this brought, it was far from adequate. She longed for some type of intimate connection.

Eingard had the habit of visiting her weekly. He was very formal, in the way of Bavarian military men, reserved in his dress and his speech, but also thoughtful, intelligent, and a surprisingly good conversationalist. It took her a while to find out this last, but once he became comfortable in her company, he was more than willing to engage in subjects of all kinds. Trudi looked forward to his visits.

He had confessed to being appalled by Sudiger's threats to force her into marriage. A devout man, he practiced his pagan beliefs regularly and adhered to their teachings. To him, the idea that Sudiger would threaten her into marriage was sacrilegious.

To Trudi's surprise, he was also a learned man. When she confessed that she couldn't read or write, he sent her a tutor to help her learn her letters. While this proved to be a useful distraction, it also made her feel ignorant, especially in his presence.

He ignored such complaints when she made them, explaining that the only thing she lacked was instruction. She found out that he was a widower and had grieved mightily over his wife's death and that sorrow provided a means for her to talk about her own loss.

She found comfort in their shared knowledge of heartache and for the first time since Odilo's death, she allowed herself to grieve his loss.

Eingard's visits became a lifeline of sorts for her. On the days he was due to see her, she woke up early, bathed, took her time brushing her hair and even wore a dress. Her one frustration with the man was that he refused to speak of council affairs. He would smile and deftly deflect her questions and move the conversation to less sensitive topics.

One day, just as the trees began to make spring apparent, he arrived at the palace door and was admitted to the grand hall. As usual, Trudi ordered servants to bring him the wine he preferred and checked her appearance in the mirror before heading downstairs to meet him.

She recognized that something was amiss the moment she saw him. He was still standing, and his eyes were filled with regret. "What is it?"

He bowed formally. "Milady, I've news from the north and from the council."

She held her breath.

"All the eastern duchies are rebelling over the massacre in Alemannia. Saxony is already on the march, rebels in Alemannia are attacking their new Frankish overlords, and Bavaria has chosen to join them."

Trudi's thoughts moved quickly to the heart of the matter. He was here to ask her for the armory.

"How many on the council voted for war?"

"It was unanimous."

That shocked her. "Even the Christian nobles?"

He nodded. "I already have the armory."

Trudi sat down. She had no leverage at all. "How did this happen?"

"Gripho is leading the rebellion in Saxony with Theodoric. He has called on the Agilolfing family to rise with him. Even the Christian nobles rallied to his cause."

Trudi's mind reeled. Gripho? It didn't make sense. Pippin had promised to offer him a role in ruling the kingdom. There was no need to rebel. Did he really think he could defeat Pippin?

But, then again, it was Gripho. Her petulant brother had always begrudged Carloman and Pippin's place in the kingdom.

She should have seen it coming. His rebellion was her doing. She had demanded Gripho's release to avoid war. And now, he was calling the rebel and pagan duchies to revolt. That he was rumored to be the pagan son of Charles Martel would not be lost on them. It was a nightmare.

Trudi swore under her breath. "I find myself at your mercy, milord."

Eingard gave her a sympathetic smile. "You may keep the palace guard, for now," Eingard continued. "The council has guaranteed your life and the life of Tassilo, but, for your own safety and my peace of mind, please do not leave the palace under any circumstances. I do not trust Sudiger and neither should you."

"I've lost everything," Trudi said. "Every choice I've made, every gamble I've taken, I've lost. No matter how hard I try to keep those I love safe, they are taken from me."

"You still have your son."

Trudi nodded, her strength leaving her. "For now." She looked up at him. "When do you leave for Alemannia?"

He shrugged. "In a week." He hesitated and then said, "I will try to come to see you before I go."

Trudi nodded. "Please keep yourself safe. Bavaria will be a very difficult place without you."

He nodded and was gone.

22

It was midafternoon when Miette arrived home. She was relieved to find that her husband had yet to return from the palace. Knowing that closing the gates would not restrict him, she quickly changed into one of her own dresses, ordered wine, and waited for him to appear.

When he did, he was livid. "Where have you been?"

Miette waved her glass of wine dismissively. "Here, of course. I waited for you in the garden but got bored with all the ladies who sit there and gossip all day. I left the palace to walk along the water and when I returned, they had closed the gates! I couldn't get back in."

He bent forward so that his face was within an inch of hers. "Drusseau's wife is missing. You wouldn't happen to know anything about that, would you?"

Miette pushed him away from her. "You know I am barred from seeing her."

"Drusseau didn't miss the fact that when the gate was closed both of you were nowhere to be found. No one saw you leave, yet both of you were gone. It's as if the two of you simply vanished."

"Did they check Childeric's rooms?"

Ragomfred wasn't amused. "You're lucky that Drusseau is so busy with the attack."

"I guess for him Charlotte isn't much of a priority."

Ragomfred grabbed her by the arm. "You have no idea how danger-ous that man is."

Miette knew. Just thinking about him made her palms sweat. She shrugged off her husband's hand and gave him her best smile. "Then, I'm lucky to have you here to protect me."

She saw her sarcasm hit home. Ragomfred slapped her. The blow surprised her more than harmed her. She turned away, not wanting him to see the fury in her eyes. The thought of killing him where he stood appealed to her but she knew that would only lead to her own demise. It took every ounce of effort she possessed to keep herself in check.

Without turning around, she made her voice sound timid. "So, Drusseau plans to seize Paris?"

With her apparent submission, her husband strutted around the room like a boy who'd just lost his virginity. "It's the key to Neustria. Once he has control, he'll name himself mayor."

"He's not worried about Pippin?"

"Pippin will be occupied with Gripho's rebellion in the east. Even if he survives, he'll be too weak to be a threat. And Drusseau will have the king's blessing."

"But first you have to take Paris."

"Pippin left only one regiment under that foolish lieutenant of his."

"Gunther?"

"The man's a buffoon."

Miette was amazed at how foolish her husband could be. She had heard others mock Gunther's ineptness at court, but Pippin valued the man's leadership on the battlefield – as had Charles Martel. Her husband never had understood the difference.

* * *

Two days later, after the palace had closed, Gunther met Drusseau's army west of the Rouvray Forest, where his men were encamped. Poised on the western edge of the city, the encampment forced Gunther to split his regiment of two thousand men in two with one part facing east toward the city where the palace guard was housed and one part facing west toward the threat posed by Drusseau's army. He put Arnot in charge of the eastern flank, facing the city, with a defensive corridor of pikemen and archers, while he took the western side. He had assigned himself more men under the assumption that he would see the heaviest fighting. Once he spied Drusseau's force, he was glad he did. They had nearly five hundred more men to deploy.

His commanders barked sharp orders while his cavalry checked their mounts, and the men of the line calmly shifted their shields from their backs, readying themselves for the confrontation. It was a cold spring morning; the air was moist and heavy so that clouds of vapor blossomed from their mouths. He was proud of the cool proficiency his troops displayed.

By contrast, the men of the Twelve Counties produced a loud discord of shouting, taunting, and complaint, as their commanders wrestled the men into position. Horns blared to get their attention while horses pranced into and out of place.

Don't be fooled, Gunther told himself. They, too, are well blooded. It's how they fight that matters, not how they look.

Drusseau offered to parley and Gunther rode out to meet him. The nobleman was quite tall and Gunther was amused by the way he drew close in an attempt to tower over him. It was a ruse tall people often used to intimidate others.

"I suggest you take these men back to the Twelve Counties where they belong."

"It's you who don't belong here," Drusseau countered. "I have the king's blessing to protect Paris and Neustria and you are in my way. And, in case you haven't noticed, Pippin is a long way from here and you are outmanned."

Gunther grunted. "Just say what you've come to say."

Drusseau spoke loud so that Gunther's men might hear him. "There is no need for bloodshed. Those who wish to still serve Neustria can do so under my banner. Those who wish to flee can yield. I will let them walk away without their arms. Those who fight will die. And I promise, I'll chase every one of them down."

"Pretty arrogant, even for you, Drusseau."

"You would do well to yield."

Gunther chuckled. "Is that Twelve Counties foreplay? 'You would do well to yield'! I'll bet that works well on the women of the Breton March."

Drusseau's eyes hardened. "Then, prepare yourself."

Gunther shook his head and laughed. "'Prepare yourself'! Even better!"

Gunther rode back to his regiment and ordered the men to match the two-column formation used by the Twelve Counties, placing his cavalry on either side of the attack. He kept a small regiment of fifty men in reserve.

With a barked command, Drusseau's army advanced with the strange stutter step common to shield walls until they crashed into Gunther's wall with a great shout.

By design, shield walls were defensive in nature. With cavalry protecting their flanks, they were difficult to displace. Cavalry horses wouldn't approach the pikemen and men on foot couldn't overcome the barrier. The only way to oppose a stout shield wall was to deploy another shield wall.

As the two armies pressed behind the shields, each of the lines strained for advantage, their voices dropping to labored grunts as the men pushed their weight into it. Once engaged, pikes and swords were thrust above and below the wall to catch an enemy eye or shoulder or foot.

Archers launched arrows into the opposing ranks, hoping to force a break in the line while the two cavalries sat patiently waiting, ready to take advantage once such a break occurred.

It was grim work but slow. Blood soaked the ground beneath the men's feet and the dead laid where they fell. Some bodies were still pinned upright by the press of the shields. By late afternoon both walls were weakening, and Gunther signaled for his cavalry to pressure the edges while he sent in reinforcements. Drusseau for his part did much the same.

Hours went by with little progress. As the sun rose higher in the sky, it burned off the morning's dampness and sent waves of hot air onto the battlefield. Gunther sent men to douse the lines with water to cool their flesh.

Drusseau was racing back and forth behind his lines, barking orders, and shouting at his men. Gunther decided to keep an eye on him. There were times when such aggressiveness was warranted, but he saw nothing that would require it now. Drusseau still had reinforcements to spare; there had been no breaks in the line, and the death count for both sides was roughly the same. It was curious. Battles like this could last days. Why would Drusseau be so frustrated?

As the sun was setting and the shadows on the battlefield grew long, a cry went up from the Twelve Counties army and reinforcements poured into the back of their shield wall for a late-day push. Gunther's wall bulged inward and he quickly ordered his own reserves forward. Drusseau began frantically signaling to his cavalry.

"They're going to charge!" Gunther shouted. "Pikes forward! Pikes forward!"

Drusseau's cavalry circled behind their own ranks and drove straight at the bulge.

"Pikes forward!" Gunther spurred his horse and reached the back of the line in seconds. "Hurry, goddamn you!"

A gap formed in the wall just as Drusseau's cavalry reached it. Gunther's pikemen planted the bases of their pikes in the ground and lifted just as the cavalry thundered through the gap. Dozens of horses were skewered. They reared and fell, taking their riders with them. More riders came through and Gunther's pikes greeted them.

But not all. A number of Drusseau's mounted knights made it through unscathed and they turned to butcher the back of Gunther's line.

"To me! To me!" Gunther cried, signaling for his own cavalry to follow. And then he was among the fray, chopping at the opposing knights with his broadsword. His presence forced several to abandon their attack and refocus on the threat he posed. They converged on his position.

Gunther pulled an ax from his saddle and threw it at the horse of an approaching knight, catching it on the snout. The animal careened into the rider next to it and Gunther drove at the third rider to his right. Their blades clashed in a succession of blows. Both warhorses stepped back to reset and the Twelve Counties nobleman drew on his reins, forcing his horse to rear. The mare's forelegs clawed the air before Gunther. He spurred his own mount to the left of the descending warhorse and thrust blindly with his blade. It caught the nobleman in the shoulder and knocked him off his horse.

Gunther's cavalry swept past him to dispatch the rest of those who had charged the line. Gunther moved back to the rear, stunned by Drusseau's recklessness. Clearly, he had grown frustrated by the slow pace of the battle and nearly devastated his cavalry on a hopeless charge. Even if Gunther hadn't intervened, his cavalry would have outnumbered those pushing through the shield wall. The gambit was doomed to fail. All that Gunther had done was reduce the numbers of casualties his men had suffered.

* * *

Miette's husband had been animated all day. "That fool Gunther withdrew everyone guarding the city. The Knights in Christ have taken command of Paris. It's just a matter of time before Drusseau defeats what's left of Pippin's army."

He had ordered a feast prepared for Drusseau and his lieutenants to celebrate seizing the city. His entire house was lit with candles, and the tables in the grand hall were filled with meats, cheese, and flagons of wine.

Miette listened to the servants' gossip for any scrap of information she could attain about the battle west of the city, but the stories were far-ranging: Pippin was dead; Carloman had stormed the battlefield in a monk's cassock; Gunther had surrendered before the battle had begun.

What kept her on edge, however, was the fact that Drusseau was coming. She couldn't seem to catch her breath; it came in shallow, rapid, and high in her chest; she wrung her hands repeatedly and found herself jumping every time someone came through a door. She tried to use the training techniques Hélène had taught her but couldn't calm herself.

Ragomfred was so giddy he didn't notice her angst. He made her change her dress twice to find one that would impress Drusseau. It disgusted her that he was so enamored by the nobleman. It was nearly nine bells before the bastard arrived. He strode into their home, signaling to a servant to pour him wine. Several of his lieutenants trailed in behind him. They were already inebriated and looked more like highwaymen than nobility.

"You should have seen it, Ragomfred! We nearly defeated them on the first day. Our cavalry devastated them and nearly captured that oaf of a commander, Gunther."

"To your victory!" Ragomfred saluted with his drink.

Drusseau downed his wine in one quaff.

"Eat up, gentleman!" Ragomfred ordered their guests.

Miette stood to the side of the room hoping no one would notice her. The men regaled each other with their military exploits, crowing about one part of the battle or another. Miette listened carefully for details but there were few, and none were favorable to Pippin.

With a frown and a nod of his head, her husband signaled that she should join the festivities. Swearing under her breath she joined him. "Is the battle done?"

"It will be soon, but this is just the start. Once we defeat Gunther, the fight will move east to where Gripho is leading the rebellion."

"So, you have yet to beat Gunther."

Drusseau cut in. "It's only a matter of time. We'll have him before the next day's out."

Their boasting continued as did their drinking and Miette let enough time pass before drifting away once more to the perimeter of the room. She wouldn't get more information out of this lot. They were too busy singing their own praises and dancing around each other, desperate for recognition. A messenger arrived for Drusseau, who was well into his cups. They all were. Every one of them had their chests puffed out and laughed too loud. She let her mind wander, wondering about Pippin's campaign in the east and whether he would return to find anything left of the army he left behind.

"Where is she?" Drusseau's angered voice jolted her from her reverie. He was two steps behind her.

A trickle of fear slithered down her spine. "Who, milord?"

"Don't lie to me, bitch!" He leaned forward, menace pouring from his eyes. "I've just been given word that servants saw the two of you together."

She desperately battled the fear that engulfed her. "Servants will tell you anything if they're afraid."

He grabbed her arm, twisting it till it hurt. "How about noble-women?"

"Please, milord, I don't know where she is."

He slapped her and the sound of it drew the attention of everyone in the room. "Liar! I have a witness. She's in the enemy camp. And you took her there."

Miette's husband took several tentative steps toward her, clearly torn over how he should react. In the end, the pathetic man just stood there, a pitiful dog afraid of his master. She grew furious at his impotence. At least the man could protest! But no, the bastard was too afraid.

But then, by a curious shift of perspective, she grew furious at herself. What had she done but cower before Drusseau? Her face still stinging from the slap, she grew defiant.

"Does hitting women make you feel powerful? Does it make you feel more like a man?"

He hit her again, this time with a closed fist, and she fell back against a table.

"You dare to mock me?" He raised his voice for the benefit of the men in the room. "You?! A traitor and a whore?"

She tried to get up, but he shoved her back against the table. "Giving my wife to the enemy proves your treason. It proves your alliance with Pippin – or should I say your *dalliance* with Pippin." Looking down at her, his eyes seemed to latch on to her breasts and a change came over him. A smirk took his face, and he looked around the room. "How many times did you fuck him?"

He seemed to enjoy the laughs this gathered. "How many times did you suck Pippin's cock?" He made a show of fondling her breasts.

She struggled to get up, but he caught her by the throat and slammed her back down on the table so hard she nearly blacked out.

"My question is this: With my wife now in Pippin's camp, who will fulfill her wifely duties?"

"Fuck her!" someone shouted.

Drusseau chuckled, still squeezing Miette by the throat. "Lord Ragomfred, I demand recompense for the loss of my wife's conjugal obligation!"

He gripped her legs and shoved them apart. Looking around the room, Miette knew there would be no one to stop him. All the men were either laughing or leering.

As her mind ran through what would happen next, a quiet calm descended upon her. She recognized that, in the next few moments, she would die in this room. She had no intention of letting Drusseau take her. No man would ever do that to her again.

Sliding a blade from the back of her dress, she took solace in the knowledge that he would die first. Rather than struggle against him, she pretended to be afraid and allowed him to get close.

His eyes hooded with lust, Drusseau dropped his pantaloons and lifted Miette's dress. She gripped the knife, seeing the spot beneath his left jaw where it would go, and imagined the blade thrusting up into his brain.

"Milord?" Ragomfred finally had decided to intercede. From the look of him, Miette knew it to be a fool's errand. Tentative, weak, and ineffectual, he took three steps to stand beside Drusseau. She almost laughed at him, knowing there would be no stopping Drusseau's lust.

"Just a word?" Ragomfred leaned forward, his face pale and glistening with sweat, and whispered in Drusseau's ear.

To Miette's surprise, Drusseau's face fell with shock, and he backed away a step. "In truth?"

Her husband nodded. "Unfortunately, so."

Fury took her tormentor's face. He turned back to Miette. "You miserable cunt!" He seized the edge of the table and flipped it over, spilling Miette and a dozen plates of food to the floor.

By the time she crawled out from under the detritus, Drusseau and his lieutenants were storming from the room. Miette stood, stunned by the turn of events.

Ragomfred gave her a weak smile. "I'm afraid your dress is ruined."

She looked down; she was covered in spilled food and wine.

"What – How did you?"

"I told him that Childeric gave you the pox."

A bark of a laugh escaped Miette and then it turned into a chuckle and then she was snorting with laughter. When her hysterics had run their course, she embraced him. "Sometimes, husband, you amaze me!"

"Sometimes I amaze myself." He smiled and pointed to her right hand. "You can probably put that away, now."

She was still clasping the knife she had intended for Drusseau. Her mood sobered. "He won't let that be the end of it."

Ragomfred shook his head. "No."

"I'll have to go into hiding."

"I suppose you should." He hesitated and then took her hand in his. "I know we've had an unusual relationship and that it has not always been cordial, but you have always kept my secrets, when it would have been easy for you to malign me. In that regard, you've always been faithful."

"It is no one's affair but ours."

"Would you allow me to keep one of your secrets?"

"What do you wish to know?"

"When Childebrand was attacked at Lady Hélène's ball, did he really best those four soldiers by himself?"

She laughed. "You don't believe I killed them, do you?"

He looked at the blade still in her hand. "I'm no longer sure of what to believe."

23

Regensburg

For a week the rain had been unrelenting, pummeling the city with a thrashing torrent that whipped through every open space in the palace. Trudi hated it. She was cold; Tassilo was miserable. They hated being cooped up inside. She had done her best to amuse him, sitting on the floor, rolling hoops, and spinning tops, but nothing seemed to satisfy him, and her frustration grew with each passing day.

Being trapped indoors only heightened her awareness of their isolation, which had grown intolerable with the departure of Eingard. Half the city's nobles had accompanied him to Alemannia to defend Lantfrid's claim. Now, no one came to visit her. No news was relayed.

Making matters worse, Sudiger had remained behind, requiring her to be forever vigilant against his threat. She felt powerlessness trapped in the palace. The rain only made it worse.

Tassilo had taken to sleeping in her bed, curling up against her stomach so that her arms could surround him. Invariably, he awoke first and took great delight in poking his finger in her ear to awaken her.

One morning, he surprised her by jumping up and down on the bed. "The sun! The sun!" he shouted.

It took Trudi a moment to open her eyes and register what he was saying, but his joy began to infect her, and she jumped out of bed, scooped him into her arms, and carried him out to the balcony where they could see the eastern horizon. True to her son's word, the sun was lifting low off the river, its light dazzling the Danube's water with sparkling light.

"You're right, Tassilo. The sun is shining!"

"The sun!" he said, pointing.

A temperate breeze swirled around them as if the spring was declaring its arrival, and Trudi luxuriated in its warmth, wondering how she had ever lived without it.

She kissed Tassilo and, lifting him in her arms, she twirled him around. "Let's go play outside!"

She didn't bother to dress and the two of them ran down the stairs to the palace courtyard in nothing but their night shifts. The rain had transformed the garden, turning the grass a deep green and bringing many of the flowers to bloom. They ran through the pathways, chasing each other around the fountain and walkways, laughing with a giddy joy she hadn't felt in years.

In time, other members of the household joined them, just to bask in the warm rays of the sun. Tobias arrived with his wife in tow, and they danced a short jig, much to the woman's embarrassment. Tassilo was running in circles with a handful of children, so Trudi stood aside to watch, amazed at the change the warm weather had brought.

She was about to call Tassilo to take him for breakfast when she heard a commotion coming from the direction of the palace gate. Every head in the courtyard turned toward the noise.

A trickle of fear slid down Trudi's back. "Tassilo! Tassilo, come here!" She looked around the courtyard for her palace guard and seeing none, she grabbed Tobias. "Fetch the palace guard. Do it now!"

She sprinted to grab Tassilo, but her son thought she was still playing and ran from her. "Tassilo! Come at once!" But he laughed and ran to the other side of the fountain.

A phalanx of armed men led by two of her palace guards marched into the courtyard from the direction of the palace gate.

"What is the meaning of this?!" Trudi demanded.

The phalanx separated and Sudiger stepped forward. The shock of his presence stopped everyone in their place.

"Grab the boy!" he commanded and one of her own palace guards responded.

Trudi ran to intervene, but the soldier was closer. He picked up Tassilo, wrestling with him as he began to kick and scream. He carried him back to Sudiger. Trudi tried to follow but was intercepted by two armed men who barred her way. She tried to launch herself past them, howling in rage and fear. "You can't do this. You promised our safety!"

Sudiger didn't bother to acknowledge her presence. He made a circular sign with his hand and his men turned to leave. One of the guards holding her struck her on the side of her head and she fell to the ground. In a moment the soldiers and Sudiger were gone. To Trudi's utter desolation, so was Tassilo.

She stood in the courtyard, stunned at the loss of her son. Although everyone in the courtyard was watching her, Trudi's mind couldn't function. She stared at the tunnel to the palace gate. When Tobias returned with Hans and several members of the palace guard, Trudi finally found her voice. "Where were you! They've taken my son!"

"We've been betrayed, milady. Two of our men guarding the gate opened it to Sudiger. We had no warning."

"Go get him back."

"We don't have enough men to lay siege –"

"I said, 'go get him'!"

"Yes, milady."

Hans took twenty men with him to chase down Sudiger. Trudi could tell by the look on his face, he thought it was a fool's errand, but she didn't care. She had to try.

Feeling vulnerable in her night shift, she went back to her room to dress. Once inside, she bolted the door and howled her frustration as if it might block out Tassilo's loss. She was furious with her impotence to save her son.

Everyone was being taken from her. Tassilo's game hoop laid close by on the floor and the reality of his loss struck her. He was gone. Tears stung her eyes. She tried to push back the despair with her hand, holding in front of her face to ward away the grief, but it came for her nonetheless.

* * *

When Trudi descended to the main hall, she had bathed, combed her hair, and donned a dress to fortify herself for what lay ahead.

Hans had failed to retrieve Tassilo. He reported that Sudiger had planned the capture well in advance and took the boy to his estate, which was well fortified. When the captain of her guard had finished relaying his news, Trudi refused to speak with him. She angrily waved him away with her hand.

Sudiger approached the palace the next day. Keeping herself hidden, Trudi stared down at him from a second-floor balcony. The bastard was so arrogant, he didn't even bring a guard. He waited outside the gate, a smirk on his face, expecting Trudi to admit him.

She strode out onto the balcony. "It was reckless of you to come alone."

Sudiger shrugged. "If I don't return within the hour, your son's life will be forfeit. As long as you cooperate, he will be safe. I've no intention of harming the boy, but please realize that I don't harbor the same allegiance to his succession as do some of my compatriots. To me, he's just a gaming chip on the table."

"Why are you here?"

He opened a hand as if offering her a boon. "I've come to inform you of my current demands."

Trudi briefly weighed her options and then nodded. Turning on her heel, she called out to the palace guard. "Let the bastard in."

She didn't see any other option. She needed to know if Tassilo was safe. She went to the main hall and awaited him there seated on Odilo's ducal seat. She was relieved to see Hans take up a place behind her.

Sudiger strode into the room in a military uniform, his opulent stomach testing the garment's limits. He seemed pleased with himself, his eyes alight with mirth and his smile as condescending as Sergius's.

He had failed to bow to her in greeting, failed to address her as "milady." He was treating her as if she were a servant. She frowned to express her displeasure but nodded for him to continue.

"I will keep this short."

Trudi could barely control her anger. "I won't wed you."

He chuckled, shaking his head. "Oh, my proposal of marriage has been withdrawn. I no longer have need of you. Acquiring your son will more than suffice."

"The what do you want of me?"

"You misunderstand me, my dear Trudi. I'm not asking. With the authority granted me by the council, I've named myself acting regent."

"Eingard would never agree to that."

"Alas, he is away at war and I am here to protect the home front. Your role as guardian is revoked. You will vacate the palace immediately."

"And if I don't?"

Sudiger grunted. When he spoke, his voice carried a condescending lilt as if he were weighing his options. "Let's see. I could take the palace by force – but that, of course, would require bloodshed – *or* I could remove one of your son's fingers."

Trudi grew pale at the thought. "You wouldn't dare!"

"As I have said, he's only a gaming chip on the table. And I can assure you I've done much worse to those in my debt."

"And if I agree?"

"You will live comfortably in one of my estates."

"I'll be your prisoner."

"My guest. Of course, you will be required to remain on the premises."

"I will not live in the same house as you."

Sudiger moved closer, his face suddenly fierce. Hans stepped forward to keep him at bay, but it did little to soften the vehemence in the man's voice. "Oh, I would love to find out how far you'd go to please me with your son's life hanging in the balance. But, alas, I won't be living with you." He waved in Hans's direction. "And you can keep your personal guard. I promised Eingard that I would ensure your safety and I won't risk his ire – at least as long as he leads an army. For now, I just want you out of the way."

Trudi was trapped. She kept her face blank but was reeling inside. As long as he had Tassilo there was little she could do.

"First, I must know that Tassilo is safe."

"Tomorrow morning, I will bring him into the courtyard outside the palace. You can see him from your balcony."

Trudi nodded. "That will do."

Sudiger turned to leave, again failing to bow.

Trudi waited until he was gone. "Bastard!"

* * *

Sudiger was true to his word. He arrived the next morning with Tassilo. He held the boy's hand as they entered the courtyard. An armed contingent followed them in. Trudi nearly cried out upon seeing her son. Tassilo looked docile and pale to her. She could tell he was frightened.

She stood outside the gate and waved them forward. "Bring him closer where I can see him."

Sudiger led Tassilo toward her.

"Tassilo!" Trudi cried. "Are you well?"

"Maman!" He burst into tears, collapsing on the ground.

As Sudiger bent to retrieve him, Trudi signaled to Hans. Soldiers poured into the courtyard from an alleyway, cutting off Sudiger from his men.

Sudiger yanked Tassilo from the ground and held aloft a knife.

"Halt!" Trudi cried.

"Do you think I'm foolish enough to come unprepared?" Sudiger spat on the ground. "You underestimate me, woman."

Trudi waved Hans back to the palace. "I was hoping you underestimated me." Her last gambit having failed, she had little choice. "I will vacate the palace peacefully. But, if anything happens to my son, your life will be such a hell that you will beg me to kill you."

This time Sudiger bowed before taking his leave.

24

Paris

Gunther rose early to muster his men for another day's battle. Much like the two days before, the morning was bright and cool and the air was heavy with moisture. The men moved with the same quiet proficiency into their two columns. Shields with pikes faced forward and were flanked by cavalry as the sun lifted off the horizon. Their formation matched that of the Twelve Counties men who arrayed themselves on the western edge of the battlefield.

Horns blared and the drums began to beat, and the men of both armies marched forward, their shields held high. As the two shield walls slammed together, something struck Gunther as odd. As much as everything seemed the same from one day to the next, he was sure there was some factor he'd missed.

He scanned the battlefield. Everything was where it should be. The men of the shield wall strained in place, their pikes and swords lunging to maim and wound the enemy. The cavalry pranced behind them, waiting for an opening to exploit. Nothing was out of place, and yet it was. He just couldn't figure out what was amiss.

He called for Laurent. Carloman's former champion now served as his second while Arnot covered the eastern pickets of the army's encampment. The tall lithe swordsman joined him at the rear of their deployment.

"Huh-ya, Laurent."

The man nodded. It was one of the things Gunther liked about him. He only spoke when he had something to say.

"I've got this nagging feeling that something is amiss, but I can't seem to figure out what it is. Everything looks the same as it did yesterday. Do you see anything that's changed?"

Laurent frowned and turned his eyes to the battlefield. Gunther watched as the man scanned each portion of the battlefield. When he was done, he shrugged.

"What do you see?"

"Drusseau's banner is in the lead, but it is being carried by Pierre de Rouen. He is in command. He was a fellow Knight in Christ. A good soldier. Drusseau, however, is not there."

"Is that it?"

Laurent shook his head. "They also have several hundred fewer men in the field."

Gunther stood in his stirrups to confirm the assessment and sat back in his saddle, a sense of alarm building inside him. "Jesus Christ! They must be attacking from the east."

Laurent made the sign of the cross.

"I'm leaving you in command here. I'm taking three hundred men and half the cavalry."

Laurent nodded. "We'll be vulnerable late in the day but should be able to hold."

Gunther began shouting orders, hoping he wasn't too late.

* * *

Miette's appearance during the dark of night didn't surprise Bertrada so much as that she bore no wounds from her confrontation with Drusseau. Bertrada had assumed that he would blame Miette for his wife's disappearance.

She made room for the woman in what was turning out to be quite a menage of women and children within the military camp. Fortunately, Gunther had given her his large command tent. She and

Charles, Catherine and her two children, the Lady Hélène, Charlotte, and now Miette graced their new abode. She just wished Pippin had left more than one regiment to protect them. While she had great faith in Gunther, she worried that Pippin had underestimated Drusseau and his Knights in Christ.

As large as their tent was, it was cramped for five adults and three children. Gunther had provided little in the way of furniture: a chair and cot for Bertrada, due to her condition, bedrolls for the others, a large cross in a stand behind her chair, and several rugs to serve as a floor. These last, Bertrada had brought with her, knowing what life in a military camp was like. There were limits in her willingness to share the life of a soldier.

Located at the center of camp, they had the benefit of being near the food wagons but, unfortunately, were far from the latrines. They also had the benefit of a large fire outside their tent that helped to keep them warm through the cold nights. During the day, Bertrada insisted that her guests help with preparing food for the soldiers and tending the wounds of those injured in battle. At night two soldiers guarded their tent.

While still discomfited by Miette's presence, Bertrada was grateful for the news she had brought. No one seemed to think keeping her informed was a priority. Everything she had learned was from the wounded soldiers she tended to.

It was still dark when she rose to help with the early meal. The men were in good spirits, confident of their victory despite their lack of numbers. She gathered that none of them expected much to change while the shield walls continued to press for advantage. After helping to police the campsite after the meal, she decided to use the latrine. She hoped the journey would ease the pain in her back. Her pregnancy was proving to be a difficult one.

She left Charles in the care of Catherine's daughter and struck out for the edge of camp. As she drew near the pickets, she heard shouting and drew closer to see what was amiss.

Overwhelmed by a massive column of men, the line protecting the eastern side of the camp was collapsing. Arnot's cavalry crashed into the enemy column while he screamed for men to shore up their line. Bertrada was no expert on military matters, but she knew they couldn't hold long.

She fled back to the way she had come, hampered greatly by her condition. All around her, men were screaming to reinforce the line. A cramp seized her just as she reached her tent and Catherine helped her to her chair. "We're under attack from the east," she forced out between groans. "It's too large to stop. They'll be here within minutes."

Hélène ran out of the tent and returned moments later with two long staffs and a sword. She threw a long staff to Miette and handed the sword to Catherine.

"Where's mine?" Bertrada asked.

Hélène pulled a knife from somewhere in her dress. "You're in no condition to wield a sword. This will have to do."

Bertrada took the weapon. "We must evacuate the children."

Hélène frowned. "We won't get far. Our only hope is that Gunther will realize the threat and counterattack. All we can do is try to hold out until he arrives."

"What if he doesn't?" Bertrada asked, dread filling her.

"We pray Drusseau will take us hostage."

Bertrada didn't like the sound of that.

Catherine began giving orders. "Charlotte, help me roll up these rugs. We'll use them as a barricade to keep the children protected." Although Charlotte helped, Bertrada could see that the woman would be of little use. Her eyes had a glaze to them as if she were in a stupor.

Miette and Hélène stood on either side of the tent flap, long staffs in hand. Silence took over the group while they waited. A minute went by, then two. One of the children started to cry. Catherine began to lead them in the paternoster, which seemed to help calm them, but the prayer put Bertrada on edge.

She began to tremble. There was no way they could save themselves from such a force. She looked at Hélène and Miette and thought how ridiculous they looked. What could they hope to accomplish against soldiers?

In the distance, she heard horns blaring. Hélène stepped outside to look. When she returned, she nodded. "It's Gunther's men. They're streaming through the camp from the west to meet the threat."

"Are we saved?" Bertrada asked.

Hélène shook her head. "Not yet. Drusseau's men are everywhere. He'll have to sweep the entire camp before we're safe."

A soldier appeared in the tent flap. He wore the red doublet of a Knight in Christ. He appeared surprised to see them and opened his mouth to shout, but Hélène hit him in in the face with her long staff and he keeled over backwards.

Again, silence stole over the occupants of the tent and again Bertrada trembled with fear. She had never felt so out of control. Another cramp took her. She prayed it was false; it was far too early for the babe. It would perish if she had it now.

Another soldier entered the tent and died with a knife in his throat. It was so fast, Bertrada didn't see who had thrown it, but from the smirk on Miette's face, she could guess.

Outside, grunts and shouts competed with the sounds of blades and shields colliding. It was clear the fighting was nearing their tent. She found herself reciting the paternoster silently to herself.

A third soldier appeared in the tent's opening but pulled back before Miette's knife found him. He must have been forewarned by the bodies lying at their doorstep. Hélène tried to follow him out into the melee but returned, shaking her head.

"Lost him" was all she said.

The fighting was all around their tent, the noise and shouting surpassed only by the children crying and Charlotte keening. She was kneeling near the back of the tent, swaying back and forth as if she'd been possessed. Catherine stood, stepped away from the children, and with a stern countenance, lifted her blade to stand next to Miette.

* * *

Laurent was worried that he'd given Gunther too many men. Twice, he had to shuffle men to back up his shield wall and still it was failing. Even with his cavalry harrying the opposing wall, he watched with alarm as his shields lost ground.

There was too much of the day left and he was losing too many men. In his heart he feared they wouldn't have enough. Desperately, he searched his mind for a solution, but finding none, mentally prepared himself for the carnage to come.

"Yield!" It was Pierre de Rouen shouting across the field at him.

Laurent considered it. They both were experienced enough to see where the battle was headed. His chances of victory were slim. Only a lopsided melee or an act of God would change that fact.

"Yield," Rouen cried again, but Laurent knew he wouldn't yield. He said a silent prayer and rode forward to assist the cavalry.

When the horns blew behind him, Laurent's fear spiked. Either Gunther had returned or Pierre de Rouen had him surrounded. He prayed it was Gunther. Pulling on his reins, he turned to face his fate.

What he saw didn't make sense. It was an army the size to his own and it was thundering toward him. A quiet moment of panic seized him until he saw the lead banner. It was Childebrand.

But that made no sense. Childebrand was with Pippin. Yet his banner led an army that advanced like a giant wave over the field. A great shout went up from Laurent's men as Childebrand's army crashed into the enemy's shield wall. Within minutes it was overrun, their cavalry overwhelmed. Laurent briefly felt guilty that he didn't leave an opportunity for Pierre de Rouen to yield, but the rout had happened so fast, there was little time. The battle had become a slaughter.

Childebrand rode up next to him. The man towered over him. "Where's Gunther?"

Laurent took a moment to frame his words. He still couldn't accept the turn of events. "Drusseau mounted an attack from both the east and the west. It caught us off guard. Gunther took several hundred men to counterattack."

"Where's Bertrada?"

"In the camp."

"Jesus Christ!"

Laurent made the sign of the cross.

Childebrand ordered horns to blow and flew banners calling for a retreat. When his lieutenant hesitated, Childebrand shouted, "We've already won. I don't care how many of them escape. There's a second front. We must save the encampment."

Laurent knew that it would take too much time for Childebrand's men to return. The bloodlust was upon them. They wouldn't hear the horns or wouldn't choose to hear them. He hurried into the field to rally what he could of his cavalry and men. They would be exhausted but grateful the day was saved. He only hoped they would be in time to save the camp.

* * *

When Drusseau's soldiers came, it looked to Bertrada as if they were vomited through the tent flap. Four went down in a succession of blows from the long staffs, but more pushed through, forcing Miette and Hélène backwards. Catherine stabbed forward with her sword, gutting one of the attackers through the stomach, but she had trouble freeing her blade and fell back without a weapon. Bertrada handed her the knife she held, and Catherine retreated to stand before the children.

Miette and Hélène fought with a vengeance Bertrada had never seen in women. She marveled at their bravery and tenacity. Their staffs were a blur, spinning and landing with incredible accuracy, blocking blades, smashing heads, and crippling soldiers at the knees. At times, they fought in tandem, at others, they separated to fight alone. But in the end, there were too many soldiers. Miette was stabbed by a blade in her midsection and Hélène was hit from behind with a shield. Both fell to the ground and soldiers held them at sword point. Recognizing the futility of opposition, Catherine dropped the knife and the soldiers left her and the children alone.

Once the fighting stopped, Drusseau entered the tent like a conquering hero. He even swirled his cape. Bowing formally, he met Bertrada's eyes. She nodded, hoping that would be the end of the violence.

"It is my pleasure to meet you, milady." He smirked.

Bertrada hated him immediately.

"Although I have heard nothing but good about you, I have to question the company you keep." He stepped over to where Miette laid, bleeding. "A whore?" She groaned as he lifted her up by her hair and spat in her face.

Miette fell back to the floor when he released her. "Bastard," she said as he walked away. He next turned to the unconscious Hélène. Again, he lifted her by the hair. "And an assassin?"

He tossed her aside and stepped toward the children. Bertrada rose from her chair.

He held up his hands. "I'm no child killer," he assured her. He made his way to Charlotte, who still was rocking back and forth, softly mewling to herself. "What do we have here? Why, it is my wife! Why would she be in your tent, milady, when she should be at home with me?"

"She sought refuge," Bertrada said.

"Yet, she is my property!"

"She is a child of God."

He lifted Charlotte by the hair to make her stand. Screaming, she pulled away and grabbed the knife Catherine had dropped and tried to stab Drusseau. He blocked her easily and threw her to the ground at Bertrada's feet.

"You bitch! You think you can leave me?!" He hit Charlotte in the face with a closed fist. "You are mine! You are nothing without me!" He hit her again and again until her blood splashed over him as her face began to collapse.

Horror swept over Bertrada. "Stop!" she shouted.

Drusseau turned; he was smiling, his face streaked with Charlotte's blood, but he didn't let go. "This is just the beginning." He turned to beat her again.

It was too much. Bertrada couldn't stand by and watch such depravity. Anger like she'd never experienced seized her. Every muscle and sinew in her body screamed for action. Searching around her she found no weapon, but her eyes landed on the large cross behind her chair. Without hesitation, she grabbed it by its base and, turning, swung it over her head. It was heavier than she had imagined so she put every bit of her fury behind it.

Shouts of warning came from Drusseau's soldiers, but they were too late to stop her. She swung it down on Drusseau's head like she was chopping wood. He turned in time to see her strike and tried to raise his arm, but it was too late. One arm of the cross sank fully into his skull. His eyes looked at her with shock, and then they grew dull as he crumpled to the ground.

She heard Miette whisper, "Justice!" before one of the soldiers knocked her unconscious.

Bertrada wasn't sure if she had blacked out or was simply dazed, but somehow Gunther was there with his men. They were removing Drusseau's soldiers from the tent. When she sat up an enormous pain assaulted her head. "What happened?"

Gunther looked embarrassed. "I'm sorry, milady. I should have seen it from the beginning. We came late and had to fight our way to your tent."

"At least you're here now."

Catherine was on the ground holding Charlotte and wiping away the blood. The right side of the poor woman's face had swollen to nearly double its size. She was almost unrecognizable.

Catherine's children were still near the back of the tent with their arms around little Charles. Hélène was beside Miette, cradling the younger woman's head in her lap. Miette looked pale as a specter.

"Will she be all right?" Bertrada asked.

Hélène shook her head. "I don't know. The wound is deep. They've sent for a doctor."

Miette opened her eyes and they locked onto Bertrada. She struggled to speak. "My fault for bringing Charlotte."

"No!" Images of Drusseau beating Charlotte flashed before Bertrada's eyes and an acute anger coursed through her. She fought for control. In a calmer voice she said, "No, I'm glad you did." She laid a hand on Miette's arm and smiled. "Now, I understand why it was so urgent. What you did was heroic. I owe you an apology."

Miette's smile was weak. "You're the one who saved her."

"I don't understand."

"You're the one who killed Drusseau."

The statement stunned her and a wave of nausea nearly made her vomit. That it was true was obvious. She just hadn't thought of it in those terms. She merely had tried to stop Drusseau from hurting Charlotte. She could still see the cross in her hands, still feel its weight and the effort it took to swing it toward the bastard's head. She could still see it descending toward him and puncturing his skull, the light fading from his eyes. She had killed him...murdered him. Her heart wailed. She had committed a mortal sin.

She staggered to her feet intent on fleeing the tent when Childebrand walked in. His huge form confused her.

"What – What are you doing here? You are supposed to be with Pippin."

"He sent me back with a regiment to help Gunther defeat Drusseau."

"And to protect me and Charles."

"Well, yes...in part."

"But that leaves him with half the army to face the Saxons!"

Childebrand nodded.

"You have to go back."

"It's too late. I might be able to meet him in either Alemannia or Bavaria. But getting to Saxony before he battles Theodoric is impossible."

"How will he succeed?"

Childebrand shrugged. "That's what I asked him."

"How did he reply?"

"He said he would have to improvise."

25

Schöningen

Pippin began to hear rumors about "Gripho's uprising" long before he entered Saxony. The "pagan son of Charles Martel" made for good storytelling, and from everything Pippin could learn, the tale was spreading rapidly east of the Rhine. That, along with the shock from the Alemanni massacre, was creating a religious furor throughout the countryside that was almost palpable. Everywhere they went people avoided them, drew runes of warding in the air, and spit on the ground after they had passed.

He was surprised, however, that Theodoric had embraced the idea. Twice in the past three years he had defeated the Saxon and done it soundly. It was hard to imagine Theodoric would risk a third try. Surely, Gripho didn't provide any new advantage to help him succeed. He had no additional troops to offer, no command experience. Did Theodoric think Pippin would refrain from attacking his own brother?

It was foolish. Yet here he was on the banks of the River Meissau near Schöningen waiting for the Saxon to attack.

He had taken a risk sending a regiment back to Paris with Childe-brand. It left him with less than twenty-five hundred men and gave the Saxons an advantage in numbers. That would further embolden Theodoric. But Pippin couldn't afford to wait. He had to kill the power of the rumor quickly. If he didn't, he'd spend years fighting a religious war east of the Rhine. Taking his younger stepbrother into custody was the best way he could think to achieve it.

But first he had to defeat Theodoric. He had spent half his journey east considering how. At first, Theodoric had avoided him. Pippin spent weeks chasing sightings of the Saxon's army, knowing that Theodoric was trying to exhaust him and string out his supply lines.

Recognizing his vulnerability, Pippin changed tactics. He laid waste to Eastphalia, attacking the largest estates, raiding their stores, and burning their crops. Theodoric would be forced to respond if for nothing other than to maintain his credibility as a leader.

In less than a week, the Saxon had arrived with four thousand men to confront him in Schöningen. Theodoric signaled for parley and Pippin rode out to meet him. The Saxon looked much the same as he had a year earlier, He was a large man, with blue eyes, light hair, and a scraggly beard. He was a hard man, who had clearly earned the scars that covered his body.

"You are brave to come with half an army, Pippin."

"You are foolish to make me come."

"Had I known you were so few, I wouldn't have made you chase me throughout Saxony."

"You need better scouts."

Theodoric spat. "You need more men."

"You swore allegiance last year and, as we agreed, I left you alone. I only asked for tribute. I didn't take your palace in Seeburg; I didn't take hostages. I won't be so sparing this time."

Theodoric grunted. "You won't win this time."

Pippin smiled. "Where's Gripho?"

"Raising men in the south."

"Leaving you to fight his war."

He nodded the briefest of nods.

"When did he leave?"

"When he first heard you were coming."

"And that's who you're fighting for? A coward?"

Theodoric spit. "I fight for Saxony. Gripho brings allies and splits your armies into smaller pieces." He pointed at Pippin's men. "It's hard to win with so few."

"Yet, I plan to." Pippin turned to ride back to his line.

They retreated to their respective armies, formed their men into columns, and urged the shield walls forward. On the face of it, Theodoric was correct. Pippin couldn't win with the men he had brought from Paris. But, having fought in and around Saxony twice in the past two years, he had other resources upon which he could draw.

Prior to laying waste to Eastphalia, he had summoned troops from Frisia and bribed tribes from the Wend region, near the lower Saale River and the upper Elbe. Promises were made and gold exchanged; all that remained was for them to arrive on time. If they didn't, Pippin wouldn't last a week.

The Frankish and Saxon shield walls met and the two armies strained against each other. Pippin's one advantage was in fielding a sizable cavalry that kept the Saxons from outflanking them. The Saxons tried early to press their advantage at the wall, adding extra lines, but the Franks held firm. The strain, however, required Pippin to reinforce regularly. As the day labored forward, neither side had a real advantage.

Just as the sun was three fingers above the horizon, the Frisians arrived. They pushed into Theodoric's rear, forcing him to split his troops to counter the assault. He reacted quickly and had enough men to fend off the attack, but it weakened his shield wall, and the Franks began to press forward, one step at a time. Progress was slow, but Pippin had seen enough battles to know it was significant.

When the Wends came from the east dressed in their animal skins, Pippin sighed in relief. They stampeded across the battlefield like a screaming horde. Theodoric didn't have enough shields to form a third line. The Wends slammed into the Saxon flank and Theodoric's shield walls collapsed. Pippin threw all his reserves into the ensuing melee and drove his cavalry toward Theodoric's position in the rear.

They never made it. The Saxon horns blew and what was left of Theodoric's army laid down its arms. While Pippin rode forward to confront him, the Wends plundered the battlefield for armor, swords, and coin.

Theodoric looked furious as Pippin approached. Roaring like a wounded animal, he sheathed his sword and removed his scabbard. With a muttered curse, he tossed it to the Frisian commander. It should have been offered to Pippin. Aware of the Saxon discourtesy, the Frisian dismounted and retrieved it for Pippin.

Although he had planned his attack for weeks, Pippin only now realized how angry he was. In the past, he had tried to show mercy. He had tried to establish a structure where the Saxons could continue to rule within an allied relationship. Instead, oaths had been betrayed repeatedly, much like Theudebald in Alemannia.

It took Pippin a moment to realize that all eyes were upon him and that he was expected to address Theodoric. He came close to imitating the villagers who had spat at his feet. Instead, he examined the Saxon sword with disdain and tossed it to the turf as if it were garbage.

That insult wasn't lost on Theodoric.

"As long as I've been alive," Pippin began, "the eastern duchies were considered allied independent duchies. We accepted your hands in fealty, expected you to pay tribute and fight when we called, but we let you rule your territories without interference. That ends today. Alemannia is gone, Saxony is mine, and Bavaria will be next.

"Your army is forfeit. I'm taking them with me. They will be impressed into my regiments permanently. I'm also taking your palace at Seeburg and whatever treasure it holds. It now belongs to the Franks."

Theodoric looked unbowed. "Let's just get to the cross kissing and be done with it."

"I won't ask you to convert by sword but Gripho's rebellion is dead. If you champion his banner again, I will send so many priests to Saxony that you won't be able to piss without making a confession."

He turned his horse away from Theodoric, dismissing him from his mind. He had other problems to address, most notably finding Gripho.

26

Regensburg

Despite Sudiger's assurances, he had forbidden Hans from accompanying Trudi to the estate where she was confined. He also refused her any companions, so that with the exception of the servants who came and went, she was alone.

The house had six rooms, the furniture was cozy, but her accommodations held little import for her. Her only coherent thoughts were of Tassilo. She took some solace in the fact that Eta was with him. Trudi hoped the woman would calm his fears and act as her surrogate until she was freed.

As the days passed, however, Trudi became desperate to see him, desperate to hold him in her arms, to play with him, to kiss him, cradle his head in her lap. Those desires – and her inability to achieve them – assaulted her endlessly, leaching away her soul. She had never felt so powerless.

With nothing to occupy her hands and mind she grew listless and took to walking the grounds of the estate just to pass the time. Spring was in full bloom around her, the trees and flowers filling the landscape in a lush display of nature's beauty, but none of it touched her.

In time, she stopped walking, then she stopped dressing and combing her hair, letting a simple shift suffice for her wardrobe. She saw no reason to do otherwise. The only people she saw were the servants who cared for her. She longed for conversation but couldn't imagine confiding in them the way she had with Tobias or Eta. Anything she might say would be reported back to Sudiger.

One morning, she saw the servants in the kitchen, their voices pitched high and their hands fluttering in the air with excitement. Curious, Trudi stood behind the door hoping to overhear what prompted such enthusiasm.

"Are you sure?" one of the women asked.

"They say he'll be here in a week! Can you imagine? A pagan mayor?! He has every territory east of the Rhine in revolt."

"I've heard he's handsome."

"And brave."

Although Trudi found it hard to imagine any woman being excited by her younger brother, she welcomed the news that Gripho was coming. She had not been close to him, but their relationship always had been cordial. She was certain he would end her isolation and restore Tassilo to her.

That hope carried her for days. She dressed each morning and coiffed her hair, patiently waiting for news of his arrival. Having abandoned hope for so long, its return filled her with anticipation and excitement. Unfortunately, as day followed day, the delay became unbearable. She paced relentlessly, watching the road back to Regensburg for any sign of change. When her expectations collapsed each evening, she fell back into bed crushed with disappointment.

A full two weeks after she overheard the conversation, a carriage pulled up to the house of her confinement. It was Sudiger. Heaving his great bulk, he quit the carriage with some effort and followed a servant to the house. His man opened the door and bowed to Sudiger like one would a king, and then her captor strode into the residence as if he expected her to bow as well.

Trudi crossed her arms to show her disdain. "How is my son?"

"Tassilo is well – quite the celebrity," Sudiger said as he opened a cabinet and poured himself some wine. "But do you know what I find interesting? No one asks about you. It's as if you never existed. You should have accepted my offer. You'd still be with Tassilo. And you'd still be regent."

"And I'd still have to suffer your nightly visits to my bedchamber."

Sudiger tilted back the flagon of wine and smacked his lips in appreciation. When he turned to her, his eyes were dark with menace. "You would do well to alter your tone with me. While I promised Eingard that I would ensure you safety, I'd be happy to suffer his wrath to still that tongue of yours."

"You mean you'd rape me." Anger filled Trudi with a strength she hadn't felt in months. "I'll rip off your manhood before I let that happen."

"We shall see." The smirk on his face suggested a secret he was anxious to convey. "The game is finally getting interesting."

"So, Gripho is here?"

Sudiger frowned. "How did you hear that?"

His surprise delighted her. "This is Gripho's war, isn't it? Why should I be shocked when he comes to lead it."

Sudiger sighed and put down his flagon. "He demands your presence. I'm here to gather your things and take you to the palace."

Trudi stood and picked up her packed bag.

Sudiger frowned and hesitated, seemingly unprepared for her preparedness.

"Let's go," she said. "I've been ready for weeks."

* * *

Sudiger escorted her to the palace and into the main hall. A feast was being prepared and already dozens of nobles were in attendance, milling around the large fireplace while they drank flagons of wine. Heads turned as she entered; most looked surprised to see her, but a few stopped to acknowledge her presence.

She tried to head upstairs to Tassilo's rooms, but Sudiger held her arm with more force than she thought him capable.

"He's not there. You will see him later tonight; I can assure you. For now, you'll have to wait."

As more people gathered, the room took on a festive air. Food was brought in as was another barrel of wine. Most of the guests were men and their voices grew more boisterous as the wine was poured.

At the far end of the main hall a door opened, and a half dozen nobles entered. Once inside the hall, they turned and lined the doorway like an honor guard. After a pregnant moment, Gripho marched through the doorway carrying Tassilo on his shoulder. A cheer erupted throughout the room. Trudi couldn't tell whether it was for her son or for Gripho.

Her half-brother brought Tassilo to a place by the fire. "To Duc Tassilo!" he shouted, raising her son high in the air.

The room erupted in shouts and applause. Tassilo looked like he was going to cry.

Trudi tried to run to him, but Sudiger grabbed her arm. "Not yet!"

She slammed an elbow into his midsection. It loosened his grip, and she wrested her arm away from him to run toward her son. "Tassilo!" she shouted.

He saw her and started to cry. "Maman! Maman!"

Seeing her come, Gripho smiled and offered Tassilo to her. "My sister, Hiltrude!" he announced to the crowd. Although they cheered, perhaps out of respect for Gripho, it was decidedly less enthusiastic than their applause for Tassilo.

She didn't care. She had Tassilo in her arms and that was all that mattered. They both were crying as she stroked his hair and whispered into his ear.

"Thank you, Gripho," she said when the crowd had quieted and turned their attention away. "It's been months since I've seen him."

"So I've heard. That ends tonight. Your friend Eingard strongly suggested that I come to Regensburg to intercede on our behalf. He worried that you were being used as board pieces in someone else's game. I'm naming myself regent and guardian over you and your son. You'll live here with me in the palace."

The relief she felt was palpable. "Where is Eingard?"

"I left him and Lantfrid in command of the army."

She and Tassilo sat next to Gripho at the table during dinner and he toasted their health to the room. In time, nobles came to pay their respects and she accepted them each in turn. It struck her as a bizarre turn of events. She had been so isolated for so long she had difficulty comprehending her sudden restoration to prominence. Part of her resented that her acceptance hinged on Gripho's assurance – that she didn't carry the same weight of authority – but after months of confinement and isolation from her son, she embraced the change wholeheartedly.

Eta came to take Tassilo to bed and Trudi took the opportunity to pull her aside.

"How is Hans?"

Eta looked crestfallen. "He was dismissed from the palace guards and sent to the stables. For the time being, he's living with his brother."

"And Tobias?"

"He lives in town. He refused to consider leaving until he had news of you."

"Can you get word to the two of them?"

"Yes, of course."

"As much as I'm happy that Gripho freed me, I don't trust him or Sudiger. You, Tassilo, and I need a plan to escape. Tell Hans and Tobias to plan accordingly."

* * *

Sudiger officiated the ceremony to name Gripho regent the next day. Trudi held Tassilo's hand until he was ushered to the ducal seat. The gathering of nobles chuckled at how the huge chair dwarfed the boy. He looked like a carved doll perched among its plush blue cushions. Gripho stood triumphantly behind him.

Sudiger stepped forward and in a sonorous voice announced, "The symbols of Bavarian power date back to the time of the Romans. They are inviolate representations of duty, nobility, and honor."

He lifted a blue mantel, displaying it to the crowd. "The mantel of ducal responsibility!" He turned and draped it over Tassilo's shoulders before lifting it again to place on Gripho's. "You are charged with defending Bavarian soil, protecting Bavarian lives, and honoring Bavarian laws and traditions."

"I accept," Gripho said.

Sudiger next lifted a golden scabbard. "The sword of Bavaria!" He turned and placed it on Tassilo's lap, before lifting it again to hand to Gripho. "May honor strengthen your sword."

Gripho drew the blade and held it aloft. "And may truth guide its way."

The crowd applauded and Gripho sheathed the blade. Nodding for Trudi to join them, he lifted Tassilo until he was standing on the ducal seat. With him at the center, the three of them stood together holding hands as Sudiger proclaimed Gripho's regency.

"Duc Tassilo and his regent, Gripho, son of Sunnichild of the Agilolfings and Charles Martel, Mayor of the Palace."

The crowd roared its approval. With a mischievous smile on his face, Tassilo raised Trudi's and Gripho's hands in celebration.

That night a dinner was held to honor the naming of Tassilo's regent, and again Trudi and Tassilo were seated next to Gripho. Watching him interact with the nobles, Trudi found the change in her half-brother remarkable. He always had been a sullen child, resentful of his two older brothers, but here in Bavaria he was confident, buoyant, almost charismatic. She felt as if she didn't know him. She had dozens of questions for him but felt it important first to express her appreciation.

"I want to thank you again for freeing me from isolation. I couldn't stand being parted from Tassilo."

Gripho waved off her gratitude. "I'm glad I could help."

"If I might ask, what happened between you and Pippin? When last Odilo and I spoke to him, he had agreed to free you from Neufchateau."

Gripho put down his knife. "I suspected it might have been you and Odilo who prompted my release. I owe you my thanks in return."

"And Pippin?" Trudi prompted.

Gripho's face darkened with fury. "The bastard wanted to exile me to the Breton March. 'Master of the March' he called it. Charles named me mayor. Mayor! I have every right to rule as much as Pippin. Who is he to deny me my birthright?"

A familiar fear pricked the back of Trudi's neck. She had felt it every time Odilo spoke of war with Pippin. For all the bravado that went into their speeches about honor and courage, all she heard was lunacy. They couldn't beat him. Gripho should know that. He'd seen Pippin in battle. "Maybe I can speak to him. Perhaps we can negotiate better terms. Please don't go to war with him."

"What do I have to lose?"

"Everything! You can't beat him. He's too strong."

Her plea only served to stoke Gripho's anger. "What do you know of it? Do you think dressing up like a soldier makes you one? I've rallied half the kingdom. Pippin has had to split his army to fight Drusseau. If he survives Theodoric in Saxony, Lantfrid and Eingard will weaken him in Alemannia. And if that doesn't bring Pippin to his knees, we will battle what is left of his army when he reaches Bavaria."

Trudi ignored his anger. "I was here when he last battled Bavaria; we are still suffering from the losses."

"I don't expect him to fight," Gripho said. "I expect him to negotiate. There's no reason we can't share the kingdom the way he and Carloman did."

"That didn't work out well for Carloman," Trudi said, almost to herself.

"I'm not Carloman."

After the dinner Eta came to retrieve Tassilo while the tables were cleared.

A new barrel of ale was tapped to a rousing cheer and the nobles broke into small groups of celebration. Trudi shook her head; she had never gotten used to the volume that the Bavarians could consume.

She tried to reconnect with several of the nobles who had once been kind to her but found no one who had more than a couple words to offer her. Frustrated, she decided to seek out Gripho. She searched the room and found him standing with Sudiger by the fire.

As she approached, she saw Sudiger and Gripho smirking as if they'd just heard an indelicate jest. "What is so amusing, brother?"

Gripho smiled. "Sudiger and I have just agreed to a lucrative transaction."

She looked from one to another, fear snaking up her spine. "What have you sold him?"

A twinkle touched his eye. "Your hand in marriage. As your guardian, I've decided you will wed Count Sudiger."

His words struck Trudi like a thrown stone. She couldn't breathe. She looked at the two men in disbelief. Yet, Gripho's face was earnest and Sudiger's triumphant.

"I will not," she managed to stammer.

"I'm afraid the choice is not yours," Gripho said.

She grew desperate and angry. "If I could defy Charles, what makes you think I won't defy you?"

Gripho didn't even blink. "Oh, I doubt that you'll leave in the dead of night to traipse across the kingdom."

"Why not?"

"I have Tassilo."

The blood drained from her face. Sudiger had planned this. Without a second thought, Trudi slapped Sudiger in the face. "You bastard!"

Sudiger was smug, even with a red handprint on his face. "It has never been a good bet to underestimate me."

She turned back to Gripho. "I've already refused him."

"As I am aware, sister, but the rebellion requires gold and my good Count Sudiger has plenty of it. I've seen many political marriages made for far less."

"I won't do it."

"Yes, you will. The date is set for a fortnight from tonight."

Trudi turned to storm from the room. But before she could come up with an appropriate curse with which to leave them, a commotion near the doorway drew everyone's attention.

The crowd parted and Lantfrid and Eingard strode through the amassed nobility. Instead of the arrogant youth she had come to detest, Lantfrid looked embarrassed, if not frightened. His eyes were rimmed with red and if she had to bet, she'd wager he was about to cry. Eingard looked uncharacteristically stricken.

Gripho stared at them like they were specters. "Why are you here?"

Lantfrid threw one of his gauntlets to the ground. "We've been defeated. As were the Saxons."

A murmur swept through the crowd of nobles. Trudi could see the panic grow in Gripho's eyes. He spoke loudly to regain control of the room. "As unfortunate as this news is, we understood the risks. Our strategy has always been to weaken Pippin before he reaches Bavaria. We will meet what is left of his army here and defeat him. That will restore our allies to power."

He focused on Lantfrid. "Where is your fallback position?"

The Aleman looked confused. "Milord?"

"When your men retreated, where did they establish a new line? We'll send reinforcements."

Eingard stepped forward. "There is no line – no fallback position. We were routed. The Saxons were routed. What's left of our army is on its way here."

Sitting next to him, Trudi could see a line of sweat roll down her brother's temple. It was one of the most satisfying things she'd ever seen.

Gripho stammered, "What are you saying?"

Eingard's voice sounded like a death knell. "Pippin is coming."

* * *

The nobles in the room erupted into a cacophony of shouting and curses. Several bolted from the room as if it already was under attack. Gripho raised his hands and called for calm before grabbing Sudiger, Eingard, and Lantfrid and pulling them into a corner.

Sensing an opportunity, Trudi calmly walked out of the main hall and sent a servant to fetch Eta and Tassilo. Returning to her rooms, she changed into a plain shift she had set aside for just such an opportunity and waited for Eta to appear. Minutes later the woman arrived with Tassilo in hand.

"Is it time, milady?"

Trudi nodded.

"I've sent word to Hans. We'll meet him in the stables."

They made their way down the stairs to the interior courtyard and turned toward the palace door.

Sudiger was coming from the other direction and nearly knocked Trudi over as he turned the corner. The confused look on his face disappeared within the space of a moment. He seized Tassilo from Eta's hands. Trudi threw herself at him, reaching for her son, but Sudiger wrapped his hand around the boy's neck.

"I'll kill him!" he shouted. "I'll snap his neck!"

Trudi backed away, fear gripping her.

Sudiger's voice lowered to a growl. "The three of you aren't going anywhere. I'm moving up the wedding day. I've sent for a lore-master to officiate."

Trudi couldn't allow her despair to slow her thoughts. He was using her as a shield against Pippin's ire, expecting that Pippin wouldn't harm him if they were wed. She forced out a disdainful laugh. "It won't matter. Pippin won't recognize the marriage unless it's officiated by a priest."

"Then we'll get a priest." He started toward the door. When Trudi hesitated, he turned back, holding Tassilo in front of him. "If you want to see your son alive, you had better come with me."

With her free hand, Trudi pushed Eta away from her. "Run!"

Sudiger moved to restrain her, but Eta was too far away; she ran for the palace door. Howling his frustration, he shoved Trudi ahead of him and they followed Eta into the courtyard. Tassilo wailed and cried the entire way.

The church was in the old section of the city, a short distance from the palace. Sudiger led her through the streets, ignoring the shouts of onlookers recognizing Tassilo. Shoving open the doors to the church, he shouted, "Priest! Priest! I need a priest!"

A befuddled priest came from the sacristy via a door that led to the altar. He grew more confused upon seeing Tassilo struggling and screaming. "How – how may I help you, my son?"

With a furious grimace, Sudiger barked, "I'm not your son! You will address me as 'sire.' Sire!" Looking at Trudi he shook his head with disdain. "How you Franks let common men demean you like this I'll never understand." He turned to the priest. "You will perform the rites of marriage for me and this woman at once."

The priest's eyes were wide with fear and dismay. Trudi could see that he clearly had recognized her. "It's – It's not that simple."

"I didn't ask how hard it was."

"But you aren't a Christian!"

"Neither was Odilo."

Trudi knew the priest was stalling, looking for an excuse to delay.

The priest bowed deeply. "I will send for the bishop. I'm too lowly a priest for such nobility as you."

"Can you perform the rite or not?" Sudiger shouted, leaning over the poor man, using his size to intimidate.

"Yes, of course, but for nobility such as you, the bishop –"

"Fuck your bishop. Perform the rite!"

"I – I –"

Sudiger drew a dagger from his belt and held it out before the priest's face. The man's face grew pale.

"This is God's house. Put away that weapon." A voice boomed from the doorway to the sacristy. It was Bishop Gaibald. He stepped in front of the priest and with a straight back faced Sudiger. "You will not defile this church."

"I will do whatever I please. Now, one of you will perform the rite of marriage or I'll have this church burned to the ground."

Trudi was happy to see him. The bishop had been a regular guest of hers at the palace and Trudi considered him a friend. Appointed by Boniface five years earlier, he was not one to be intimidated by blustering nobility.

"We cannot. Gripho has been named her guardian. And he is not here to offer her hand to you."

"He has approved the marriage," Sudiger shouted.

"So you say." The bishop opened his hands with a gesture of helplessness.

Sudiger waved the dagger in front of the bishop's face. "I'll cut your throat."

The bishop didn't blink. "You forget, milord, that we worship a martyr."

Anger took Sudiger and he shifted Tassilo to his hip with one hand to bring the knife up before the bishop. "Then, I'll be happy to let you become one –"

Trudi kicked Sudiger's knee from the side and snatched Tassilo from his arm. Sudiger lunged wildly at her with his blade. Under normal circumstances, Trudi could have easily ducked beneath the blow, but holding Tassilo, all she could do was turn away, using her body to protect her son. Sudiger's blade cut into the flesh of her shoulder. She ran to put some distance between them but knew she would ultimately have to fight the man. Carrying Tassilo impeded her ability to get away. She set him down and pushed him toward Gaibald before turning to meet the threat.

Sudiger was on her before she could set her feet. Using his size as a weapon, he rushed her, lowering his shoulder in an effort to knock her to the ground. Trudi spun to her right, letting the left side of her body absorb the blow but quickly giving way before it. Sudiger barreled past her and Trudi shoved him to throw him off balance.

Her shoulder was in pain and blood from the wound covered her right arm, but she set her feet to await the next rush. Sudiger hadn't trained to be a knight. He was big but carried more fat than muscle. Sudiger faced her, this time more cautiously. He kept the blade low before him, flicking it back and forth as if he already was cutting her to ribbons.

Since he was using his right hand to hold the blade, Trudi circled left, limiting his range of motion. As she had hoped, he slashed backwards at her. She easily sidestepped the blade's arc and stepped forward, punching up with the heel of her hand. She caught his nose and heard it break. Blood poured out of his nostrils and he stepped back, lifting his left hand to try to staunch the blood.

A warrior would never have done that. She stepped in and kicked his knee, shoving it backwards in its joint. Sudiger stumbled away from her, exposing his left side. Trudi kicked again, disabling his other knee. This time, Sudiger went down. Trudi didn't waste another moment; she turned, found Tassilo, and made for the back of the church.

Before she reached the doorway, three armed men burst into the church and Trudi's heart sank. Gripho stepped in behind them. He walked down the aisle of the church to where Sudiger lay whimpering in pain. Shaking his head, he turned to Trudi. "You did this?"

She was too furious to respond.

Gripho shrugged. "I'd hate to see him on your wedding night. Unfortunately, we don't have time for this," he said. "Our scouts just arrived. Pippin's army will be here by tomorrow."

"You can't beat him."

"Hopefully they'll be so bloodied that he won't want to fight."

27

Regensburg

All night long, Bavarian soldiers – survivors of the battle in Alemannia – returned to Regensburg. Trudi watched from the rampart as Eingard reformed them into fighting units alongside the household retainers of the Bavarian nobles. These were augmented by several units of Slavs and Serbs who filled out the rest of the ranks, leaving Eingard with a force of about fifteen hundred men. It wasn't enough to face Pippin, thought Trudi. If Gripho meant it as a show of force, it was a pretty meagre one.

The bulk of the Bavarian nobility were waiting for Pippin on the rampart. It reminded Trudi of waiting for her father to come home after a campaign. Gripho was restless, pacing back and forth across the stout wall facing west. Lantfrid attended him, answering his questions and arguing over defensive strategies. The Aleman looked haunted with bags under his eyes and his face drained of color.

Eingard joined them late morning; he looked like a soldier destined to be hung but determined to face his demise bravely. Trudi pulled him aside so that they could speak privately. She wasn't sure what to say to him. He seemed a far different man than the one who left months ago on campaign.

"I'm happy for your return," she ventured.

He nodded. "An inglorious homecoming to be sure."

She put a reassuring hand on his arm. "All my life, I have been surrounded by the great and terrible men who rule Francia. Most of them, at one time or another, were beaten in battle by my father. Charles never lost. By the end of his life, few dared to challenge him and save for the Saracen, the kingdom was at peace. Each of them still ruled their own territories. All they had to do was place their hands in commendation, pay an annual tribute, and fight alongside him when he called.

"When Charles died all the great and terrible men of the kingdom rose to challenge his sons. Rather than keep the peace, they chose war. Rather than continue to rule their own lands and pay tribute, they chose war."

Anger filled her voice. "I know the cost of war. I bound the wounds of those who survived it and closed the eyes of those who didn't. I comforted the mothers who lost their sons and the wives who lost their husbands. They are the ones who paid for the arrogance of their leaders."

Trudi looked Eingard in the eye. "I hold our friendship in high regard, and I am truly glad that you've come home, but I beg you to sue for peace. Pippin is much like my father. Some say that on a battlefield, he is better. He doesn't lose."

Eingard shook his head. "Gripho thinks he won't fight; he thinks Pippin's army will be too bloodied and that he'll negotiate."

Trudi shook her head. "You fought with Lantfrid in Alemannia. What do you think?"

"Even bloodied, Pippin could beat all that we can muster."

A commotion interrupted them at the rampart wall.

"They're here!" Lantfrid shouted. "They're here!" He was leaning way out over the wall, straining to see the full extent of the threat they faced. Long minutes passed as Pippin's army came into view. Coming down off the wall he looked to Gripho and Eingard. His face was as pale as a ghost.

"What is it?" Gripho asked.

"Pippin's army is twice the size of what we faced in Alemannia. Childebrand is with him."

* * *

Pippin had chased what was left of the Alemanni and Bavarian troops all the way to Bavaria but stopped north of Danouwörth upon receiving word of Childebrand's approach.

"Less than two days," the messenger reported. He was one of Childebrand's top lieutenants. Pippin searched his mind for the man's name.

"Mattis," Pippin guessed.

"Yes, milord."

"Why did Childebrand send you rather than one of the regular messengers?"

"There is much news to relate, and it was thought you might have questions that a messenger could not answer."

"Did Childebrand arrive in time?"

"Yes, milord. At least to defeat the Twelve Counties men in battle. Unfortunately, Drusseau's main attack was on the camp itself. They drove deep within our camp before a counteroffensive could be made."

"Was Drusseau defeated?"

The man nodded. "Paris is secure. Drusseau and the Knights in Christ have been defeated and the king imprisoned in the palace."

Pippin held his breath. "And Bertrada?"

The lieutenant hesitated. "She is safe as is your son Charles. Although their tent was attacked, she and most of her party survived unscathed. Only the Lady Ragomfred and the Lady Drusseau were harmed."

Childebrand had warned him that Miette might try to rescue Drusseau's wife. "I take it Miette freed the Lady Drusseau?"

"Yes, milord. They and the Lady Hélène sought refuge with Lady Bertrada within Gunther's regiment."

"I'm sure Drusseau is livid."

Again, the man hesitated. "He's dead, milord."

Pippin was surprised. "In battle?"

"No, milord."

"What are you not telling me, Mattis?"

"The Lady Bertrada killed him, milord."

The words struck Pippin like the boss of a shield. He couldn't bring himself to believe them. Drusseau was a trained warrior. How had Bertrada come to kill him? Why would she kill him? He couldn't fathom her holding a weapon, much less using one. Hélène had told him that Bertrada was stronger than she seemed, but she had always abhorred violence. Something profound had changed and Pippin feared it was not for the better.

"How badly was Lady Ragomfred injured?"

"It is a serious wound, a sword thrust to her body. When we left, it wasn't clear she would survive."

The news shook him. He tried not to show it. "And the regiment?"

"Intact and on its way, milord. Although we suffered casualties, less than two hundred men died, mostly in the shield wall and in Arnot's defense of the camp. Childebrand's arrival broke the battle's impasse and the Twelve Counties men surrendered."

"And the Knights in Christ?"

"Most have been apprehended. Those guarding the palace and the king remain in place."

Pippin's gamble had succeeded. Paris, and therefore Neustria, was secure. Theodoric and the Alemanni had been defeated, and with the addition of Childebrand's regiment, they would have more than enough to confront Gripho and the Bavarians.

The news about Bertrada, however, gave him pause. Either she had changed beyond recognition or she was suffering terribly from guilt. Neither scenario was a welcome one.

Relieved that he would have Childebrand's legions to augment his own, he dismissed Mattis and sent men out to forage. He let the rest of the army enjoy the warm spring day. Gripho could wait a day or two.

When Childebrand arrived, the relief Pippin felt was palpable. His uncle's leadership ability was beyond value. The two had fought together so often that they required little communication between them.

Each understood the strengths and weaknesses of the other and compensated accordingly.

After giving orders to encamp, the giant of a man dismounted and hugged Pippin with both arms. Pippin felt lost within his embrace.

"Well met, uncle!" Pippin laughed when Childebrand released him. "You must have left Paris the moment the battle ended."

"That I did. I was worried I'd miss all the fun."

Pippin quickly described his battles in Saxony and Alemannia and his decision to impress most of the Saxon army. "Gripho and Lantfrid are both here. I want to take them into custody. We need to end this talk of a 'pagan mayor' rebellion."

"When do you want to attack?"

"Give your men a day to recoup. I've got men out foraging for supplies and Gripho won't be going anywhere."

When their conversation hit a lull, Pippin said in a soft voice, "Tell me of Bertrada."

Childebrand frowned. "In a surprise attack, Drusseau diverted a substantial number of men to assault our encampment, while our armies clashed in the field. By the time we routed their shield wall, he had control of most of the camp. We had to redeploy to drive them out. Ultimately, we found him in Bertrada's tent, where his wife was hiding."

"You had said Miette might try to rescue her."

Childebrand nodded. "Miette and Lady Hélène fought off Drusseau's men until they were overwhelmed. Miette was wounded and Hélène knocked unconscious. From what Miette told me, Drusseau found his wife and began beating her until her face was unrecognizable. With no one else to stop him, Bertrada intervened. She hit him with a heavy cross and crushed his skull."

Pippin shook his head. "It's hard to believe."

Childebrand nodded. "She's wracked with guilt, believing she committed a mortal sin."

"Surely a priest would disavow her of that."

The large man frowned. "Some priests hold people hostage to their sins."

Pippin swore. "I'll talk to Boniface. Maybe he can help her."

Childebrand nodded.

"How's Miette?"

"Very weak when I left."

The thought of her wounded made Pippin angry. "She's so reckless!"

Childebrand chuckled. "She called it 'justice.'"

Pippin grunted. "So I've heard."

* * *

They rode south and east to Regensburg, bringing their army before the massive Roman fort. Once in place, they flew a flag to offer parley. It took several minutes for the gate to open. When it did, a lone rider came forth. It was a woman. When she drew closer, Pippin realized it was Trudi.

Exchanging a look of confusion, Pippin and Childebrand rode out to meet her.

"Trudi," Pippin acknowledged.

"Brother," she said and turned to Childebrand. "Uncle."

"Where's Gripho?"

"He and the army fled yesterday when they saw Childebrand's banner."

Pippin's uncle chuckled. "Would be nice if that happened more often."

Pippin frowned. "Where did they go?"

"Eingard suggested that they head east towards Passau, using the Inn River as a line of defense."

"We heard you were imprisoned. Are you well? Is Tassilo?"

"Tassilo and I were held captive by Count Sudiger of Nordgau. He convinced Gripho to agree to an arranged marriage with me."

"Gripho?"

"He named himself regent and my guardian. If you hadn't arrived when you did, I'd likely be the Comtesse de Nordgau."

"Is Sudiger still here?"

Trudi shook her head. "He's no soldier but fled with the rest of them. He didn't want to be here when you arrived." She motioned to the city gate. "You're welcome to what hospitality I can muster."

"A wise choice on his part. I'll accept your hospitality after dealing with Gripho."

After a moment's hesitation, Trudi grinned mischievously. "Would you mind if I came with you?"

* * *

They followed the Danube's course east. It took three days for them to reach Passau. By the time they arrayed themselves along the shore of the Inn River, Gripho's army already had crossed to the other side. This posed a problem for Pippin as his men would be vulnerable when they crossed.

He was about to pull Childebrand aside to discuss strategy when Trudi touched his arm and pointed. A delegation from Gripho's army rode forward under a flag of truce. Commandeering two boats from the shoreline, the delegation rowed across the river to meet with Pippin.

"It's Eingard," Trudi said. "He will deal with you fairly."

"Come with us," Pippin said, as he nodded to Childebrand. The three of them dismounted and walked out to meet the Bavarians.

To Pippin's surprise, the delegation carried several chests with them. They laid the chests at Pippin's feet. One man stepped forward; he was stern looking with military bearing.

"What's this?" Pippin demanded.

"Milords Pippin and Childebrand, milady Hiltrude. I am Eingard, general of this army."

"Where's Gripho?"

Eingard looked embarrassed. "Alas, he, Lantfrid, and a number of Bavarian nobles have left the army in my hands."

"They fled?" Pippin asked.

Eingard nodded.

"What about Sudiger?" Trudi asked.

Again, the Bavarian nodded.

"Why the chests?" Pippin said.

"Your sister once counseled me that if you came to make war, I should sue for peace." He pointed to the chests. "I believe it is the right choice for this moment in time." He opened the chests. They were filled with silver and gold denarii.

Pippin heard Trudi's breath catch upon seeing the treasure. "What is it?" he asked her.

Trudi shook her head. "That's more than we had in the treasury. Where did you get it?" she asked Eingard.

"I suggested that Count Sudiger could make his escape faster without it."

Pippin frowned. "My sister has told me that you will deal fairly. While I accept your offer for peace, it comes at a higher price than this."

Eingard conferred with his compatriots before turning back to Pippin. "Your terms, milord?"

"I require hostages of my choosing from each of the noble families and enough treasure to pay for their care. Bavaria will return to their former level of tribute and my sister Hiltrude will regain her regency for Duc Tassilo. I will stand witness as each of your nobles offers her their hands in commendation. Those who refuse will be executed for treason. I also name myself her guardian and any threat to her will be considered a threat to me."

"Is that all, milord?"

Pippin shook his head. "I'm also offering a bounty of one hundred gold solidi for the capture and return of my brother Gripho. Do you agree to these terms?"

After receiving a brief nod from his delegation, Eingard bowed deeply. "Yes, milord."

"Then, I charge you with the administration of these conditions and ensuring that the Bavarian army surrenders unconditionally to my sister's authority."

Trudi leaned over and kissed Pippin on the cheek.

28

Paris

Although it took weeks for Pippin's army to return to Paris, the journey proved trouble free and the mood of the men remained buoyant. Each evening they celebrated their victories against the Saxons and the Alemanni and drank to the wisdom of the Bavarians for surrendering without a fight.

The news of their success preceded their journey home and long before they reached Paris, their march became a parade. Cheering throngs lined the roadway to greet the advancing cavalry and then fell in line behind the infantry to march for a moment as if they themselves had been a part of the army's victorious campaign. Musicians played, young women danced, children kept pace with the marching soldiers, and priests blessed their passing.

Once inside the city limits the cheering became a roar of approval that carried them all the way to the city's center. Even Pippin couldn't ignore the adulation. He and Childebrand chuckled at the extensive outpouring.

Childebrand tried to say something, but Pippin couldn't hear him. Laughing, they led the army to the encampment at the Rouvray Forest where Gunther had maintained a regiment to control the city. When they arrived, Pippin saw a green and red signal flag, flying above the entryway. It meant that Boniface had important news that required his immediate attention.

Leaving the army's management to Childebrand, Pippin returned to his family compound, his euphoria waning with each step closer to home. Although curious about the news from Boniface, he was far more worried about Bertrada.

She was waiting for him at the door when he arrived. Exhaustion marred her face and her eyes were haunted as if she hadn't slept in weeks. She ran to him and kissed him, tears streaming down her face. "I'm so thankful you are home," she said.

"I'm here now. Everything will be all right."

Shaking her head, she began to pull away from him. "It won't. It won't ever be all right."

The despair in her eyes unnerved him and Pippin took her face in his hands and kissed her on the lips. "Yes. Yes, it will!" he insisted. "We're here and alive and together." Looking around him, he called out, "Where's Charles?"

"Here, milord." It was Catherine. She led Charles out of the house by his hand.

Pippin laughed and picked up his son and pulled him into the embrace with Bertrada. "See! We're all together!"

Charles immediately started wailing and flung his arms around his mother. A slight smile found Bertrada's face. "He'll have to get used to you again."

"Have I been gone so long?"

Her smile turned into a smirk. "That and you really need of a bath."

Pippin laughed outright and saw a glimmer of amusement in Bertrada's eyes. It didn't wash away her despair, but it did offer him hope.

Turning toward the door he found the entryway filled with people welcoming him home. In addition to Catherine and her children, Gunther, Lady Hélène, and Boniface stood waiting for him. Pippin embraced each of them in turn.

Boniface immediately tried to pull him aside. "Bishop Burchard of Würzburg and Fulrad have returned from Rome," he whispered.

Pippin's eyes widened. "And?"

"They will only speak to you."

Pippin's heart was racing. "Where are they?"

"They are staying with me at Saint-Germain-des-Prés."

"Send for them, immediately." Seeing Bertrada frown, he hesitated. "I will meet with them this afternoon." He squeezed Bertrada's hand. "But first I need a bath."

Returning Charles to Catherine's care, Pippin led Bertrada to his rooms. They spoke quietly while his bath was being prepared.

Pippin wasn't sure where to start. "Childebrand told me of your encounter with Drusseau."

Bertrada's eyes grew hard. "You mean my murder of Drusseau."

"You saved his wife!"

"Miette saved his wife. I killed him." Her throat constricted when she said this and her tears started anew.

"You defended a woman being beaten. It was a righteous act."

Her haunted eyes looked up at him. She shook her head. "It is a mortal sin. I have damned myself to hell."

"What priest has told you this?"

"Father Morreau."

"Speak to Boniface. I doubt he would characterize it that way."

"The commandment only says 'thou shalt not kill.' It doesn't say 'unless you are defending a woman being beaten.'"

This shocked Pippin. "Do you believe I've committed mortal sins?"

Bertrada slowly nodded. "You don't?"

Her answer both confounded and infuriated him. "Of course not. I keep the peace."

"By conquering everyone else. That's the definition of a tyrant." She held up her hand when he began to protest. "I had made my peace with your role as mayor, Pippin. I understood that you must stop evil men like Theudebald. I've tried to believe that I could abhor the office but still love the man. But after I killed Drusseau, I've come to believe that one's purpose does not justify the deed."

Pippin shook his head. "If we don't confront evil it will rule the world."

"That's something Carloman would say."

The rebuke stung him. "My brother believed he was the Blade of Christ here on earth. He saw good and evil as absolutes."

"They are."

Pippin stopped to think. He could see her reasoning but sensed there was a flaw in it. "Good and evil may be absolutes, but our choices are not. If you had not acted when you did – if you had let Drusseau kill his wife – would that not have been evil?"

Bertrada nodded. "But it would have been his evil, not mine."

"And if he had continued his savagery? If he had killed Miette or Lady Hélène? At what point does your responsibility begin for allowing his evil to continue?"

"You don't know that he would continue. I didn't."

Pippin tried a different tack. "Do believe it is a sin to defend yourself?"

Bertrada shook her head no.

"Then why would it be a sin to defend another?"

In a small voice she said, "But I didn't just defend her; I killed him."

Pippin pulled her into his arms. "Bertie, he was a trained soldier. If you didn't kill him as you did, you could never have stopped him."

Her tears returned. "I just don't know if I can live with myself."

"Talk to Boniface. He'll help you see the truth." While Pippin hoped that was true, he doubted it would be easy.

* * *

After his bath, Pippin came downstairs to find Boniface waiting for him. He asked his godfather to speak to Bertrada before turning to matters of state.

"Father Morreau has got her twisted into knots. She can't see that her actions were justified."

"I will speak to her. I can't imagine Morreau would be so damning."

Pippin frowned. "I can. How many priests use absolution as a leverage for power? You saw what Heddo did to Carloman."

"Be at peace, Pippin. I will attend to Bertrada's atonement myself."

"You've already missed the point. For what does she have to atone?"

Boniface held up his hands signaling surrender. "I agree with you, Pippin. But, if she believes she has sinned, we must offer her a way to forgive herself. Penance can be very helpful in restoring the soul."

Pippin struggled to keep the emotion from his voice. "She's struggling, Boniface. She believes I'm damned as well. You must help her."

Boniface wrapped his arms around Pippin. "I will. I promise I will."

Although surprised by Boniface's gesture, Pippin returned the embrace. He had carried Bertrada's angst alone for so long, it was a relief to have help. After a moment, he coughed and broke free.

"Burchard and Fulrad?"

Boniface waved Pippin toward the sitting room. "They're waiting for you."

Pippin hesitated. The outcome of this meeting would determine the path of his life for years to come. Although he prayed that the pope would grant him the legitimacy he would need to rule, he prepared himself to be rejected.

It was the likely outcome. He had gambled, intimating that unless the pope sanctioned his right to rule, he would withhold military support if the Lombards attacked the Holy See. It was an empty threat, and the pope likely knew it. Pippin couldn't allow King Aistulf to have such power over the Church.

A rejection would force Pippin to rule without the sanction of the crown or the papal see. It risked excommunication. Pippin stared into a future where his only legitimacy came from military power.

"Doesn't that make you a tyrant?" Bertrada's words haunted him. She believed he'd committed mortal sin. He, like his father and grandfather, had spent the greater part of his life in battle. Together, they had brought to heel every warlord from the Pyrenees to the Carpathian

Mountains. Could such relentless ambition be justified? He needed to know before the meeting.

"Pippin?" It was Boniface. He appeared confused.

Pippin held up his hand; he needed more time to think. Carloman had used the Church and his faith to validate his pursuit of power, but what did Pippin count as his own reasons? He had opposed Childeric because the man was evil. But is that enough? What justified him seeking the throne?

Bertrada would call it arrogance, but at the heart of it, Pippin had a broader perspective. He had seen his father's unyielding resolve to establish a strong central power for the kingdom. Without it, they were vulnerable to attack from without by the Saracen and from within by the pagan territories. Over the course of their reign, the Merovingians had become weak, and Charles had stepped into the breach to shore up their power.

But in his heart, Pippin knew his quest wasn't about power alone. The truth was he didn't trust anyone else to wield such authority. He knew none of the other nobles could hold the kingdom together or rule it justly. He had to do it – with or without the pope. There was no other choice. That was his justification for seeking the throne.

Nodding to Boniface he said, "I'm ready."

Burchard looked much the same as when Pippin had seen him last – more blacksmith than bishop. The large man stood and clasped forearms with Pippin. "Well met, milord."

"Well met." Pippin nodded to Fulrad. "Any trouble on the road?"

"A bandit or two. Nothing we couldn't handle."

"How did Zachary respond to Pippin's message?" Boniface blurted out.

Burchard raised an eyebrow. "*His holiness the pope* said this was to be delivered only to the mayor." He produced a scroll and handed it to Pippin.

Pippin took the document, trying to ignore the dread stealing into his stomach. To keep his emotions at bay, he read it slowly.

"What is it?" Boniface urged. "What does it say?"

Pippin held the scroll up and read aloud. "Mayor Pippin, you ask, 'whether 'tis good, or not, that the kings of the Franks should wield no royal power?' We ordain that: it is better to call him who has the royal power than the one who does not."

Pippin's shoulders slumped. He had been rejected. He felt the weight of the coming years bearing down on him.

"I don't understand," said Fulrad.

"It's a nonanswer." Pippin sighed. "He is being intentionally vague."

"Yet," Boniface said, clapping him on the shoulder. "It is enough." Pippin's godfather chuckled almost to himself. "I always suspected this day would come."

Pippin turned to him, confused. "I don't understand."

Boniface was grinning. "He's leaving himself room in case you fail. He can always say you misinterpreted him."

"And if I don't fail?" Pippin said.

"Then it will suffice. He'll claim the decision was his all along."

Fulrad looked bewildered. "I don't understand."

"It means I won't have to fight for legitimacy," Pippin said.

Boniface put his hand on Pippin's shoulder. "It means we're going to Soissons."

* * *

As the news swept through Paris, church bells rang in celebration and Pippin's compound flew into turmoil. Given Bertrada's melancholy, Boniface and Catherine bent to the task of planning the coronation, relegating her to the task of dispatching messengers to the kingdom's nobles inviting them to attend the ceremony at Soissons.

Pippin ordered Gunther to seize the palace and, on the advice of Boniface, usher Childeric to the monastery in Saint-Omer. Once that task was underway, he felt like he had been abandoned. Everyone close to him was engaged in some aspect of his elevation. He decided to check on the progress of Miette's recovery.

She greeted him sitting in a chair, her torso wrapped tightly in a bandage. Although she was pale, thin, and weak to his eyes, she maintained that she was well and would soon be ready to resume her training with Hélène. He asked her to recount her rescue of Drusseau's wife and she had regaled him with her exploits escaping the castle.

When she told him about being asked to clean the bedpans she laughed so hard it sent a spasm of pain through her. She clutched her side in agony.

Pippin could see blood seeping through her bandage. "I'm so sorry I wasn't there. I should have protected you and Bertrada from Drusseau."

She smiled. "We did well enough on our own, especially Bertrada."

"She's wracked with remorse."

"Shouldn't be. It was just."

Pippin nodded. "Still, I owe you a debt for protecting my family."

She waved her hand, dismissing his words. "It was the right thing to do."

"Nonetheless, it was very brave."

She smiled at him, her eyes suddenly glassy. "Remember when we first met? I came to your messy room. You couldn't keep your eyes off me."

"I remember."

Tears leaked from her eyes. "We had quite the dance, you and me. You thought I was manipulating you."

"You weren't?"

"I was, a little. It wasn't hard." She shook her head. "But I knew at once I loved you. I should have seduced you, then. Before Bertrada –"

"Miette –"

"I just need to say it!" she insisted, then shook her head. "You're right." She smiled weakly. "Forget I mentioned it."

Pippin had no idea what to do. He couldn't deny having strong feelings for Miette, but he had made his choice. He felt guilty and embarrassed for her all at the same time.

She stood. "I apologize, but I need to rest a bit."

He rose. "If there's anything I can do –"

She waved away his offer. "I'll be fine. But I do have a favor to ask: Would you mind if I missed your coronation? I've got something important that needs doing."

Pippin couldn't imagine anything more important than his coronation but was somewhat relieved at her decision. If she needed time to accept his marriage, he would give her however much time she needed.

* * *

Pippin and Boniface sat next to each other in the sacristy of the Abbey Saint-Médard of Soissons waiting for the coronation to begin.

"Do you think we'll be safe here?" Pippin quipped. As large as a city, the abbey was a bastion protected by stone walls, turrets, drawbridges, and moats. Within its confines, the abbey housed a dozen gardens and cultivated fields, a granary, a church, a residence hall, a stable, and an armory. It was nothing less than a fortress.

Boniface kept a straight face. "There are more humble abbeys."

They had delayed the coronation for six weeks after receiving the pope's letter to provide ample time for the kingdom's nobility to witness the ceremony. While this was not a necessary convention – Boniface could have performed the ceremony at any time – Pippin wanted the pageant to help solidify his power in the minds of the nobles. He also hoped that a large showing of nobles from throughout the kingdom would discourage opposition to his rule. If, however, there were large gaps – territories absent – Pippin feared it would send the opposite message.

"How many do you think will come?"

"Nobles?" Boniface frowned. "Most of Austrasia, and Neustria, of course. Your sister brought a contingent from Bavaria. Warin and Ruthard are here representing Alemannia."

"Saxony?"

Boniface shook his head. "Theodoric refused. How about Aquitaine?"

Pippin frowned. "Waifar slew the messenger. I suppose this group will have to suffice."

"You can deal with Waifar next year."

"And the decade after that." Pippin smiled wryly. "It's what I get for naming myself king."

"It's too late for remorse," Boniface chided.

"I just wish the pope had been more explicit."

"He left himself a way out. If you fail as king, or if you refuse to come to his aid against the Lombards, he can say you mistook his words to name yourself king."

Although Pippin understood the logic, he was angry because the pope's gambit would cost him years of bloodshed. "When I save him from the Lombards, I'll insist he come to Francia to crown me himself."

Boniface laughed. "He'll never leave Rome."

"Mark my words, godfather."

Horns blew declaring the beginning of the coronation. Although Pippin couldn't see the procession of nobles filing into the church, he could hear their names announced as they walked down the aisle to take their seats. More horns sounded and Boniface nodded for them to step out onto the altar. Pippin watched as a parade of bishops advanced toward them behind a large cross carried by Aidolf of Auxerres.

Pippin whispered, "I thought he opposed me."

"I wanted to send a message. You can't afford a divided clergy."

"Kyrie eleison," Aidolf intoned.

"Kyrie eleison," echoed the bishops, chanting the opening lines of the Litany of Saints. They progressed through two dozen names before finding their places on the altar. When they had finished, Boniface took charge of the ceremony, offering mass and the eucharist to those in attendance. Pippin waited patiently for the actual coronation rite to begin, surprised at his own lack of emotion.

It struck him as sad that, other than Trudi and Childebrand, none of his original family were present. Carloman was in Rome, Sunnichild had passed away in her abbey, and Gripho was on the run. Three generations of his family had fought for this moment and almost no one was present to see it.

He took comfort in Bertrada's presence in the front pew. She was growing large with their second child and holding little Charles in her lap. Boniface had helped to ease her guilt over Drusseau's death, but she still wrestled with the morality of it. Pippin took it as a good sign that she had agreed to celebrate his coronation. Filling out the rest of the pew reserved for his family were Lady Hélène, Catherine, and Gunther.

Pippin was so focused on them that he almost missed Boniface's motion for him to take the throne. He bowed to Boniface and sat. In unison, the entire congregation stood. It was at that moment the magnitude of his family's accomplishment – his accomplishment – struck him. His mind cascaded through the battles he had fought with his father and the stories of the battles fought by his grandfather. At the same time, he also envisioned the next hundred years where his son and his grandson would be kings.

Boniface dipped his thumb in the holy oil. "On the day Clovis became king, the holy dove brought oil to christen him king. So, too, do we christen thee."

A dove was released from behind the altar as Boniface pressed his oiled thumb to Pippin's forehead. Aidolf handed the crown to Boniface, and together they held it above Pippin's head.

"In the name of the Father, the Son, and the Holy Ghost," Boniface said in a voice that carried the entirety of the church, "as legate of the Holy See, I crown thee Pippin the Second, King."

As one, the congregation roared their approval. For once, Pippin allowed himself to enjoy the moment. He took in the applause, the cheering, and the pride expressed by the nobility and an overwhelming sense of relief flooded through him. Despite the hard work ahead, he had fulfilled his father's dream.

Boniface and Aidolf lowered the crown on his head. He was surprised at how heavy it felt.

29

Endings

Gripho was furious. He was running out of options. Once he realized the Bavarians couldn't beat Pippin, he had taken the nobles loyal to him to Aquitaine to seek Gascon support. He had been sure that Hunoald would welcome his war against Pippin. Unfortunately, the duc recently had abdicated and left the duchy to his son Waifar, who didn't see much difference between one of Charles Martel's sons and the next. They had been lucky to leave unscathed. Only the promise of a broader rebellion had saved them.

His only remaining possibility of sanctuary was King Aistulf of the Lombards. Aistulf had a long-standing resentment for Carloman and Pippin, as he had been promised Trudi's hand in marriage. It was a political union meant to ally the two kingdoms through their family bloodlines. When Trudi had fled Charles's court to marry Odilo, Aistulf had felt betrayed.

Gripho's problem, for the moment, however, was avoiding capture while they crossed Francia to reach the Roman Peninsula. He had a half dozen nobles with him, including Lantfrid and Sudiger, along with their retainers – another twenty men-at-arms. As such, they were a formidable fighting force, at least for travelling the Roman roads across southern Francia. He had completed the bulk of his journey by avoiding the more populous cities.

They were near the end of their journey. Nestled among the Alps in the southeast corner of Francia on the river Arc, Saint Jean-de-

Maurienne was their last stop before heading south to Turin. It had rained for much of the day, drenching their party to the skin, so Gripho decided that they would spend a night at an inn rather than camp out in the cold.

Once their horses had been tended, the men agreed to meet in the main hall of the tavern for their evening meal. Gripho went upstairs and attempted to dry out some of his clothes. When he came downstairs, he found his men clustered around a large fire along the back wall drinking wine.

"To our mayor!" Sudiger raised his flagon. Lantfrid and the others followed suit. The toast drew looks from some of the other tables, but Gripho's stare returned them to their places. He poured himself a cup and cautioned his men. "Let's keep such accolades to ourselves, until we leave Francia."

A waitress brought out stew for each of them and was quick to keep their flagons filled. As the night wore on and their clothes dried, the group became boisterous.

Lantfrid boasted about retaking Alemannia once they had Aistulf's army behind them. Sudiger frowned at this and Gripho was quick to point out that Bavaria had to be first. It was a persistent issue between the two men. Gripho found the argument absurd given their current circumstances.

As was their habit most evenings, Sudiger drew out a pair of dice and the men began to gamble. Sudiger was wise enough to let the others win occasionally to prevent resentment among the group. Still, Gripho noted, Sudiger never lost very much.

After an hour, Lantfrid left the game with a curse and made his way to where Gripho sat, spilling his wine as he came. When he was deep in his cups, the Aleman's eyes became angry, staring from under his brow at everyone who passed.

"I'm going to gut that brother of yours, Gripho."

Gripho smiled, humoring him. "Which one?"

The Aleman looked surprised. "Carloman!"

"Take your revenge on Pippin," Gripho said. "Carloman can do us little harm tucked away in the clergy."

It took some time for this thought to penetrate Lantfrid's wine-induced fog, but eventually he nodded. "You're right. I'll gut both of 'em."

Gripho clapped him on the shoulder. "Just make sure I'm there to see it."

An argument broke out among the gamblers and Gripho quickly stepped in to settle the dispute. The last thing he needed was for them to draw unwanted attention; they still had another day before they crossed the border. He ordered the men to bed and, although several grumbled, they obeyed.

The next morning, they left the inn just after dawn to make their way south. Fortunately, the rain had stopped, and the day promised to be a cool one, perfect for their trip to Turin. Majestic mountains to the east and west towered over them to as they left the city following the Arc River through the valley. As was their practice, Sudiger led the contingent to allow Gripho to remain hidden among the nobles.

Just as they reached the Roman road, they were confronted by a group of armed men. Gripho counted no more than thirty barring their way.

"State your name!" ordered their lead knight. He was a tallish man with a northern accent.

Sudiger rode forward to meet them, Lantfrid beside him. "Count Sudiger. These men are my cousins and their retainers." Sudiger sounded polite but mildly irritated. "Who the hell are you?"

"Theodoenus of Vienne." The lead knight pointed to a second. "And that is Frederic of Transjura."

"Both of you are far from home," Sudiger said. "Why are you barring our way?"

"We are searching for the outlaw Gripho."

Sudiger made a great show of spitting. "Well, I hope you find the bastard. He's caused enough trouble, hasn't he?"

"You were overheard last night toasting to one of you as 'mayor,'" Frederic said, his eyes scanning their faces. "Which one of you boasts of such a title?"

Sudiger shook his head and chuckled. "Your source must have had too much drink. We toasted Mayor Pippin, of course."

"No," Theodoenus said. "I heard it myself. One within your group is the outlaw Gripho and you'd be advised to surrender him now or we'll take him by force."

Sudiger appeared unruffled. "I can assure you that –"

Lantfrid drew his blade. In response every scabbard in both parties emptied. Silence captured the road as the men poised for battle.

"Christ!" Gripho whispered, riding forward. In a loud voice he stated, "I am Gripho, son of Charles, son of Pippin of Herstal. I was named mayor of the palace by my father. Who are you to name me 'outlaw'?"

"It is your brother Pippin who names you."

"Then who are you to judge which of us is in the right? If you are a noble, Theodoenus of Vienne, you are from a minor house as I've never heard your name. You're also far from home and acting far above your station. Why would you take such a risk?"

Theodoenus seemed a bit unsure. "It is by order of Mayor Pippin."

"Let me guess," Gripho said. "He offered a bounty. You're here for the bounty. How much did he offer?"

"One hundred gold solidi."

Gripho feigned shock. "Only one hundred?!" He shook his head. "Pippin was never good with gold. I can promise you two hundred gold solidi if you let us pass. Otherwise, there will be a battle and you and Frederic will die today, and I will still make my way to Turin."

Theodoenus hesitated and looked to Frederic for input. Their eyes locked. "Two hundred?"

Lantfrid spurred his horse forward and lunged, his sword catching Theodoenus in the neck, ripping away his throat and knocking him off his horse. Frederic was quick to react, slashing down with his blade, sinking it deep into the Aleman's shoulder.

Both companies spurred forward, meeting in a crash of horses and a clang of blades. With Theodoenus down, Gripho attacked Frederic, thinking that if they could kill both leaders, the attack might end.

Frederic, however, was a veteran fighter and quick with his blade. They exchanged blow after blow, with neither finding advantage. Gripho reared his horse to try to throw the man off balance, but the noble calmly pulled his horse aside and resumed the attack.

Although frustrated, Gripho remained confident. He had been trained by Fulrad and there was none better. All around him the fighting continued. Sudiger fell, his stomach sliced open from one end to the other, but the retainers fought well, giving Gripho hope. His only focus now was Frederic. If he could defeat Frederic, he was sure the battle would end. He ducked under a sweeping blow that passed inches above his head and punched forward with his sword catching Frederic in the side. Hearing the man grunt, Gripho smiled and launched an attack to end the contest.

Frederic fell back; all his efforts bent on deflection. Gripho felt a rush of euphoria as he saw the opening for a killing blow. He took it, slashing down on Frederic with all the strength he could muster. His blade caught the man just to the side of his head, sinking deep into his chest. It was finished.

With a cry, Gripho doubled over as severe pain erupted from his stomach. Confused, he looked down to find Frederic's blade deep in his belly. For the chance to catch him off guard Frederic had left himself open to a killing blow. With horror, Gripho watched his blood draining from him, as he tried to wrest the blade from its hold.

He no longer could hear the fighting around him. Looking up, he found soldiers from both companies watching him.

"Bastards!" he swore. "You think to watch me die?" He continued to struggle with the sword until the world seemed to tilt on him, and he found himself on the ground. The blade was still wedged in his stomach. He tried to stand but his feet couldn't seem to find capture.

A shiver took his body, and he wondered how the day had grown so cold. He looked around for someone to help him up, but no one moved. He could see the resignation in their eyes.

"I am mayor!" He tried to shout, but his voice sounded so weak. He closed his eyes. "I am..." he said as his last breath left him.

* * *

After the coronation, Bertrada and Pippin returned to Paris and again their arrival was cause for celebration. After tolerating several fetes commemorating Pippin's elevation to the throne, they moved into the palace.

Bertrada was grateful for the opportunity to lose herself in the transition. She long ago had reconciled herself to Pippin being crowned king but hadn't considered the implications of becoming queen. While she always had been paid some amount of deference due to her association with Pippin, the esteem afforded her as queen was in many ways alarming. Men bowed and women curtsied every time she passed. Everyone waited for her to recognize them before speaking. And when they did speak, they always deferred to her opinion. It was dreadful.

All the nobles affiliated with Childeric's reign had left the palace, most by their own accord. With Pippin's input, new residents were chosen, including, of course, all their household from the compound on the West Bank.

Bertrada also oversaw redecorating the building using Pippin's colors of green and white as well as repurposing several rooms to display the many works of art already housed within the palace but tucked away in the living quarters.

She threw herself into the transformation, knowing it was a way of avoiding the issues that still haunted her waking hours. She had come to some sort of truce with Boniface. Although she had acquiesced to his process of penance and pardon, she had a hard time believing it released her from all responsibility.

She also still feared for Pippin's immortal soul. How could he survive the Lord's judgement day with so much blood on his hands? And now that she was his queen, to what extent was the responsibility hers?

Hélène was helpful at quieting her mind. Although Bertrada was getting far into her pregnancy, she joined Hélène each morning in her daily ritual of moving through her series of poses. Together they flowed soundlessly from one posture to another. It took every bit of Bertrada's concentration to keep up the pace set by her friend.

One morning after they had finished, Bertrada sat next to Hélène, letting her body cool in the early daylight. Hélène brought her some water to drink and the two sat in silence. Bertrada had come to appreciate Hélène as more than a friend. The woman exuded a wealth of confidence and passion that Bertrada wished she could emulate. She also didn't curtsey or call her "milady." Hélène still called her by her name and Bertrada could kiss the woman for it.

"Your poses were troubled this morning," Hélène said. "Your mind is unsettled."

"It is." She wanted to say more but didn't know where to begin.

"Was it the babe?"

Bertrada chuckled. "He did kick me a few times. But that isn't it."

Hélène waited.

Bertrada tried to find gentler words but couldn't. "How do you live with the blood on your hands? How do you justify the killing you do?"

If Hélène was offended by her question, she didn't show it. She seemed to weigh her words carefully. "I understand the context of my actions."

"I don't understand."

"When you think of killing Drusseau, you see the act itself as a sin."

"It is."

"I have been trained to see the purpose surrounding such deeds."

Bertrada frowned. "To excuse them?"

"To determine if they are just. When Salau came for you at the abbey, were Agnès and I wrong to attack him? Was I wrong to save your life?"

"No."

"Then, how is that different from you defending Charlotte? You took Drusseau's life to stop him. It was a selfless act. You put yourself in harm's way, attacking a knight trained in combat, to save the life of another. If you examine the deed alone, it is murder. If you examine the context, it is righteous."

Bertrada sighed. "Even if it is, I'm not sure I can live with murdering Drusseau."

Hélène took her by the hand. "Justice is a dark path."

Bertrada had heard the words before but hadn't understood them. Now they settled within her mind, erecting a bridge between her abhorrence for violence and the moral need for wielding it. It allowed her to see that killing Drusseau, even if abhorrent, was the right thing to do. Pippin had been right; good and evil may be absolutes, but the choices we're given are not.

Despite this revelation, accepting the premise that such violence could be justified frightened her. "But how can defining a moral need for violence be anything but subjective? Carloman certainly thought he was justified at Canstatt."

Hélène nodded. "You need a moral framework for making such decisions."

Bertrada suspected that the answer was forming in her mind but wasn't sure she had the right questions. "Tell me about justice."

Hélène's mouth curled into a smile. "It's complicated."

* * *

It was a late summer evening but the hallways of the monastery at Saint Bertin felt cool to Miette. She had waited until after Compline before slipping quietly past the gothic outer doors, through the nave, and down the hallway to the residence hall. Dressed in black, she moved so soundlessly she could have been mistaken for a specter. She counted the doorways, stopping at eight, and slid the latch to open the door.

Childeric was sitting in a lone chair by a fire, his face illuminated by a single candle on the table next to him.

Although surprised by the intrusion, Childeric smiled when he recognized her. "Miette! How delightful. Have you come to play?"

She closed the door. "I've come to watch you die."

He frowned. "How curious! I would have expected Lady Hélène." He pointed at his bed. "I apologize for my lack of accommodations. Please, sit."

Miette sat.

"I'm stunned it took Pippin so long!" Childeric twirled his hand. It was a gesture she often had seen him do when his fingernails were long. They, along with his hair, had been shorn when he'd taken the tonsure. He seemed to realize they were missing and closed his hand.

"So, you've been expecting this?" she asked.

"It is said that we Merovingians can forecast the future, but an idiot could predict my murder. As long as I live, I'm a threat to your master."

"I have no 'master.'"

"Yet, you're here at Pippin's bidding."

Miette shook her head. "He doesn't know I'm here. I'm come to claim a debt for the murder of a woman named Agnès and the violence you did to me, Lady Brevet, and Lady Drusseau."

"I've never even heard of Agnès."

"Your man Salau killed her along with several nuns while hunting Bertrada."

Childeric waved his hand contemptuously. "As you well know, Salau could be quite excessive. I only asked him to find her, not harm her. So, if there's a score to settle, you'll have to settle it with him." He feigned sudden surprise. "Oh, but you already did!"

"The fault doesn't end with him. You bear responsibility for your man."

"And who are you to judge the actions of a king?"

A righteous calm filled her. "I am justice."

Childeric grunted. "And how am I at fault for what happened to you and the rest of those women? You were more than willing! You invented half the games we played and always begged for more."

Miette stood, the anger getting the better of her. "Until I didn't. And then you nearly killed me."

Childeric rolled his eyes at her outrage. "What you call 'justice' sounds very much like 'revenge.'"

"Vengeance is the Lord's work. I just help balance the scales."

Childeric grunted dismissively before pointing to her midsection. "For someone coming to kill me, you seem to be doing all the bleeding."

Miette looked down. Blood was seeping through her bandage. Her wound had never fully healed and the ride to Saint Bertin had torn it anew.

"It won't stop me."

His smile was patronizing. "And how will you do it? I doubt you could subdue me even if you were armed."

"Oh, I'm well armed. And I can think of three ways to kill you without getting off this bed."

He chuckled. "What then? A knife across my throat? Such a murder in this place would arouse a great deal of suspicion." His hand went to his chin. "Suffocation? Strangulation?"

Miette sat down again. "It's already been done. I'm just waiting for the end."

Childeric's eyes widened. "Poison? I should have guessed."

His indifference to his own death bothered her. She wanted to see him beg for his life, weep for his soul. She wanted to see him humbled. "You don't believe me?"

"On the contrary. But I'll admit to some disappointment. It's an ignoble way to die."

"You don't seem upset by the prospect."

Childeric winced in pain and stared at his fist. He watched it open and close several times before returning to her question. "I've had ample time to prepare. I saw my death years ago."

"Is it true, then? You can see the future?"

"We Merovingians aren't all-knowing, but we're given glimpses into what's to come. I once warned Pippin that, if he didn't bend his knee to me, he'd be doomed to a lifetime of war. I wasn't lying. I saw the crossroads of his choices and knew where it would leave us."

Miette rolled her eyes. "So you say."

Childeric sat forward in earnest. "Had he submitted to me, the kingdom would have been at peace for his lifetime and mine! He would have had to suffer...my indulgences...but he would enjoy the love of his family and live a life of comfort."

"And now that he's refused?"

"He's doomed himself to war for the rest of his days. It'll take twenty years to defeat the Gascons and even then, he won't be done. He'll waste his life on a dream he'll never live to see."

Childeric sat back in his chair with a sigh. "His refusal also ordained that I would die in this room."

"Then why try to kill Bertrada and their son?"

"They, too, represented crossroads. Without either of them, he would have failed. And I wouldn't be sitting here with you."

Childeric's face grimaced and his body clenched in a seizure. His eyes grew wide in surprise as his back arched in pain and a howl escaped through his teeth.

She sat patiently until the spell passed, watching his body slowly relax and his breathing return to normal.

"You bitch." He tried to unclench his hand. "That was painful."

Miette finally felt some satisfaction. "It's going to be very painful." She went to the washbasin across the room and returned with a small towel.

Another seizure hit him, and his hands drew back toward his chest, his fingers curling into odd shapes. His back arched and his teeth began to gnash down on his tongue. Twisting the towel, she waited for his mouth to open and thrust the towel in to prevent him from shouting.

Again, the convulsion passed, and, again, his eyes returned to her. They were wild from the pain but alight with a malevolence she found arresting. He pulled the towel from his mouth and gripped her arm to pull her close.

"The irony is" – he smiled, blood dripping from his mouth – "Pippin will be forgotten. He will conquer a kingdom not seen since the time of the Romans and all his sacrifice, all his triumph, will fade from history.

"But his son?" Childeric's voice grew giddy with laughter. "All Pippin's fame and glory will accrue to Charles. Pippin's name will be lost among the multitude of names that cascade through time but his son's will live for a thousand years!"

Another seizure, a powerful one, started and Childeric's face began to panic at its onset. An agonized scream seemed to wrench itself from his lungs.

Miette watched dispassionately while his back arched and his limbs contorted until some of his smaller bones snapped. This time she didn't help with the towel. She kept her eyes on him, watching wave after wave of pain wrack his body until he breathed his last.

Only then did she allow herself to groan with pain. Holding her hand to her side, she slipped from Childeric's room, leaving a rivulet of blood in her wake.

* * *

Pippin followed Bertrada through the palace to see the logic of its transformation. They walked from room to room as she explained what functions each would hold and why she had chosen the decorations on display. Although he was exhausted, he was very complimentary of her choices and nodded appreciatively at the works of art she had gathered together to exhibit.

It dawned on him that this had always been her way of expressing affection. Despite their differences, she had always been hostess to his home, always been there at his side. Even though she loathed the violence associated with his family, she had never let go of that connection to him. It was her way of demonstrating her commitment.

They worked their way through the kitchen to the residences. She noted which nobles were to reside where and explained her choices for the hierarchy she used in assigning them.

She ended the tour back in the ballroom, which she had reoriented by putting the throne on the long wall to create a less imposing entrance.

"I want people to love you, not fear you," she said.

He chuckled at that. "I'm afraid that as king, I'll need a little of both." He took her in his arms and hugged her. "You've done a wonderful job. It's beautiful."

Although there was no music, he lifted her hand and led her in an impromptu dance. She followed his lead, resting her head on his shoulder and aligning her body alongside his as they made their way across the floor.

"Are you happy, my love?" Pippin whispered. Now that he was king, it was the only doubt that truly plagued him. He wasn't sure he could carry the weight of the kingdom without her.

Her eyes squinted in thought. "I'm finding my way to it. It may take me some time, but I will get there. Are you happy now that you're king?"

He chuckled. "I don't think kings can afford to be happy."

She pushed him playfully. "Liar! You defied the odds, outmaneuvered the Church, and achieved your life's ambitions. Don't tell me you're not happy."

He smiled but shook his head. "I'll admit to some joy at the achievement but being king will cost us much. It will be years before the realm will be at peace. I've accepted a great and grave responsibility that I can't take lightly."

She stopped dancing and looked up into his eyes; the challenge he found there offered no compromise. "Tell me you'll be a just king."

His own gaze never faltered. "I will."

She nodded and rose onto her toes to kiss him. "Then our lives will be well lived and we will find happiness."

She let him go, spread her arms wide, and twirled. "So, you like your new palace, my king?"

"It's beautiful."

She heard the hesitation in his voice and stopped twirling. "But?"

He gave her a tired smile. "I know it took us a long time to get here, but all I want now is to go to Quierzy. Let's take Charles and go tonight. I'll leave Childebrand in charge. We'll have the new babe there and have some time to ourselves before returning to all this." He waved his hand at the ballroom. "We can be king and queen of all Francia when we get back."

A huge grin spread across her face. "You're right," she said. "Let's go home."

In the author's note of the previous two books of this series, I catalogued the history of the Carolingians' rise to power from Pippin of Herstal through Charles Martel, the civil war between his children, the imprisonment of his second wife Sunnichild and their son Gripho, as well as the flight of his daughter Hiltrude to marry the rebellious Duke, Odilo of Bavaria. I also acknowledged where my fiction diverges from the history for the sake of storytelling.

Rather than repeat that history here, I've chosen to focus solely on the events described in *Crown of a King*.

As in the other two books, most of the main events taking place in the novel are matters of history. Carloman's slaughter of the Alemannians and his subsequent abdication have long been debated among historians. It was certainly controversial at the time prompting him to make a rare public expression of his regret "with a heavy heart...as they were Christian." Some speculate that it was purely a ruthless political move that supplanted a rebellious nobility with a more sympathetic Frankish cohort.

His abdication as mayor, however, suggests more than regret. Carloman was still a young man at the time and at the height of his power. He had the support of the Church and the king (Childeric acknowledged him alone as the one "who put us on the throne") so it is hard to imagine that he would give up the role and take the tonsure without a compelling reason. As he was a deeply religious man, I chose to portray his decision as a crisis of conscience.

The Bishops's Council at Estinnes did take place, resolving a long-running dispute between the mayors and the church over the land confiscated by Charles Martel a generation earlier. The conclusions of the Council are as I've described them, but there is no evidence that it played the pivotal point in the confrontation between Carloman and Pippin as I have described.

There also is some question as to the date of Charlemagne's birth, leading some to believe he was born out of wedlock at an earlier time than is recorded. I accepted this theory for the sake of the story in *Wheel of the Fates* and suggest that it was kept secret to help explain why Carloman felt safe to turn over the reins of power to his brother (with the assumption that his son Drogo eventually would inherit the kingdom).

As might be expected, there were consequences to the massacre. One of the first decisions Pippin makes as the sole mayor of Francia is to free his brother Gripho. Some have used this gesture as evidence that Pippin wasn't complicit in Carloman's civil war with their half-brother (and stepmother) and was merely righting a wrong. It also may have been a preemptive move to placate the eastern duchies in the wake of the Alemannian massacre. Hiltrude's husband Duke Odilo of Bavaria (who likely would have negotiated such a concession) unfortunately died shortly thereafter, leaving Pippin's sister alone in Bavaria to defend her regency for their son Tassilo.

Regardless of Pippin's motive for freeing Gripho, the move back-fired as, instead of commanding the Breton Marsh as Pippin had hoped, Gripho stoked rebellion first in Saxony and then Bavaria (where he claimed guardianship over his sister Hiltrude and her son Tassilo). Pippin mobilized to defeat both rebellions. Gripho then fled to Aquitaine where he failed to recruit the Gascons before heading to Lombardy to try his luck with King Aistulf. He was killed on the road to Turin by Frederic of Transjura and Theodoenus of Vienne. Counted among Gripho's band of rebels were the ousted Lantfrid of Alemannia and Comte Sudiger of Bavaria.

Aistulf's rise to power in Lombardy, succeeding the more conservative King Liutbrand, proved to be a problem for Pope Zacharias. King Aistulf began usurping papal lands once protected by the Byzantium emperor in Constantinople. His appeal for aid provided Pippin an opportunity which he exploited by sending Bishop Burchard of Würzburg and the chaplain Fulrad to inquire "whether it was good or not that the kings of the Franks should wield no royal power."

The pope's response, that it was "better to call him who had the royal power than the one who did not," was rather vague but deemed enough by Pippin and Bishop Boniface to usurp the throne, crown Pippin, and banish Childeric to a monastery in Saint Bertin.

I took several liberties in recounting this story which are worth noting. The most significant of these relates to time and omission. The events described in *Crown of a King* actually take place between the years 744 and 753. To keep the story interesting and comprehensible, I felt it necessary to pare down much of the history and collapse the events into a two-year time frame to give it urgency. Most notable in my omissions are the Gascon sack of the city of Chartres and the burning of the Church of Saint Mary. The two brothers joined forces shortly thereafter to conduct a campaign across the Loire to punish Duke Hunaold.

Miette and Lady Hélène (and her sister Catherine), as is noted in *Wheel of the Fates*, are fictitious characters who somehow kept showing up as my story unfolded. Drusseau and his wife of the Twelve Counties are also fictitious as are the battles within Paris between the (again fictitious Knights in Christ) and those loyal to Pippin. While Pippin's uncle Childebrand is an imposing figure in history, his sidekick Gunther and Arnot are inventions as is Carloman's man Laurent.

Hélène's religious calling requiring her to champion one of the seven virtues, which first was mentioned in *Wheel of the Fates,* is fabrication. In the novel she chose "justice" and referred to it as "the dark path." In *Crown of a King*, I decided to expand on this storyline and searched around for sources that could help me better define justice in a way that would put some flesh on the bones. I stumbled upon an online course conducted by Harvard professor and author Michael J. Sandel. Taped live in a Harvard auditorium, his first class held me rapt and I ended up watching the entire course.

Fitting such a complex subject into a novel based in the eighth century proved challenging. Although the class covers Aristotle's dissertations on the subject, most of the course material post-dates my heroine. Given that her calling was based on her faith, I also needed to give it a religious connotation. I used the concept that we are all "God's children" as a means to introduce the subject. As I began to flesh it out, I struggled with how much to explain – it is a truly complicated topic – even when made understandable by Sandel. That's why I included the inside joke among those who are recruited by Hélène that, "it's complicated."

Writers of historical fiction often struggle with how much detail to include in our stories. Along the way we learn enormous amounts of minutia about our subjects that can either help ground the story in a time and place or (as often happens) weigh down the plot so that it grinds to a halt. I chose to use the concept of justice in a fairly rudimentary form but wove it through the novel as a way for Pippin to grapple with his motivation for seeking the throne and for Bertrada to reconcile her abhorrence for violence inherent in her husband's role as mayor.

Childeric does not live long after his confinement in Saint Bertin and it is suspected by many that he was killed to prevent a challenge to Pippin's ascension. I gave this task to Miette (as opposed to Lady Hélène) to bring justice to the character that had abused her and several other noble women in the novel.

As alluded to in Childeric's premonition (the Merovingians were rumored to be prescient) at the end of the book, Pippin was embattled for the rest of his life but succeeds in conquering all of Aquitaine, securing the Papal lands from Lombard aggression – the "Gift of Pepin" defines the papal lands to this day – and the unification of much of what is now the European continent under one rule, a truly remarkable feat for which he is rarely acknowledged. His reign paved the way for his son Charles's coronation by Pope Leo III as Holy Roman Emperor in 800.

Milton Keynes UK
Ingram Content Group UK Ltd.
UKHW012122210923
429156UK00013B/136/J